CW01496564

About the Author

Roger was educated in a grammar school in Coventry and gained a background in engineering. Around this time was when he bought his first business. Most recently, he has worked in management for a major chemical company becoming an energy consultant.

Roger Parkes

THE SECRET'S HOLDER

AUSTIN MACAULEY
PUBLISHERS LTD.

A CIP catalogue record for this title is available from the British Library.

ISBN 9781786129932 (Paperback)
ISBN 9781786129932 (Hardback)
ISBN 9781786129956 (E-Book)

www.austinmacauley.com

First Published (2016)
Austin Macauley Publishers Ltd.
25 Canada Square
Canary Wharf
London
E14 5LQ

Contents

INTRODUCTION

The setting: A Midlands village in the summer of 1947.

The storyline: Ben Spencer's continuing fight against the thriving post-war black market business, set against the background of the Spencer family, especially the children Polly, Maisy, Daisy and George aged 13, 8, 7 and 5 years, who enjoy an idyllic lifestyle, living in the countryside.

However, Mr Spencer's work during the war years, and his continuing activities afterward, will have significant and dangerous consequences for the whole family, especially Polly.

His efforts put him into direct conflict with criminal gangs, making his family a target for the criminal underworld enjoying rich pickings from their illegal black market activities.

Black market racketeering during the war years posed a great danger to the nation's survival. Despite the government employing some 900 inspectors, introducing fines of up to 500 pounds, prison sentences up to five years and offenders having to pay back three times the value of the goods they were selling; the black market continued to flourish.

Mr Spencer is actively involved in, pursuing the criminal racketeers and bringing them to justice.

These points are the basis for the story that will unfold against a background of the effects of his activities on the lives his family.

CHAPTER 1

(In which the children discover The Secret's Holder)

Our story begins with the regular activity of the children feeding the chickens and collecting the eggs. As usual, Polly is in charge, she is very much the mother hen herself, so Daisy, does her best not to break any. Polly is a mature girl for her age, and bears the responsibility for looking after the others very well. But she can be a bit bossy sometimes!

"Do hurry up, Daisy," says Polly, "I want to go to the shops with Mummy later."

"I am going as fast as I can."

George and Maisy, meanwhile, are playing with the dog by the stream which borders their garden, when Rusty, their dog, seems to be excited over some discovery...

"Come on, Rusty, it's almost dinner time," shouts George.

But Rusty is occupied with his find, a metal box which he has dug up. The box is about the size of a biscuit tin and, from its condition, has not been in the ground very long.

So what is in the box, what does it have to do with Mr Spencer and what 'secrets' does it hold about Mr Spencer's activities?

Polly tries to open the metal box but is unable to do so. She takes it to the workshop and uses a chisel to carefully loosen the lid. Inside the box are papers with lists of names, places and dates. Some of these dates refer to events and transactions that occurred during the war.

"Maisy, quick go and fetch Mummy," urges Polly.

"What is it Poll?" asks George. "Is it valuable? Can we get a reward for finding it?"

"It may be important that is why I have told Maisy to fetch Mummy," replies Polly. She looks at the pages briefly and can't help noticing her father's name, Benjamin Spencer, on some of the pages.

"What is it, Polly? I really am busy at the moment."

"Look Mummy, look what Rusty found down by the stream," shouts Daisy.

"I helped him find it, too," says George.

"Yes children, alright, let me look at what all the excitement is about" Mrs Spencer remarks. On briefly viewing the contents, she appears visibly shaken.

"Where did you say you found this?" she says, with concern in her voice.

"Down by the stream, Rusty pulled it from behind the big bush," George and Maisy reply.

"What is it, Mummy? What does it mean?" asks Polly, wanting to know more about the contents.

"It's probably just some old papers dropped by someone a long time ago," she replies trying to sound unconcerned about the find, but which is obviously causing her concern. Just then Mr Spencer arrives home rather unexpectedly.

"Daddy, Daddy look what we've found," the children all say excited at their find.

"The children found it at the bottom of the garden, Ben," explains Mrs Spencer.

Mr Spencer glances at the papers handed to him and appears rather startled by what he sees. "Go along and play, children, I need to speak with Mummy."

"But, Daddy, what are all these papers and why is your name on them?"

"Polly, all of you, please go into the garden, I need to speak with your mother," Mr Spencer replies firmly. Mr Spencer closes the back door and slumps into a nearby chair.

"What is it, Ben, tell me, you look as if you have seen a ghost."

"I do not understand how these papers have come to light, Margaret, they should have been destroyed years ago."

"Well they haven't been destroyed so what are you going to do with them?"

"Sit down, Margaret, I need to tell you something."

CHAPTER 2

(Mr Spencer explains
The Secret's Holder contents)

"During the early war years, you will remember that I was attached to The Ministry of Information? When The Ministry was dissolved in 1946, I was asked to continue with my work from The Central Office of Information.

"My time at The Ministry was spent investigating a number of people suspected of fraud and racketeering of food stuffs and ration books. It was considered the best place for me to investigate under the umbrella of this information organisation, since it allowed me to move about freely into other government departments

"When the War ended there were still many people involved in black market criminal activities because of the shortages of food, clothing and raw materials generally. I was asked to investigate, by any means at my disposal, and close down as many sources of black market trading as possible, by any means necessary, and advise the authorities of their activities. This has meant me having to compile information about people I have worked for and worked with and also collaborating with some unsavoury characters. The information was compiled over a number of years, naming contacts and places where transactions may have taken place or were supposed to have taken place. They were filed away securely by my contacts at COI.

"I have to assume that someone has found out about my role in the department and it was felt necessary to remove the information. Quite why they decided to bury the evidence at the bottom of the garden is a mystery, again perhaps it was considered too dangerous to approach me direct, and hand me the documents, for fear of discovery. I will have to contact the London office for advice on what best to do about this. The information is key to my investigating black market activities. I have so much more to do and cannot risk the operation being compromised internally. There are a lot of desperate people involved, Margaret, who would stop at nothing to see my investigations fail and be dismissed.

"In the meantime, do not mention this to anyone, since I am now unsure just how my position has been compromised. Call in the children, I will speak to them," Ben concludes.

"Very well," says Mrs Spencer, looking worried and tense.

The children crowd into the parlour looking towards their father in anticipation.

"What is it, Daddy?" asks Polly adopting the role as the oldest member of the four children.

"Children, I have to go away for a little while to attend to some Council work. I am not sure how long I will be gone, but hope you will all look after Mummy."

"But what about the box of papers?" asks George trying to sound important.

"Yes, Daddy, you have not said anything about that, are they important, and why did someone bury them in the garden instead of bringing them to the house?" asks Polly.

"You must try and forget about finding that box for the moment children, and not mention it to any one, do you all understand? There will be a very good reason for it being left there, but for now best that we forget about it. It may be that someone wanted to hide it for a short while during the war years, I don't know, but for now let's keep the discovery to ourselves will you do that for me, please?"

"Yes, Daddy," they all answer in unison.

Just then there is a knock on the front door of the house. The children look startled and Polly goes to answer.

"I'll go," says Mr Spencer moving to the hallway briskly.

He opens the door to see a Police Constable and another man standing in the doorway.

"Mr Spencer? I am Inspector Perks. I have been asked to collect you by your office, there seems to be some sort of emergency situation you need to be aware of, will you come with us, please?"

"Can I ask what it is about?"

"It's just some information we would like you to help us with, sir, it will not take too long," the officer replies.

"Very well, I'll get my coat and inform my wife, please wait, I'll only be a moment."

"Margaret, I have to go to the office help with something, not too sure how the police are involved, but I'll not be too long, should be back for supper I hope," Ben says trying to sound matter of fact, but is rather concerned.

"Tell the children I will be back soon."

"Very well, dear, I hope it isn't anything too serious I will let the children know where you are."

CHAPTER 3

(Mr Spencer is taken by police officers)

"Polly, Maisy, George, Daisy, can you come inside please?

The children dash into the parlour in anticipation.

"What is it, Mummy? Where's Daddy?" asks Polly.

"Daddy has had to go and help a policeman with something and will be back later."

"Is it about that box we found?" asks Maisy.

"'Course it's about the box and the papers. I bet Daddy is going to help catch some robbers and put them away," says George.

Mrs Spencer is alarmed at how quickly the children have assumed that the visit by the police is somehow to do with the finding of the box of papers in the garden.

"Children, please, stop it, this has nothing to do with anything found in the garden, so do stop going on about that," she replies with her voice raised as if to emphasise her comments.

However, she is not altogether convinced herself that the two events are not somehow linked to each other. But Ben was most insistent that they forget about the discovery in the garden. She is sure he knows more about how it got there than he has said, but trusts him to tell her when he is ready. She is very aware of how important his work was towards the end of the war and since. It has occupied him completely, meaning he has had to go away a number of times, not knowing for how long. She is also aware of the dangers involved as rationing of just about everything has meant shortages of food, clothing, fuel and items for manufacturing. These shortages are being exploited by racketeers, enjoying a luxury lifestyle at the expense of everyone struggling for work and to buy enough food to feed their families. She can only hope that Ben can continue with his work without being exposed to any danger and speaks to the children again about the find in the garden.

"You remember what Daddy said about the box that was found?"

"We must forget about finding it and not mention it to anyone," replies Polly, reciting what Mr Spencer had told them.

"But it must be about that box," replies Maisy, "else why would a policeman ask Daddy to help them after we had found it?" she points out with determination.

"I think Daddy is going to solve all the policeman's problems and catch the bad man," chirps Daisy, anxious to get involved in the discussion.

"I think Daisy is right, Daddy is going to help the police catch some very bad men," adds Maisy, keen to be part of the discussion also. "And anyway, he will be back soon and tell us all about it," she adds with a little frown on her face.

"Maisy is right, Daddy will be able to tell us all about it at supper time," George replies.

The four children move off towards the garden and leave Mrs Spencer to her thoughts. She thinks the children may be right in their assumptions about her husband, but she tries hard not to get too concerned. She sits down and tries to remember what her husband had told her regarding his activities during the war years and after, and asks herself, what exactly did he actually do? He has always tried to keep his work private, using the excuse that it was important not to burden her with his problems. He would simply say it was very important and that he had to keep it that way. It was obviously secret in some way and he did not want her to be concerned. Now she is beginning to wish she knew more about what he did then, during the war years, and since.

In the meantime, it was important that she should look after the family and he would be okay. Now she was not sure about anything and found herself in the study, removing the box of papers from the desk drawer and looking more closely at its contents. There were many names that she did not recognise, but there were also names of politicians and some local government officers. Mrs Spencer had worked on council business for a while and knew of the names from that time. There were meeting places and sums of money alongside consignments of foodstuffs such as butter, cooking fats, tinned foods and meat and alcohol. Disturbingly, there were also medical items listed such as penicillin and morphine. Petrol coupons also were mentioned. There were places listed with times and dates. Many of the places were in the London area, but there were also a number of sites listed in Birmingham and Coventry, two areas that had suffered extensive shortages and would be ideal for setting up black market activities. Birmingham and Coventry had suffered especially from bombing during WWII, Birmingham being the most bombed city outside of London. Mr Spencer's name was alongside many of the sites in Birmingham and Coventry as was detailed sums of money.

Despite all the propaganda, about traitors and saboteurs holding the nation to ransom, that was put out during the war years, despite all these efforts to cut out the business, it was still flourishing. The black market was thriving in all the big cities even if it was not so obvious in the countryside. Even the stiff penalties that were imposed did not deter the organised criminals, it merely punished the small businessman trying to make a living and satisfy his customers' requirements. Most food and drink items were still controlled by government rationing, so the public were still looking for more of everything to carry on with their lives. Rationing continued for a number of years. This, coupled with wages increasing as manufacturing and house building moved forward, meant that people had more money and wanted a better standard of living, giving the racketeers more and more business. The organisers of the black market operations would continue to enjoy the spoils of their dirty business for some time yet.

CHAPTER 4

(Mrs Spencer makes a disturbing discovery)

Mrs Spencer was concerned at what she had read and feared that her husband was involved in something far more dangerous than she could begin to understand. What he was involved in was the pursuit of highly organised professional criminals, ruthless and determined in their exploitation of the nation's shortages. These men would not allow anyone to get in their way, including her husband. Meanwhile she would have to continue life as normal. She put the box away in the locked drawer and went through to the kitchen to see what the children were up to in the garden. They seemed to have already forgotten the events of earlier and were amusing themselves.

Polly was keeping a watchful eye on proceedings while reading a book, Maisy and Daisy were chasing each other around the flowerbeds and George was playing with Rusty. She was relieved to see them all occupied. Just then, Polly looked up.

"Mummy, how long before tea, I'm hungry?"

"I'm hungry, too," shouts Maisy.

"Me, too," calls Daisy, not wanting to be left out.

"Come along then, I'll make some sandwiches."

And so the children sit down and enjoy their tea, and even some cakes that Mrs Spencer has baked. Thankfully, the family were not feeling as many hardships from the restrictions that the rest of the country was under because of rationing.

"I have used my coupons for margarine for this month, children, so enjoy these cakes!" says Mrs Spencer, as if to restate the problems that rationing imposes.

After tea, Maisy, Daisy and George return to the garden. Polly, however, remains.

"What is it Polly?"

"Have you heard from Daddy?"

"I don't expect him to call Polly when he said he would be home for supper, do you?"

"I don't suppose," replies Polly and goes and sits in the conservatory with her book.

Mrs Spencer glances at the clock and realises that her husband has been gone since before lunch and indeed she has had no word from him as to his whereabouts. She quickly moves into the study and picks up the telephone.

"Number please?" says the operator.

"Put me through to the police station please."

"Trying to connect you, caller," the operator responds.

"Hello, Police Station, Sergeant Wilson here," says a voice abruptly.

"Good evening, Sergeant, it's Mrs Spencer from The Gables on Crab Tree Lane."

"Oh hello, Mrs Spencer. What can I do for you?"

"I was wondering if you might be able to tell me when my husband might be coming home?"

"Your husband, he hasn't been to the station today or for some time to my knowledge."

"But didn't your Inspector Perks accompany him earlier today?"

"Inspector Perks? There is no Inspector Perks in this station or any local station that I am aware of," the Sergeant replies with an air of authority.

"Oh, I must have been mistaken, sorry to have bothered you, Sergeant," she replies, replaces the phone, sits down in the chair and bursts into tears. Her imagination now begins to run riot. What has happened to her husband? Where has he been taken and who is responsible? She is in despair and does not know what to do next. Just then Maisy and Daisy burst into the study:

"Mummy, Mummy Rusty has got out of the gate and is running down the lane with George," they call out together. Mrs Spencer gets up quickly and goes from the study to the hallway and out of the front door in time to see George has caught up with the dog and is leading him back to the house.

"George, what happened who left open the gate?"

"I didn't, it wasn't me, Mummy, honest it wasn't."

"I think Daddy came in that way a couple of days ago," Polly replies, joining them from the house.

"Why would Daddy use the side gate instead of the front door?"

"Mummy, who are those men staring at us from the end of the lane?" Maisy enquires looking towards a black car parked about 200 yards away.

"Go inside now, children, George, bring in Rusty, and Polly, please see that the side gate is locked and bolted," she replies with some authority, but with anxiety showing in her voice. They all move swiftly inside closing the front door and the inside door behind them.

Who are the men in the lane? What do they want? And do they have any connection to Mr Spencer's disappearance? Mrs Spencer is most concerned and her imagination begins to run wild. What should she do about her husband's disappearance? Should she contact the police? The way that Mr Spencer was led away by men posing as police officers has alarmed her, but she decides not to inform the police at present, but wait and hope that her husband returns safely. Instead she finds herself checking doors to make sure they are locked especially at the back of the house. The back door and door to the garage are most vulnerable since they are in the rear porch and washroom area which is quite isolated.

"Mummy what are we having for supper?" asks George. A question which brings her back to reality, which she is grateful for after the concerns of the last few hours.

"We have a meat pie, or a chicken stew whichever you prefer, George followed by some fruit from the garden."

"Pie for me, Mummy," Maisy calls.

"Me, too, please Mummy," says Daisy.

"Polly, will you help me with this please?"

"Yes, Mummy, are you going to make enough for Daddy as well?" she enquires.

"Yes, there will be more than enough for Daddy when he returns." And so the family go about their everyday business with thoughts about Mr Spencer very much occupying their minds. After dinner, the children, except for Polly, go up to the playroom for a while before bedtime. In the playroom, they have toys and games to occupy themselves for as long as they want. Polly, meanwhile, begins to ask questions.

"Mummy, what does Daddy do?"

"What do you mean, Polly?"

"What does he do, where does he go to work, why is he not here now, Mummy, I need to know what is happening," says Polly, anxiously.

"My dear Polly. Daddy will be home shortly, I am sure. As for what he does for work, most of the time it is probably quite boring office work. Unfortunately, he sometimes has to go to offices in other towns so has to stay away."

"But what can he be doing that the police want to know about if it is only office work?" replies Polly, as if to emphasise her anxiety.

"Well, Polly, it is just possible that Daddy may be able to help with evidence of wrongdoing by someone who the police want to talk to. As you know, there are still many household items in short supply, and people who will try to sell them to make money. Sometimes, what they are doing might not be honest and legal, so records are kept regarding sales and movement of goods, petrol, alcohol and many household items. The departments that Daddy is involved with, will have details that could help the police control and watch how many items are moved around, especially if they are doubts about whether they have been obtained with proper documentation. It is very important work, Polly, but probably a bit boring since Daddy has to check on so many movements of items throughout the Midlands. He has to be sure that those that are moving them and those that are receiving them have authorisation to do so."

CHAPTER 5

(Mr Spencer returns)

"Mummy do you think Daddy is in any danger because of his work?"

"I really—"

Just then, there is a loud banging on the door at the back of the house.

Mrs Spencer hurries across the hall, through the kitchen and into the back porch.

She can see that it is her husband at the door.

"Ben, thank goodness it is you," she says tearfully.

"Daddy, Daddy where have you been?" asks Polly, also with a tear in her eye.

"I really am fine, please will you let me in!" he laughs.

They move into the parlour and are joined by the other children;

"Daddy, Daddy I knew you come home soon," says George,

"We have missed you, Daddy," chorus Maisy and Daisy hugging Mr Spencer tightly.

"Children, I'm alright, please don't fuss, I've only been gone a few hours."

"Margaret, can you make some tea? I need to sit down and talk with all of you."

"Polly, can you go with Mummy and check that the back door is locked and bolted please?"

Mr Spencer relaxes in an armchair whilst the children sit patiently on the sofa. Mrs Spencer returns with a pot of tea, places it down on the table and begins to pour a cup for Mr Spencer and herself. The children wait anxiously for him to speak.

"First of all, children, I can tell you that I left this morning at the request of the people I work for, who thought it would be best if I were escorted.

"Daddy has not done anything wrong, it was just decided that the easiest way to get in touch with me quickly, was to have the police escort me.

"I shall be spending some time with council and government officials, over the coming weeks so I may have to stay away from home sometimes, so you all will have to help Mummy."

"But, Daddy, why do you have to go away? I want you to stay and play with us, you always used to play with us."

"Please don't cry now, Daisy, I won't be away all the time, just the occasional night. I have to be at any meetings that the council wants me to be involved with since I have a lot of information that could be useful to them."

"What sort of information Daddy? Why did those men pretend to be policemen and ask you to go with them, I don't understand?"

"Polly, I am sure that Daddy has had a very long day, and you and I should go and get supper ready," Mrs Spencer says hoping to ease the situation for her husband.

"Oh alright, but I still don't understand, you will tell me soon, Daddy please, won't you?"

"You will all know soon enough; now off you go and help Mummy with the supper."

With that, Mr Spencer sits back in the chair and closes his eyes whilst going over the day's events. Then, after supper, Mr Spencer speaks to the children.

"Children, I have to speak with Mummy, so will you go into the playroom for a while?"

"But, Daddy, I want to stay with you. I really need to speak to you," pleads Polly.

"Yes. Perhaps it might be best if you did remain, Polly, but Maisy, Daisy and George will have to go to the playroom for a short time," Mr Spencer confirms.

"From today, and until I am satisfied that all is well, you, Polly, and your sisters and brother will be accompanied to and from school each day. Mummy will take Maisy, Daisy and George and Mrs Poulton will go with you, Polly. Mummy and I have known Betty Poulton for many years, she has lived in Milton Parva all her life, and will take good care of you I am sure. Should Mrs Poulton not be at your school, at home time, you must wait until she arrives, do you understand?"

"Yes, Daddy."

"A colleague of mine with The Ministry, Mr Peter Forsyth, will stay at the house during the day, acting as gardener and handyman, so that the house is not left unattended. I am concerned that someone may try to enter the house if no one is here, so Peter will be here at all times.

"And it is important that you watch for any suspicious people in the lane and nearby when you are travelling to and from school, too, Polly."

Suddenly, Polly bursts into tears, she really cannot understand what is happening. Whilst she is a mature girl for her age, she is only 13 years and enjoys their close family way of life.

"What is happening, Daddy? Who are these people?" she says through her tears.

"They are very bad people, Polly, selfish and ruthless, who are stealing valuable foodstuffs, fuel and even medicines to sell illegally and at high prices. Their actions are making the lives of many people harder and more difficult than they are already and they will stop at nothing to protect their operations from anyone interfering."

"What about the police, can't these people be arrested?" Mrs Spencer asks.

"The police do not have the manpower to pursue these very organised gangs, and can be handicapped by rules and regulations. I, and people like me in government, do not have to be necessarily guided by rules and regulations.

"We have spent years tracing these gangs, looking for enough evidence to close them down. We cannot stop until they are all put out of business and behind bars. I know this is worrying and a lot to take in, but while this is happening I have to know that you are all safe. Only when I am sure that you are all as safe as possible that I can do my job without unnecessary worry. Now, Polly, I think it is now time for you and the children to start getting ready for bedtime, so no more questions for now."

"Yes come along, Polly, I will follow you upstairs to put the others into bed," says Mrs Spencer.

She is anxious to resume the conversation with her husband, as soon as the children are all in bed, especially to discuss what exactly is in the box found in the garden! What about trips into town? Mrs Spencer often goes into Carswell when she cannot purchase something from the village. And the children always enjoy the trip. Most worryingly is the responsibility that Mrs Poulton has taken on. Does she know just how desperate these criminals could become, and the danger to herself in all this? Mrs Spencer spends some time with the children telling them how she will be accompanying them to and from school from now onwards. She tries not to worry the children, but has to be sure they understand how important it is to be safe. Polly is a concern because she has to travel so much farther, using two buses to get to Carswell Secondary School. She is very independent and being escorted will mean that she will not be travelling with her friends. Just how will she react not being allowed to go anywhere on her own? She is a very sensible girl, but can be stubborn sometimes, and will not like the restrictions that she will have put on her every day movements. Mrs Spencer is a little apprehensive on how Polly will react when she eventually realises just how many restrictions have to be put in place to keep the family safe. She knows that her life, and that of her children, is about to change, and not for the better. But she will do whatever is necessary to protect her family in these difficult and dangerous times and stand by whatever decisions her husband has to make. He would not be placing these restrictions on everyone unless he was sure that it was necessary. Safekeeping

CHAPTER 6

(Mrs Spencer explains to Mr Spencer)

When Mrs Spencer eventually returns downstairs, Mr Spencer is in the study looking at the papers from the box.

"I will take these papers with me tomorrow, the information is vital to the authorities fighting the criminal racketeers. I am sorry that I cannot tell you more about the contents, Margaret, but it really is for the best, my dear," he says with some concern in his voice.

"But what exactly is your connection to some of the names mentioned in the papers, Ben? Are you in trouble, could you be prosecuted for any part you may have played? I have only glanced at the contents, but recognise some of the names, and am worried about your connection with them" says Mrs Spencer with some alarm in her voice.

"I really do think it best that you only know what I have told you so far, Margaret."

"But won't these people try to make contact in some way, Ben, they must know that you have information that could put them in prison for a very long time?"

"That is why I have taken the steps to protect you and the children, so please try not to be too concerned."

"I can't help be concerned and frightened, Ben, what little information you have told me has scared me and I am worried for the children."

"I think we should sleep on all this for now my dear, and talk more in the morning."

Polly meanwhile, who had been listening from behind the door to the hall, dashes back up the stairs to her room. She sits on her bed, her mind racing with all the information that she has just heard. So what exactly is Daddy investigating? Has he become involved with these people just to expose them, or is his role more complicated? She has always looked up to him and loves him dearly. So she is determined to try and find out for herself. She feels sure that if what she heard was correct, then all the members of the family could be in danger. She knows that, as the oldest, she will have to look out for Maisy, Daisy and George. They will not know just what danger they may be in, and will look on this as just another adventure. Polly, however, must try and help her Daddy, and protect her family as best she can. She must try and find out more about the container. *Why do they now have to be so careful of where they go, and who they speak with? What Polly would like to find out is just exactly who these people are that could be a danger to her family?* And with these thoughts racing through her head, Polly lies back and drifts into a fitful sleep with many questions still uppermost in her mind.

Mrs Spencer is up early, and finds herself looking out of the front windows and from the parlour overlooking the garden. She doesn't know what she expected, but all is peace and quiet. Normal in fact as it usually is.

"Good morning, dear," says Mr Spencer entering the parlour.

"Morning, Ben, I have just made some tea. Would you like an egg for breakfast?"

"Yes please, that would be nice."

"What time are you leaving?"

"I am being collected at 8 o'clock, I have to travel to Coventry and possibly Birmingham, so I will take some things with me to cover a day or so away."

"Will you let me know when you will be able to return?"

"Yes of course, Margaret, as it is Friday today, I hope I am able to return before the end of the weekend."

Meanwhile, the children have all arrived for breakfast. They chatter as they enjoy their breakfast, and Mr Spencer is grateful that they do not begin asking more questions. Polly, however, is rather subdued, and when Mr Spencer moves into the study, she follows him.

"How long will you be gone, Daddy?"

"Two days at the very most, Polly," he replies, giving her a reassuring hug.

"You will remember what I have told everyone about being careful and watching for strangers?"

"Yes, Daddy, but is there nothing else that I can do to help you?" she pleads.

"Just be careful, Polly, do not wander off anywhere on your own, not even into the village."

"I have Guides this evening; shall I ask my friend Valerie to call on me so that we can go together?" Polly enquires.

"Yes, very well, but be sure that you also return with her."

"Now I must pack a few things before I go."

And with that, Mr Spencer hurries from the study. Polly notices the metal box on his desk and places it back into the drawer and the returns to the parlour to see what the others are up to. She has already decided that she will have a look through Daddy's desk, if she gets a chance, to see what she can find. She is determined to try and do what she can to find out about these people. She is not afraid, but angry that their lives are about to be so restricted. She has already made up her mind to find out just who they are as soon as she is able. Mr Spencer, meanwhile, is saying goodbye to his wife as his car has just arrived.

"Bye, everyone, I should be home tomorrow afternoon."

"Bye, Daddy," echo the children and move to the door to see Mr Spencer depart.

Nobody notices the car at the end of the lane!

Mr Spencer duly returns on Saturday afternoon, having cut short his meetings, because he had forgotten to take some of his documents. He met with senior officials at the council offices, who reminded him how dangerous the people he was investigating have become. There was an official badly beaten in Coventry, and another almost run down by a truck in Birmingham. His colleagues at The Ministry were asking for even more diligence since they were concerned at the level of violence that the criminals were resorting to in their pursuit of profits. He was made very aware of the danger he was in and reminded how important the task in hand was if they are to win this 'war' with the criminal gangs of racketeers. Naturally, Mr Spencer did not mention any of these accounts to anyone in the family, merely saying that progress was being made in the breaking down of the organised black market operations. Mrs Spencer, however, wanted to know more details, but he dismissed her concerns, repeating what he had said about being careful and not straying away from the house alone. She could tell he was hiding something, but decided to leave the questions for the time being. Polly, however, having looked at some of the papers, was more insistent.

"Daddy, how well do you know some of these people, do they trust you, and do you trust them?"

"Polly, I have to trust them to trust me and hope that we can all stop their illegal activities as soon as possible. Can I trust you to accept that and not ask any more questions for the time being?"

"Yes, Daddy," says Polly, and leaves the study. She had examined the contents of the metal box. She does not understand what it all means and is upset and frustrated that the information is not clearer to her, that is why she has been asking so many questions. She is very concerned about the references to her father, especially as it seems that he could somehow be involved in some of these activities! Polly idolised her father, and thoughts of him being involved with criminals scared her. He would only talk with these people if it was his last possible way of getting the important information that he has to have in order to bring these people to justice.

It was inconceivable to Polly that her Daddy could be anything more than her dear Daddy.

CHAPTER 7

(Polly is taken!)

However, on Monday morning things take a turn for the worst. Polly is abducted by two men as she waits by the bus stop with Mrs Poulton. Mrs Poulton is deliberately distracted by someone asking directions, and while this is happening, Polly, despite fighting desperately, is bundled into the back of an old van and driven away at high speed.

She is taken on a journey which lasts about 45 minutes. On arrival at a big old house she is bundled inside and questioned by the men who snatched her from the bus stop. They are very threatening, demanding to know where her father is and what she knows about his work. Some of the threats are particularly nasty, and Polly is really scared.

"Come along, young lady, what has Daddy been saying to you then about his work lately, he must tell you where he is going and who is meeting with? We don't want to hurt you, but we need some information about some papers he has. We can keep you as long as we have to, but we need that information one way or the other do you understand?" the older man says quietly.

"A pretty girl like you doesn't want to get bruised and battered just for not telling," the younger of the two says, as he stares at Polly. When Polly refuses to answer they push her into an old cellar and follow behind her. She is covered in dirt and dust and has bruises and scratches on her legs from the floor of the van and from the cellar.

"Take off her jacket and tie her to that old bench," the older of the two men says.

"Don't touch me, you horrid man!" she screams as they wrestle with her to remove her jacket.

When they finally get her jacket off they tie her hands behind her and to the bench.

"If you know what's good for you, you'll tell us what we want to know. And if your Daddy is sensible he will cooperate," the younger man says as he grabs Polly by her hair. "Like I said, a pretty girl like you doesn't need to get hurt, but we mean to get some answers from you one way or another," he adds.

Polly does not understand what he means and turns away from the men shutting her eyes.

"We'll be back later, and you had better tell us what we want to know or else it'll be the worse for you. And it's no good shouting and screaming 'cause no one will hear you in here."

And with that the two men go back up the steps and lock the cellar door behind them. Polly, collapses sobbing with relief that she is unharmed, but fearful of what they might do to her when they return. She realises that these men intend to hold her until they get the information they are after by any means. She must somehow try to escape before coming to any harm. But how? She is locked in a cellar in a big old house situated well off the road.

Mrs Spencer, meanwhile, tries to contact her husband using the number he gave her to use in an emergency, but unfortunately, the number only puts her into contact with the office that he uses They have to pass on any relevant messages. When she explains what has happened they make contact with Mr Spencer, and he arranges to return home immediately. There is panic in the household over Polly's abduction, and poor Mrs Poulton is distraught at what has happened.

"Please do not blame yourself, Betty, these men are very determined and would have kept trying had they not been successful this time," says Mrs Spencer trying to console her.

"I just keep wondering if there was anything I could have done to stop them," says Mrs Poulton.

"You should go home now, Betty, we will let you know the moment there is any news," says Mrs Spencer, trying to console her.

"But is there nothing I can do to help? I feel so responsible."

"Well perhaps you could help me with the supper if it will take your mind off what has happened, but what about Mr Poulton?" asks Mrs Spencer.

"He insists I stay with you and help where I can, he will make himself something until I get home."

Maisy, Daisy and George keep asking about Polly and why Mrs Poulton has not brought her home.

"Daddy will explain when he gets home children, so please go and play outside while we get supper ready.

"Are we going to wait for Polly, before we have supper, Mummy?"

"We'll see, Daisy," answers Mrs Spencer, hoping that will be enough to satisfy the children's questions for the time being.

Just then, the front door opens and Mr Spencer arrives home.

"Ben, is there any news?"

"Everything possible is being done to find her Margaret, the Police and my colleagues are rounding up all known criminals that may know something, but at the moment there is no news I'm afraid. It may be that these men are not local and have been sent from London.," responds Mr Spencer with a degree of concern in his voice. And with that, he moves towards the study.

"I have to make some phone calls. I will let you know as soon as I hear any news at all," says Mr Spencer.

"Please find our daughter, Ben, please."

Mr Spencer sits at his desk with a feeling of despair. What has happened to their daughter? Why has she been taken and why hasn't anyone made contact with him?

CHAPTER 8

(Polly tries to escape)

Polly, meanwhile is becoming anxious. It has been sometime since the two men left her and she is getting cold and hungry. She is determined to say nothing to these men, she knows very little anyway! Whilst she is very scared, she does not believe the men mean to hurt her. They appeared agitated when they spoke with her and preoccupied with other things. But, if she is of no use to them what will they decide to do with her? Polly screams out as loud as she can:

"Help! HELP! Somebody please help me!" But all she hears is dripping water and a drone which sounds like vehicles passing overhead. No one, it would seem can hear her cries for help. She tries desperately to free herself, but succeeds only in ripping her skirt on a nail on the bench seat and scratching herself quite badly on her bottom. After several minutes, she gives up, realising that she has been tied too tightly to be able to free herself, and has succeeded only in badly chafing her wrists as well as scratching herself. The ropes have dug into her wrist which is now bleeding. She sits on the bench and screams as loud as she can, more out of frustration than anything. She is cold and hungry, her clothes are dirty and dishevelled and her skirt is badly torn. Her hair is also matted from being dragged by the men who abducted her. Her hands and face are dirty also her legs are covered in bruises.

"I am in a terrible mess!" she says to herself, and begins to sob uncontrollably. However, she still continues to try and escape, pulling and tugging at the ropes that bind her to the bench. She tugs so hard that she slips from the bench seat and pulls the bench with her collecting even more scrapes and bruises from contact with the stone floor. With her hands tied tightly behind her, she is now flat on her face. Her shirt buttons have been torn off in her struggles and she has somehow managed to scrape the skin on her tummy on the hard uneven cellar floor. Her knees and legs are badly scraped and bleeding, and her shoulders are hurting as a result of her arms being stretched tight behind her. She is now bleeding from her cuts and lacerations and lies there in despair, sobbing fearful that her injuries may be serious. Then, after what appeared to be an age for Polly, the cellar door opens and the two men reappear. They are visibly shocked at the sight of Polly, dirty and dishevelled and covered in bruises.

"What the hell has happened, you stupid kid?" the older one shouts, obviously shaken by what he sees. "Get her back onto the bench and untie her, Jimmy," he says to the younger man.

"Jesus, you look a mess, girl; we've got to clean you up before we can take you back," he says.

"What the hell are they gonna say when they see her like this, Don, they'll think that we've done this, I'm scared, I never expected this to happen."

"Take it easy, Jimmy, I'll get some water and a cloth to clean her up."

"Here are some buns and something to drink, I expect you must be hungry," the older one adds.

Jimmy stands in front of Polly and says:

"What did you think you could do? You couldn't escape because I tied you up too tight. You must be really stupid to get yourself into this mess."

Polly looks at him fearfully, and is relieved when the cellar door opens and the older man enters. He is carrying a bowl of water to tend to Polly's cuts and bruises. Polly washes herself as best she can, and realises just how badly she is bruised from her attempts to escape.

"I need you to take off what's left of your shirt to clean the wounds on your stomach and shoulders," he adds. When the dirt and grime have been washed from her legs and arms, she can see they are a mass of bruises and cuts some of which are bleeding.

"This will hurt a bit, but we have to get the dirt from these cuts, and this one is particularly nasty," he says, pointing to the cut at the back of her leg where the nail pierced her from the bench. Polly, flinches as he lifts her skirt to reveal a nasty gash on her bottom. He gently bathes the cut and the area around the cut, smiling reassuringly.

"Thank you," says Polly as she puts her torn skirt back in place.

"Your shoulder is also badly bruised and the skin is scraped raw. This is a waste of time really, you are in a mess, which is your own fault," says the older man sounding annoyed.

"I told her that and I bet the law will think we did this to her!"

"And we know we didn't so don't keep on about it," the older man says becoming agitated.

"When are you going to let me go?" asks Polly trying to calm things down.

"We're leaving as soon as it is dark, but you will have to stay here overnight because someone else is using the van."

Polly's heart drops, since although the two men have not harmed her in any way, she does not like the idea of being away all night.

"Please let me go and I will get a bus home."

"Shut up, sit down and eat your food, you are not going anywhere and for God's sake don't try and free yourself again," the older one says firmly.

"Polly moves away from the two men into a corner, finding an old box to sit on and waits for the morning to come, alone and in the dark. The night seemed to go on forever, but finally the two men return and take Polly from the cellar. They put her in a van and drive back to the bus stop, in town, from where she was taken. She is then released, unharmed. A passer-by, seeing how badly bruised and dishevelled she is, calls for a policeman. At the sight of friendly but concerned faces, Polly collapses into tears of relief. When the police arrive, they want to take Polly to hospital, but she insists that they contact her father.

"Very well, Miss, if you insist," says the officer and goes to phone Ben Spencer.

CHAPTER 9

(Polly arrives back home)

Ben contacts Doctor Wilson, the family doctor and asks him to attend and look at Polly when she is brought home from Carswell When Polly arrives home, her parents gasp when they see the state that she is in.

"I'm okay, Mummy and Daddy, really I am."

"Oh my God, Polly, you look wretched. What on earth did those men do to you?" asks Margaret.

"They did not hurt me, Mummy, really, I did most of this trying to escape," she replies, but her father is not at all convinced that her injuries were caused by Polly herself.

"I think we should let the Doctor look at you and hear what he has to say before we go any further. After that, the police will want to interview you," says Ben.

Polly goes upstairs with her mother to wait for the Doctor to arrive. Mrs Spencer helps her to remove her shirt and skirt and gasps with dismay at the mass of cuts and bruises Polly has all over her legs, arms and body. She would prefer to give her a bath first, but decides to wait and hear what the doctor has to say. Doctor Wilson examines Polly thoroughly and asks her just how she managed to get so battered and bruised all over her body.

"Did these men harm you in any way, Polly?" he asks after she explains falling off the bench whilst still tied.

"No, Doctor, the youngest one, the one called Derek, grabbed my hair, but that is all. The older man was very gentle with me when he bathed some of my wounds."

"Yes I can see that the deep scratches at the back of your leg and the shoulder abrasions have been cleaned."

"And you are quite sure that they did not put their hands on you anywhere else?"

The Doctor asks, looking directly at Polly.

"They did not hurt me in any way, Mummy, really!"

"That's a relief my dear Polly," the Doctor responds.

"Now I think it best if you get into a warm bath, Polly, and then get some rest.

"I will wait downstairs in the study, Mrs Spencer," says Doctor Wilson as he leaves the room. Mrs Spencer takes Polly to the bathroom for a well-deserved bath. When Doctor Wilson enters the study he is met by Mr Spencer, a uniformed police officer and two other men.

"Would you like me to make some tea, Mr Spencer?" enquires Mrs Poulton, who has remained behind to help with the children.

"That would be very kind, Betty, thank you very much,"

"How is Polly, Doctor, will she be alright?"

"She should be okay after a bath and good night's rest," the Doctor replies.

"What about her injuries, Doctor, those villains must have given her a terrible beating?"

"No, Ben, I believe Polly's injuries were a direct result of her desperate attempts to escape, and she assures me that neither man touched her except to put her in the van and tie her up in a cellar," the Doctor responds with conviction.

"However, I do believe that her injuries were caused as a direct result of her being taken away and held against her will, and I will be emphasising these points in any statement I make."

"Well if you are satisfied, then so am I, James," Mr Spencer replies to the Doctor with relief. "There is really nothing you can do until tomorrow, gentlemen, so I suggest we leave it there for now," Mr Spencer says addressing the two police officers directly.

"Very well, sir, we'll call you tomorrow, good bye for now, we'll see ourselves out." And with that, the two police officers leave the room and depart through the front door. The door closes and Philip Landers, who has been waiting patiently, turns to Mr Spencer and asks:

"Do you mind telling me what the hell is going on here Ben?"

Phil Landers is a civil servant at the Central Office of Information, and Ben Spencer reports to him regarding any information that he believes is pertinent to their investigations.

"I'm sorry, Phil, I just have not had time to report because of Polly being taken."

"I understand how difficult recent events may have been for you, Ben, and of course your family must come first, but now that your daughter is home safe, perhaps you can fill me in on events?"

Mr Spencer tells him about the container found in the garden, and Phil Landers browses its contents whilst listening to Mr Spencer's version of events up to the return of Polly.

"So that's about it, Phil, we need to catch these people and put them away where they can do no more harm," Mr Spencer comments forcibly.

"You're absolutely right of course, Ben, I need to talk with your daughter to see what information she may be able to give us regarding the two men who abducted her, and the place where they took her. If we can pinpoint where she was taken, it might lead us to their hideout," Phil Landers comments.

"We will talk about it tomorrow, Phil, after Polly has rested."

The next morning, after breakfast, Ben asks Polly to come along to the study.

"Polly, I want you to meet Mr Landers, we work together at The Ministry."

"Hello, Mr Landers."

"Hello, Polly, how are you feeling this morning, do you think you might answer a few questions?"

"I am feeling much better thank you, and yes I will try and answer your questions, but I am not sure I will be of much help."

Mr Landers began to ask Polly about her time kept in the cellar, hoping she will remember something that will help pinpoint its location.

"Firstly, Polly, how long do you think the journey was before you stopped, and were you able to recognise any buildings from the van windows?"

"I am not sure about the time, about 45 minutes maybe longer, but I am sure it was Coventry, because I saw several buses on the way, and saw the names Wykin and Walsgrave on them, and I know they are not in Leicester are they?"

"That's very good, Polly, Wykin and Walsgrave bus routes would have to be passed through going into Coventry the most direct way by road," Mr Landers confirms.

"And just before we stopped, I saw a picture house, I think it said Alexandra, we turned alongside the picture house and stopped straight afterwards."

"There is an Alexandra picture house in Ford Street in Coventry, well done, Polly."

"Do you remember anything about the place where they took you to at all, large, small; did it have a long driveway, anything at all would be most helpful?" Mr Landers enquires.

"It was a big house, but I didn't see anyone and was taken straight to the cellar which was dark and smelly," Polly shivers remembering the cellar.

"I don't think anyone else had been down there for a long time, there were cobwebs everywhere. There were a lot of pipes down there, big pipes leading to a big heating boiler, similar to ours but much bigger, and it was cold."

"So it was obviously a big house, unoccupied, but available to these people if needed."

"I would say that is correct, Ben," Mr Landers concludes.

"I think we will leave it there for the moment Polly, you have been very helpful. Perhaps you should go through to the parlour now, meanwhile Daddy and I will look at what we have here," Mr Landers says.

"You will need to give a statement to the police sometime today, Polly, as well."

"Yes, I understand that, Daddy," replies Polly and she proceeds to leave the study, closing the door behind her.

"I think I know who the men are who took Polly, Ben."

"Jimmy Spiers and Don Wilson fit the descriptions and both are operating in the Coventry area, so would know where to hide someone. We know they belong to a gang that have hijacked lorries carrying vital stores, and have raided banks in the Birmingham area. Can I use your phone, Ben? The sooner we can arrange to pick them, up the better chance we will have of finding out where Polly was held, and finding out where they are storing their contraband."

"Please carry on, Phil," Ben Spencer replies.

Whilst Phil Landers is busy on the phone, Ben goes through to the parlour to have a word with Polly. However, just as he is about to enter the parlour, the doorbell rings.

Mr Spencer answers the door to find the two police officers from yesterday.

"Good afternoon, Mr Spencer, D.I Wishart and PC Parsons again, I wonder would it be possible to speak with your daughter now, if she has fully recovered from her ordeal?"

"Please come in officers, would you wait in the dining room please?" Ben says, and shows them into the room, closing the door behind them.

He returns to the study to find Phil Landers preparing to leave.

"I am going back to my office, Ben, to see what can be arranged in Coventry, you would be better off remaining at home for the rest of the day: there isn't anything that can be done until arrangements have been made, and you should spend the time with your family after what has happened."

"Yes, thank you, Phil, the police are here anyway wanting to talk with Polly, so I will need to be with her for that."

"Say goodbye to Mrs Spencer, Ben, I will be in touch."

And with that, Phil Landers leaves the house and drives towards the main road.

"Polly, can you come in please? The police would like to have a word with you."

"This is Detective Inspector Wishart and Constable Parsons, Polly," he says as he points towards the two officers.

"Hello, Polly, I hope you are feeling better today?" the Detective Inspector asks.

"Yes thank you, sir," Polly answers.

"There are just a few questions I need to ask about what happened to you."

Polly answers the officers' questions, which are similar to those asked by Phil Landers.

"Thank you for being so helpful, Polly, I think that is all for now, Mr Spencer."

"Ben, would you like some tea, before I start supper?" Mrs Spencer calls.

"Thanks, dear, I will be in the study, ask Polly to bring it in please."

When Polly returns with the tea, Ben speaks to her.

"Sit down a moment, Polly, I just wanted you to know how proud I am of the way you have coped with all that has happened to you, and to thank you for answering all the questions from Mr Landers and the police. It is important that you continue to be careful when you are away from the house, 'though I very much doubt if those men will try to contact you again."

"Thank you, Daddy, and I will be careful, I promise," Polly replies with a nod and a smile.

"I'm going outside with the others before supper. They haven't said anything yet so I expect they will ask all sorts of questions.

"Be careful what you tell them, Polly, we don't want them worrying about you."

"Okay, Daddy, I will be careful not to worry them," Polly replies, and leaves the study by the kitchen door and moves out into the garden.

"Polly, Polly, what happened to you? Where did they take you?" they all chorus together.

"We were terribly worried about you Polly," says Maisy.

"Yes we really were, and I was frightened that something horrid may have happened," says Daisy with a concerned look on her face.

"I hate those nasty men," George adds.

"Nothing really happened to me, they just kept me overnight to warn Daddy what they could do if they wanted to."

"But, Polly, weren't you scared, I mean really scared that they might hurt you?" asks Maisy expecting Polly to reply in more detail.

"I was scared, Maisy, of course I was, but the men didn't hurt me really they didn't," Polly replies, trying to sound confident, but inwardly thinking of what might have been.

"Come on let's play a game and not worry about what has happened, I want to try and forget it," says Polly.

And with that Polly runs off towards the bottom of the garden with Maisy, Daisy and George and Rusty, the dog, in hot pursuit. Polly feels so much better for spending time with them and, for a little while at least, forgets about the events of the past few days.

"Polly, I will contact Mrs Williams and explain to her the circumstances of your being absent, and tell her that you will be off for a few more days yet. You cannot return to school with so many bruises showing, too many questions will be asked that you will not be able to answer," says Mrs Spencer over supper. Schools were used to children being absent for a number of reasons at the time, with so much uncertainty in people's everyday lives. Mrs Spencer will not be able to inform Polly's school of the actual reason for her absence, just enough to satisfy the register.

"I will find you something to do in the house in the meantime, and perhaps a visit into town might be arranged."

"I would like that Mummy, I need a new shirt and skirt anyway if they can be found."

And so the next morning, Mrs Poulton takes Maisy, Daisy and George to school, and Polly stays at home with her mother. Mr Spencer leaves around 8 o'clock and is not sure whether he will be back that evening.

"I will have to let you know, Margaret, as soon as I am able, when I will be home," Mr Spencer calls as he leaves from the front door.

In fact, Mr Spencer does arrive back that evening, since there has been no real progress, by the police, in tracking down Polly's abductors. Polly, meanwhile, spends a leisurely day with her mother and gets a new shirt and skirt from their visit to the town. She decides that Polly should return to school on Thursday, having fully recovered from her ordeal. Virtually all of her bruises are covered by her school uniform, so she will not have to explain them to anyone. The fact that she wears long socks also helps since these cover most of her legs below her skirt. Polly is delighted, since she has spent her time at home making plans as to how she can help her father track the men who abducted her. She has decided that she will go to Coventry herself. She will use the school library to find out bus times, since she is sure that is where she was taken. She has also determined that a bus will take her to Pool Meadow bus terminus, and that is not too far from The Alexandra Theatre. Since she often spends time in the school library, Polly is confident that no one will question what she is up to.

She distinctly remembers Mr Landers, mentioning The Alexandra Theatre in Ford Street in Coventry, so that is where she heads for. She is confident she will be able to recognise the house where she was taken. She told Valerie that she would be unable to go to Guides this week so she would not need to call on her. Instead, she asked Valerie to go into town with her on Saturday. Valerie agreed, but was very curious why Polly wanted to go off on her own. Polly said it was something she had to do for her father, but could not be specific since it was to do with his work. So Polly has just to wait for Saturday so that she can begin her plan to help her father catch the men who abducted her. The rest of the week was uneventful and the family could almost forget the difficult situation they were in. Mr Spencer returned home each evening, and Mrs Spencer was running the household smoothly as she always had done previously.

The children simply carry on enjoying their way of life playing games and having fun with Rusty when, Rusty suddenly gets agitated and barks furiously at the bottom of the garden.

"What's the matter with you, Rusty?" asks George running towards the dog who is getting more and more agitated over something in the fields.

The other children arrive and notice two men at the field's edge watching the house through binoculars. They see the children looking at them and run off. A few moments later, a car engine is heard in the distance. Polly and the others return to the house and tell their parents what has happened. Just when everyone thought they could forget their situation, this has reminded them of how difficult their lives are now. After they had recited the events they sit down in the parlour for a drink and suddenly realise that Rusty has not returned with them to the house. They go back to the bottom of the garden calling him as they do so.

"Rusty, Rusty where are you, silly dog?" calls Maisy, but Rusty is nowhere to be seen.

However, the gate at the bottom of the garden is open and this is always kept shut, especially now since Mr Spencer had told everyone to be careful. Polly calls her father, who goes into the field to see where Rusty has gone. He ventures towards the side gate leading to the road and sees Rusty apparently lying down in the long grass. However, he does not move or respond to Mr Spencer's calls.

Rusty is in fact dead, he appears to have been poisoned and the children are completely distraught over the death of their beloved dog.

"Why, Daddy, why would anyone want to hurt Rusty?" Maisy and Daisy ask in floods of tears.

"He was my very best friend, Daddy," sobs George.

"I know children, now come along back to the house, Polly you take them, and I will bring Rusty." Mr Spencer says with a degree of sadness. The dog had been part of the family for a number of years, and Ben feels he is responsible for what has happened. Polly meanwhile has escorted the children back to the house and tried to console them as best she can whilst holding back her own tears. Ben carries the dog back into the garden, through the gate, and covers him with a sack momentarily, before returning to the house. The family sit quietly through supper, and Ben prepares to bury Rusty.

"Children you remain in the house until I am finished then Polly will bring you to say goodbye."

He lays Rusty in a hole at the bottom of the garden in a secluded corner and makes a cross from some timber oddments in the garage. Polly brings out the children who walk down the garden to where Rusty is buried still very tearful but being very brave over their loss. After standing by the side of the mound where Rusty is buried for a few moments, Polly says:

"We must get some flowers from the village tomorrow and bring them to Rusty."

"Yes, and can I choose?" George asks, he has been especially upset by it all.

"I am sure Mummy will let you choose some," Polly answers.

After saying their goodbyes, the children go back inside.

"Daddy, Valerie and me are going into town tomorrow, will that be okay?"

"I would prefer that you stayed home, Polly."

"But, Daddy, it will mean having to make up more excuses to my friends about not being able to go out, and I will be with Valerie all the time."

"Oh very well, but do be careful and don't be away for too long," Ben relents.

"Thank you, Daddy," says Polly, and returns to the house.

CHAPTER 10

(Polly returns to the house where she was taken)

The following morning, Saturday, Polly is up early ready for her trip to Coventry.

She spends time with Maisy, Daisy and George keeping them occupied so as they do not get too upset again over the loss of their dog.

"Will you be going into the village later, Mummy?" enquires Polly.

"Yes, please, Mummy, so that we can get some flowers for Rusty," Maisy, Daisy and George all chorus.

"Very well, children, as soon as I have finished in the kitchen, and as soon as I have spoken with your Daddy."

"Thank you, Mummy," they all reply.

Polly's friend, Valerie, calls around 9.30 a.m. and the two girls go off towards the main road to catch the bus to town. When they arrive in Carswell, Polly arranges to meet with Valerie around 4 o'clock by the bus stop back to the village.

"I wish you would let me come with you Polly," Valerie says, concerned that Polly is going off on her own.

"I have to do this by myself Valerie, I am so sorry I cannot explain any more, you are my best friend, but this is about my family, please try to understand."

"I do understand, Polly, I am just worried for you."

"I will be fine, really, what are you going to do today anyway?" asks Polly.

"I am meeting up with Veronica and Clare, we'll probably have a good look round the shops and have something at the cafe later," Valerie replies, as they reach the bus stop where Polly will catch the bus for Coventry. She is a bit apprehensive, but determined to carry her plan through.

"Have a good time, Val," she says as the bus arrives.

And with a wave Polly gets on the bus that will take her to Coventry and, she hopes help her to find out where she was held earlier in the week. The bus is crowded, so nobody notices a young girl travelling alone which is unusual. Polly, meanwhile, settles down to look out of the window at views that she is unfamiliar with on her way to the City of Coventry.

"I am taking the children to buy some flowers for Rusty, I won't be long."

"Very well, dear. I'll see you when you return," he replies.

Mr Spencer was on the phone in the studio when Mrs Spencer entered.

"Are we any closer to finding these men, Phil?" he asks Phil Landers.

"We have every available man looking for them Ben, they must be hiding out somewhere, we just have to keep looking. We have carried out a number of checks at warehouses and found some discrepancies in paperwork, but nothing significant. I believe they may be trying to set up legal businesses, and using them as a way of creating artificial shortages."

"Yes, that is a tactic that I have been looking at Phil, but it is extremely difficult to prove. Most of the criminals set up the business in false names. Often, by the time you determine that the business is a front for crime, they have moved on."

'We have to get someone involved on the inside, how are you with informants, Ben?" Phil asks.

"I may have someone in Birmingham that could help. He uses the pubs around The Bull Ring, there are quite a few but he shouldn't be difficult to find since he spends most of his time doing business from pubs around the market," Mr Spencer replies.

"Can you trust him, Ben?"

"He has given me some useful information in the past, providing there is something for him."

"In that case you need to get over to Birmingham and meet up with him on Monday, we have to break this chain of illegal operators. Meanwhile, I am to question a number of council officials next week who we believe, have been implicated in illegal activities from their positions in office. We will talk again Sunday evening ready for next week, Ben, bye for now."

"Yes, bye for now, Phil," Mr Spencer replies as he puts down the phone.

As soon as Mrs Spencer returns from shopping, the children go into the garden with the flowers to place on the plot where Rusty has been buried, still tearful about what has happened.

"I am going into the field to see what those horrid men were doing," says George tearfully.

"I'll come too," replies Maisy.

"And me," says Daisy, and they all go through the gate into the field and head toward the spot where they found Rusty. As they walk towards the gate at the side of the field, which leads to the lane, Maisy notices something shiny in the long grass. She leans over to take a closer look: lying in the grass is a cigarette case, and next to it a key.

"Look what I've found, I bet those horrid men dropped them as they ran away."

"What is it Maisy?" asks Daisy.

"Let me see Daisy," George says with excitement.

"It looks like a case and a door key, we must take it to Mummy straight away."

George runs ahead calling:

"Mummy, Mummy look what Daisy has found," he says as he dashes into the kitchen.

"George, stop running in the house, what are you going on about so?" she enquires as she holds on to him to stop him running any further.

Daisy and Maisy follows him in and Daisy shows Mrs Spencer what she has found. Mrs Spencer examines the cigarette case and the door key.

"Where on earth did these come from?"

"They were by the gate to the lane in the long grass."

"They must have, somehow, been dropped by one of the men when they ran off after Rusty barked at them."

"We must show these to Daddy right away," says Mrs Spencer, as she walks through the door from the kitchen into the study.

She hands the two items to Ben, recalling how they were found in the field by the lane gate.

"Will these be of use to you at all Ben?"

"Well yes, I am sure they will be, I notice that the case is engraved with the initials DRJ, that could be the initials of the older of the two men who took Polly, namely Don Jones, and the key is probably for some storeroom. Where is Polly, by the way?" he suddenly asks.

"She has gone into town with Valerie Oakes, she will be home later."

"I would have preferred if she hadn't gone Margaret," says Mr Spencer.

"I understand Ben, but we really cannot keep her in all the time, the poor girl will not like it at all. We must allow her some freedom, you know that she is sensible and will not do anything silly."

"I understand Margaret, I just worry about her, you know how special she is to me."

It was true to say that Polly had always been close to her father, and he loved her dearly.

"Yes dear, now are you ready for some lunch?"

"I'll just inform Phil of our find, then I will be through," replies Ben.

Polly, arrives in Pool Meadow Bus Station, and asks a friendly looking elderly lady for directions to The Alexandria Theatre.

"Go straight down Ford Street to the crossroads with Cox Street and you will see the Alex on the corner my dear," the lady replies.

"Thank you very much."

When she reaches the Alexandra Theatre, she instantly recognises it and is sure she is in the right place. She turns alongside the Theatre and starts walking. She was sure that the van had to cross the road to enter a driveway so looks at the houses on the opposite side. The houses are all large properties, with gated entrances and long driveways. Suddenly, she remembers, when they turned into the driveway, they drove over a wide hole causing the van to tilt and Polly to fall across the floor! She examines the pavements, and there is the large pothole outside a house called 'Primrose Lodge'.

Polly peers inside the driveway to see if there are any cars or vans. There is nothing in the driveway, so Polly tries the side gate which is unlocked. She ventures inside and hurries up the drive and looks through the glass front door, but there does not seem to be anyone inside.

Polly tiptoes around the back of the premises and looks through the windows. She sees a large room, but no furniture and the garden is overgrown with weeds.

Polly continues to move round the side of the house, and notices a small window not completely shut. She pushes the window which opens freely and clambers up the wall and through the window into a washroom and storage area. Once she is accustomed to the light, she moves into the house and is confronted by boxes of margarine, tea, sugar, jam and alcohol. She moves out of the room into the other room at the back of the house and discovers drums of paraffin, and a box with pistols and ammunition. Somewhat overwhelmed by what she has discovered, she decides that it would be best if she left as soon as possible. Just then, she hears a car in the drive and doors opening and closing. Then she hears the front door open and goes cold when she recognises the voices of the two men.

"We gotta start moving this stuff, Jimmy, are there any orders that need to be filled?"

"Not that anybody has told me, Don, you need to ask the boss," Jimmy replies.

"Yeah right, I was hoping to move some stuff into the cellar, but I lost the damn key."

"While we are here, do a quick check on what we have in case anyone asks."

"Okay, Don," replies Jimmy moving toward the back room of the house.

Polly has been hiding in the room she first entered, and realises that she has to leave the same way, and somehow escape from the bottom of the garden. She clambers back through the window, and pauses to see how she might escape unseen, from the house. There is a path at the edge of the garden shielded for the most part by overgrown bushes. She follows the path and goes out through the unlocked gate at the bottom into an alleyway that runs behind the houses. She dashes along the alleyway and reaches the main road alongside a public house, looks around her, then runs across the road, back towards the bus station. After a short wait, she gets onto the bus for Carswell, relieved that the trip is over and she can return home safely.

Ben Spencer telephones Phil Lander to tell him of the items found by the children in the field at the bottom of the garden. He is surprised at the find, putting Polly's abductors so close to the house. Why were they there?

"Ben, I believe you need to be very careful, they must be looking to break in to look for the documents," he suggests.

"I understand, but I believe my safe is the best place for this sensitive information, I do not want to rely on the security at the office and I have Peter Forsyth helping me during the day, watching over the house and garden."

"Did you have any more thoughts on how the documents ended up in your garden, Ben?"

"I had been expecting someone to contact me on this Phil, since I had originally filed the papers away in a safe place at COI. As I haven't been contacted, I can only guess that the opportunity has not yet occurred."

"Do you have any idea who it might be?"

"At the moment, I am keeping an open mind on that, I think it best to wait and see, don't you?" Ben Spencer replies.

"I understand, we'll talk again tomorrow as we suggested, bye Ben."

"Goodbye, Phil," Ben replies replacing the receiver.

He sits for a while pondering the conversation, and decides that there is only one person who would make the decision to move the documents, and then bury them in the garden rather than contact him direct. But why hasn't she made contact yet? Ben decides he will contact her because he has to know the background into the decision to leave the container of documents in his garden.

Polly arrives back in Carswell safely, and meets with Valerie to catch the bus back home. Valerie has been shopping and is anxious to show Polly a dress she has bought.

"That is really nice, Val," Polly comments keen to make sure that Val does not ask her any questions about her day.

"Was it very expensive?"

"I've used all my coupons Poll, but it was worth it even though I'm not sure what Mummy will say!" replies Valerie with a smile. Many everyday items were subject to rationing and "fashion on the ration" was the description used by advertising. However, there were still shortages from the war years so most items of clothing were subject to a number of points, four for a skirt, seven for a dress, three for stockings, eight for trousers and so on. Valerie had used a shop that knew her family and so allowed her to use the ration book allocated to her mother. Although this was not allowed, the law was somewhat relaxed outside of essentials such as food and fuel.

"Thank you for helping me today, Val, thank you very much," says Polly as they arrive back in the village.

"I am your best friend, Poll and will always help you if I can, you know that don't you?"

"Thanks Val, I'll see you at school on Monday," says Polly as they reach her house.

"Yes, bye Poll."

And with a wave to her friend Polly enters the house front door.

"Hello Polly did you have a good day in Carswell?" asks Ben.

Polly has walked into the parlour to get a drink since she has not had a drink all day.

"Yes thank you, Daddy, can I speak with you about that, please?"

Mr Spencer looks at her with an enquiring note and asks.

"What is it that you want, Polly, I was hoping to make some phone calls before supper."

"This is very important Daddy, really it is."

"Oh very well, come with me into the study," he says, leaving the parlour and crossing the hall before entering the study, with Polly close behind him. She sits down and proceeds to relate to him that she has been to Coventry, found the house where she was held and discovered a large amount of goods presumably earmarked for sale through the black market. Mr Spencer's reaction goes from initial shock at what Polly did, anger because of the danger she had put herself in to finally admitting that her exploits had uncovered what he had were looking for, namely the opportunity to catch a gang of criminals and close down their operation.

"Polly, this information really will be very useful, but to act as you did was very, very silly, do you realise what could have happened to you if you had been caught by these men?"

"I am sorry for worrying so much, Daddy, but I just had to do something to get back at those horrid men who took me away. I want to be able to help you catch these men before they steal any more things that are needed by everyone. You do understand don't you?" she says, almost pleading with Ben.

"Yes I do, so for now let's leave it, I will tell Mummy what happened when I get a chance, you must not tell Maisy, Daisy and George any of this," he replies firmly.

"No of course not, Daddy, I promise."

"Now go along and help Mummy with supper, I have an important telephone call to make."

And with that, Polly goes through the door to the kitchen to help prepare supper and hear about the discovery in the field at the bottom of the garden.

Ben searches through his pocket book looking for the private number of Beatrice Carrington. Beatrice Carrington was Ben Spencer's confidante and mentor from his early days in the Central Office for Information. They met while he was compiling data relating to racketeering in Central London and was most helpful. She was able to help in with paperwork required to access confidential documents and assist in determining which department was responsible for what in government. Her position, in what was effectively an internal affairs department monitoring government personnel, gave her the authority to seek whatever she felt may be required to break up racketeering and activities against the state. She had authorisation from the highest level to monitor criminal activity in all government departments. Ben Spencer contacted her only when all other efforts failed and he needed information quickly and was struggling with protocols. No one knew of their relationship, which Ben had hidden from all his colleagues, because of her position and the sensitivity of the information that she was able to offer. She had been able to assist him many times, giving him names of personnel suspected of involvement in black market activities. He was able to openly pursue them whereas Beatrice would have had to reveal her identity. When he began to compile the dossier of names places etc., he realised the importance of keeping it safe, and asked Beatrice if she would hold it in safekeeping until he was able to act on its' contents. It was imperative that this information be kept secret until he had every piece of evidence needed to break up the racketeering gangs. Beatrice agreed to hold on to the information for him, and he had not made any contact with her regarding this for some time. It was agreed that the less they made contact the less chance their relationship could be compromised. Ben dials the number and listens to the dialling tone.

"Hello, Beatrice Carrington."

"Beatrice, it's Ben Spencer."

"Ben, I had been expecting your call, how are you?"

"Yes Beatrice, I'm fine it was good of you to drop off those papers," he says, referring to the documents clandestinely.

"Circumstances meant that I had to move them quickly, I believe someone may be watching me and who I meet with, I meant to call you but have not had a safe opportunity to do so."

"I see, you obviously did the right thing, do you have any idea who may be watching you," Ben asks with concern.

"I believe it may be someone attached to your end, but I have no proof, I am just being careful."

"Is there anything I can do at all?" he asks.

"Just keep your eyes and ears open for any unusual meetings or discussions generally, but do not take any chances, Ben."

"You be very careful also, Beatrice, I will contact you again only if I have pertinent information for you, goodbye for now."

"Thank you goodbye, Ben." Ben sits there pondering his conversation with Beatrice Carrington. It had been at her suggestion that the family moved out of the capital during the war, partly because of the bomb devastation, but also because it was felt that Ben could be more useful to the government's efforts to stamp out corruption by operating from the provinces ideally The Midlands. The Midlands was the hub of a huge racketeering operation out of Birmingham, and someone was needed to head up a team, and be locally based. Beatrice had put Ben's name forward, unofficially via her contacts, believing him to be the best possible man for the job. His family were happy to make the move, Mrs Spencer was delighted to be able to move the children to the countryside, and be nearer to her sister Pauline and brother John who both lived in Leicester. Ben was pleased to be running his own team at least for the duration of the war years. When war ended he was content to be part of a new set up with wider powers. His remit was to advise local councils of how to rebuild their economies and what funding they might be eligible for to complete their rebuilding programmes. This was his official position which everyone one around him was led to believe. In fact, whilst he was able to advise, what he was actually doing was often quite different. His position allowed him to walk through just about any door in any council office, and this was what he had to be able to do in order to access and pinpoint any unusual activity in a department which may require further investigation. No one ever knew how many investigations had been highlighted and from where the information had come. Nor would anyone suspect him since he operated 'in plain sight' of everyone!

During his time at The Ministry for Information, Home Publicity Division, he made several contacts with people with dubious backgrounds. They gave him valuable information which he brought to the Central Office of Information in the Midlands. These contacts fed him sources and details of robberies, distribution drops and other illegal activities such as counterfeit ration cards. In order to maintain a low profile, he reported to Phil Landers any information that he acquired which was not too sensitive. In fact, he was constantly monitoring the movements of the main players in criminal activities involving the sale and purchase of goods that the public requires to live and work in post war Britain. Phil Landers was Controller for The Home Publicity Division. His remit covered monitoring goods and services in and out of the Birmingham and Coventry areas. Ben did not know what his background was and, until recent events, had not had a great deal of contact with him.

He was a typical civil servant who tended to be blinkered to a great deal of what was going on. This suited Ben, since it gave him all the latitude he needed to carry out his activities. Ben reaches for the phone and calls Phil Lander. He recites Polly's activities to him, and suggests a raid on the house on Monday morning.

"Right, Ben, I suggest we meet at Coventry Police Station at 8 o'clock tomorrow."

"Fine by me Phil."

"Good, I will see you then."

On Monday morning, Ben leaves the house early for Coventry Police Station, arriving at 7.45. Phil Landers and his men are already inside, and upon Ben's arrival meet in a conference room to be briefed for the raid at the house that Polly has identified. After outlining their plan of action they leave The Station, Ben in Phil Lander's car the rest of the men in an unmarked police van. Two men are placed in the alleyway at the back of the property, the rest drive in through the front gate. They rush to the front door and force it open with a crowbar, before dashing inside. Two men go upstairs; the remainder go towards the back of the house where Polly had said the items were stored. To the dismay of everyone, the place is empty, save for a couple of cartons containing tinned fruits, that have been discarded because of damage, probably by the rush to move the goods. Phil Landers sits on an old box and shouts: "What the hell happened here? How did they know we were coming at such short notice?"

How indeed? thinks Ben Spencer before adding, "My guess is they panicked over what happened with Polly, and moved the stuff as soon as they were able. They were unaware that she had returned, so the items have literally just been moved. You can still smell paraffin in the next room."

"You may be right, Ben, but this is a major setback for me," Phil adds with obvious disappointment in his voice. The two men sit in silence on the short journey back to the police station, Ben asking himself again, were the gang tipped off about the raid this morning?

Polly is escorted to school by Mrs Poulton and thanks her at the school gate.

"See you at 4 o'clock Mrs Poulton, bye," she says as she runs into the school to meet up with some of her friends in the driveway.

"I will be waiting for you. Polly," Mrs Poulton replies, still worrying about the events that led to Polly's recent abduction. Polly meanwhile settles down to a routine school morning and is relieved when lunch break arrives. There is not much choice in the school shop, so she settles for an apple from the school orchard with some crusty bread and sits outside on the school playing field with her friends to enjoy her lunch.

"Poll, there is a lady at the gate asking for you, something about Mr Spencer meeting you after school?" Claire mentions to her.

Polly looks puzzled and wonders what Daddy can possibly want with her. She wanders to the gate where a middle-aged woman is waiting. She is wearing glasses and has a hat on which shields her features. Dressed in a long coat she looks rather austere, and Polly watches her with apprehension as she approaches.

"Hello, Polly. My name is Margery Wilcox; I hope I haven't alarmed you calling on you like this."

"What do you want and how do you know my Daddy?" Polly enquires sharply.

"I know your Daddy very well, and have been trying to make contact with him. I wonder if you would give him this letter? It is very important."

"Why can't you just leave it at his office or post it to him?" Polly asks suspiciously.

"Because the information is too important not to give to him personally. I am sorry, I told your friend a story about a meeting, but I had to be sure you would meet me."

"Yes, of course I will give him the letter," says Polly.

"That is all, Polly, nice to have met you, goodbye."

Polly places the letter in her pocket and returns to her friends on the school field, suspicious of what the letter might contain.

CHAPTER 11

(Mrs Spencer has visitors)

Mrs Spencer, too, has an eventful visit when she returns from taking the children to school. She has just gone into the kitchen to put down her shopping, when the front door bell rings. She assumes it is Peter Forsyth, but had she looked into the garden she would have seen him tidying up the sand pit. She opens the front door to be confronted by a man and woman with a clipboard and ID tags around their necks.

"Good morning, madam, we are from the food rationing distribution offices, I wonder if we might ask you a few questions."

"May I see your identifications please?"

"Yes of course," the man replies and shows her what looks like an authentic identification, although she would not really know if it was genuine or not.

"May we come in, it will only take about ten minutes, and it is very important that we secure the information about the rationing of food," the woman confirms.

"Oh very well, this way," replies Mrs Spencer and leads them into the parlour.

"You have a beautiful home; tell me do you grow any food yourselves?" the man asks.

"Yes, we grow carrots and beans, and we have some apple trees."

"And what does Mr Spencer do?" the woman asks. "And is he away much?"

"Why do you want to know how often he is away?" replies Mrs Spencer.

"Because, Mrs Spencer, it could affect your allocation of certain items if your husband spends a lot of time away," the woman responds firmly.

"Oh, I see well my husband works in local government advising on how to secure quotas of any items the council may be entitled. This means he may be away the odd night but that is all."

"And does this mean he keeps information at home that may be useful to someone who wants to influence him on their entitlements?" the man asks.

"I really have no idea what documents he may bring home with him; my place is in the home. I thought you were going to ask questions about food rationing, why so much interest in my husband's work?" Mrs Spencer asks suspiciously.

Just then, Peter Forsyth enters from the conservatory.

"Who are you?" the man asks rather brusquely.

"I am the gardener."

"Oh I see, well I think that will be all for now, Mrs Spencer, thank you for your help. I hope we have not been too much of an inconvenience," she adds as she and her companion cross the hall toward the front door.

"Good bye and thank you once again."

Mrs Spencer returns to the parlour to talk with Peter Forsyth.

"Thank you for a timely entrance, Peter," says Margaret and recounts to him the strange and suspicious interview.

"I think it may be an idea to write down what you remember of the descriptions of the two strangers, Margaret, while the memory is fresh in your mind. I will contact Ben and tell him what has happened."

When Peter returns he looks worried.

"I have left a message for Ben, I expect he will make contact as soon as he hears what has happened. Those people were obviously trying to get information about him and used the excuse of a food ration survey to get into the house. Did they go into any other rooms?" Peter asks anxiously.

"No, I brought them straight to the parlour."

"On a positive note, they must be getting concerned about what Ben knows and are trying everything they can to get information on how and where he operates."

"I have made a few notes describing them, I hope it helps," says Margaret.

"Any information could prove useful, Margaret."

"Would you like some tea Peter, I know I would after all that talk?"

"Thank you, Margaret, then I am going to check the garden area and the field beyond."

As Margaret is making tea, the phone rings, and Peter answers. It's Ben responding to the message Peter had left for him. Peter, tells him of Margaret's visitors and Ben is just so very relieved that he had installed Peter in the house. Ben tells Peter of the disappointment over the raid in Coventry and they both agree that the gang could have been tipped off. After lunch, Mrs Spencer sits down in the parlour and goes over in her head the morning's events. She is worried for the family and what might happen next, but knows she must not burden her husband with any of this. She has to carry on as usual and hope that eventually they will get back to normal.

However, since there are still many restrictions on so many food items she realises that that time may be some way away. She must have drifted to sleep, because she is woken by Peter reminding her it is time to collect the children from school. She hurries off to collect the children, and is relieved to see Ben upon her return.

"My dear Margaret, are you okay? I am so sorry that you had to go through that unpleasantness," he says with concern.

"I'm fine, Ben, really," she replies hugging him with relief.

"Daddy, Daddy, what happened to Mummy, have those bad men been here?" asks Maisy.

"I wish Rusty were here, he would have barked and frightened them away," says George, obviously still upset over the loss of their dog.

"Children, everything is fine, Mummy had an unwelcome visitor, but she was quite safe with Peter in the house."

"But what do they want, Daddy, why can't they leave us alone?" asks Maisy tearfully.

"You will look after us won't you, Daddy?" Daisy asks clutching at Ben for reassurance.

"Of course I will look after you, Daisy, soon all this will be forgotten, so please try not to worry about anything. Mummy and I, and Polly, will take care of you and not let anyone harm you in any way, do you understand that, children?"

"Yes Daddy," they all answer together.

"Good, now go along with Mummy to the parlour, I have to speak with Peter."

"Keep them occupied while I talk with Peter, Margaret, you and I will catch up on what happened later," he says as he disappears into the study with Peter Forsyth.

"What do you think, Peter?" asks Ben of his close friend.

"I think these people are becoming increasingly desperate to find out what you know," Peter replies.

"You are absolutely right, Peter, I will speak to London about this, I do not feel confident keeping it local anymore, I am sure we have a leak somewhere."

"You could be right, Ben, it was some coincidence that they found out soon enough to move everything so quickly."

"That's what worries me, Peter."

"I'll go and have another look around outside before I leave, unless you want me to stay on?"

"I think we will be fine, Peter, you go when you are ready, and I will see you tomorrow no doubt," says Ben.

Peter moves from the study just as Polly comes in from school, followed by Mrs Poulton. "Daddy, I have to speak with you most urgently," Polly says with excitement.

"Polly, calm down what is it that you want now?" asks Ben wearily.

"Mrs Poulton, would you go through to the parlour, please?"

"Yes of course, Mr Spencer, bye, Polly."

"Good bye, Mrs Poulton, and thank you for taking care of me today," replies Polly as she follows Ben into the study.

Polly tells about her meeting a woman at the school gate, and hands over the envelope to Ben.

"What does it mean, Daddy, what do these people want, why do they keep bothering us?" she asks with some anxiety for someone so young.

Ben takes the envelope, opens it and scans the contents.

"Polly, I wonder if you would do me a favour?"

"Yes of course, Daddy, what do you want me to do?"

"Would you go to the garden and ask Peter to come to the study, then stay with Mummy in the parlour while I talk with Peter about this, will you do that for me, please?"

"Yes, Daddy," says Polly and leaves the study closing the door behind her.

Ben sits at his desk and again reads through the contents of the letter.

'Hello, Mr Spencer, in view of your constant interference in my business affairs, I believe that I should talk with you to clarify my position. You are very aware of my determination not to allow anyone to jeopardise my activities, the abduction of your daughter is proof of that, and yet you continue to cause me problems. Please be aware that my organisation is far too big, stretching to the highest levels of government, to allow your amateurish efforts to curb my business operation. Be content with your modest successes to date. I am happy to give you some small success from time to time to satisfy your superiors. I know that there are some losses that have to be absorbed in any operation. But any further attempts to attack my business from the inside will be met with severe consequences. I suggest that we meet to discuss what you can and can't do in the future, in fact what you will be allowed to confiscate with my blessing. You will be contacted presently to discuss a suitable venue. Meanwhile, Mr Spencer, curb your enthusiasm and enjoy the benefits that your lovely family have to offer. Please, be warned I do not make statements that I cannot back up with whatever actions may be necessary

Overlord.'

Mr Spencer sits and ponders the contents of the threatening letter, for that is indeed what it is, and he accepts that fact, as Peter Forsyth enters the study. He hands the letter to him.

"I think we are beginning to get under the skin of these crooks Peter," he says with a satisfying grin.

Meanwhile, Polly and her mother are exchanging notes regarding their day and what has occurred. It soon becomes apparent that the woman that handed Polly the letter for Ben, Margery Wilcox, was the same woman that came to the house with a man both posing as collectors of information for the food office. Margaret Spencer becomes quite fretful when she realises that these people are able to contact them in broad daylight without any fear of being discovered or of being brought to justice.

"I will have to speak with your Daddy about this as soon as he is free. Betty, I wonder if you would mind arranging some supper, I am so sorry to impose, but I must find out what Mr Spencer is doing about all this," she says wearily.

"Don't you worry, Margaret, I will organise supper with Polly and the children, you go and sort out your business with, Mr Spencer."

"There are potatoes that can be boiled and perhaps we can make some dumplings and use some of our carrots and parsnips?"

"That sounds wonderful, Margaret," Mrs Poulton replies.

Margaret enters the study, anxious to talk with Ben about the day's events.

Ben is looking through the letter Polly delivered as she enters.

"Is that the letter handed to Polly, Ben?"

"Yes, it is," he answers and hands it to her.

Margaret reads the contents and sits down wearily saying.

"These people get more threatening each day, Ben, I am fearful of what they may try next."

"I believe they, too, are fearful in a way, scared of what we have achieved, we must continue this fight, Margaret," Ben answers firmly.

"I understand, Ben, really I do, I just wonder how it is going to end?"

"This is a war we have to win, Margaret."

And after more assurances from Ben, although he also remains apprehensive, he asks, "Now what do we have for supper this evening, I am quite hungry after a very busy day?"

After supper, Mr Spencer returns to the study to phone Phil Landers and updates him on events. Why is he wary of telling Phil too much information? He doesn't know but wary he is. After telling him of the letter sent via Polly, and the visit to the house in his absence, Phil Landers responds.

"We must set up the meeting as soon as possible, Ben, I believe that the racketeers want to make some sort of concessions here," he says enthusiastically.

"Yes, I believe you are absolutely right about that, Phil."

He has already decided to speak with his contact in Birmingham, Bill Holder, but decides against mentioning this fact to Phil Landers. Best see what he has to say first. He hopes his contact will be able to give him some background into 'Overlord' whoever he might be.

"Let me know as soon as he makes contact, Ben, I want to join you at any meeting that Overlord arranges."

"That may not be the best way forward Phil, the last thing we want to happen is for him to have another target, don't you think?"

Phil Landers pauses, then replies, "Yes of course, and you can pass on the information so that we can coordinate a firm plan of action to bring down these crooks as soon as possible."

"The Nation has suffered enough, Phil, we need to be able to purchase freely everything we need at a fair price, not be held to ransom by a small number of gangsters."

"Well said, Ben, I will be in touch tomorrow, is there anything else I should know about?" he adds.

"No, that is it for now, Phil, goodbye."

"Goodbye, Ben," Phil answers and puts down the receiver.

Mr Spencer sits and ponders what his next move will be in this sordid business involving black market goods and racketeering and other unsavoury activities. The following morning, he is bombarded with questions from Polly.

"What did the letter say, Daddy? Who was it from? Why did those people come to the house and question Mummy?" she fires questions, almost nonstop.

"Slow down, Polly, the letter was from a man who wants to meet with me but wanted to keep it secret, I can only guess what Mummy's visitors were after, possibly checking the house to see how to get in and out quickly if necessary," Ben replies as honestly as he can without giving too much away.

"Will you meet with these people here, Daddy? When will this happen, will it be soon?" Polly continues with her endless questions.

"Why are they always bothering us, Daddy, I am scared?" Daisy asks.

"I think we should tell the police to lock them up for ever," says George firmly.

"One day, we will be able to do just that George, now run along and get ready for school. Polly, I am waiting for a message as to where and when I am to meet with the people concerned, I do not want them in our house again and will resist any suggestions to meet here. Now off you go and prepare for school, Mrs Poulton will be here shortly," Ben replies, relieved it is time for Polly and all the children to get ready for school.

He understands that there will be questions, especially from Polly, who seems determined to find out more about what is happening with her father's activities. He decides he must talk with her about this, reassure her, but make sure that she does not go off again looking to help him and putting herself in danger. With these thoughts in mind, he leaves for his office, telling Margaret he may be late this evening. It is his intention to make contact with Bill Holder, in Birmingham, hoping he will be able to tell him more about 'Overlord'.

After a quiet day in his local office, Mr Spencer leaves to catch a train for Birmingham. New Street station, in Birmingham is a busy hub being close to the centre of the city. Extensively damaged by bombing in the Birmingham Blitz, it was actually repaired, ready for use again, using surplus war materials. Mr Spencer leaves the station and sets off on the short walk to The Bull Ring market area. He looks at his watch; it is just after 6 o'clock.

The Bull Ring dates back to the time of Henry the second who granted the charter to allow the area to trade. The name derives from when bull baiting by dogs was popular in the 16th century. Mr Spencer knows that Bill Holder will be in one of three pubs, The Woolpack Hotel, The Royal George or The Board Vaults, known locally as The Cod's Head because of its proximity to the fish market! These are the only pubs where Mr Spencer has ever met with him. Bill Holder has worked on the market for many years, and has always been a useful source of information, about what is going on, for a price. Mr Spencer first met with him at the end of the war when he was arrested for handling goods on the black market. He kept him out of prison in return for his providing information.

The Bull Ring pubs were known to be frequented by many villains operating outside the law. Most were small time, just making a bit extra, but there were those that moved large consignments of food items, cigarettes and alcohol. The authorities had been trying for some time to catch these people but had never been able to catch them with anything illegal. Mr Spencer was hoping that his letter from 'Overlord' might be just what he needed to catch the main movers of black market goods throughout the Midlands and even beyond. He enters the Woolpack, and

Bill Holder is sitting down, alone, at a corner table facing the door. Bill spots Mr Spencer immediately and beckons to him to go and join him.

"Hello again, Mr Spencer, how've you been, it's been a while?" he enquires with his strong local accent.

"Yes it has been, Bill, so I hope my visit will be worthwhile, for both of us," he says, looking around to see if anyone is showing any interest in him. He has dressed himself as plainly as possible to avoid anyone noticing him, and hasn't shaved today, so, having a dark beard, he looks a little unkempt.

"How is business, Bill, still keeping busy I trust?"

"Very busy, Mr Spencer, that is what I wanted to talk to you about."

Ben Spencer glances around the room once again, but there are not too many drinkers yet since it is still early. No one seems to be taking any notice of these two men sitting in a corner. Bill Holder tells Mr Spencer that movement by road is now being replaced by movement by canal. The roads are still being used, but the gangs operating out of London and Birmingham, having realised that checks on barges are minimal, have started moving more and more by barge. So far, not one shipment has been confiscated, so the villains have not been too concerned about their losses from transporting by road. The barges are able to mingle with family boats carrying small shipments of timber and coal as they have done for many years. No one takes any notice of one or two additional boats going through the locks. Bill Holder has family that work on the barges, and he can visit them when they are in dock without anyone taking any notice of him, especially as he will stay overnight occasionally.

"Are the boats easy to pick out among the others on the canals?"

"Yeah, they're freshly painted, and are bigger than most, and the cockney accents stick out among the Brummie twang an' all."

"Any names being mentioned at all, Bill?" asks Ben.

"Yeah, Bob Danvers and Nick Wilson, both cockneys and really mean characters. Danvers is the older of the two very big, and Nick Wilson always has a knife handy which he is not scared to use. They are always there when any boats dock, and organise unloading."

"Any possibility you could find out any more about these two and when any other shipments are due?" asks Ben with anticipation.

"Okay, Mr Spencer, but this info' will cost you. I will have expenses because I will have to leave some of my other business," Bill Holder responds.

"You will be well rewarded if your information is solid, Bill," replies Ben as he hands an envelope to him beneath the table.

"Meanwhile, here is something for your trouble."

"I'm obliged, Mr Spencer, now how do I make contact with you if I need?"

Ben hands him his telephone number, which Bill puts into the lining of his cap, before finishing his drink.

"Goodbye, Bill, and thank you," says Ben as he gets up from the table and leaves.

Ben returns home that evening to assess the information from Bill Holder, concerned of the new method of shipment that is now being used so successfully. No one had mentioned barges being used by the gangs to move large amounts of illegal goods from London to the Midlands. For the moment, Ben decides to keep this information to himself, until Bill Holder contacts him with details of a new shipment. And he decided not to ask about 'Overlord' in view of this new information about barge shipments. He has yet to hear from 'Overlord' whoever he is with his proposals, which he has no doubt will be unacceptable. So there was very little he could have said about him to Bill Holder and would prefer him to concentrate on watching what is happening with the barges. Ben enjoys a quiet supper with the family, and actually has time to sit down and look at the local newspaper. Polly has schoolwork to attend to and the other children are upstairs amusing themselves in the playroom. Margaret has clothes to iron and has vegetables from the garden to clean and store for tomorrow.

"Hello, Daddy, have you found out about those people who came to the house yet?" asks Polly as she burst into the parlour.

"Nothing yet, but I am sure they or someone else will make contact when they are ready. Meanwhile, we shall get on with things and not worry about what has happened. I will do everything possible to see that you and all of the family are safe and in no danger from anyone. Do you understand Polly?"

"Yes, Daddy, I know you will keep us all safe," Polly replies.

"Polly, can you call the children down it is nearly bedtime?" says Margaret entering the parlour.

Ben says goodnight to them and takes them upstairs to get them ready for bed.

"It has been such a long time since we have been able to sit down without anything happening," says Margaret as she returns to the parlour after seeing the children safely tucked away for the night ... or so she believes.

"I would enjoy some tea before we go up, Margaret if you have finished."

CHAPTER 12

(Polly disturbs intruders)

Polly wakes up suddenly hearing what sounded like breaking glass. She sits up in her bed, her ears straining to pick up any sound. Because the house was situated in a lane, the night was normally very quiet apart from owls. So any unusual sound was almost magnified. Polly opens her door and listens from the landing. There was definitely someone downstairs, *if only Rusty were here*, she thinks. She moves toward the stairs, listening for any more noise then goes down stairs and listens at the door of the study. There was definitely someone in the study, and she could see the shadow from a torch beneath the door. She turned the doorknob and slowly opened the door.

"What are you doing in my house?" she shouts, as she switches on the study light.

Two men, the same two men who abducted her, look at her in amazement.

"Jesus, Polly, when are you gonna learn to mind your business?" says Jimmy Spiers.

Polly suddenly realises how vulnerable she is standing there clad only in her nightshirt.

The other man, who is Don Jones, grabs her and puts his hand over her mouth.

"Please don't struggle, Polly, we are not going to hurt you, we are looking for some papers that your Daddy has," he says holding her tightly around her waist.

"There ain't nothing here what we were told about Don, just figures no names or places." Jimmy says to him, obviously annoyed at being disturbed.

"Let's get out of here," says Don as he drags Polly toward the kitchen door.

"We are leaving by the back door, Polly, give us time before you start shouting do you promise?" says Don releasing his hold on Polly.

"Get out, get out!" screams Polly in tears.

Jimmy Spears slaps Polly hard across the face as he pushes her to the ground.

"Don't you ever learn, girl?" he says menacingly.

"Come on let's get out of here, Jimmy, before Spencer arrives," Don urges.

Polly screams again after being hit and falls to the floor. The two men, meanwhile, make off across the garden. After what seems forever, Ben and Margaret dash into the kitchen to find Polly trying to get up from where she fell after being struck.

"Good God, Polly what on earth has happened?"

"Oh, Daddy, I tried to stop them," says Polly and bursts into tears.

"My dear Polly, what were you thinking? Margaret, we must call the police."

Margaret goes into the study to call the police.

"Are you hurt, Polly?" he asks noticing red marks on her face.

"I'm okay, Daddy, just a few scratches."

"The police will be along as soon as possible, Ben," says Margaret returning to the kitchen.

The study has been ransacked, but the papers there are not sensitive, just accounts relating to recommended purchases by various council departments. The safe is discreetly hidden behind the wall clock on the adjoining kitchen wall. Ben leaves things as they are for the police and returns to the kitchen where Margaret is making some tea.

"Is Polly okay, Ben? She really should have called you," she says with concern in her voice.

"I am sure she is fine save for a few bruises, but I worry about her insistence on trying to be so helpful."

Polly, meanwhile is in the bathroom examining her bumps and bruises. After washing, she dresses and returns downstairs as the doorbell rings. She answers the door to D.I Wishart and PC Parsons.

"Please come in, we have had a break in," she says and shows the officers into the study.

Margaret decides she should check on the children who seem to have slept through all the activity. They are in fact still sleeping, which is some relief to her, so she returns down stairs to the study. Polly gives a detailed statement to the police, recalling what happened but not mentioning who the two men were. She can always mention this later, but decides to see whether Ben would prefer not to inform the police at this stage. He also omits knowing who the men were, and for the moment is content to let the police treat the episode as a simple robbery attempt. He passes these thoughts onto Phil Landers when he calls him at 9 o'clock.

"You are absolutely right not to inform the police about these men Ben, it would not help them and could complicate matters for the department. How is Polly, your daughter is really a brave young lady."

"She is fine thanks, just a few bruises," says Ben.

"No news on this 'Overlord' character I suppose?" Phil Landers asks.

"Not yet, but I expect him to make contact soon since we have been damaging his business."

"Okay, Ben, I may see you later today?"

"Yes, I will finish cleaning up then I will be on my way," Ben replies replacing the receiver.

He sits back in his chair reflecting on the night's activities and again ponders over Polly's actions. He has nothing but admiration for his daughter, but does despair sometimes at her actions. But what he is sure of is that she is unlikely to change, Polly has always been determined and very independent. He realises that his family are now very much involved with his activities, and he must take all necessary steps to protect them. In his gun case he has two old 12 bore shotguns, family heirlooms, used for rabbiting and killing vermin. Both were in working order when he checked them, and he has an ample supply of cartridges. In the bottom drawer of his desk, which is always locked with a key he has with him at all times, is a semi-automatic Waltham P.38 pistol from the war years. He can't remember how he came about the weapon, or whether he has authorisation for it, but is happy to know that he has something which might help protect his family as a last resort.

"Good morning, Peter, am I glad to see you?" says Ben as Peter arrives and proceeds to tell him of the night's activities and also comments on not mentioning knowing who the intruders were.

Peter listens intently and asks, "Do you think they will try again, they seem desperate to find those documents?"

"I really don't know what they will do next, Peter, but we must be prepared for whatever they have in mind. I am waiting for this Overlord character to call me so that I can get a better idea of what we are up against."

"Ben, when will you be leaving for work?" Margaret asks from the kitchen, having returned from taking Maisy, Daisy and George to school.

"Very shortly, dear, I am just bringing Peter up to date with the events of last night," he replies and closes the door.

"Peter, can I ask do you still have any weapons at your disposal?"

"Well, I still have an old Browning semi-automatic pistol from the war, and the family has shotguns used for shooting trips."

"Can I ask that you carry the Browning with you when you are at the house? I want to be prepared should events turn ugly."

"Very well, Ben, I will pop back home and collect it right away," says Peter, leaving the study.

"Thanks, Peter, we will talk again later no doubt."

He sits down at his desk and reflects on what he has just requested of Peter. *Is it really that serious, am I contemplating using firearms to protect his family? Yes, it is, it would seem.* In fact, his decision makes good sense considering Polly's abduction, the visit yesterday and the break in last night! The events of the last few days have strengthened his resolve and made him more determined to destroy the people who would hold the country to ransom for their own gain both during the war years and after up to present day. And he knows that no one person can close down the black market business. But he will continue to do everything he can, using his contacts gained over a number of years, to supply the information needed to break down as many illegal operations as possible. He will keep the pressure on these people, seizing their goods at every opportunity and bringing the culprits to justice. There will be a time when rationing of essential goods will end and the public will be able to buy as much as they want of anything. But until that happens, racketeers and gangsters will continue seek to exploit the shortages for profit. These people do not care about shortages, only the money they can make from exploiting those shortages, and they will not let anyone get in the way of their business. And shortages are still evident in everyday essentials: Fresh eggs, egg powder, butter, sugar, jam, sweets and meat especially. And criminals are regularly using firearms in robberies, weapons continuing to be a most menacing import. It is for these reasons that Ben Spencer asked Peter to carry a weapon while he is at the house, and Ben will himself have his pistol to hand when he is at home. He will continue the fight and be prepared for the risks that he and his family will face. And with those thoughts he leaves the house for his office.

Margaret is hoping for a quiet day at the house after the events of the last evening. The children went off to school safely, and it was decided that Polly should also go to school rather than have to explain another absence.

Polly is relieved that she does not have to miss any more time from school so soon after her time off to recover from her abduction. And Margaret wants her to be able to continue normal life as much as possible. This is not going to be easy if recent events are anything to go by, and Margaret is sure that they have not seen or heard the last of the people who have entered their lives so dramatically over the last few days. Meanwhile, she has arranged for a local tradesman to replace the broken window which he does that afternoon. She is relieved to see Peter Forsyth return and finds him in the garage securing the tools that the intruders used in their attempts to break into the house. Peter also uses the shed next to the garage as his refuge against any bad weather. And it gives him a full view of the grounds and the field beyond.

"Peter, I am off to the village to see what I can find for supper, you know where everything is if you need anything?"

"Thank you, Margaret, I will see you when you get back," Peter replies as he stands at the door of the garage and looks out over the garden and the field beyond. Because the garden has a natural slope away from the house, he can see clearly across the adjoining field to the lane. At the far end he has noticed a car has been parked for some time. He collects a spade and moves down the garden towards the gate stopping behind the large bush. He peers through the bush, with his binoculars, toward the car. There is only the driver in the car who is sitting there watching the house. Peter, watches from behind the bush, until he sees Margaret walking down the lane toward the car. He moves toward the gate to the field, concerned what the man in the car might do, but stops when the car drives away.

Margaret continues her walk to the village and Peter occupies himself in the garden, now carrying his Browning pistol tucked in to the back of his chords. It has been sometime since he has used the pistol, and he decides he must check it as soon as possible, and fire off a few rounds to get the feel of the weapon. The remainder of the day is uneventful, Margaret collects Maisy, Daisy and George from school as usual and Polly arrives soon after having been collected by Mrs Poulton.

Ben returns around 5.30 p.m., as Margaret starts to prepare supper. Just as she is about to call everyone for supper, the telephone rings.

"Hello, Ben Spencer speaking."

"Mr Spencer, hello again, I hope you and your family are well and not too shaken up by that unfortunate business last night," says the voice of the man calling himself Overlord.

"I wondered how long it would be before you made contact again, sorry that my daughter upset your men, she is very determined as you know."

"You have a responsibility to your family Mr Spencer, and need to stop your daughter from meddling, do you understand?"

Ben pauses before replying.

"My daughter does not meddle, sir, she was merely confronting intruders in our house!"

"Anyway, Mr Spencer, I want to arrange this meeting, are you free tomorrow to travel to Birmingham?"

"I will make time tomorrow," Ben replies bluntly.

"Can I suggest The Woolpack Hotel, Moor Street in The Bull Ring?"

"What time?" Ben replies.

"Shall we say 3 o'clock?"

"Very well, I will be there for 3 o'clock," Ben responds and replaces the receiver.

He immediately contacts Phil Landers and makes him aware of the meeting.

"Thanks for letting me know, Ben, we will discuss what we are going to say at the office tomorrow before we leave."

"Yes okay, Phil, I will see you in the morning," he replies replacing the receiver.

"What we need to find out is just how much this Overlord character thinks he knows and hope to find out just what he is up to," Phil Landers says when he meets with Ben the next morning at the office. Ben has not told him about his meeting with Bill Holder, so simply agrees that they must find out what they can.

"Let's see what he comes up with, we know he is not going to tell us anything about distribution or supply, but we do know that they are looking for some sort of agreement regarding our constant seizing of their so called assets," says Ben.

"So you think he is going to try and get some deal worked out for his operation to continue?"

"Yes, Phil, I think he is, remember he was the one that asked for this meeting, and he is the one who has so much to lose."

"So all we need to do is listen and learn, Ben?" Phil Landers replies.

"Yes, I believe that is the best way to deal with this meeting."

So, after due discussion, they eventually catch the train for Birmingham. Ben had taken time to ring round last evening, after his telephone call, to contact Bill Holder and warn him not to go anywhere near the Woolpack this afternoon. It was important that his contact remained a secret to him, and that no one could link the two men, Bill Holder and Ben Spencer. He suggested that Bill go down to the canal and find out anything he can about any deliveries. Bill Holder thanked him for the warning and said he would go and visit his colleagues on the barges to see what he can find out.

Ben and Phil Landers arrive at the Woolpack on the stroke of 3 o'clock. Unknown to Phil Landers, Ben Spencer has taken the precaution of tucking his pistol into his inside pocket. He really does not know what to expect at this meeting, so is rather apprehensive of what he will find. He knows he is dealing with ruthless men and that his actions have been directly responsible for severely damaging their business. So it makes good sense to take the precaution of protecting himself.

CHAPTER 13

(Ben meets with Overlord)

They walk into the main room of The Woolpack and notice three men sitting in the corner who are looking straight at them as they enter.

"Mr Spencer?" one of the men asks.

"Yes, I am Ben Spencer, and you are?"

"I am an associate of Overlord, who apologises for his absence, and has asked me and my colleagues to listen to what you have to offer?"

"I think you must have been misled, sir, just what did you expect of me and my colleague, this is Phil Landers by the way?"

"We are hoping that you can offer some sensible ideas relating to your constant raids on our business operations so that we do not have to resort to further action on our part," a second man replies with some threat in his voice.

"We have the resources and the men to overcome the difficulties that you may have created, and will not put up with your constant interference."

"The authorities have no problems with legitimate business operations, but we do have a duty to prevent racketeering in the country. Your businesses are no more than a front for moving stolen goods, essential to the people of this country in order to feed and clothe their families. You are holding them to ransom with your actions."

"Mr Spencer, you need to offer us something that we can take back to our boss, it is what we all expect. Some of your raids have caused us severe hardship and we cannot allow this situation to continue, I am sure you understand."

"Yes, I understand that you have previously enjoyed running your operations unhindered since the war, and you want to continue doing so whilst the general public are forced to suffer rationing restrictions," says Ben angrily.

"We offer a service to those that can afford to pay, people want what we have to offer."

"As I have said, providing you are operating legally, and your goods have been purchased legitimately, then you will receive no bother from the authorities."

"Mr Spencer. You will go back to your superiors and tell them, that unless they cease significantly their raids on our warehouses, they and you will suffer the consequences do you understand?"

And with that threat ringing in the ears of Ben Spencer and Phil Landers, the three men get up from their seats and leave The Woolpack Hotel.

"Well that was pretty much a waste of our time Ben don't you agree?" says Phil Landers. He had sat listening to the conversation and realised that these men were hoping for Ben to offer them some sort of truce to continue with their illegal business, something which, he knew Ben would never sanction.

"It was certainly a waste of their time, Phil, what we have proved is that the gangsters and racketeers are losing the battle and trying to get concessions from the authorities. This will not happen, and I hope that is the message that those three men take back to Overlord."

On their way back to the office in Carswell, Ben continues the conversation.

"Providing we have the resources we can and will defeat these people."

"As a well-known member of the government team from Central Office of Information, you need to be careful, Ben, these people are ruthless as they have already shown you and your family."

"I have taken every precaution, Phil, but appreciate your concerns," says Ben.

"I am sure that their boss will make contact with me quite soon, meantime we keep up the pressure on their operations using the information we are getting from our network of contacts in The Midlands and beyond."

"Okay, Ben, well keep me up to date and let me know how I may be able to assist in any way."

They arrive back at Carswell station safely, and say their goodbyes. Ben returns to his car and has an uneventful journey back home arriving good time for supper. Margaret is very pleased to see him and looks forward to the family being able to all sit down together and enjoy their evening meal. Ben meanwhile, goes into the study and calls Peter Forsyth.

"Peter, hello it's Ben; do you have a moment?'

"Yes, Ben, what is it?"

Ben goes over the meeting in Birmingham earlier then asks, "Peter, I wonder if you would consider staying on longer some evenings? I would feel a lot more secure if both of us were in the house."

"Certainly, Ben, I can come over now if you wish."

"Thanks, Peter, and will you remember to bring along your pistol?"

Ben feels better for talking with Peter, knowing that his expertise would be invaluable if there were any real trouble. During the war years and immediately afterwards, Peter Forsyth had served a period in Military Intelligence after a successful campaign in North Africa. He was present for the Western Desert campaign, which resulted in the Italian defeat at Tobruk, as well as taking part at El Alamein. It was there he received injuries from shrapnel and a bullet in his shoulder. He was subsequently sent home and attached to the War Office, where his ability to speak fluent German was useful in prisoner interrogation and listening to German radio messages. While he was no longer a member of Military Intelligence, he had numerous contacts that he could turn to for advice of all sorts. An outwardly quiet man, Peter Forsyth is as tough as they come and a good man to have on your side in a crisis. Ben had first met with him during the war when he was attached to the Ministry of Information, and they had remained close friends ever since. Ben enjoys the evening meal of fish pie followed by some stewed apples topped by custard. Margaret has excelled herself and Ben had not realised how hungry he was.

The children chatter throughout the meal, and usually Ben would have told them to stop, but this time, he enjoys the chat which takes his mind off the day's proceedings.

"Daddy, where have you been today?" asks Polly. Ben had wondered how long it would be before Polly started the questions.

"I've been to Birmingham, with Phil Landers, and met with some unpleasant characters."

"It was a waste of my time since these men were hoping I would give in to their demands."

"But why do they always pick on you, Daddy? Is there no one else they can bother about all this?"

"It is my job, Polly, to find out what these people are up to and, if it is illegal as it often is, stop them and see that they are punished. Please try and understand that I have to do this to rid the country of evil criminals who only see profit in the present situation of rationing and restrictions.

"When there is enough food for everyone to buy as they wish, and no more restrictions on any goods that we need, and plenty of fuel for everyone, then these men will have no market to sell into. But that time is little way off I'm afraid."

"I will try and understand, Daddy, and think that you are doing a marvellous job."

"Daddy, will you read a story to us you haven't read a story to us for ages and ages?" says Daisy.

"Very well which one?"

CHAPTER 14

(Concerning the Spencers' house invasion)

Mr Spencer is interrupted by a loud banging at the front door.

"Who can that be making such a noise?" he says as he moves from the parlour into the hall and toward the door.

Mr Spencer opens the front door, and is confronted by four or five men, the foremost of whom enquires:

"Mr Spencer, my name is Montague Galbraith, I believe you know me as Overlord may we come in?" he says as he pushes past into the hallway followed by the other men.

"What do you think you are doing, barging your way into my house in this way?"

"I will ask the questions, Mr Spencer, shall we use the study, I believe it is this room isn't it, you men take the rest of the family upstairs, except Billy, you come with me into the study?"

Montague Galbraith issues orders with a confidence that singles him out as a leader. A big man in every respect very well dressed, definitely not in any war surplus materials. Galbraith sits down at the desk and beckons Ben Spencer to do the same.

"Mr Spencer, you are becoming very irritating to me, I sent my colleagues to meet with you to arrange some sort of agreement, and you completely refused to talk with them. They were angry at you over this, and so am I, so am I."

Galbraith looks hard at Ben, anticipating some response, but he simply stares back!

"Well don't you have anything to say?" says Galbraith.

"Yes get out of my house!"

"I am going nowhere until you talk some sense to me, Mr Spencer, I want you to stop your interfering in my business affairs right now."

"Do you think I am the only person seeking to break up your illegal activities?" says Ben.

"I am sure that you have help, but it is you with your knowledge and contacts, going back to the war years, that run the operation from The Central Office of Information," Galbraith replies.

"You are correct, I have the contacts and control the operation, but there will always be others when I am no longer here," says Ben firmly.

"But don't you see, you stupid man, that there is enough for everyone, no one need get hurt and I will give you just enough information to break up small operations and keep the Ministry happy?"

"I'm afraid I don't operate like that, Mr Galbraith."

"That's a pity, Mr Spencer, Billy, go and fetch the oldest daughter Polly from upstairs," replies Galbraith with a degree of menace in his voice.

"Wait, what do you want with my daughter?" Ben asks with some concern.

"Because she might help you to make up your mind, sir!" he replies as Billy leaves the room.

Mr Spencer's mind begins to race; this is a move he was not expecting. He cannot imagine how Polly's presence can make any difference to their discussions, unless Galbraith is contemplating something so sinister that he does not want to think about it.

Billy and a colleague, meanwhile returns with Polly, barefoot and dressed only in her underwear.

"So you are Polly, my name is Galbraith, I am trying to convince your father to help me with my business, and you are going to help him make up his mind," says Galbraith, grasping Polly toward him.

"Let go of me, you horrid man," says Polly, and proceeds to grab his right hand and bite it."

"Ouch, you little bitch!" shouts Galbraith and slaps Polly hard across the face.

Mr Spencer dashes to Polly's side, picks her up from the floor and helps her to a chair.

"I swear to God, Galbraith, you touch my daughter again and I will kill you for it," replies Ben, livid with rage.

"I believe you, Mr Spencer, and I believe you understand my intentions. You two, take her into the room across the hall, do whatever you have to do."

"Yes boss," Billy replies with a smile grabbing Polly by the hair.

"Now then, Mr Spencer, shall we begin again?"

The two men take Polly into the dining room and shove her into a chair. She is very scared and screams at the two men.

"Don't you dare touch me or my Daddy will kill you I promise!"

"Shut your mouth, girl, you should have been dealt with when we had you at the big house, now I am going to teach you a lesson that you won't forget," Billy replies.

The two men grab hold of Polly again and push her towards the table, holding her by her hair. Polly struggles loses her footing and rips her vest on the corner of the table as she falls to the floor. One of the men grabs her arms and holds them across the top of the table, the other holds her round her waist pulling at her underwear.

"This will be a lesson you will not forget you little brat," says Billy as he leans over Polly ripping her pants and pulling her towards him. Suddenly, the door bursts open and Peter Forsyth moves into the room shouting:

"Get your hands off her and move away, I mean it or I will shoot you where you stand," says Peter pointing his pistol at the two men.

"Polly, are you alright?" he asks with concern.

"I am alright, Peter, thank you."

"Here, take my jumper and cover yourself, then tie them both together as tightly as you can, you two face the wall."

Polly enjoys being able to tie up the two men who had treated her so badly. She shudders, partly with feeling cold and with an element of relief on Peter's timely intervention.

Peter then marches the two men across the hallway, followed closely by Polly, and pushes them into the study.

"You! Move away to the far wall and raise your hands above your head," he instructs Galbraith.

"Ben, is your pistol handy?"

"Yes I have it here," says Ben as he takes his pistol from the drawer.

"You keep these two here, you, sir come with me," he instructs Galbraith.

And with that he marches him to top of the stairs and instructs him to call his men from where they are holding Margaret and the children.

"Please do not attempt anything while I have a weapon pointing at you, if you do I will shoot you," Peter informs Galbraith with an almost casual air. Galbraith's men are marched down the stairs with him and Peter calls Ben to bring the other from the study. All the men are searched for weapons. Three of them including Galbraith are carrying pistols which Ben passes to Polly and asks her to place them on his desk in the study.

Ben Spencer speaks direct to Galbraith in the hallway while Peter watches his men.

"Mr Galbraith, be in no doubt that I will continue to pursue you until I can bring you and your organisation to justice. I see no point in handing you over to the police at this time with what little evidence we have. But be advised, sir, if you ever set foot in my house again or threaten any member of my family, I will shoot you dead before I hand you over to the authorities do you understand?"

Galbraith nods as Ben and Peter usher them toward the front door.

"Good, now get out of my house, all of you."

And with that, Galbraith and his men leave the house and move away in their cars. Ben watches from the door as they disappear up the lane toward the main road.

He goes back inside, locking and bolting the front door after him.

"My dear Polly, are you okay?" he says as he embraces his daughter.

"Yes thank you, Daddy, thanks to Peter, without him I do not know what would have happened."

"Peter, how can we ever repay you for your timely intervention?"

"It was as well that you asked me to return, Ben, I saw two cars at the front and suspected they might be uninvited guests. Then I heard Polly scream and decided to move."

"Is everyone else okay? Margaret, children are you alright?" Ben asks.

"Daddy, Daddy, are you going to shoot those nasty men for what they did to Polly?" asks Maisy.

"I think you should Daddy, I really do," replies George holding Margaret's hand tightly.

"Yes okay, children, I think we should all go into the parlour for a hot drink, Polly, I expect you would like hot bath, you do look a bit of a sight," Ben adds.

Polly is covered in bruises on her arms, legs and back and her underwear is ripped and dirty from her being dragged by the two men who took her into the dining room. Ben makes some tea while Margaret goes upstairs with Polly. He makes a warm milk drink for Maisy, Daisy and George to settle them before they go back to their beds. It has been an eventful period since supper and Ben is anxious to talk with Peter as soon as Margaret settles the family down. Once again she finds herself looking at the bruised body of her daughter and struggles not to burst into tears. She has bruising on both arms, her neck and her waist and the tops of her legs are scratched from struggling with the two men. She also has a nasty weal on her face. Her beautiful daughter has probably been subjected to more physical abuse over the last couple of weeks or so than most people will experience in a lifetime. But she is very resilient and will bounce back from this Margaret is sure. That does not detract in any way from what she has endured, but she goes off to her room with a cheery good night to Margaret.

"Say goodnight to Daddy for me, Mummy, and please thank Peter again for rescuing me," she says as she disappears into her bedroom.

She closes the door behind her, runs to her bed, drops down and bursts into sobs and tears. She sobs for a little while before drying her eyes and reliving the events of the evening. She shudders as she recalls the comments passed and how the two men handled her before Peter arrived. She can only guess at what they intended. It would seem that they wanted to force her father to make concessions by threatening her. She is already escorted to and from her school and dare not go anywhere alone, and now she has been attacked in her own house. However, for now she is just glad that it is all over. As she drifts off into a fitful sleep, she knows that this is not the end of desperate men seeking to exploit the shortages caused by rationing, nor the end of her father's efforts to destroy their evil activities.

After enjoying a welcome cup of tea, Ben goes into the study with Peter to discuss the evening's events.

"Peter, once again, thank you for turning up when you did, especially when Polly was in such danger from those men."

"My pleasure, Ben," says Peter.

"Your help has been invaluable, especially as my family has obviously been targeted by Galbraith. If you can continue with this role I would be very obliged, and of course your input and comments on their activities will be appreciated."

"They are organised and widespread Ben; I can talk to my contacts in London. Is there anyone you can call that may be able to assist?"

"As a matter of fact there is," Ben replies, thinking of his confidante Beatrice Carrington.

"Good well, I will get on to my colleagues in the morning."

"You will stay the night now, Peter, we have plenty of room, and it is getting late?"

"Very well, Ben, thank you, I will send for some of my things tomorrow so that I do not have to leave the house."

"Can you take care of these weapons for me, Peter, you are probably more familiar with guns than I am?" Ben asks, pointing to the weapons they took from Galbraith's men.

Peter takes the weapons and moves out of the study with Ben toward the parlour.

"I thought you might like something a little stronger than tea as a nightcap Ben," says Margaret, reaching for a bottle of whisky and three glasses.

"Thank you, Margaret, that's just what we need, Peter is staying the night by the way, can you fix the spare room for him please?"

I have already prepared your room, Peter, I expected that you would be staying after this evening's activities."

"Thank you very much, Margaret."

"And thank you very much, Peter, for saving Polly from those awful men, we shall be for ever in your debt, Polly too thanks you very much," says Margaret, with relief sounding in her voice.

"Polly played her part very well when I asked her to tie those two men, considering what she had been subjected to, she was very brave."

"She is a wonderful daughter, Peter, and we love and cherish her very much."

The three chat for a while about the evening's events, then retire upstairs as soon as they finish their drinks. The following morning, after the children had been seen off to school, Ben goes to his study to make some calls. Again, it was decided to let Polly go to school, in spite of her ordeal, so as to keep things as normal as possible for her. Since she did not have any games or P.E. today, none of her bruises or scratches would be evident so she would not be subjected to any awkward questioning by her friends or her teachers.

However, as a precaution, it was decided that Peter would use Ben's car and take her to school, leaving Mrs Poulton to go along with Margaret and Maisy, Daisy and George.

Ben and Peter had decided to carry their weapons at all times, after the events of the last evening, so Peter had his Browning with him when he escorted Polly to school, although he was careful to make sure it was not on show.

Ben, also, had his weapon close at hand in the study. Just as he was about to call Phil Landers, the phone rang.

"Hallo, Ben Spencer speaking."

"Mr Spencer, it's Bill Holder here, I got news," the voice at the other hand said.

"Bill, good morning, what have you got for me?" asks Ben

"There's a boat load arriving full of foodstuffs and alcohol."

"Do you know when exactly, Bill?"

"Best I know is tomorrow 'else Saturday, my guess would be Saturday when the docks are quiet," Bill Holder replies.

"That's very good, Bill, I suggest you keep low for the next day or so, when it's all over, and you will be well paid for this information if it is true."

"Thanks, Mr Spencer," Bill Holder replies and puts down the receiver.

Ben now has a difficult decision to make. He is concerned about a possible information leak from his local office, and considers making the necessary arrangements with Birmingham Constabulary. After consulting with Peter on his return, Ben makes the decision to consult Birmingham Constabulary direct. He wants to be absolutely sure that maximum damage is done to the criminal gang that is bringing the boat from London, and, at the same time, ensure that there is no leakage of information. He speaks with Chief Inspector Bernard Jamieson and outlines what Bill Holder told him regarding the shipment due within the next day or so. Ben asks that the Chief Inspector talk with him direct and not to make contact with the office because of a possible leakage of information.

"That will not be a problem, Mr Spencer, I will start things moving my end and contact you as soon as I have any news. Tell me do you wish to be involved in the operation direct if and when we go in to arrest these people?"

"That will not be necessary, Chief Inspector, it will be your operation to carry out as you see fit, but I would appreciate an update when you have one."

"Absolutely, and thank you for your information, Mr Spencer, goodbye for now."

Ben has decided that, officially, he will have no knowledge of the operation when it takes place. That way, no one will question why he did not consult at the local office.

However, it is time that he contacts Phil Landers to apprise him of the evening's events so that he is made aware of just what they are up against. Also it will show everyone involved at the office just how much Ben and his family are having to endure in order for him to continue the fight against black market racketeering.

"My God, Ben, are you sure your family is alright?" Phil Landers replies when Ben recalls to him the events of the previous evening.

"Everyone coped remarkably well considering, especially Polly, who suffered most from the intrusion."

"Yes you have an amazing daughter Ben you must be very proud of her," Phil answers.

"Do you think Galbraith will return, Ben?" he adds.

"Who knows, given the visit of last evening, anything is possible: what I do know is that we will be ready for them if they do return," Ben replies.

"You be very careful, Ben, and keep in touch, anything I can do you let me know."

"Thanks, Phil," replies Ben, replacing the receiver. After pondering for a moment, he decides it is time to talk with Beatrice Carrington again to see if she can give him any information. She is shocked to hear what has happened and offers her sympathy.

"The intrusion into your house must have been very frightening for your family, Ben, and your daughter Polly in particular. She is a very brave young lady and you must be very proud of her."

"Yes indeed, Beatrice, it was quite an ordeal but we managed to overcome the criminals in the end, and I left Montague Galbraith in no doubt what would happen to him if he attempted to set foot in my house again."

"Good for you, Ben, intimidation has to be met with firmness and conviction, and you and your family demonstrated that perfectly, now how can I help you?"

"I really need to know who is pulling the strings of men like Galbraith, Beatrice. I have to start attacking the operations from the heart rather than the outside perimeters."

"I have four names you might like to look into: Miles McKenzie, Giles Williamson, Toby North and John Devonish. McKenzie and Williamson worked in The Food Ministry during the war and are well connected.

"I am sure they had contacts in The Ministry, so may have access to sensitive information. They have both been suspected of using their contacts from the war years to move food and drink on the black market, but they have never been arrested and some of their colleagues have gone underground recently suggesting they are becoming edgy. Both these men are ruthless in their pursuit of profit and will stop at nothing to protect their operations.

"North and Devonish were in the manufacturing of arms and equipment, and were known to be importing large quantities of electrical goods and cloth for black market distribution. I believe they are also involved in trading counterfeit petrol coupons. Both men are known by the police to have been involved in a number of serious assaults on small time operators, but no one was prepared to give evidence against them," says Beatrice.

"I believe that you may have mentioned McKenzie and Williamson previously. I am sure their names are in the documents you left in the garden."

"Yes, I believe they are," mentioned Ben.

"All four men sound pretty ruthless, Beatrice, do you have any ideas how we may get to them?" asks Ben.

"Only if someone in their organisation offers you any information can we hope to bring them to justice, unless you can find any documents linking them directly with illegal activities," Beatrice answers.

"What about Galbraith, I might be able to pressure him after his intrusion into my house?" Ben suggests.

"How would you do that?"

"By threatening to go to the police and have him charged for violent assault against Polly and forcefully holding the family against their will."

After pondering Ben's suggestion for a moment, Beatrice replies:

"That might just work, Ben, threatening his freedom might be exactly what is required to bring him to heel, then use him to our advantage, how would you get in contact with him?"

"Oh I believe he will get back to me sooner rather than later, he has so much to lose by my meddling in his affairs," Ben replies and outlines the planned raid on barges entering Birmingham along The Grand Union Canal.

"My goodness, Ben, if the police are successful in confiscating a barge load of goods that Galbraith has commissioned, the consequences for his operation locally could be catastrophic," Beatrice replies enthusiastically.

"Well I certainly hope that will be enough to draw him back to another meeting very soon," Ben replies.

"Do let me know how you get along, meanwhile I will continue to keep my ears open this end, goodbye, good luck and please be careful."

"Thank you, Beatrice, and goodbye," Ben replies and replaces the receiver.

After pondering over his conversation, Ben walks through to the kitchen and into the garden looking for Peter. He finds him in the shed inspecting the weapons that were taken from Galbraith and his men.

"Can you recommend a good locksmith, Peter, I think it would be an idea to increase security in the house and grounds?"

"I can arrange that, what do you have in mind?" Peter replies.

"Some lighting in the area at the back of the house, a reliable alarm and better locks on the back door and garage."

"I will get on with that immediately, can I use your phone?"

"Yes of course, thank you, Peter," Ben replies and goes back into the house. He has not really had time with Margaret since the activities of the previous evening and needs to reassure her that everything that can be done is being done to keep the family safe.

"I am sure you are doing what you can, Ben, I just hope and pray it will be enough," Margaret replies anxiously and wraps her arms around Ben holding on to him tightly.

Peter makes the arrangements for the new locks, floodlighting and alarm system to be fitted over the next day or so. Now that he is staying with the Spencer's it will be easy for him to oversee the installations without being concerned about security when Ben is not around. With the weekend just around the corner Ben is hoping to spend time with the family, especially the children. They all adore their father and enjoy being with him, and Ben tries very hard to give them as much time as he can. Sadly, of late, that has not been possible so any opportunity to make up time has to be taken and cherished. The weekend begins with Peter arranging the security measures which means that the children will be asking lots of questions and enjoy the company of the two men who are carrying out the work.

"Daddy, how many lights will we have in the garden, will they flash when we walk by?" ask Maisy and Daisy.

"What about the alarm, Daddy, will it make a lot of noise, if it does it will scare me," says George.

"No the lights will not flash, those close to the house will be on during the night, others further down the garden will only come on if anyone enters the garden when it is dark and don't worry about the alarm, George, it will not be frightening I promise," Ben assures them all.

"Where is Polly?" he asks, somewhat anxious that she is nowhere to be seen!

"She is in her room, Ben, perhaps you should go and talk with her," replies Margaret.

"Is she not well, what is wrong?" asks Ben with some concern.

"No she is not unwell, I think it is a reaction from all that has happened, I don't know," Margaret replies with a worried look on her face.

"Very well, Margaret, I will go to her now," Ben replies and goes up the stairs and taps gently on Polly's door.

"Yes, come in."

Mr Spencer enters Polly's room, and Polly dashes toward him in tears.

"Daddy, Daddy I was so scared of those men, what they said, I keep thinking about it and what else could have happened if Peter had not arrived, I can't help myself," she says as she holds on tight to Ben, still in her night clothes.

Ben hugs his daughter, concerned that she is reliving the events of two nights ago over again.

"My dearest, Polly, I understand you must still feel frightened over what happened, I will never forget and I don't suppose any of us will forget for some time. You must try not to dwell on it too much, it will only make you unhappy, and the Polly I know is not usually unhappy, she is strong and determined and a valuable member of our family, and especially valuable to me," he tells her planting a kiss on her forehead, then holding her at arm's length, he goes on:

"I suggest you go and have a hot bath and relax while we are having the locks and alarms and lighting fitted."

"Yes okay, Daddy," says Polly as she goes off toward the bathroom.

Mr Spencer watches her and can't help noticing some of the bruises and scrapes she has on her legs and shoulders. Polly did indeed go through a lot that evening and the physical and mental scars will take some time to heal. Meanwhile, the family enjoy a lunch of sandwiches and a cake that Mrs Spencer had found time to make in spite of everything. Ben notices how close to Peter Polly was keeping He obviously gave her confidence and she regarded him as a kind of guardian angel after what had happened. For his part, Peter was happy to talk with her and explain what the security measures were.

"You will remember to be careful of where you go, Polly, and avoid ever going anywhere on your own from now on, you do understand don't you?"

"Yes, but you are going to be here, aren't you, Peter?"

"I will be helping your Daddy with security issues and will stay over as often as I am wanted. Now I need to get back to arranging the security lights so that they will be working for this evening."

Polly seemed reassured after speaking with Peter, and went off to see what Maisy, Daisy and George were up to. It was so nice to be able to spend time as a family and forget the terrible events of the last few days, at least for a while any way! Whilst the children were all together outside, Ben took the opportunity to speak with Margaret. He was sure that she, too, had been very much affected by the recent events and wanted to reassure her, as much as was possible, that the family would be safer from now on.

"We will all cope, Ben, but I do worry about what these men might do next, they must be getting desperate with you and your success. Do you have any idea what they might do next?" she asks with some concern.

"I don't think that Galbraith will bother us again, but I cannot speak for his bosses, that is why I am hoping to use him as a lever for more information."

"Really, how on earth are you going to do that?" she asks with interest.

"By threatening to inform the police of the events of the other evening unless he cooperates," replies Ben.

"But how will you get in touch with him?"

"Well if events go according to plan, he will be contacting me very shortly, and will be desperate to cooperate to save his own neck," replies Ben.

"So you have a plan, I do hope it works out for you, by the way what did Polly have to say?"

"It was a reaction over what happened to her the other evening and what could have happened, but for Peter's intervention. I think she will be fine now, you know she is a tough girl?"

"I do, Ben, I also noticed how close she stayed to Peter, do you think she is forming an attachment to him?"

"Probably, she sees him as her knight in shining armour over what happened."

"Well that's understandable in the circumstances, and she will certainly listen to anything he has to say to her. We are very fortunate to have such a dependable friend," says Margaret.

"We are indeed, and he will be on hand until this business is settled, you do know that he is carrying a weapon, Margaret?" Ben asks.

"I didn't know but I can understand your caution, I assume you have your own pistol as well?"

"Yes, it is in the study, available at all times," he replies.

"A sad reflection on our times Ben, but I am relieved that all precautions that can be taken have been taken."

The rest of Saturday passes by uneventfully for the Spencer family, and by evening, the security lights are working, the locks have been replaced on the garage and garden doors, leaving just the alarm to be fitted on Monday. Peter asks Ben if he is okay with him collecting a change of clothes and some additional personal items, telling him he will be back Sunday evening.

"That's fine, Peter, you are obviously free to come and go as you wish, I am very appreciative of the assistance you have offered to me and the family."

Peter decides he will have a word with Polly before he goes to assure her he will be back tomorrow.

"I will be away for only one night, Polly, and you have all the family here with you," says Peter.

"And you promise you will be back tomorrow?"

"Yes I promise," Peter replies and gives her a hug for reassurance.

"Okay Peter, I will come to the front door with you and say goodbye."

Peter leaves the house and Polly returns to the parlour to help Mrs Spencer with the supper.

"Peter will be back tomorrow, Mummy," she says with confidence in her voice.

"We are very fortunate to have such a good friend to watch over us."

"I do believe we might all venture to church in the morning, Margaret, we have not been together for a week or so."

"Yes, Ben, it will be a very pleasant change for us to all go together."

After supper, Margaret carries on with household jobs while the children go outside. Ben browses through the local paper which he has not been able to do for some time, and Polly goes to her room to finish some school work.

"I'll answer that, dear," says Ben on hearing the phone ring.

"Hello, Ben Spencer speaking."

"Ben, it's Beatrice Carrington, I am sorry to call at this time, but I have only just received some rather disturbing information."

"That's okay, Beatrice, what is it?" says Ben with concern.

"I believe you and your family may be targeted over your recent successes. Your activities have not gone unnoticed and are obviously hurting a lot of people. A colleague of mine heard your name mentioned in Giles McKenzie's office," says Beatrice.

"God, just as I was beginning to believe there would be no more violence directed toward me and my family," he replies with concern in his voice.

"Perhaps your local police can keep an eye on things Ben?" Beatrice suggests.

"So far, I have not involved them any more than necessary, so long as the new security measures are effective, we should be safe enough, especially with my colleague Peter Forsyth being on hand, and we both have our own firearms," Ben replies.

"Good, I hope that will be enough, Ben, but please, be careful."

"I will indeed, Beatrice, and thank you very much for being so prompt with the information, Goodbye now."

"Goodbye, Ben," says Beatrice and replaces the receiver.

Beatrice Carrington's revelations bring Ben back to earth with a bump, so much for the peaceful weekend! After thinking over what she had said, Ben decided it was too soon for anyone to mount any form of operation against him, as it was Saturday evening and government departments would be closed for the weekend, so he decides to leave things as they are for now, and make any further decisions after the family return from church tomorrow.

"Who was it, dear?" asked Mrs Spencer as he returns to the parlour.

"Just some information I will act upon tomorrow after our visit to church," he replies.

So, on the Sunday morning, the Spencer family do attend church together and give thanks for being safe, although, unknown to the family, Ben is carrying his pistol, just in case! After lunch Ben contacts Peter Forsyth to update him on the information he has received, and asks him how soon he will be able to return to the house.

"I will be with you in time for tea, Ben."

"Thanks, Peter, I do appreciate that, I will see you then."

Ben then relates the details of Beatrice's conversation to Margaret.

"Really, Ben, for a moment, I thought we were being allowed to enjoy a normal life," says Margaret with a sigh.

"For the moment let's enjoy a typical Sunday afternoon while we can."

Just at that moment, the telephone rings.

"Hello, Ben Spencer speaking."

"Mr Spencer, Chief Inspector Jamieson Birmingham Constabulary."

"Chief Inspector, do you have some news?" asks Ben.

"I do indeed Mr Spencer, you will be pleased to know, that acting on your information we seized a barge in the early hours which had a full load of foodstuffs, Tea, Coffee, Sugar, Canned fruit, Alcohol, a large consignment of counterfeit coupons and a number of firearms," Chief Inspector Jamieson replies.

"That is very good news indeed, anyone we know?" Ben asks.

"Not that I could identify, just agents expecting their cut from the delivery. We will be questioning all the men in more detail tomorrow."

"They put up one hell of a fight, and tried to set fire to the boat alongside as a diversion. There were five men on the boat and about ten at the wharf side waiting to unload and after a fierce scuffle some of them got away. Three of my officers were hurt, but thankfully no shots were fired," the chief inspector adds.

"If any relevant names do emerge from your questioning, I would be obliged if you would let me know."

"I will indeed, Mr Spencer, and thank you again for your help," replies the Chief Inspector.

Ben sits back in his chair and contemplates the consequences of this seizure from the barge in Birmingham. *I expect I shall be receiving a call very shortly,* he says to himself. Meanwhile Peter Forsyth returns carrying a kitbag with everything he may need for a prolonged stay at the Spencer's home. This includes an automatic pistol and an old Beretta sub machine gun! Peter also has a length of rope which could prove useful should there be any more intruders that need to be restrained. Ben updates him on the information from Beatrice Carrington, and tells him of the successful seizure of the barge, by Birmingham Constabulary. He is, however, most concerned on hearing of a possible threat from another source, and discusses how they might prepare for this.

"Your being here, together with the security preparations we have in place, should be more than sufficient, especially with your arsenal of weapons, Peter," Ben comments.

"Let us hope that Galbraith contacts you soon and we can get some information about possible suspects issuing these threats. Once we have an idea of who they are, we can take whatever additional action is required," replies Peter.

"My concern, is that these threats were determined before the seizure of the barge, so Galbraith's superiors will be even more furious now."

Meanwhile Margaret has prepared some sandwiches for Sunday tea.

"You will have some tea with us, Peter?"

"Thank you, Margaret, I would like that."

"Peter, you are back it's so good to see you again," says Polly sitting beside him at the table.

She is obviously forming quite an attachment to him and asks him if he is going to stay, and if so will he be taking her to school again tomorrow.

"I don't see why not, but we must not forget Mrs Poulton," he replies.

"Yes that's true, Polly, it will stop any questions about Peter, I'm sure he has been mentioned at school?" asks Margaret.

"I told Valerie and the others he was a friend of Daddy's staying with us for a while," replies Polly.

"That was a good idea, Polly, well done."

"Thank you, Daddy, you will be staying with us won't you, Peter?"

"I will be staying as long as I am needed, Polly, so don't you worry, your Daddy and I will take care of all of you," he replies with conviction.

After tea, Peter takes his kitbag up to the room and unpacks his extra clothing items along with his shaving requirements. He places the automatic pistol beneath his pillow, and leaves the Beretta in his haversack. The Browning remains on his person, as always, at all times. He then returns downstairs to meet up with Ben in the study.

"Hello, Peter, have you settled in okay?"

"Yes thanks, Ben, I would have liked that alarm to have been active for this evening, so I have decided to stay downstairs in the parlour tonight, just to be on the safe side."

"I will tell Margaret of course, but I won't mention it to the children, so as not to worry them, and Polly would only want to stay down with you!"

"I think you may be right," replies Peter also smiling.

Peter has become all too aware of how Polly is staying close to him, but knows that if his being there gives her added confidence, it can only be a good thing after her recent ordeals.

"You said that the new alarm will be fitted tomorrow, Monday, Peter?" Ben asks.

"Yes, they will be along at 9 o'clock sharp so it should be working by lunchtime I hope."

"I will be here to let them in and leave it to you after you arrive back from taking Polly to school."

CHAPTER 15

(A furious Galbraith makes contact)

Then, quite suddenly, the phone rings. Ben lets it ring four or five times before answering.

"Hello, Ben Spencer speaking."

"Spencer, Montague Galbraith here, what the hell are you up to confiscating my boat on the Birmingham canal? I warned you about this."

"Before you start making accusations, Galbraith, I had nothing to do with that operation, perhaps you should check that you don't have an informer," Ben responds.

"That's nonsense, none of my men were involved," Galbraith responds, but Ben detects an element of doubt in his voice.

"Are you quite sure about that?"

"Somebody has to pay for this, Spencer, and right now I am holding you directly responsible."

"What are you suggesting, Galbraith?" Ben asks.

"I am suggesting another meeting to give you the opportunity to put forward some ideas on how you and I can work together here."

"I am always willing to listen to what you propose, Galbraith, this time, however, I will choose the place and time," Ben responds.

"Whatever you like, I will call you tomorrow afternoon, be sure to be at home," Galbraith responds and replaces the receiver.

Ben, sits back to digest what Galbraith has said, and is satisfied that he is in control of proceedings and will make the arrangements as soon as he goes into the office tomorrow. He would have preferred to be accompanied by Peter Forsyth to the meeting, but decides that Peter's presence is required at the house in case of any incidents relating to family. Ben has a brief phone conversation with Phil Landers, informing him of the conversation with Galbraith, and tells him that he will meet with him tomorrow around 10 o' clock to arrange the meeting. He does not elaborate and no mention is made of the Birmingham raid on the canal boat.

Monday morning sees the children going off to school, Maisy, Daisy and George with Margaret while Polly travels with Peter and Mrs Poulton, before Peter returns to find the tradesmen ready to fit the alarm. Ben enters his office around 10 o'clock and asks that two of his colleagues, Rupert Bolton and James Taylor to sit in on his meeting with Phil Landers.

"Good morning, Phil, I have asked my two colleagues Rupert Bolton and James Taylor to sit in because we shall need them when we meet up with Galbraith. Rupert and James are from the C.O.I. security division and we have known each other for a number of years. I fully intend to negotiate from strength, when we meet with Galbraith leaving him in no doubt that I am in control of the situation."

"Good idea, Ben, I am with you on that, any ideas where we might arrange to meet?" asks Phil.

"Yes I have; I shall suggest Castle Bromwich on the outskirts of Birmingham. I visited the Castle Bromwich Aircraft Factory during the war, so know the area. I was there last year for the annual Battle of Britain Display, and know of a number of pubs that we could use in the centre of the town," replies Ben.

"What are you going to propose to Galbraith, Ben, he is going to ask you to stop meddling and probably issue further threats; I am concerned about you and your family's safety in this," Phil replies with obvious concern.

"I do appreciate your concern, Phil, and I have taken further steps at home, the last of which is being completed today, to ensure the family's safety. We have to find out who is operating the black market operations, talking to middle men only slows down their activities, I want to be able to bring the ringleaders, those at the very top, to justice. We have to get Galbraith to give us the names of his superiors, those that are pulling his strings, giving him instructions and reaping huge rewards from their operations. I am going to suggest to him that unless he gives me some real information, names, places, etc., I shall inform the police of his visit to my house, and have him charged with serious physical assault on Polly, as well as issuing threats and holding my family prisoners against their will. The charges for the serious assaults on Polly would put him and his men, away for a very long time."

"My God, Ben, that is some threat to put forward. Do you know it might be enough to make him talk?" Phil replies with a smile.

"I hope so," Ben answers.

For the benefit of Rupert and James, Ben briefly outlines the events of a couple of nights ago.

"Gosh, Ben, that daughter of yours sounds a very special girl, you must be so proud of her?" Rupert replies after listening to Ben recalling the visit of Galbraith and his thugs.

"I am very proud of her, Rupert, but I do worry about her and the rest of my family, that is why we have to break up these criminal gangs quickly and stop them from holding the country to ransom and issuing threats against me and my family," replies Ben.

"Now I have to return home to wait on Galbraith's call, once he has called me we can finalise arrangements, are there any questions before I leave?"

"What about weapons, Ben, shouldn't we be prepared?" James asks.

"Ah, yes absolutely, I meant to mention weapons, I suggest it will be prudent to arm yourself with a pistol and extra rounds of ammo, you do all have weapons?"

They all nod in confirmation, and leave the room.

"I will call you as soon as Galbraith makes contact Phil, you will be in your office later?"

"I will wait on your call, Ben, bye for now," replies Phil as he leaves the room.

Ben reflects on the meeting on his way home, he is pleased that Rupert and James were available. He has known both men for many years, solid and dependable, just the sort you want by your side if there is trouble. Both are ex -army and Rupert spent some time in Europe after the war on unofficial business watching what the Russians were up to. He is also a trained marksman.

James was a training instructor on all types of activities, and is still active when required. Ben is satisfied that he has picked the best possible men to back up Phil Landers and himself at the soon to be arranged meeting. On returning home, Ben enjoys a sandwich, whilst Peter shows him how the alarm will operate. Any attempt to enter the house illegally, breaking a window, forcing a door, will set off the alarm. There is a camera fitted to the rear door and the front door which also has an intercom setup. There is also a sensor fitted on the door from the conservatory to the parlour, since the conservatory is particularly vulnerable to a forced entry.

"I'm impressed, Peter, the family should feel very secure with the arrangements you have put in place, and we have the added bonus of yourself in residents!"

"Thanks, Ben, I believe we have done all we can, and cannot see anyone penetrating the level of security that we have put in place."

"Now, I have to wait on Galbraith's phone call, so come and have some lunch, Peter."

Ben goes into the study to wait on Galbraith's phone call, going over how he will approach his obvious hostility to any suggestions that Ben puts forward.

The phone rings and, after a short pause, Ben answers, "Hello, Ben Spencer here."

"Spencer, Galbraith here, when are we going to meet to discuss your bloody intrusions into my business, I hope it will be soon?" Galbraith asks.

"Tomorrow, midday in Castle Bromwich, the Hotel on the High Street," Ben replies promptly.

"Very well, Mr Spencer, I will see you then," replies Galbraith and replaces the receiver.

Ben contacts Phil Landers, Rupert Bolton and James Taylor, telling them of his conversation with Galbraith, and sets up a meeting at the office for 9 o'clock before they set off to Castle Bromwich. Ben reflects on the importance of the meeting, and knows that if Galbraith calls his bluff, he will end up with nothing for his efforts. However, he is sure that will not happen, since Galbraith will not want to risk Ben carrying out his threat, and he must be aware that the treatment of Polly especially, could have serious consequences for all concerned. She was subjected to a nasty assault, and but for Peter's timely intervention could have been seriously harmed. It is because of the harm done to his daughter that Ben will not hesitate to carry out his threat unless Galbraith can give him the information he demands. Whilst it is not ideal that his family have been directly affected by his work for the government, it has happened and Ben is so very concerned that he is determined to see that everything that can be done will be done.

Meanwhile, with all the added security in place, he is satisfied that he can overcome whatever any outsiders may attempt on his home and family.

The children return home from school, and Polly is excited about the school hockey match.

"Mummy, Daddy, I am in the hockey team for tomorrow's match in Coventry, if we win, we will be in the county finals."

"Well done, Polly, I am sure you will do well," replies Margaret. She has always encouraged Polly to take part in sport, and is delighted for her.

"Which school are you playing against, Polly?" asks Ben.

"Stoke Park, Daddy, the last time we played against them, we beat them so I hope we can win again and get into the finals."

"Well good luck, I am sure you will do well, just be aware wont' you?" Ben replies.

"Of course, Daddy, and there will a bus load of girls and teachers with me," Polly responds.

Peter, tests the alarm system after supper, much to the delight of the children. George is particularly puzzled by the alarm going off as he opens the back door to the garden.

"Won't we be able to go in the garden anymore to play, Daddy?" he asks with a frown.

"Of course you will still be able to do everything you have always done, but not once the alarm has been set, and you will all be in bed when this happens," he replies smiling.

"But, Daddy, if we wake in the night will we have to be very still in case we set it off?" Daisy asks.

"No, Daisy, everything will be as it has always been, the alarm and the other precautions are to stop anyone trying to enter our house unless they are invited. The precautions are to keep us all safe from nasty people who would try to break in and harm us. You should carry on having fun and playing in the garden as you have always done."

"Children, I think that is enough questions for now don't you? Now off and play before bedtime," says Ben.

Peter goes into the garage to clear the bits of material left over from the recent installations to be followed by Polly.

"Peter, how long will you be able to stay with us?" she asks.

"I will stay as long as your Daddy believes I should stay because of his work bringing some danger to you and all your family. You really should not worry, Polly, I will be here for you and the family as long as I am needed. Is there anything that you are especially worried about?"

"I can't stop thinking about what would have happened to me if you had not turned up when you did. How can you be so sure that those men won't come back and try again, how can you be really sure, Peter?" she asks tearfully.

"We can be as sure as it is possible that they will not return, your Daddy is meeting with them tomorrow and will threaten to expose their visit here unless they agree to what he has to say."

"They are coming here again, no, Peter, please tell me they aren't, please?" she replies tearfully.

"No, Polly, your Daddy is meeting them in Birmingham, well away from the house."

Peter is a little concerned at her reliance on him as her guardian angel in all this. For now, however, his comforting her seems to be working.

"Oh good, and you will be here all the time won't you?" she asks.

"Yes I will, my dear Polly, now off you go and look after Maisy, Daisy and George."

"Thank you for taking care of me, Peter," she adds as she goes into the garden to see what the children are up to.

Ben meets with Phil Landers, Rupert Bolton and James Taylor at 9.30 a.m., a little later than he arranged as he had waited at home for Peter to return.

"My apologies for being late gentlemen, are we ready for today?"

"Yes, Ben, I have the times of trains to Birmingham, and I have arranged for a car, from New Street Station, to take us to Castle Bromwich," replies Phil Landers.

And with that, the three of them get into Ben's car for the trip to Carswell Station.

"My plan is to hear what Galbraith has to say first, he will no doubt bully and threaten as he has done before, and then to tell him what I propose we do if he does not cooperate. He is too intelligent not to take notice of what I am to say to him, and he has too much to lose anyway."

"Not only that, Ben, but should he be arrested, his own life may be threatened by his superiors, the last thing they would want is Galbraith talking to the police."

"Good point, Phil, I will make him aware of that, too. Do we all have our weapons to hand just in case?"

"Yes, Ben," they all reply as Ben parks the car in the station car park.

The journey to Birmingham passes uneventfully with little conversation since everything that needed to be said has been said.

"I am not expecting any trouble from Galbraith, but please be on your guard. He may have men outside the hotel, or we may be followed after our meeting. Remember, he believes he is going to get concessions from me, and will be livid when I threaten him with the police."

"Do you really believe he may try something today, Ben?" Phil asks with concern.

"The man is capable of anything, Phil, he showed that when he invaded my home and assaulted Polly. I just want to be sure that we are all on guard against any surprises he may be planning."

"Point taken, Ben, if he does try any intimidation we will be ready," Phil comments.

Ben is in no doubt that all operations against the racketeers from now on will become increasingly dangerous, as they become more desperate over their losses. He needs intelligence about senior figures responsible and sees Galbraith as his way of tracking them down. The sooner he can break down the major players, the sooner his life can return to some sort of normality. He frets about the family's wellbeing, and hopes that today's events will be encouraging and help to move his operation forward.

CHAPTER 16

(Ben meets with Galbraith)

Ben and his colleagues arrive at The Hotel in Castle Bromwich at about 11.45 a.m. and go into the lounge. Galbraith is already seated at the far end of the room accompanied by two other men. He stands as Ben approaches and points towards vacant chairs.

"Good morning, Spencer, I have been waiting for you."

"Hello, Galbraith, I have brought along two more of my colleagues, and you know Phil Landers, I hope you don't mind?"

"What I mind, Spencer, is your meddling, and since we spoke I understand that one of my boats has been seized by your men? Dammit, Spencer you are asking for real trouble, you don't appreciate who you are mixing with," he says with anger in his voice.

"Firstly, Galbraith, I have no idea what you are talking about regarding the Birmingham raid. I can only assume that Birmingham Constabulary carried out the seizure and arrest. What I will say to you before we go any further is that any threats will be dealt with accordingly and will most certainly stop me and my colleagues from further discussion. So can we proceed in a civil manner, or do we get up and leave?"

"Yes, yes alright, Spencer, perhaps I did overreact, but you have to understand the pressures I have to deliver, that is why you must be able to offer me something to take back to my superiors," Galbraith replies.

"I am sure we can come to some amicable agreement on what we confiscate and what we allow to go unnoticed," Ben replies thoughtfully.

"That's more like it, I knew you would see sense, Spencer, what do you suggest?"

"There is just one thing before we go on with details, Galbraith," Ben goes on.

"Yes what is it, anything to sort out this business," replies Galbraith.

"Well, I shall expect something in return for turning a blind eye to black market activities, it could prove very embarrassing for me and my colleagues if this information got into the wrong hands."

"Yes, of course I understand that, Spencer, what do you have in mind from me, some sort of share in the profits for example?" Galbraith replies with a smile.

"No nothing like that, what I what I have in mind is something quite different. I want you to give me the names of your superiors that issue you with the instructions about shipments of goods, I want their names and I want the addresses of their distribution sites. I want you to give me these details in exchange for me allowing specified shipments to be delivered without interference."

"Are you insane, Spencer? Why on earth would I give you such information?" Galbraith gasps.

"I haven't finished yet, Galbraith. If you fail to supply me with this information, I will inform the police of your visit the other evening, and how you kept my family prisoner and violently assaulted my daughter. You and your colleagues will go away for a very long time. Make no mistake, Galbraith, if I do not get what I want, I will inform the authorities," Ben concludes.

Galbraith stares down at the floor and Ben watches for any movement of the men with him, but they appear visibly shocked at what Ben has threatened.

"Have you any idea what you are asking of me, do you know what will happen if they find out I have given you their names, they will kill me?" says Galbraith with genuine fear in his voice.

"The only way they will find out is if you or one of your colleagues tells them, I certainly will not, I have all I need to get you to cooperate."

"Very well, Spencer, but what about my shipments will you leave me alone?" Galbraith asks.

"I will let through two shipments per week by road, no boatloads, whilst we are rounding up anyone that you give us, together with what we confiscate. We will give you grace for four weeks only, unless I arrange differently. The moment I hear that you have passed this information onto anyone else, then the arrangement will cease."

"That doesn't sound like I am getting much for my money, Spencer, you are asking me to risk my life for a handful of shipments," Galbraith replies.

"You, sir, are being given eight shipments free of any fear that they will be confiscated, that is eight more than you could have hoped for and you are being allowed to keep your freedom."

"Yes, alright, I will get you what you want, but you must let me know how you propose to keep me out of this," Galbraith responds.

"Providing you are not with the men, or at their depots when they are raided you have nothing to worry about," Ben replies.

"Very well, Spencer, I really have no choice in this, I will get you the information you require and contact you around 8 o'clock this evening, I just have to check on the depot whereabouts," Galbraith replies.

"Thank you, I look forward to your call," Ben replies, as he and his colleagues get from their chairs and leave the Hotel. They hurry back to their car and make the short journey back to Birmingham New Street to catch the train back to Carswell.

"Well, gentlemen, I think that went rather well, providing Galbraith comes up with the information," says Ben to his colleagues.

"I'm sure he will, he dare not risk calling your bluff about contacting the police," Phil replies.

"Yes, I'm sure you are right, Phil, I am really looking forward to listening to what he has to say."

Polly meanwhile is preparing for her trip to the Hockey match in Coventry.

"Come along, girls, get onto the bus as quickly as you can please," calls Miss Jones the sports teacher.

Polly is excited at the prospect of playing for the school in a match which, if they win, will give them a place in the finals

"How far to Stoke Park School, Miss?"

"About half an hour or so I believe Polly, we should be there in plenty of time for the 2 o'clock start," Miss Jones replies.

The girls are really confident that they can win this match and progress to the finals.

Polly is especially excited to have been chosen since she is the youngest member of the team, and has worked especially hard on her game so as to be chosen. The journey is uneventful, and no one pays any attention to the large saloon which has followed them from Carswell. The entrance to the school is from Dane Road just off Walsgrave Road. The playing field is adjacent to the entrance gates. The bus pulls into the gate and pulls round to the changing rooms, about 50 yards from the field and the girls rush off the bus into the changing rooms.

"Alright, girls, do stop rushing, get changed and meet me on the playing field," says Miss Jones.

The girls go into the changing rooms and change into their hockey kit before emerging to go out to the pitch. There is lots of chatter as they have been looking forward to the match for some time. No one pays any attention to the large saloon car that has driven into the school then reversed ready to go back through the gates, close to the school entrance. It stops and the three occupants, two men and a woman remain in the car. The girls pass out of the changing rooms in ones and twos and head for the playing field. The occupants of the car are obviously not there for the hockey match, but seem to be looking for someone. Then the woman gets out from the car walking towards the girls, then calls out to Polly.

CHAPTER 17

(Polly is taken a second time!)

"Polly Spencer, there is a message for you at reception, this way please," she says.

She catches Polly completely off guard, who starts to walk with her then realises, too late, that something is wrong. One of the men has got out of the passenger side of the car and moves toward them. He grabs Polly and with the woman's assistance bundles her into the back of the car, which speeds off through the school gates. The whole thing is over in a matter of seconds as the car speeds down toward Little Heath. Polly struggles frantically, but the woman has her hand over her mouth and the man is stopping her from escaping pinning her arms by her side.

"Stop your struggling, you little brat," says the man as he slaps and manhandles her roughly.

"Don't hurt her, she will be no use to us dead," the woman yells at him.

"A good slap will do her good, pretty girls appreciate a good slap it puts them in their place doesn't it, Polly?" he says as he grabs her legs to try and keep her still as they continue their trip through Walsgrave toward the City centre.

Polly knows that her struggles are a waste of energy, and only serve to give the man holding her the excuse to manhandle her, which he enjoys. Finally, they pull into a large driveway and Polly realises that she has been brought to the same location, in Cox Street Coventry, namely Primrose Lodge, as she was previously. She shudders at the thought of what happened to her last time.

The car pulls up to the side of the house, so that is unseen from the road and Polly is dragged into a side door and marched down into the cellar as before.

"Sit down, Polly. Behave yourself and you will not be harmed," the woman tells her.

"What do you want, why are you doing this to me, you horrid people," Polly sobs.

"Stop whining, you little brat, come here," the older of the two men says.

The two men grab her, one twisting her arm, the other puts his arm around her waist.

"Don't struggle, Polly dear, and nothing will happen to you, we don't want to hurt you do we, Jim?" the older man replies pushing her against an old table.

"Leave her alone, you two, we have been asked to hold her here, nothing else," the woman replies. She is obviously in charge, and Polly is indeed relieved that she is there.

"Either of you lay a hand on her and I will tell McKenzie, and you don't need me to remind you of what his men are capable of," the woman adds.

"Okay, Missus, we was only having a joke, we didn't mean her any harm," the older man responds and immediately releases Polly on hearing the threat about McKenzie.

"Now, Polly, promise me you will not try to escape, and I will leave you untied."

"Yes, I promise," says Polly, with relief in her voice.

"Very well, I will get you some chocolate and a glass of water."

"But why are you doing this to me, I don't understand?" Polly asks in tears.

"It will not be for long, Polly, you must just be patient, come along, you two, we have work to do."

The woman turns and walks up the steps followed by the two men. After the woman returns briefly to give Polly a chocolate bar and some water, she is left alone in the cellar to reflect on her dilemma. For a second time she has been taken from her friends and family, and manhandled and abused by her captors. This time, but for the timely intervention of the woman, the consequences could have been far worse. She shudders as she recalls the events just before the woman told the two men to leave her alone with threats of telling someone called McKenzie. She just hopes that the woman does have enough power to keep them under control by threatening to tell of their behaviour towards her. She looks around and tries to guess how long she has been held and so work out what time it is. She thinks it must be about two hours since she was taken, so the police will be searching for her throughout the city. Now that she has had time to settle without fear of any abuse, she feels quite cold wearing only her hockey kit which is dirty and torn. Her gym shirt is torn, her hockey skirt's zip has broken and she has had her plimsolls and socks taken from her. Polly, she says to herself, you are a frightful mess. She reflects that at least she is not so badly battered as she was last time. But what do they want with her this time. They could still inflict more damage on her unless she is rescued quickly. After what Polly guesses is about an hour, the cellar door opens and the two men who abducted her move down the steps. Polly moves towards the back of the cellar, fearful of what they intend.

"You stay away from me, I will tell the lady about you if you hurt me in any way," she screams desperately.

"She won't hear you, Polly she is at the front of the house on the telephone," the younger one says as he grabs Polly and pushes her down to the cold stone floor.

"Keep still, you little brat," says the older man slapping her across her face.

"Hold her down while I'll sort her," the older one shouts, as both men wrestle with Polly to hold her down on the floor. Her skirt has been ripped off in the struggle as the two men manhandle her. She closes her eyes and screams as loudly as she can at the same time biting the hand that is clamped over her mouth. The other man meanwhile has stood up and removed his thick leather belt. He raises his arm to strike Polly again...

"What the hell do you two think you are doing? Get off her, you bloody fools before I shoot you."

The woman shouts pointing an automatic pistol at the two men. Polly jumps up from the floor and runs toward the woman, collapsing into her arms.

"Get dressed, Polly, it's okay we are leaving now, you two go and bring the car round to the front of the house now!" the woman instructs the two men.

"I am sorry about the behaviour of those two, I will see to it that they are punished, Mr McKenzie gave very specific instructions that you were not to be harmed in any way. My God you look awful, Polly!" the woman says with concern.

Polly brushes away her tears and tucks what is left of her shirt into her skirt which she has to hold up since it is badly torn. The woman hands her back her socks and plimsolls, and wraps her jacket around her as Polly is shivering with cold.

"Thank you for helping me. Can I ask you your name?" Polly says with relief and gratitude.

"My name is Rebecca Faversham."

"Thank you very much, Miss Faversham."

"We have a long journey ahead of us, would you like to wash before we leave?" asks Miss Faversham.

"Yes, thank you I do feel very grubby."

They walk to the top of the cellar steps into the hallway just as four police cars roar into the driveway. A number of police officers emerge, some armed and overpower the two men who have just brought the saloon round to the front of the house. They burst inside the house and take Miss Faversham away to a waiting police car.

"You must be Polly Spencer; my God you look terrible. Are you alright?" one of the detectives asks. "I'm Chief Inspector David Burt and this is Sergeant Holt by the way, you are quite safe now, Polly," the Chief Inspector adds.

"Thank you, sir, I am alright now you are here, though I know I probably look worse than I really am."

As Ben and his colleagues get back into their office to begin discussing their meeting, Ben's secretary and close friend Maureen Potter is waiting anxiously with a worried look on her face.

Ben has known Maureen since she joined the service just after the war ended and trusted her completely.

"Ben, I am so sorry, your daughter Polly has been taken from a school in Coventry about an hour ago, around 2 o'clock."

"Oh my God not again. We have just left Galbraith. I cannot believe he could be so stupid after what I told him I would do if he made any more threats to my family. The man has really overstepped the mark this time, and will pay for his actions with a long prison sentence. What other information do you have, Maureen?" Ben asks, furious at what Galbraith has done despite their arrangement discussed only a couple of hours ago.

"The police say there were two men and a woman who made off towards Coventry City centre in a large saloon. There are some fifty officers, some of them armed, that are looking for Polly, I am sure they will find her soon, Ben."

"Can you get me in touch with Coventry Police Headquarters, Maureen? I must find out what is happening, and if we can assist in any way."

"Right away, Ben," replies Maureen leaving the room.

Ben slumps in a chair covering his face with his hands; he cannot believe what is happening.

"I must call Margaret and tell her what has happened."

Margaret Spencer had already been informed by Polly's school, of the abduction, and was very glad that Peter was on hand to console her.

"Peter, I'm afraid our lovely daughter may be suffering again at the hands of desperate people, who will stop at nothing it seems, to get at Ben and his work," she responds with an air of desperation in her voice.

"It must be very worrying for you, Margaret, I am so sorry, but I am sure Ben will be doing everything possible to get her back. You must stay close to the phone in case there is any news."

"First I must call Betty and ask her if she is free to collect Maisy, Daisy and George for me," Margaret replies.

Betty Poulton is happy to help and informs Margaret that she is available for as long as she is needed. Margaret tries to occupy herself by preparing for the evening meal whilst listening for the phone to ring. Eventually, the phone rings and Margaret is so relieved to hear Ben's voice. She tells Ben that the school has informed her of Polly's abduction and continues:

"How much more of this are we going to have to endure, Ben, I feel as if we have been singled out to suffer as much pain as possible?"

"Let us concentrate on getting Polly back above everything else for now at least, Margaret," please," Ben replies pleading with his wife to focus all her energy on Polly's safe return.

117

"Yes, of course, Ben, you are absolutely right, let us pray for Polly's safe return."

"I have to go now, Margaret, I want to speak with Coventry Police to see if I can help in any way, I will call you the minute I have any news, goodbye for now and try not to worry."

Ben talks at length with Coventry Police, and decides not to go over unless they have any positive news. He sits down with his colleagues and tries to figure out why Galbraith has taken this negative step, which must have been arranged before their meeting.

"It doesn't make any sense, Ben. He has nothing to gain from taking Polly. Galbraith is a businessman; he is only interested in how he can protect his profits; this move is counterproductive."

"You're right, Phil, I am not so sure that Galbraith did plan this, I can't see how he would have had enough time."

"So who has taken Polly then?" James Taylor asks somewhat puzzled by what has happened.

"At this moment, I am not sure, but it has to be someone involved in the black market operations, someone above Galbraith, angry at losing so much business recently?" replies Ben.

"You may be right, Ben, but how do we find out?" asks Phil.

"We wait for the names that Galbraith gives us, that is all we can do at the moment," Ben replies with resignation.

"Can't you make contact with Galbraith Ben and see what he can offer you now, all we need is a name?" asks Rupert Bolton.

"I have no way of contacting him direct; I have to wait for his call this evening. In the meantime, I will get Maureen to contact Coventry Police again to see if they have any news." Ben looks at his watch; it is just after 4.30 p.m.

Meanwhile, the police take Polly, the two men and Rebecca Faversham back to Coventry Police Headquarters. The three abductors are held for questioning, and Inspector Burt arranges for W.P.C to take care of Polly. The officer takes note of Polly's injuries for evidence. She has extensive bruising to her back, legs thighs and arms. Almost all of her bruising was caused by the men holding her over the table and struggling with her on the cellar floor. There are red marks across her waist at the back, her legs have extensive scratches from Polly struggling, and there are red wheals across her midriff. She also has bruising to her face from being slapped hard. The W.P.C is visibly shocked by her injuries, and decides that the doctor should examine her. In the meantime, she manages to find her some clothing and keeps hold of what she was wearing, again as evidence. Polly is given a warm drink and some food and thanks the W.P.C for her help.

"You are amazing, Polly, how you managed to survive your ordeal I do not know," she says.

"It really could have been worse, Miss Faversham was very kind and stopped those men from hurting me," replies Polly.

The doctor examined Polly thoroughly and decided there was no lasting damage other than the severe bruises and scrapes.

"You will need a few days' rest, Polly, you have been badly treated and need to heal in your own home," the doctor tells her.

Ben, meanwhile calls Maureen into his office and asks her to contact Coventry Police again.

"Ben, I was just on my way to you, they have found her she is safe and well," Maureen tells him.

"That is wonderful news, Maureen, can you get my home number for me now that you are here please?" Ben asks, as his colleagues rush to congratulate him on the news.

Ben speaks briefly with Margaret, has a word with Peter asking him to watch over her until he gets home.

"Do what you have to do, Ben, I will be hear when you return."

"Thanks, Peter, I need to find out when Polly is being brought home, then I will be on my way," Ben replies and replaces the receiver. Ben then talks with the officer in charge, Chief Inspector Burt, who confirms that Polly is safe and will be driven back home as soon as possible.

"You have a remarkable daughter, Mr Spencer, how she has survived this assault is a miracle, I will not trouble her for her statement details now I will send someone round tomorrow if that is alright with you?"

"That will be satisfactory Chief Inspector and thank you for your consideration," Ben replies.

"I have to get home now, Phil, to be with Margaret when Polly returns, can you do the report on the meeting, and I will let you know what Galbraith says when he calls this evening?"

"Yes of course, Ben, you go home and wait for your daughter and good luck."

Ben thanks his colleagues Rupert and James for their help and leaves the office for home. The short drive seems to take for ever, as Ben churns over the events of the last few hours. First, the success. he thought, over the meeting with Galbraith with his commitment to supplying names and places in the racketeering operations. Then the despair on hearing of Polly's abduction. Again his daughter has been used as a pawn to attempt to stop him from bringing down the criminals in racketeering. Whilst he is devastated by what has happened to his daughter, he is even more determined to bring the men responsible to justice if only for the sake of Polly. Ben enters the front door and Margaret rushes towards him with tears in her eyes.

"Oh, Ben, when is this all going to end, why do these men keep taking Polly from us, she is only a girl, who has done them no harm?" she sobs.

"I know, my dear, I feel so wretched about all this, and am desperate for it all to end," he says with more than a trace of a tear in his eyes also.

"Peter, thank goodness you were here with Margaret, I do appreciate that so much," Ben remarks.

"Glad I was here for you and Margaret," Peter replies.

"Daddy, Daddy, what has happened to Polly?" the children all ask running into the hallway.

"Polly will be with us shortly children, let's all go and have some tea while we wait for her," Ben replies, not wanting the children to ask too many questions at present. Ben enjoys a welcome cup of tea with Margaret and Peter before asking Peter to come into the study for an update. Margaret, meanwhile keeps herself busy, with the children, getting supper ready. Ben is anxious to go over the events of his meeting with Galbraith and wants Peter's comments on whether he thinks another party responsible for abducting Polly. He still isn't sure himself, although it would be the obvious answer.

"I don't think Galbraith took Polly, Ben, in fact I am almost sure. He would have nothing to gain, you had given him concessions, and warned him of the consequences of direct interference with the family, why would he be so stupid as to take Polly while you are talking to him; it makes no sense?"

"The more I talk about it the more I am convinced that he had no knowledge of the abduction. So who did arrange and carry out Polly's abduction?" asks Ben.

"Perhaps you will get some idea this evening," says Peter.

"Let's hope so," Ben replies as the doorbell rings and he goes to answer.

Ben opens the front door confronted by a W.P.C and two other officers together with Polly. Polly hugs her Daddy and bursts into tears.

"Daddy, oh Daddy, I was afraid I would never see you again," she cries.

"Come along, my dear Polly, come in officers, let's go through to Mummy," Ben says with a tear in his eyes.

Peter directs the Police Officers into the study and asks if they will wait a moment.

"Yes of course, sir, we will wait for you and Mr Spencer," the W.P.C replies.

Polly goes through to the parlour clinging to Ben almost afraid to let him go. As soon as she sees Margaret she bursts into more tears.

"My dear Polly, no more tears, you are safe at home now, goodness what are you wearing?"

"The Police gave me these clothes because mine were ripped and torn, so they have kept them as evidence."

Polly is wearing an oversize jumper over a dress which is a loose fit but adequate.

"Let me go and see the police officers out then we can sit down and talk, Polly."

"Very well," replies Mr Spencer as he leaves the room, crosses the hall and goes into the study.

"Thank you very much for bringing my daughter back safely, and Polly asked that I especially thank you for being so kind toward her," he says to the W.P.C.

"Very happy to be a help, sir, your daughter has been through a terrible experience," replies the W.P.C.

"Yes she has, and not for the first time," says Ben.

"I believe your Chief Inspector will be coming to interview Polly tomorrow, would you mind coming along; too she seems to feel comfortable with you?" Ben asks.

"Of course, sir, I will see you tomorrow," The W.P.C replies as all three officers depart to return to Coventry Police Headquarters.

"I think it might be a good idea to have a soak in the bath before supper," Margaret suggests to Polly.

"I would like that very much; I feel so grubby."

Margaret goes upstairs with her daughter to run her bath. As she goes with her into her room she is visibly shocked to see Polly's battered body as she removes her clothes. There is virtually nothing left of her vest and her pants are black with dirt and grime. As she looks at her daughter, she sees more bruises and scrapes than she has ever seen on any person before. How Polly did not break any bones is a miracle, but it will take some time for her body to heal, and she cannot imagine how much longer Polly will need to get over what has happened to her.

"My dear Polly, what on earth did they do to you?" she asks.

"It probably looks worse that it is, Mummy, I am alright now that I am home, and I am looking forward to this bath," she says as she puts on her dressing gown and moves to the door.

Margaret takes her daughter to the bathroom and watches her wince as she steps into the bath. The bruising on her face is now quite prominent, and Margaret is really concerned about the bruises all over her legs and arms as if she had been held down forcibly. There were other bruises over her front which were a concern, but Margaret decided that she would not ask any questions until after she had bathed and eaten. Margaret leaves her daughter to her bath and goes down stairs back into the parlour. She sits down on the chair and fights to hold back the tears, fearful that Polly has been assaulted, the visible scars suggest she may have been, and concerned at how she will cope if that is the case. She goes into the study and voices her fears to Ben and Peter going over in some detail the state of the bruises on Polly's body.

"My God, Margaret, if they have harmed her I will kill them, I swear. There was no reason for them to have behaved so brutally toward her, no reason at all," he replies with a voice full of anger.

"Let Polly tell you in her own time Ben, I am sure she will, for now you both need to be as normal as possible with her," says Peter.

"Yes, you may be able to coax some details from her when the time is right, Peter, she is so very fond of you as you know."

"I will certainly try when the time is right, Ben," says Peter.

"Good, now let's go and see what the children are up to arrange some supper," Ben replies.

Polly, meanwhile lies in the bath trying not to look too closely at her bruised and battered body.

Once again she has been violently assaulted by criminals as revenge for her father's activities.

This last assault has deeply affected her and she finds herself weeping at the sight of her bruised legs, arms and body. She is relieved that the police kept her clothes, so that her parents were not able to see them. Ben and Margaret would have thought the worse from seeing her clothes together with the bruising and scrapes on her body. It will take some time for the bruising to heal, and even longer for Polly to get over her ordeal. As she lies in the warm bath, she starts reliving some of the events that happened. She realises how fortunate she was that Rebecca Faversham was there, for her actions saved Polly from a severe beating, and probably much more. Then, she recalled her mentioning a name, McKenzie, *I must remember to mention this to Daddy,* she thinks to herself. He must be important, since mention of his name, by Rebecca Faversham, prompted the two men to leave her alone. They were obviously shocked by her threat to tell him of what they were doing.

"May I come in, Polly?" asks Margaret through the door.

"Yes of course, Mummy, come in," replies Polly.

Margaret enters the bathroom and is overcome with dismay at the sight of Polly's injuries.

"Oh Polly, you poor girl, what have they done to you?" she cries out.

"I'm okay, Mummy really, please don't cry. I have finished in the bath, so will you help me to dry?"

"Yes of course," says Margaret and in helping Polly sees up close just how badly her daughter has been beaten. She tries hard not to cry, so as not to upset Polly too much.

"I really do think that Doctor should have a look at you Polly, just to be sure." She says with some concern.

"But, Mummy, the police doctor has already examined me and said I was okay."

"Yes I know, dear, but he would only have been looking for abuse, he would expect you to let your doctor give you a more detailed exam and recommend how your wounds might be treated."

"Well okay, if you want me to Mummy, I will see him," Polly replies with a sigh.

"Now off you go and dress, I have put some clothes on your bed," replies Margaret, relieved that Polly has agreed to see the Doctor.

Polly dresses in trousers and a jumper so that all her bruising is hidden save for the marks on her face. The children ask her lots of questions which Polly tries to respond to without going into any real detail.

"Might I have a quick word, Daddy?" Polly asks after they have all finished supper.

"Yes, of course, I was just about to go into the study with Peter, I am expecting a phone call."

Polly follows the two men into the study, and tells Ben the name that Rebecca Faversham mentioned.

"McKenzie, are you sure it was McKenzie Polly?"

"Yes I am sure, Daddy, the mention of that name stopped the two men from doing anything to me, that is why I remember it so well," he replies.

Polly leaves the study, and Ben and Peter discuss the significance of Polly's comment.

"So, it would seem that Galbraith did not arrange Polly's abduction after all Peter?" Ben comments, and Beatrice Carrington's warning was correct.

"I think we both agreed that he would not be foolish enough to take Polly again so soon after his agreement with you," replies Peter.

"He will not know what we know about McKenzie's name being mentioned so I will let him believe that I am going ahead with my threat. It may just be worth it long-term. I just hope that he has some real information that I can act upon, currently we are losing the battle with the criminals Peter," says Ben.

"You can only do so much from your Midlands base Ben, you need intelligence on the operations directed from London, and this is what Galbraith should bring to you. You seem to be well organised your end, but you need to stop the operations at source, before they have begun, that way the supplies will eventually dry up," Peter concludes.

"Yes you're absolutely right, Peter, and with you in place here, I can go after these people and not have to be concerned that I am exposing my family to more danger."

"I will take care of your home and family, Ben, rest assured of that."

Ben knows Galbraith has to come up with names and places as quickly as possible so that he can start to plan a definitive strategy against the ringleaders. Beatrice Carrington has given him names, he has to substantiate that information, from Galbraith, and secure addresses from where they are operating. Just as he was beginning to think that Galbraith will not be calling, the telephone rings.

"Mr Spencer, Galbraith here, and before you say a word, you need to know that I had absolutely nothing to do with the abduction of your daughter in Coventry."

"My God, Galbraith, you had better be right, or I will hunt you down for this, I swear," Ben answers, with a degree of venom in his voice.

"What on earth would I have to gain by such an act so soon after we had met and discussed an agreement?" Galbraith responds.

"I will consider carefully, your comments after you tell me what you have for me Galbraith?"

"There are two men that you should be investigating, namely Miles McKenzie and Giles Williamson. Both men have contacts in government departments, and have access to planning rationing and distribution. They have both been in positions of influence, dating back to WWII," Galbraith continues.

"Williamson has a cottage close to Rye in Sussex, this area was key during the war, and ideally situated to operate his business. The cottage is apparently occupied by his mistress, but I have discovered that it has a large cellar. My guess is that cellar has details of illegal imports and shipments. McKenzie organizes transportation, he knows that some of the coastal areas in Sussex are still unused since wartime, and so are safe to land cargo. In fact, it is rumoured that there are secret underground tunnels down there that were to be used by government if we had been invaded, that McKenzie is now using for his illegal storage depots."

"What about security at these tunnels Galbraith, are we talking a small army or just a few men?"

"Both these men have a small army at their disposal mostly from London, some of them are deserters from WWII, and they would be heavily armed to keep away any intruders," Galbraith replies.

"What about the cottage, do you have any idea how often Williamson goes down there?"

"Not as often as he would like, apart from weekends, I imagine, because of his position in London, so his mistress spends some time alone there," Galbraith replies.

"Okay now I need one more thing from you," Ben goes on.

"I assure you I have no more information Spencer, do you have any idea how much danger I have put myself in by passing on this information to you?" Galbraith responds with fear in his voice.

"I really do not care about any danger you have brought upon yourself because of your actions toward my family and the consequences for you," Ben replies harshly.

"I may need you to find me two local men who can assist with the geography of the area, ideally ex-military who would know how to handle firearms. All I need are names and I will make the contact myself."

"I will see what I can find out, but it may take a day or so," Galbraith replies.

"Shall we say Thursday 8 o'clock Galbraith, that gives you two days?" Ben says.

"I will do what I can, Spencer, goodbye."

Ben looks at Peter, who had been listening to what was said, and looked at the names and places that Ben had written down.

"What do you think, Peter?" asks Ben.

"I think you have done far better than you could have expected, you have enough information here to go ahead and mount a major operation in the south, and smash this black market ring forever."

"I must confess, I never expected Galbraith to come up with quite so much information."

"He wants to protect his own interests Ben, and is prepared to do whatever he has to do so that his business can continue," Peter replies.

"I think this calls for a drink, don't you?" says Ben reaching for a bottle of whisky in his drawer.

"My only disappointment is that you will not be with me on these raids Peter, your expertise would be invaluable."

"Yes I would have liked to be involved, but I can help you with personnel, I know of a couple of my colleagues that are still very active."

"Active in what way, Peter?"

"Well both men are attached to a department within the Defence Ministry responsible for investigating possible deserters who are being used by subversive operators. There is a lot of concern about Communist agitators and the government is using whatever tactics are necessary to fight this dangerous situation. The two men are Daniel Bottomley and Conrad Wilberforce, both men are weapons experts and have served time in with me in Africa. Since the end of the war they have spent some time in Europe. "

"How soon can you make contact with them?" Ben asks.

"I will call them tomorrow; shall I arrange a meeting here?"

"I think that may be best, Peter, I would prefer that their presence in this operation is kept as confidential as possible."

"If they can come along, then together with local law enforcement, we should be able to get both Williamson and McKenzie. I also have to consider Phil Landers, I expect he will want to be involved," Ben continues.

"Do you have any knowledge that Phil Landers may be implicated in some illegal activities Ben?"

"No, I do not, just a nagging doubt since I know so little about him, is there any way we might make some detailed checks outside of the office, Peter?"

"Yes, I know someone in London who can do that for you, Ben, I will call them also tomorrow."

"Then I think that is about it for this evening unless there is anything else?" says Ben.

Just then there is a tap on the door and Polly enters, looking better for her bath but still showing scars from her ordeal. She has taken off the oversized jumper and trousers, and put on one of her summer dresses.

"Hello, Daddy, I wondered if I might speak with Peter before bedtime?"

"Of course, Polly, I will be with Mummy in the parlour," replies Ben as he leaves the room.

"Polly, how are you?" asks Peter, somewhat dismayed at the sight of Polly's injuries.

"I am feeling much better thank you. What I wanted to ask, Peter, is will you be here while I am off school this week?"

"As I have just been discussing with your Daddy, I will be here for as long as I am wanted. I know how worried your Daddy is over what has happened, especially to you Polly, and together we have done everything we can to make sure all the family will be safe. My part in this is to be at the house at all times, so that your Daddy can go about his business unhindered. So you do not have to worry, Polly, I will be with you at all times, I promise," Peter reassures her.

"Thanks, Peter," replies Polly and kisses him lightly on his cheek before leaving the room.

It's as if Polly has to confirm Peter's presence on a regular basis to give her peace of mind.

At 9 o'clock prompt on the Wednesday morning, Doctor Wilson arrives as arranged, to look at Polly. He follows Margaret upstairs to Polly's room where she is waiting.

"Now then, Polly, I understand you have been in the wars again," the doctor says with a pleasant smile.

"Yes I'm afraid I have, Doctor."

"Well let's have a look at you," the doctor asks.

Polly slips out of her clothes and stands in front of the doctor, who is shocked by what he sees.

"We shall have to give you something to treat some of this bruising, Polly," he says looking closely. He then takes a closer look at the marks on her chest and shoulders and at the tops of her legs and thighs which show scratches and bruising and he is concerned that Polly may have been subjected to a serious physical assault.

"Polly what exactly happened to you in the cellar?" the doctor asks with concern.

Polly relates what happened in the cellar in as much detail as possible. The doctor then asks, "And how did you get these bruises on your thighs and round your wrists, were you held down?"

Polly recalls being held against the table top before Rebecca Faversham threatened the men with her pistol.

"So there was no other physical contact between you and the men?" Doctor Wilson asks.

"No, Doctor, now please can I get dressed, I am cold," replies Polly tearfully.

"Yes of course, my dear, I have finished now get yourself dressed and I will go down with your Mummy and see you in your parlour before I leave."

"Your daughter has been subjected to a fearful beating, Mrs Spencer, and I believe that she was within a whisker of a much more serious assault if the woman had not intervened," the doctor tells Margaret.

"She will need to be kept off school for the rest of this week, I will give you a note for some cream that should help to bring out the bruises, and I will prescribe a mild sedative to help her sleep, because I imagine she will be reliving those terrible moments for some time," the doctor adds.

Polly enters the parlour and the doctor recaps on what he has prescribed for her.

"Unless you feel bad in any way Polly, you should be fit for school next Monday, please do not hesitate to get Mummy or Daddy to contact me if you need to talk with me about anything, anything at all," Doctor Wilson says to her.

"Thank you, Doctor, shall I see you to the door?"

Ben enters his office at 10 o'clock. He had waited to hear the doctor's findings regarding Polly's injuries before going into work. He calls in Phil Landers and gives a detailed account of his conversation with Galbraith telling him that he will begin talking with the London Headquarters to set up a team for raids on the south coast. Ben had asked Peter to arrange for his colleagues, Bottomley and Wilberforce, to come to the house as soon as possible, but does not mention to Phil any details relating to these two men for the time being.

"It looks like your plan has worked brilliantly, Ben, how can I help?" Phil asks enthusiastically.

"Well, Phil, I am going to be away from the office for a while once this operation takes off and will need to know that everything is being attended to as it occurs. We still have some operations in The Midlands that will need coordinating, if you can look after them, I will be obliged."

"You leave all that to me, Ben, make a list and I will attend to everything while you are away."

"Thanks for that, Phil, now I need to make some calls."

CHAPTER 18

(Ben makes contact with Major Baxter)

Ben contacts the London Headquarters of The Ministry of Information and asks for Major Jeremy Baxter, Head of Special Operations at The Ministry. Ben had met him a couple of times, a hardnosed Scot with a reputation of getting the job done whatever it takes. Ben was sure the Major would want to head the operation, but was unsure of how he would react to having to use the local police force to assist.

"Major Baxter, good morning it's Ben Spencer from Carswell, how are you?"

"Spencer, good God it's been awhile, how the devil are you getting on up there in The Midlands? I have heard word about some of your successes, but not without some unpleasantness toward your family, I understand?"

"Yes we have had some success, and some unpleasant repercussions, but we are getting on with it, Major."

"Good to hear, Spencer, now how may I help."

"I have some leads on key players in black market operations in the south, and want to put a team together to hit their hideout and distribution warehouses, I was hoping you and I could head the operation, Major?"

"Just what are you wanting of me Spencer?" the Major replies.

"Well you have a reputation for getting the job done. Can you put together a team to assist me in taking down the ringleaders whilst at the same time closing down their illicit operations? The authorities have had little success and are restricted by their rules. We can operate unimpeded and finish these people off once and for all. How do you feel about that, Major?"

"I think your plan is bold, and with the right people, together with myself, I believe we might just pull it off, Spencer. You can count on my support," the Major responds in his usual positive manner.

"Thank you, Major, I have some arrangements to make this end, to cover my absence, but hope to make contact with you again early next week to arrange to meet up with you in London."

"Look forward to your call, bye for now," the Major adds replacing the receiver.

Ben is pleased with the response from the Major, and decides there is nothing more to be done today at the office, so leaves for home. There will be a lot of planning to do, not least being sure that Peter is in place, at the house, for the duration of his absence in London. He now has to arrange a meeting with Peter's associates who he will have to rely upon very much in the days to come. He will also need to meet with Galbraith's men when the time is right, but first he hopes that the Major will have some suggestions from his own contacts. Ben pulls up outside the house and goes inside calling Margaret.

"Margaret, I'm home."

Margaret emerges from the parlour, and Peter greets him from the study door.

"Hello, dear, dare I ask if you had a good day, or would that be too much to expect," Margaret says with a sigh.

"It has been a good day, and I am ready for some tea, could you perhaps bring it into the study. I have to speak with Peter," says Ben as he moves toward the study entrance.

"Hi, Ben, I have managed to set up that meeting for this evening with Daniel Bottomley and Conrad Wilberforce. "

"That is good news, Peter, what time can we expect them?"

"Around 7 o'clock depending on the trains, I would think."

"By the way, I hope Polly has not bothered you too much today, Peter, being off school."

"She has been interesting company, Ben, we checked the alarm system and spent some time in the garden. She seems to have overcome her ordeal for the time being anyway, and I think she is on the mend. The main thing is for her life to get back to normal."

"That is good to hear, Peter, after her ordeals of the last couple of weeks what she really needs is to be a normal school girl again."

Margaret brings in a pot of tea for the two men and Ben asks her if she might prepare something later for his two guests.

"I will arrange something as soon as we have had supper," says Margaret.

After a quiet supper, Ben and Peter go into the study to wait on Peter's colleagues from London. Ben is trusting in Peter's judgement regarding these two men, because he will have to rely on them completely if he is to succeed in the operation he will be planning. He will also have to be sure that they are okay with Major Baxter who can be rather overpowering. Then, on the stroke of 7 o'clock the front door bell rings and Ben opens the door to Daniel Bottomley and Conrad Wilberforce.

"Come in gentlemen, please follow me to the study, I trust you had a good journey?"

"Yes thanks, a bit slow, since we had to catch the local train," Daniel replies.

They enter the study to be warmly greeted by Peter Forsyth.

"Daniel, Conrad it's good to see you, how long has it been?" he enquires.

"It must be over a year, wasn't it that reunion dinner we all went to last spring?" Conrad replies.

"Yes, I do believe it was, well good to see you both again, how have you both been, busy I bet?" says Peter.

"Peter, I will give you a moment with your colleagues while I organize some tea, my wife has made some sandwiches gentlemen so I'll see when they will be ready," says Ben as he leaves the study.

He goes into the kitchen and helps Margaret with the tea and sandwiches for their guests. He is anxious to get on with proceedings as soon as possible, with so much to discuss about the operations to take place over the coming weeks. After about ten minutes or so, Ben returns with the tea and Margaret follows with sandwiches.

"Daniel, Conrad, this is my wife Margaret," says Ben as they enter the study.

After the introductions, Margaret leaves the study, and Ben opens the conversation whilst the two men tuck into the sandwiches provided.

133

"Peter will have briefly outlined why I asked him to bring you on board? I am putting together an operation, primarily on the south coast, to shut down a major black market trafficking group run by men who operate from their positions within government departments. I have had some success in The Midlands, I am sure Peter will have touched on the problems my family has had to endure over this, and now I want to 'cut off the head of the beast' so to speak."

"Peter told us about your family difficulties, Ben, especially what has happened to your daughter, how is she by the way?" Daniel asks with concern.

"Polly is healing, Daniel, the bruises will soon clear, but it will take a while for her to get over her ordeals of the last week or so. But for Peter, it would have been far worse, I am sure," Ben replies. He briefly recaps on Peter's timely intervention with Polly, when Galbraith and his men forced their way into his house.

"Good show Peter, always there when a damsel is in distress," Conrad smiles.

"It was a very unpleasant experience for all the family, and we are all indebted to Peter for his help. Now let me give you some details of how I propose we go about this and what is needed to get things moving. I have asked a colleague of mine, Major Jeremy Baxter to spearhead the operation with me, do either of you know him by the way?"

"Yes, I know him, you couldn't have picked a better man for a war than the Major, he has a fearsome reputation for crushing anyone that gets in his way in a firefight. There are stories of some of his special operations stretching to the Baltic and as far as Turkey. If anyone can kill this beast you talk of Ben then it is the Major," Daniel replies.

"Peter has also told me of his exploits, Daniel, so how do you and Conrad feel about working under him, any reservations?"

"We are military minded, Ben, and understand how former soldiers like the Major think, we will work well with him, indeed I think I can speak for both Daniel and myself when I say we much prefer to work with ex-military than civilians, nothing personal you understand?" says Conrad.

"I understand perfectly, Conrad, and feel confident that we shall work well together and achieve the ultimate goal, namely closing down these criminal enterprises and seeing the ringleaders put behind bars. Now, have you made arrangements for an overnight stay?" Ben asks.

"Yes, Peter arranged that for us, we are at The Bell in Carswell," Daniel replies.

"Okay, well can I suggest we meet up again tomorrow, back here might be best so that Peter is able to offer any suggestions, shall we say at 9 o'clock?"

Just then, Polly enters the study. "Daddy, how long will you be Maisy, Daisy and George are asking for you?"

"We're just about finished, Polly, let me introduce you to Conrad and Daniel two friends of Peter's."

"Hello, Polly, Peter has told us about your terrible ordeals recently, how are you?" Daniel asks.

"I am very well, thank you; Peter has been taking care of me."

The two men get ready to leave as Polly and Ben go out into the hallway toward the parlour. Peter sees them out as they bid goodbye to Polly, while Ben and Peter return to the study. Ben meanwhile says goodnight to the children and promises to see them in the morning. Polly asks questions about Daniel and Conrad which Ben avoids by asking her to talk to Peter about them, after which he returns to the study just as the phone rings. It's Galbraith, who tells Ben that he has not yet been able to find anyone suitable for his needs. Ben suggests that he call him back when he has done so. He then sits down with Peter to discuss the conversations with Daniel and Conrad.

The two men arrive back at the house the next morning at 9 o'clock sharp, and join Ben and Peter in the study.

"Can I first confirm with you both that you have been cleared by your department to join me on this venture? I believe Peter had spoken with you about this, but I need to be sure"

"Yes we both been granted leave of absence indefinitely to complete the operation," says Conrad.

"The first priority is to determine just where exactly the cottage that McKenzie uses is situated, so that we can take a look inside, hopefully it should reveal some interesting details of his business."

"Why don't Daniel and myself get down there as soon as possible and see what we can find out? I will get the office to drum up some cover for us to use, and find a hotel in Rye."

"That sounds a very good idea, Conrad, you need a cover that will allow you to move about with ease, and allow me to join you a little later without creating any suspicion," Ben replies.

"You will need to carry weapons for this operation, so be sure to get your documents in order," Peter adds.

"Goodness, I had forgotten about red tape, gentlemen, thanks Peter," Ben replies.

"We will attend to that as soon as we return, we can get the midday train and be back in the office in time to make arrangements," says Daniel.

"Well, unless there are any questions, we can leave it there for the time being, will you let Peter know when your arrangements are in place, and I will see you in Rye as soon as everything is arranged," Ben concludes.

And with that the two men are shown out by Peter, after thanking Ben for his hospitality the previous evening. Ben makes a quick call asking Phil Landers to arrange a meeting around noon.

"I believe we are moving toward a successful conclusion Peter, providing the documents that Galbraith says are at the cottage, we should have their details next week. Then we can look to making raids on the distribution sites and round up the McKenzie's and Williamson's of this world. The longer this takes, the bigger their profits and the longer I have to be concerned about dangers to my family. I have no doubt that these people will attempt another intrusion here once they know of my involvement."

"You need to concentrate all your efforts in bringing these men to justice Ben, I have the situation covered here. Nothing will happen to your family while I am here, I give you my word," says Peter with an air of determination in his voice.

"Thank you for that, Peter." Ben arrives at the office about 11.30 a.m. to brief Phil Landers. He confirms that the operation will be coordinated from London, and he Ben, will be in London to oversee accompanied by Daniel Bottomley and Conrad Wilberforce. He is unsure how long he will be away, so suggests that he officially take a leave of absence, which would make sense considering what has happened to his family recently. He impresses on Lander the need for absolute secrecy regarding what he will be doing. Nothing is to be written down, and he will make contact with Phil, by phone to his home, to avoid anyone listening in.

"How does the London office feel about you leading the operation, Ben, no moans about not being involved directly?" asks Phil.

"There will be very few people who will know of the operation, since I am using the Major's department to assist. Officially, I will be in London to report on our successes in The Midlands. My visit to the South coast area will not be discussed. Since I have always moved around unhindered in my position, no one is likely to ask questions about where I am," Ben replies.

"When will you be leaving?" Phil asks.

"I am hoping to catch a train on Sunday and meet up with Daniel and Conrad Sunday evening."

"All I will add, Ben, is that you watch your back, these men are desperate and would have you killed, I am sure if it is the only way they can protect their interests."

"Thank you for your concern, Phil, rest assured I will be very careful for my own safety and that of my family."

Before leaving for home, Ben takes the trouble to tell Maureen Potter that he will be out of the office for a few days. Maureen has been invaluable to him over the years and he does not enjoy deceiving her as to where he will be, but in this instance he decides he must.

"Enjoy your time off, Ben, how is Polly by the way?"

"She is on the mend thank you, Maureen," Ben replies and leaves the office for home after wishing everyone a good weekend. His mind is racing as he makes the short journey to his house, and he decides to make the most of this weekend before going off to London. After supper, Ben receives a call from Galbraith.

"Mr Spencer, I have a name for you regarding your request for a contact around Rye. His name is Joe Hocking. I have told him that you work for me, I hope you don't mind, but that was the best reason I could think of. If I had told him who you were, he would not have offered to help."

"I understand, tell me, how do I contact this man when I am ready?" Ben asks.

"He lives in Rye; I will give you his address."

"Thank you," Ben replies making a note of his address. "I shall need a number to contact you, Galbraith, once I have had a chance to use your information," Ben insists.

"Very well, Spencer, I will give you my home number, so only phone me in the evenings please."

Ben replaces the receiver, and leaves the study for the parlour. He is determined to enjoy as much of the weekend as possible, so goes into the garden to see what the children are up to.

"Daddy, push me on the swing, please?" asks George.

"Come and see how the vegetables are growing, Daddy," calls Maisy from the vegetable patch.

Ben gives George a push on the swing, and walks across to the vegetable patch to examine how everything is progressing. It was still difficult to get fresh vegetables; many items were still rationed, so everyone was encouraged to grow their own. Margaret, with the help of the children, had planted Peas, Potatoes, Runner Beans, Lettuce and Tomatoes ready for summer pickings.

"You and Mummy have all done very well, I am looking forward to having these on my plate children," Ben says with a smile.

Margaret joins them and is pleased with how the vegetables are all progressing.

"The children have worked really hard with the vegetables, Ben, I am so pleased that they are progressing so well. I remember the war years when we were all told to dig for Britain and we have continued to do so," says Margaret.

"Where is Polly, Margaret?" Ben asked surprised that she is not in the garden with the family.

"My guess is she is probably by Peter's side in the workshop, she never strays far from him when she is home."

Ben wanders over to the workshop come garage and true to form, finds Polly helping Peter clear some of the shelves ready to store the vegetables for the winter months. As Margaret said, Polly is never far away from Peter since he rescued her from the intruders. He has been very patient with her, but Ben realises that he must have a word with Polly before he goes away on Sunday.

"Hello, Daddy, Peter and me are making some space for the vegetables."

"I hope you are not being a nuisance, Polly. Peter does have things to do you know."

"She's fine, Ben, and I quite enjoy her company."

Ben leaves the garage and goes back into the parlour to join Margaret who has also gone back inside. He outlines what he will be doing for the next week or so, and Margaret is naturally concerned even though he does his best to assure her that he will be safe.

"You really do not know what you may be up against when you take on these people in their own backyard, Ben, God only knows what we have had to endure so far at home," Margaret responds with an air of anxiety.

"I have two men with me, selected by Peter, who I am sure will take care of me. We are only going to look at these documents supposedly stored in a cottage, so with luck, we should not meet with anyone," Ben replies trying to ease her concern.

"Just be very careful, Ben, I know how dangerous these men are and I do not want any more family casualties."

Ben sits down and reflects on what Margaret has said while she makes some tea. Polly arrives in the parlour, and Ben takes the opportunity to tell her he will be away next week. He does not go into any detail, but tells her he will probably be away for the whole week.

"You will be careful, Daddy, you haven't got Peter to look after you like me."

"I will be careful, Polly, now take Peter a cup of tea, then round up Maisy, Daisy and George, it will soon be bedtime."

On Saturday morning, Peter goes back to his house to take some of his clothing and collect clean items. He also checks his post before receiving a phone call from Daniel and Conrad, by arrangement, to confirm that they have settled in Rye.

"Tell Ben we are at The George in the High Street, I will book him a room from tomorrow evening," Daniel tells Peter.

"Thanks, Daniel, anything to report before you meet with Ben?"

"The locals are not very friendly as you would expect in a small community, Conrad and myself have simply wandered around as though we are on a break, kept ourselves to ourselves whilst keeping our eyes and ears open. So far we have not located the cottage but have the weekend to have a good look around without creating any suspicions. There will be a lot more people about at the weekend down to enjoy the time off work so we will blend in more easily."

"Okay, Daniel, my regards to Conrad, bye for now," Peter replies and replaces the receiver.

After a brief word with his housekeeper, Peter returns to Ben's home anxious not to stay away for too long.

Ben, meanwhile enjoys the day at home with Maisy, Daisy and George, while Margaret goes into town with Polly. She wanted to get Polly away from the house and siege environment they had been living for the last few weeks. She makes sure that the conversation stays with shopping and what new clothes she will buy for the children, then what to suggest for Sunday lunch, anything so as to keep Polly's mind occupied by everyday events. They return home to find Ben in the garden with Peter and the children. *Life appears almost normal for now,* she thinks to herself. The rest of the day is a very normal Saturday, everyone enjoying time together, just as Ben would have planned, before his going away to London. On Sunday, Ben has a brief chat with Peter concerning his trip to Rye. Peter has the number of The George in Rye, and Ben reminds him that any conversation that they have must be guarded since the call would go through a local exchange. Ben has an early lunch before Peter takes him to the station to begin his long train journey to the south coast. What does the next week or so hold for him and the operation that he will be controlling? Hopefully, he will see a conclusion to all his efforts over years of fighting black marketeers. He is very aware of the risks, but he is also aware of the benefits to everyone if he is successful.

Daniel and Conrad do their best to blend in with weekend visitors to Rye and move around freely. They manage to hire a couple of bicycles so as to cover a bigger area and enjoy the East Sussex scenery while searching for Giles Williamson's cottage. On Saturday, they travel southeast towards Hastings for about five miles before turning back towards Rye. They spot several probable cottages, but after knocking on the doors asking directions, none of the inhabitants fit the description of an attractive woman in her early forties. On Sunday, they go off in the opposite direction toward East Guildford. As they reach East Guildford, around noon, they notice a well-dressed woman, who appears to be unattached, coming out of St Mary's Church. They stop, looking at the map, and notice that she is joined by a man they know to be Giles Williamson. Williamson is a big man, with a moustache and greying hair. His clothes are most definitely tailor -made, and he has an air of self-importance which makes him stand out from the locals. Daniel and Conrad busy themselves over the map, waiting for Williamson to move off, hopefully to lead them to the cottage.

CHAPTER 19

(Ben arrives in Rye East Sussex)

The cottage is about 300 yards from the church set back off the road. Daniel and Conrad go back to the George for some lunch and can do no more now until Ben arrives this evening. They spend a leisurely afternoon by the river, Conrad is a keen fisherman, and get back to the George around 6 o'clock. Ben arrives just after 7 o'clock after a long weary series of train journeys, and the three men sit down to dinner just after 8.

"It sounds as if your time here has been successful thus far gentlemen," Ben says after Daniel and Conrad had informed him that they had located the cottage.

"What we must do tomorrow, to cement our cover is have a good look round the area for what might be a good place to build. I suggest that we tell the landlord that we will not be in for dinner, and stay out until it is dark enough to approach the cottage. We can assume that Williamson will go back to London in the morning, leaving his lady friend alone. We have to hope that she does not like being in alone, so that we can visit the cottage undisturbed."

The following morning, Monday, they have a leisurely breakfast and make sure that they are overheard discussing possible areas to visit, and why they will be visiting those areas. Ben knows how important it is that they blend in and no one suspects them of anything other than what they have tried to portray of themselves. He hopes to be able to make a successful intrusion into the cottage this evening and spend time over the next couple of days digesting the information, he hopes they will uncover then planning how to move forward. The day drags somewhat since they are all preoccupied with the evening's business. Around 6 o'clock, after looking at several 'suitable building sites' they find a pub where they can have some dinner. The conversation is somewhat muted over dinner, each one of them looking ahead to what they are about to embark on. They know that if they mess up or get discovered the consequences would be catastrophic for the fight against the black market racketeers.

"Well, gentlemen, this is it what I have waited a long time for this opportunity and with your help we are going to make it happen. I take it you have the necessary 'tools' to hand?" says Ben referring particularly to their weapons.

"Ben, we are ready," replies Conrad.

The three men move out of the pub as soon as it is dark. They stay off the main road, to avoid contact with any locals and locate the cottage after about fifteen minutes walking, which is in darkness. Although it is only just after 9 o'clock, they decide to knock the door just in case the occupant has gone to bed. There is no response, so the three men make their way to the back to look for the easiest way in. They find the window to the kitchen has a faulty catch, making it very easy to gain access. Daniel climbs inside and unlocks the back door for Ben and Conrad. After standing for a few moments to familiarise themselves with the layout, they decide that Conrad should remain at the front window of the cottage, to watch for the return of the owner.

Ben and Daniel go off to look for the cellar, which is located off the hallway. There are no windows in the cellar, making it quite safe to switch on the light. The cellar is full of boxes, all labelled with place names and numbers. Ben opens one of the boxes, and is astonished at what he discovers. The box he opens is labelled 'East London 1945' and details shipments of foodstuffs and alcohol. There are a number of addresses which must be drop off points for the items. There are also several names, possibly local merchants and agents. Ben asks Daniel to make a note of the labels, and list items that are referred to in each box. He decides to remove some 'samples' for evidence, confident that they will not be missed among the large amount of documentation. Both men, however, are careful to replace every box in exactly the same position as it was found. Then at the back of the cellar, Ben finds what they were really looking for, details of the storage dumps on the south coast. He is about to take details, when Conrad appears at the door of the cellar.

"Ben, Daniel, someone is approaching the cottage, we need to go now!"

The three men clamber back through the window, making sure that the catch is back in place, and make off down the lane, away from the cottage as a woman goes through the front gate.

Ben looks at his watch; it is 10 o'clock, time to return to The George. They get back to The George and settle down with a pint of beer. Ben looks at Daniel and Conrad and smiles.

"It's been a good day gentlemen?" he says raising his glass. "I suggest an early start tomorrow, straight after breakfast: there is a lot to discuss while we are out and about."

Since they are the only ones in the bar, Ben does not enter into any conversation that could be overheard by the proprietor. He merely acknowledges his question about their day by generalising on where they have been. He needs to be confident that no one is asking questions about the visitors from London or somewhere north. Locals can be very inquisitive of strangers and what they want, especially if any of the locals are involved in the black market themselves, as is very probable. Ben decides it might be an idea to get the proprietor involved so that he can tell the locals about them.

"You might be able to help us John, being a local you must know the names of the biggest landowners in East Sussex?" Ben asks.

He learns that there are two farmers that own a significant amount of land, but the biggest landowner in East Sussex is The Ministry of Defence. Ben makes a note of the two farms, and thanks the landlord for his help. He will probably have to make some sort of contact with at least one of them to maintain the reason for being in the area. He sits back down with Daniel and Conrad, and asks their advice regarding the contact that Galbraith had offered. They both agree that they hold off from contacting him until they have all the information from the cottage.

Hopefully, they can get back into the cottage again tomorrow, Tuesday, sometime in the evening. The following morning, the three men enjoy a good breakfast, before Ben gets details of the two farms from the landlord. They decide to seek out at least one of the farms, so that they can firmly establish their cover as property developers, and make it easier to return to the area when they have further information.

They find the farm, which is only about a mile away, and walk up the driveway to the front door, and introduce themselves to the farmer, Jeremiah Haines. A thickset and jovial character, he invites them inside. Ben had established a good cover story from the Central Office of Information in London, in case of any detailed checks, but the farmer readily accepts who they are, and listens with interest to what they have to say. Ben is careful not to go into any detail and talks about development of some 100 houses subject to the farmer's land being available for development.

"That may be a problem, Mr Spencer, I am not sure about covenants or any other restrictions that are on my land, I shall have to talk with my solicitor about that," the farmer replies.

"I would appreciate that Mr Haines, I am not sure how long we shall be here this week, but we are scheduled to return as soon as circumstances permit. We have to go back to London shortly, but will be in touch with you again before we go. We are staying at The George, so perhaps we can have dinner before we leave?"

Ben and his colleagues bid farewell to Jeremiah Haines, and walk back to the main road. They have all the equipment they need for another visit to the cottage, so decide to find somewhere for lunch where they can discuss their next moves. They find another public house, this time in East Guildford itself, less than two miles from Rye and have some lunch outside in the pub's garden, so they can talk without being overheard.

"We need to be able to get back inside the cottage tonight gentlemen, so let's hope the lady of the house is out again."

"How much time do you think we will need Ben?" asks Daniel, concerned about being late back to the George which may arouse the locals' suspicions.

"Why don't we get there earlier, see if anyone is around, and use the fields at the rear as our escape route?" Ben replies.

Although it was dark when they visited the cottage last evening, it was apparent that the lane led to nowhere, so there is no fear of being seen. They can walk down the lane and will probably notice if anyone is in the cottage, or go to the door to ask directions.

"Yes, I think it is a risk worth taking, Ben," Conrad replies.

So, after a leisurely lunch, they fold up the maps which they had deliberately laid out for the benefit of anyone watching, and stroll off back towards Rye. They turn down the lane adjacent to the cottage and soon determine that it leads to Camber, an area of coast used extensively by the military during WWII. Whilst some parts of the beach will still be restricted, they can determine an easy way back to the rear of the cottage without being seen. Ben decides that one of them should go back to the cottage to see if anyone is at home, while the other two wait in the dunes.

"That'll be me, if the lady is home, I'll see what I can find out about her," Conrad volunteers.

"Okay, Conrad, make sure you have plenty of maps to refer to."

"And don't get too friendly!" Daniel says with a smile.

Conrad smiles at Daniel and moves off toward the cottage hoping to find it empty but hopefully seeking as much information as he can if the owner is there. He approaches the cottage, seemingly studying a map as he walks up the path, and knocks on the front door.

A strikingly attractive woman answers the door.

"Yes, can I help you?" she asks with a pleasant smile.

"Hello, my name is Conrad Wilberforce, I am so sorry to bother you, but I seem to have lost my bearings. I thought I might be able to walk toward Dungeness via Camber, as the map suggests, can I do that?"

"Do come in a moment. I'll have a look at your map, although I am not sure whether I can help at all. I'm Katherine Meadows by the way."

"Thank you, Katherine, I'm very pleased to meet you."

Conrad enters the cottage, and notices a travel case in the hallway.

"Are you off somewhere interesting, Katherine?" he asks casually.

"Yes I am off to town later to stay with some friends. I miss London and go as often as I can."

"I see, well I hope I am not keeping you?"

"Not at all, I have about half hour before my taxi arrives at 3-30, are you from London, Mr Wilberforce?"

"Please, call me Conrad, yes I am, I am here on business with two of my colleagues, we are looking for land that we can develop for housing."

"Really? I wouldn't have thought that this was a suitable area at all."

"Many coastal areas are being considered, there is an abundance of space, and in most instances there are road and rail links already in place. We believe that there is an opportunity to develop these areas in preference to big cities. London, Birmingham etc.," Conrad answers with a degree of authority in his voice.

"Well, when you put it like that, I suppose it makes sense, but why here especially?"

"You are on the main road from Ashford to Hastings with very little in between."

145

"I see, well to answer your question, you may be able to walk to Dungeness, but I wouldn't recommend it since I don't believe it has been completely cleared of explosives."

"Good lord, I never thought of that, I will just have a quick look at the area generally, make a few notes, and concentrate on potential sites inland, we spoke to a local farmer yesterday, so he might be a possible source of land for development."

"Farmland may be your best option, I would have thought," Katherine Meadows replies.

"Well thank you very much for your help, Katherine, and enjoy your time in London," says Conrad as he makes his way to the door, then back down the path.

CHAPTER 20

(The Cottage secrets unveiled)

After about thirty minutes, they make their way back toward the back of the cottage, which they are able to approach unseen from either the lane or the main road. Once again, they break into the cottage via the side window with the faulty catch and Conrad keeps watch, while Daniel and Ben return to the cellar. Ben makes for the boxes he was looking at containing details of storage dumps, and asks Daniel to look into other boxes marked with place names and numbers. Daniel notes the details from several boxes, Central London 1946 and 1947, West London 1947 and Birmingham 1947 and 1948. Ben, meanwhile, is anxious to look into the boxes containing the details of any storage dumps. The information housed in these boxes could be all that is needed to close down black market operation that is run and operated from London government departments. The details show that the racketeers are using the New Haven tunnels as their storage dumps. During WWII, the navy built a maze of tunnels under South Heighton, north of Newhaven. The secret tunnels housed HMS *Forward* a military communications station, where activity in the English Channel was monitored and where raids on Dieppe and the D-Day landings were planned. Very few people outside of government would know of their existence, making them an ideal place to hide illegal goods of any description for an unlimited period. They could be easily guarded, since there were just two entrances, and they were exposed with no direct cover. There was a detailed map of the entrances, of which Ben made a comprehensive sketch, and details of what was stored where. The tunnels were identified as east entrance and west entrance, and he estimated that there was everything from foodstuffs through to vehicles, ammunition and petrol listed in the tunnels. He made some general notes of what was listed, together with details of what shipments were going where. Ben quickly came to the conclusion that this was far bigger than anyone had envisaged, and decided that the information should be acted upon as speedily as possible.

"Are you ready to leave, Daniel? Do you have enough details?"

"More than enough to bring down these villains, Ben."

"Right, let's get out of here, be sure to leave everything in exactly the same way as you found it."

And with a final check that everything is in place they leave the cellar, and climb back out of the window, after first checking that there is no one in the lane. They move swiftly down the garden path, into the adjoining fields then back into the lane, again checking that no one has seen them, before walking slowly back to the main road and Rye. Ben looks at his watch, it is just after 5 o'clock, they had been in the cellar for less than one hour, but the information they had secured in that hour was priceless.

"Gentlemen. We shall be able to return home tomorrow, earlier than I had hoped with more information that I could have dreamed we would find."

"What next Ben, when can you expect to raid the tunnel complex?" Conrad asks.

"At the earliest possible opportunity Conrad, I don't know how often they distribute, but I would think that they move goods of some sort on a daily basis."

When they get back to the George, Ben decides to call home.

"Hello Margaret, it's Ben."

"Ben, how are you." Margaret answers obviously pleased to hear from him. "Children, it's Daddy on the phone."

Before Ben can reply, Polly shouts, "Daddy, we are all missing you when are you coming home?"

Then he hears other voices all saying, "Daddy, Daddy we miss you."

Ben smiles and is overcome by his children's response.

"I hope to be home tomorrow children, now please put Mummy on the phone."

"Is that right, Ben, you are coming home tomorrow?'

"Yes dear, we have done what we can for now and have to wait for a response. We have been quite successful in looking at what we came for but now need to return to discuss how we move forward from here."

"When can we expect you home then?" Margaret asks.

"Well, I might have to call in the office, but I hope to be home for supper," Ben replies.

"I will make sure there is plenty for you, bye for now my dear."

"Goodbye, Margaret, I will see you tomorrow."

"John might we have some tea?" Ben asks before returning to his colleagues who are sitting in the garden.

"So, how and when do you propose we move on the storage sites, Ben?"

Ben appreciates that a lot of planning will have to go into these raids for maximum effect. They will have to be coordinated with the arrests of key personnel in London, Miles McKenzie and Giles Williamson for example. Major Baxter will be leading the raids, his leadership could be key to the success, and he will, no doubt, use his own men. The major's reputation for getting the job done will be crucial in apprehending dangerous men desperate to avoid capture. Then Ben will need to coordinate with the local police who will be responsible for making the arrests. They will have the unenviable task of documenting everything once Ben and his team have identified the ringleaders, and reported back to the government departments involved. It is a complex task, but Ben is determined to see it through to the very end.

"There is a fair amount of planning to be done, Daniel, as I am sure you are aware, we do not need to rush into anything, because the people concerned have no idea that we are on to them. I will be talking to the Major later this week, outlining what we know and asking him to begin sourcing his best men for the job. Before that can happen, we will have to return and find out as much as we can about the tunnels."

"In that case, Ben, it might be an idea for Conrad and I to stay on. We can move on to New Haven, check out the tunnels approaches, and find out how many men are guarding them? That will leave you to plan the operation with the Major."

"Good idea, Daniel, and moving to New Haven will take you away from this area. You will need to get me a detailed layout of the area surrounding the tunnels so that we can block off any escape routes. This is critical so that no one escapes."

"We will leave in the morning, Ben, and update you tomorrow evening," Conrad adds.

"In that case gentlemen, I think we can afford to relax for the remainder of this evening," Ben replies, as he pours himself another cup of tea. The next few days are going to be very busy, so an hour or two of relaxation will be welcome.

The next morning, the three men say their goodbyes and Ben gets a taxi to the station, while Daniel asks about a bus to New Haven. Ben has decided he will talk with the Major over the phone, rather than meet with him before he has the information required to plan a date for the raid. He looks forward to a few days back home with his family, who will all be glad to see him. He has only been away a few days, but they will all be missing him very much. He makes additional notes while he is on the train to add to the wealth of information secured from the cottage cellar. He now has details implicating McKenzie and Williamson, as well as memos sent to Devonish and North relating to transportation and smuggling from Europe. The smuggling operations relate to weapons and alcohol in large quantities. Such operations could only be carried out with help from government departments, securing shipping details etc., into New Haven. The more he reads, the bigger the black market industry appeared. He has also discovered that deserters, ex-army personnel, who would be more than capable handling weapons, are being used to move goods. These men would have struggled to find work when the war ended, and would be easily persuaded to take part in shipment of goods. Daniel and Conrad would be especially interested in apprehending these men as part of their official capacity with The Ministry. Ben finally puts away his notes, and dozes for the remainder of the journey until he arrives at Victoria Station, from where he must transfer to the Midland line at Euston. He makes his connection fairly quickly and is soon on his journey home. He eventually arrives at Carswell station at 5 o'clock and gets a taxi for the short journey to The Gables. He enters the front door to be engulfed by his children.

"Daddy, Daddy, you're home, we've missed you so much," says Polly giving her father a huge hug.

"Yes Daddy, please don't go away again for a long time, please!" says Daisy almost pleading with him.

"Can you play with me later, Daddy?" asks George.

"Children, please let me get inside, we will have lots of time together tomorrow and after that, I promise, hello, Margaret," he adds giving her a kiss on her cheek.

"How was your trip, dear?"

"Yes, Daddy, did you have a good trip, where did you go by the way?" asks Polly.

"It was a good trip, but I'm afraid I cannot say where I have been for the moment, Polly."

The family move to the parlour, where Ben enjoys a welcome cup of tea. Tomorrow, he will spend some time linking the information in his container with the notes he has made from the visits to the cottage in Rye.

He has some calls to make, but for the remainder of the day, he will enjoy the company of his family. It is warm in the early evening sunshine, so everyone goes outside to the garden where Ben is met by Peter.

"Did you have a good trip, Ben?"

"I did, Peter, we'll talk tomorrow if that's okay, how have things been here?"

"That's fine, Ben, everything has been quiet while you were away. I have had to make some adjustments to the lighting, as it was too sensitive, and I have given your car a bit of a tune."

"Thanks very much, can I see what you have been up to with the car; it will give us chance for a quick chat?" Ben replies as he follows Peter toward the garage.

Once inside the garage, he briefly outlines what has transpired over the last couple of days.

"Daniel and Conrad have moved to New Haven, they are to contact me tomorrow evening, hopefully, they will have discovered the tunnel entrances by then. I am hoping that we can plan the raid for early next week, the sooner the better, and the sooner we rid the nation of these parasites," Ben comments with some degree of firmness in his voice.

"You will win this war, Ben, of that I am sure, but I do sometimes wonder at what cost given what has happened recently," Peter replies with concern.

"We have taken every precaution Peter, and your presence has been invaluable."

"I will be here with you and the family every step of the way, of that you can rest assured."

"Thanks, Peter, I see you have made some changes around the garage?"

"I have strengthened the door to the utility room and for the moment, blocked it with boxes to make any attempt to enter more difficult," says Peter. "I have also placed a light above the garage door which is sensitive to any movement," he adds.

"That's pretty impressive, now let's go and see how long supper will be. I have only had a pie since breakfast."

The next morning, Thursday, Ben is up early to prepare for an early meeting with Phil Lander. He arrives at the office shortly after 9 o'clock and outlines what has happened over the past two days, and tells him what needs to happen once a team has been assembled by Major Baxter.

"I am hoping that a raid can be planned for next week; that is why the information about the tunnel whereabouts is so critical. Daniel is contacting me this evening. As soon as we have determined where the tunnels are, I can ask Major Baxter to begin assembling his team."

"It looks as though we are at last getting on top of these villains, Ben, you and your colleagues have done well," Phil replies.

"I certainly hope so, I have to admit the last few weeks have worn me down, with the abductions of Polly, the intrusion in my house and everything else associated with this operation."

"What can I do to help, Ben?"

"I will have to order certain items for the raid, camouflage clothing, balaclavas and so on, I will give you a list, and can you write up a report for the London office please, Phil?"

"Of course, anything to help."

"That's about all for now, Phil, can you ask Maureen to come in please?"

Phil leaves the office and a few moments later Maureen enters.

"Maureen, hello, tell me has there been any calls for me while I was away?"

"Yes, Major Baxter called from London, I told him you were away and I wasn't sure when you would be back."

"Did you mention the call to anyone?"

"No, I asked if I could pass on any message, but he said not," Maureen answered.

"Thank you, Maureen, what would I do without you?" Ben responds with a smile.

There really isn't any more urgent business for Ben in the office, so he decides to go home in time for lunch, before he makes contact with Major Baxter. He enjoys a quiet lunch, with Margaret, and takes the opportunity to tell her about the last few days in Rye.

"It sounds as if you may be closing in on these terrible people at long last."

"I believe so, Margaret, and no one will be more pleased than me to end this business once and for always. Now I need to make that call to Major Baxter."

Just as he is about to make the call, the phone rings

"Hello, Ben Spencer speaking."

"Mr Spencer, it's Bill, Bill Holder."

"Hello, Bill, what can I do for you?"

"Well I thought you would want to know about another boat load of goods due, I have heard there is one arriving sometime in the early hours of Saturday morning, at the usual docking area," Bill replies.

"Well thank you very much for that, Bill, any other details?"

"My contact tells me they are a different bunch from last time, and they will be heavily armed," Bill replies with concern in his voice.

"Please see that you are well away from the area for the next few days, Bill, I will send you something to the usual address."

"Thanks, Mr Spencer."

When Ben has occasion to pay Bill Holder for services rendered, he sends the money by registered letter to Bill's sister's address in Birmingham. Ben immediately contacts Birmingham Constabulary and asks for Chief Inspector Jamieson.

"Chief Inspector, Ben Spencer, I have some information for you concerning another shipment of goods by canal."

"Mr Spencer, good afternoon, what do you have for me?" he enquires.

Ben passes on the details that Bill Holder gave him, and makes the point about the men being armed.

"I will see to it that my men are prepared," Jamieson replies.

"And as before, Chief Inspector, this is an anonymous tip for you?" Ben adds.

"Of course, Mr Spencer, I will let you know how we get on, goodbye and thank you again."

CHAPTER 21

(Ben contacts the Major & receives news about the tunnels)

Ben gathers his papers and notes together and dials Major Baxter's number.

Mr Spencer, I was wondering when I might hear from you, how are you progressing, moving a pace I hope?"

"I believe so, Major, I am hoping we can move into the area next week, how does that sound to you, could you be ready in that time?"

"How many men will you need?" the Major replies.

"About twenty and yourself should be sufficient."

"Then yes I think I can round up suitable men for such an operation within a day or so," the Major goes on.

"I am waiting on final details of the exact locations, which I hope to hear this evening. When I have the locations, I will confirm with yourself so that a date for the operation can be arranged".

"We shall need vehicles to carry about twenty people together with a large saloon; do you want me to arrange for them to be available?"

"That would be a tremendous help Major, you are obviously able to access vehicles much easier than myself.

"Quite so, now what else will you need, weapons?"

"My two colleagues and myself have pistols which will suffice, I will leave it to yourself to decide what your men carry, but I do expect some armed resistance."

"I don't expect we will be needed for more than one day, so I will arrange for overnight items only, what about accommodation if required?" the Major enquires.

"Yes I will get back to you on that when I know what is involved."

"Very well, Mr Spencer, then I look forward to hearing from you shortly."

Before you go, Major, can I suggest that any future conversations relating to the operation, be referred to as Operation Keepsake?"

"Very well, Spencer, Operation Keepsake it is."

The major gives Ben his home number in case he needs to make further contact, before replacing the receiver. He has just replaced the receiver when he receives a call from Daniel.

"Hello, Daniel, what have you to report?"

"We have located the tunnels from the maps we found in the cottage Ben."

"That's brilliant, Daniel, when are you going to try and get inside?"

"Conrad thinks it may be an idea to make the attempt tomorrow evening, providing there is a delivery, if not we shall have to keep a close watch for a suitable time after dark."

"Can you determine where the trucks are coming from, is it from the port itself, perhaps you could hitch a lift from their starting point?" Ben suggests.

"That sounds like our best option, Ben, I must confess, the idea of starting from source had not occurred to me. We can go and take a look at the port itself tomorrow: I believe they do trips to Dieppe, so we can make enquiries about these while looking around."

"It is still very risky, Daniel, so do be careful," Ben answers with concern.

"I will get Conrad to make the enquiries about Dieppe, he is a very good talker, while I look around the local pubs to see what I can find out."

"Okay Daniel, well once again, I urge you and Conrad to be careful, do not take any unnecessary risks please."

"We will be careful, Ben, now I suggest we make contact again Saturday, around lunchtime?"

"I will be waiting for your call, Daniel, good hunting to both of you."
And with that Ben replaces the receiver. He is rather concerned about the
action that Daniel is planning, and voices his concerns to Peter.

"Both Daniel and Conrad are experienced in covert operations, Ben, if
anyone can get inside the tunnels without being seen, they can."

"Well it looks like Operation Keepsake is about to begin, Peter."

Ben decides to take a long weekend break, unsure of how much time
he may be away next week. He goes into town with Margaret and enjoys
being able to walk round the shops, although there is not much to see. It is
just a pleasant change to be able to do normal things for once, and it will
be good for Margaret to spend time away from the house with him. After
taking lunch in a local pub, they return home, Margaret has household
work to do and Ben has the children to entertain.

"Daddy, let's play a game," Daisy and George chorus, and run off
toward the bottom of the garden. Ben chases after them and catches them
by the gate. Everyone is enjoying themselves so much, that they fail to
notice the car parked in the lane, across the field, with two men watching
the house. Meanwhile, Daisy and George run back towards the house
laughing as they do so. Polly brings out some cold drinks for everyone,
then turns back to the parlour. She seems to be getting over the terrible
events of a week or so ago. Time is a great healer and she is a very
resilient girl. Ben is enjoying the fun with the children, as Peter calls him
from the shed next to the garage.

"Ben, we seem to have visitors in the lane again."

Ben takes the glasses from Peter, and looks in the direction of the lane
from inside the shed.

"Don't recognise either of them, Peter."

"I will keep an eye on them, Ben, you and the family carry on, I
suggest that you don't mention their presence to anyone."

"Yes, what do you think, Peter, what on earth can they want at this
time?"

"I can only think that they are watching to see what is happening and
who is in the house, whether they are planning anything is difficult to say,
I find it hard to believe that they intend to come to the house again. In the
meantime, I will keep a close watch on them," Peter replies.

The rest of Saturday passes without incident, the two men watching the house move off after about ten minutes. Daniel calls Ben around teatime and has some positive news.

"Hello, Ben, I'm pleased to report that last night was very successful. As we determined from the details we obtained from the cottage, there are two entrances to the tunnels, one from the east the other from the west. They are linked by two main corridors each one about 150 to 200 feet long. There are no real escape routes if we attack from the east and west entrances; only some old pillboxes near the west entrance, and they are not easy to access. If you access both tunnels simultaneously, and keep to the right corridors in each, you should be able to round up all the occupants. I would estimate there are up to 40 men at any one time working the tunnel complex. All the men wear a uniform, and I get the impression that the locals think they are working for the government."

"I was wondering how they might pass off so much movement of goods, but the locals will remember that the tunnels were used by the government during WWII," Ben replies.

"There is an enormous amount of goods being brought in from the continent, including meat products, which would need to be shifted quickly. They have also recently taken delivery of trucks, which I presume; they will use to move the goods northwards. I also noticed various clothing items, especially tailors' cloth. And there were significant amounts of alcohol and cigarettes."

"You have done better than I could have hoped Daniel, I suggest you and Conrad get back to London, I'm sure you need a change of clothes anyway, and we will talk again when I have had chance to report to the Major. I would think that a raid next week is now definitely on providing he can find the right men."

"Okay, Ben, you have my number, I will wait to hear from you."

"Very good, Daniel, and can I thank you and Conrad again for your sterling efforts?"

Ben passes the information to Peter, who is also amazed at the efforts his two colleagues have put into the operation.

Sunday is a beautiful sunny day, and Ben suggests they should go to Bradgate Park for a picnic.

"Yes please, Daddy; I love Bradgate Park, and we will be able to see the deer." says Maisy.

"What shall we have to eat at the picnic?" asks George, who is always hungry.

"I am sure Mummy will find all sorts of goodies for us, George, so let's wait and see it will be a surprise then won't it?"

Polly, meanwhile, is talking with Margaret.

"Mummy, I am still trying to catch up with my schoolwork, so do you mind if I stay behind, Peter will be here won't he?"

"So long as Peter doesn't mind and you don't bother him."

"Thanks, Mummy."

And so the family set off for Bradgate Park, to enjoy the beauty of the Leicestershire countryside. The terrible winter had forced everyone to stay at home, and Ben had been too busy since to take any weekend time off.

Polly meanwhile, did have some work to catch up, but made Peter some lunch which she shared in his company. He was very easy to talk to and she felt so at ease when he was around especially after her ordeals of the past few weeks. He has proved invaluable, and Ben is pleased to be able to call on his expertise whilst he continues on his pursuit of the black market gangs.

The family, meanwhile return from Bradgate around teatime worn out having walked miles or so they thought. There would be some early bedtimes for the young ones, it had been some time since they had spent the day walking and they were not used to such arduous exercise. In fact, all the family are ready for an early night, but insist on having some playtime first, after which they are suddenly hungry again! Eventually, they give in to their tiredness and Margaret takes them all upstairs. Peter and Ben discuss the day and Ben thanks him for watching over Polly whilst they were out.

"My pleasure, Peter, she is good company," says Peter as he retires after making one last check on doors and windows.

CHAPTER 22

(The Spencers' house is targeted again)

It is about 2.00 a.m. when the fire is started in the garage area. Peter, who is a very light sleeper, can smell the smoke through his open window. He looks outside and can see a large amount of smoke drifting from the garage. Just as he finishes dressing he hears a scream, it is Polly. Peter's room is next to Polly's at the end of the house. He dashes to the door just as two men turn onto the stairs with Polly trussed up inside a blanket. The men have attempted to drug her, but she had woken up before they were able to give her the full amount. She kicks and struggles and manages to free her legs as the two men reach the bottom of the staircase. Peter switches on the lights, and notices that the study door is open.

"Ben, quickly, they have set a fire in the garage, go and see what you can do."

He fires in the air to distract the men while Ben races into the kitchen to see where the fire is.

Margaret, meanwhile, reaches the top of the stairs, then realises that she must wake the children. Suddenly, a man appears at the doorway of the study and fires at Peter, who returns the fire and hits him in the shoulder. Meanwhile Polly struggles to free herself, screaming and kicking, one of the men hits her, but she manages to free herself from blanket, the second man grabs her nightgown almost tearing it from her back as they move towards the door. Peter fires again at the man running from the study and hits him in the thigh. Both men holding Polly then release her and make a run for the door. Peter fires again as the men release Polly, but misses and shatters the glass of the porch door and they escape into the night. Peter holds the other two who both have gunshot wounds.

"Polly, are you okay? Here, cover yourself with this," he says as he hands her his jacket.

Polly puts on the jacket, relieved at being able to cover herself from the eyes of the two men.

"Can you call the police, Polly, and you had better call the fire brigade as well, I am not sure what damage has been done."

He orders the two men to sit down on the floor, and waits for Polly to return from the study

Margaret, meanwhile is trying to console the children, who are hysterical with fear. She brings them down the stairs and takes them into the parlour.

"Mummy, Mummy, what is happening, why did those men try to burn down our house," Maisy asks.

"And what have they done to Polly, Mummy?" George asks with tears in his eyes.

"Children, you are safe now, wait here while I see if the kitchen is clear, all the lights are on in the garden, so I will take a look."

"We will come too, Mummy," they all answer.

"Very well, but stay close to me."

Ben, meanwhile, has managed to control the fire before it takes a hold. The damage however is substantial from the smoke as well as the flames. The wooden garage is completely gutted, including the door from the utility room, which is a charred ruin. Thankfully, Ben's car was still parked outside the front of the house, had it been inside the garage the consequences would have been catastrophic. Smoke damage in the kitchen and utility room is extensive but, thankfully, Ben managed to contain the fire before it did any more damage.

The police and fire brigade arrive together and Ben leaves the firemen to assess everything while he goes to Margaret to see if anyone is hurt. The children have calmed down a little, looking at the fire damage with amazement.

"Did you put the fire out all by yourself, Daddy?" asks George.

"I did what I could, George, now we must leave it to the firemen. Margaret are you alright?"

"A bit shaken, Ben, but you should go and check on Polly, she was the target again poor girl."

Ben goes into the hallway and sees the two injured men on the floor watched over by two police officers. There is glass everywhere from the shattered hall door and again his office is a mess. Peter is comforting Polly, in the study.

"My dear Polly, what have they done to you?" Ben asks with tears of anger in his eyes.

"I'm okay, Daddy really, Peter is looking after me."

She is covered in bruises, most of which can be clearly seen since her nightshirt is badly torn and she has red wheals across her face where she was hit by one of the men. Despite her ordeal, she appears in control, and was talking to the police officer when Ben arrived in the studio.

"We can return tomorrow, or should I say later today, to take all the details, Mr Spencer, we'll book the two men you have apprehended and get them patched up ready for court," the police officer says.

"Thank you, Chief Inspector, I will be here all day now after the fire and everything else that has happened. Shall we say after lunch?"

"Thank you, Mr Spencer, that would be ideal."

Ben returns to the back of the house as the fire brigade finalise damping down.

"It's all clear now, Mr Spencer, but you have plenty of clearing up to do I'm afraid," the fire officer says with a smile.

"Yes, thank you, officer, so it would seem."

It is now 3.30 a.m., Margaret has managed to get Maisy, Daisy and George back to bed, and makes some tea which she brings through to the parlour. Polly has got dressed and has a heavy jumper on since it has turned rather chilly.

"I think we should all try and get a few hours' sleep and sort out all the mess later. Peter, is the house secure?"

"I will check before I go up, Ben, don't worry."

And with that, Ben, Margaret and Polly go back upstairs to try and get some sleep.

Margaret is the first up, about 7.30 a.m. with the sun shining through the bedroom window. She and Ben go downstairs together, and have a look at the damage caused by the fire. The garage is burnt out, so Ben will have to try and find something to replace it. Hopefully, his colleagues at the Ministry may be able to help. The utility room door will have to be replaced as a priority, and everything in the utility room will have to be cleaned and washed, and the kitchen may need some redecoration from smoke damage. Peter joins them to assess the damage.

"Looks like we have plenty of work ahead of us, Ben."

"I will make some breakfast for us, Ben could you contact Betty, and ask if she can help with clearing up. I will keep all the children home today after what has happened?"

Ben goes into the study to make the call as Polly gets up and decides that she will have a bath to ease her aches and pains. Margaret decides to let the other children sleep in after the night's events. They will all be exhausted from what has happened and will benefit from the extra rest.

Betty Poulton arrives and is visibly shaken by what she sees, broken glass in the porch, papers and books strewn all over the study and the strong smell of smoke throughout.

"My goodness, Margaret, what a terrible mess, is everyone alright?"

"We're fine thank you, Betty, just a little tired, but thank you for asking."

Polly meanwhile comes into the parlour and looks better for her bath, although some of her bruising, especially to her face, is very noticeable. She has some toast and a glass of milk.

"Mummy shall I see if I can help Daddy and Peter today?"

"I am sure they will need all the help they can get Polly."

Ben and Peter are clearing some of the mess in the study as Polly arrives.

"How can I help, Daddy?"

"Would you help Peter remove whatever is salvageable from the garage; although I fear most of the perishable contents have been destroyed. I have to make some calls as soon as I find my desk underneath this mess."

Just as he finds the telephone, it rings.

"Hello, Ben, Spencer speaking."

"Mr Spencer, it's Chief Inspector Jamieson from Birmingham, I am calling to let you know that we had another success with a seizure of a boat on the canal on Sunday morning.

"The haul was very extensive, as were the villains' attempts to stop my men. We arrested 10 men in total and confiscated many thousands of pounds' worth of goods."

"That is indeed good news, Chief Inspector, the more we can confiscate from these people the better."

"I will send you a detailed report of what is exactly confiscated, Mr Spencer for your records?"

"That would be appreciated, Chief Inspector, thank you very much, we shall be in contact again, I am sure, bye for now."

Ben sits down and reflects on what he has just been told. The attack on his home and family was obviously instigated in revenge for the barge being confiscated. Now more than ever, he is determined to have Galbraith arrested for the intrusion on his home and the assault on Polly. He will give the police relevant details when they return after lunch. In the meantime, he calls his office and recalls the events of last night to Phil Landers.

"Good God, Ben, is everyone safe? When is this business going to end?" he answers sounding upset. "They targeted Polly again, that is an outrage," he continues.

"They will pay for this latest attack on my family both with their businesses and with their freedom, Phil; that I promise you."

"What can I do to help?"

"I don't suppose you know where I can find a new garage do you?"

I will find one from one of our departments, there must be suitable storage buildings that would suffice, leave it with me, Ben, anything else?"

"If you can just hold the fort for a day or so, until I have arranged things at home, I would be obliged, Phil."

"I will get on to it straight away, Ben, let me know if there is anything else won't you?"

"Thanks, Phil, I will be in touch, let Maureen know what has happened would you please?"

"I will indeed," replies Phil.

Ben wanders out into the garden to see the contents of the garage stacked around the path and on the grass. Most of the contents are destroyed, but at least his tools are okay, and any items belonging to Peter were in the garden shed. Ben suggests a bonfire at the bottom of the garden might be a good idea. Margaret and Betty Poulton meanwhile have been busy clearing and cleaning in the utility room.

"I have ordered you a new door for the utility room, Ben, I am hoping they will fit it this afternoon, and a glazier will be along to replace the glass"

"That's good news, Peter, thank you," Ben replies.

"We are helping Mummy in the kitchen," says Maisy.

"Thank you, children, Mummy needs all the help she can get at the moment."

"I will stay and give Peter a hand Daddy, he has so much to do," says Polly.

"Very well, Polly, I am sure you can be of help," replies Ben smiling.

Soon after lunch, the police officers arrive to get details of the night's events. Detective Inspector Wishart and Constable Parsons are joined by W.P.C. Becky Garrett. It was thought that Polly may be more comfortable talking to the W.P.C.

"Come in, gentlemen, you must excuse the mess, we still have a lot to do."

They decide that W.P.C. Garrett will interview Polly and Margaret in the dining room, while Peter and Ben give their statements in the study. In the meantime, Betty Poulton takes care of the children in the parlour. The W.P.C. asks Polly about her assault and how badly she was injured, making detailed notes as Polly outlines her ordeal.

"If Peter had not shot those two men, it could have been much worse I am sure."

"Did you say he shot two of the men?" the W.P.C. replies.

"Yes, your colleagues took them away last night," Margaret confirms.

"Is this man a family friend?" the W.P.C. continues.

"Peter Forsyth has been a close friend of my husband since the war. They met because of Ben's work for the government, and Peter's contacts who were able to help."

"What work does your husband do exactly, Mrs Spencer?"

"My husband is with The Central Office of Information. He is responsible for investigating black market operations in the Midlands and closing them down as quickly as possible by any means necessary. This has made him and our family a target for these criminals, who are obviously hoping to stop him by threats and intimidation. Peter Forsyth is staying with us to assist in the security of the family home and the children," Mrs Spencer replies, annoyed at the unrelated questions of the W.P.C.

"Of course, Mrs Spencer, I apologise for prying, it was the mention of someone being shot that startled me."

"That's quite alright officer I understand your reaction; I am still coming to terms with what has happened over the last few weeks myself."

"It must have been very frightening for you, Polly, especially with what has happened to you previously?" the W.P.C. asks.

"Yes it was, but I knew that Peter would not let anything happen to me or anyone else in my family. If he had not shot those men, I would have been abducted again."

"You have had a terrible experience, Polly, I hope you are feeling better today?" the W.P.C. asks.

"Yes thank you."

"I think I have all I need from you, and thank you for your patience, Mrs Spencer."

The officer moves from the dining room, and back to the study. Ben and Peter talk at length with the officers about the events of the early morning. Arson is just one of the charges that is discussed, along with attempted burglary and kidnapping, together with an attempt to kill Peter Forsyth. In short, they will be going to prison for a long time. The officers take meticulous notes of the events before Ben intervenes.

"There are additional charges that I want to level against a Montague Galbraith Inspector."

"Really? We know of Mr Galbraith and would be delighted to put him away, what do you have?"

Ben recites details of the home intrusion by Galbraith and his men and emphasises the terrible assault on Polly. He also talks, with much anger, at how Margaret and the other children were held at gunpoint by Galbraith's men. After noting all the details, the inspector enquires, "Can I ask why you didn't report this at the time, Mr Spencer, these are very serious accusations?"

166

"As you may know, I am with the Central Office of Information. I have an open remit to take down racketeers by every means at my disposal. To date, I have enjoyed some success, and the attacks on my family are a direct result of my actions I am sure. At the time, I considered it prudent to try and force Galbraith's hand by threatening him with exposure if he did not give me information I could use to bring down these villains who are trying to hold us all to ransom. He duly supplied information which has proved useful and an operation is ongoing. I never intended that he would be allowed to get away with his intrusion into my home, but hoped that I could get some useful intelligence from him by issuing threats."

"I understand, Mr Spencer, and appreciate what you are doing to rid us all of these dreadful people, do tell me what I can do to help?" the Inspector answered.

"Well firstly, we do need you to make the arrests, perhaps your opposite number in Birmingham, Chief Inspector Jamieson, can help with this. Any relative information, regarding the black market operations of Galbraith, would be most useful, but of course your main priority will be to secure the convictions of these people, and I do appreciate that."

"Thank you, Mr Spencer, we will move on Galbraith as quickly as possible, how would you want me to make contact with you to keep you up to date?"

"I am going to ask my colleague Phil Landers to liaise with you on this as I am going to be fully occupied with matters in London for the next week or so."

"Any information that you feel is relevant, can I ask you to refer it under Operation Seeker?"

"I understand, Mr Spencer, well I think we have everything we need for now, plenty to keep us busy, I will leave you and your family to clear up the mess left behind. You have all suffered very much and deserve some rest for a while at least," the inspector concludes.

"Thank you very much, I will see you out."

The police officers move from the study to the front door and off towards Carswell.

"I need to talk with the Major, Peter, we may now have to postpone any action on the south coast for a day or so."

"Hopefully a couple of days should be all that is needed, Ben, but you know what is best for the family," Peter replies.

"I need to speak with Margaret about this, I do not want to leave until the family are happy with my being away after what has just happened occurred, Peter. Your help has proved invaluable, but there is only so much one person can do in these situations."

"Once we have secured the garage area, and replaced the broken glass in the front porch, we should be pretty much back to normal. I have asked someone to come and check the electrical circuits that were in the garage, and also to make sure that the alarm system is okay," says Peter.

"I have asked Phil Landers to make enquiries about another building for the garage, I must call him on that before the end of the day," Ben comments.

For the remainder of the afternoon, everyone is busy salvaging what can be salvaged from the garage, and Ben asks Margaret to give him a hand tidying up the study while he talks with her about the events of the past few hours.

"How are you holding up with what has happened, Margaret, I have not had chance to talk with you about all this?"

"I shall cope, Ben, I am learning to cope with these setbacks, I just hope that the events don't prey on the children's minds too much. Polly has been marvellous; how she is coping is amazing, we really do have a very special daughter. The younger children have all but forgotten about last night's events and are more interested in sorting out the garage contents, I just hope they are not bothering Betty too much," replies Margaret.

"It has been difficult to say the least Margaret, but I believe that we will be moving forward very quickly over the next few weeks, hopefully to some conclusions. I will have to go away again as soon as arrangements can be made, and when you and I are satisfied that it is safe at home."

"I understand what has to be done, Ben, and I know that this business has been made very difficult for you with the burglary attempt, Polly's abductions and now the fire. I just hope and pray that it will soon be over for all of us," Margaret replies with a sigh.

"I'm with you on that, my dear, and I am confident that this will be sooner rather than later, if all goes to plan over the coming few weeks," says Ben.

CHAPTER 23

(Operation Seeker: Preparation)

Ben was confident that Margaret was coping well with what had happened and felt better for having spoken with her. He now had to make the necessary arrangements so that the hard work this far, and the sacrifices he and his family have made, will not be wasted. Operation Seeker must now begin in earnest.

"Major Baxter speaking."

"Hello again, Major, it's Ben Spencer here"

"Ah, afternoon, Spencer, what do you have for me, are we ready to go after these villains yet?"

"There has been a bit of a setback my end I'm afraid, but it should not hold up Operation Seeker for too long."

He then proceeds to go over what has happened during the last 12 hours or so and how it proves just how desperate these villains are becoming.

"My God, Spencer, you and your family were very fortunate not to have been killed. The sooner we rid society of these people the better for all of us," the Major comments with some concern.

"Yes indeed, Major, what has happened has made me even more determined to bring these villains to justice. Last night's events have put back my plans a day or so, but nothing to be of concern. I can tell you that my colleagues have successfully checked the entrances to the tunnels outside of New Haven, I will give you more precise details when we meet. Point of interest here Major, all of the men involved wear uniforms, and the locals have been led to believe they are government workers, an ideal cover for sure, removing any suspicions from the operation. This business is highly organised, has been very carefully planned and could only have succeeded with inside help from officials in specific departments, food supply and transport for example."

"If what you say is true, we shall have to be spot on with the timing of the raid to coincide with any arrests in any Whitehall departments," the Major answers.

"I have a plan to make arrangements for this with a trusted colleague of mine. She has definite knowledge of people who are involved, indeed it was she who gave me the names to pursue in the first place, and will be able to assist in coordinating any arrests. I will talk with her in detail about this when we have a firm date and time set aside for the raid."

"Excellent, Ben, and any arrests will be carried out by police and the flying squad I would presume?" the Major continues.

"Yes, Major, I imagine that any arrests carried out on members of government departments will be overseen by Scotland Yard. My colleague will be able to confirm this, I will contact her later today for confirmation, when would you be ready to move with your men?"

"I would need 24 hours' notice, Ben, that would give me enough time to round up my men, transport them to New Haven and get them set in position at the tunnels," the Major replies.

"Thank you, Major, I need a couple of days or so to get the repairs to my house completed. When I am certain that my family is safe, then I will be able to give you a firm date for Operation Seeker to commence. Realistically, I would think early next week. That will give me time to arrange both at home and in my office."

"You do what you have to do, Mr Spencer. In the meantime, I will sort out transport, I believe that trucks might be the best option, easier for me to get hold of, and probably less conspicuous than a bus or a large van and saloon cars. I am well known by the transport officers at MOD whereas I would have to requisition any other types of vehicles which might invite questions. I will see to it that my men are suitably clothed and have sufficient arms for a firefight which I am sure will take place. We will also carry basic rations for one day so that we do not need to mix with any locals."

"That's a good idea, Major, I will continue to arrange events from my end, and be in touch with you as appropriate, goodbye for now."

"Good bye and good luck, sir," the Major answers.

Ben walks through to the kitchen and asks Peter if he has a moment. He goes over what has been said with the Major and asks Peter for his comments.

"You appear to have covered everything, Ben, have you had any more thoughts regarding Phil Landers at all?"

"No I had completely forgotten, have you been able to find out anything about him?"

"He appears to have an unblemished record dating back to the war. He was in the RAF as a navigator flying in Wellingtons. He flew a great many sorties, before being shot down and limping back home sustaining injuries to his back. His record in your department is unspectacular but solid and reliable it would seem. I have a friend, with access to employment records who I can ask for more details if you wish."

"We'll leave things as they are for now, Peter, in hindsight I may have over reacted."

"I have just spoke with the Major and said that we will need a couple of days or so to get the house and grounds secure, before I can confirm a time and date for the raid on the tunnels."

"That should be enough to get a new door fitted to the utility room, alarms checked and some sort of structure erected in place of the garage."

"Okay, Peter, I have to get back to Phil on that before the end of the day, but first I must speak with Beatrice Carrington regarding Operation Seeker."

Peter leaves the study to continue with the clear up while Ben makes the call to Beatrice Carrington.

"Hello, Beatrice Carrington speaking."

"Beatrice, hello it's Ben Spencer here."

"Ah, Ben, I was expecting you to call, how are things with you?"

Once again, Ben finds himself outlining the events of last night, emphasising that, thankfully no one has been hurt.

"These people are getting more desperate by their actions, Ben, my concern is that your family is being specifically targeted, and your daughter Polly especially singled out for severe treatment. The fire could so easily have been fatal and done their cause no good. My belief is that there is discord between London and those running operations in The Midlands," says Beatrice.

"And that discord will get worse as I have brought charges against Galbraith for his intrusion into my house and the nasty assault on Polly."

"Good for you, Ben, that man should be put away as soon as possible. Holding back on reporting his actions was useful, but you just cannot trust men like him. So what are you plans now regarding Operation Seeker?"

"Well Beatrice, I need your help to coordinate the arrests in London with the raid on the storage depot at New Haven, and the cottage at Rye."

"I can certainly arrange for Williamson, McKenzie, North and Devonish to be picked up at any time. They are all well known, having been involved with a number of government departments over the years. I will try and find out who their close associates are so they can be detained at the same time."

"The issuing of warrants will take time, Ben, two or three days; do you have any idea when you intend to carry out the raids?"

"As soon as we can coordinate with the detention of the suspects in Whitehall and elsewhere.

"Let me be specific for you, Beatrice. I propose that the raid to take place early on Tuesday next, so your arrest warrants need to be dated accordingly. I will inform Major Baxter of the date. I thought that the date might be helped by Monday being a holiday."

"That should give me ample time to brief my colleagues on the operation and confirm the whereabouts of the key personnel who need to be detained. You will need to be extra careful in the run up to the operation, Ben, these men may target your family again, anything to slow down your operation against their activities," Beatrice adds.

"I appreciate your concerns, Beatrice, and I am doing everything possible to protect my family during this difficult time."

"Okay, Ben, well I'll leave you to it and wait for you to get back to me with final details?"

"Thank you, Beatrice, for all your help on this, I will be in touch."

Ben makes one more call to Phil, and asks about a new shed. Phil has some good news.

"Ben, I have located a supplier of a prefabricated structure, ideal for a garage, he will be making contact with you in a day or so."

"That is good news, Phil, I will be in the office tomorrow, so will talk it over when I see you, tell me is Maureen about at all?'

"I will transfer your call to her, Ben, see you tomorrow," Phil replies.

"Hello, Maureen Potter."

"Maureen, it's Ben, are you free to talk?"

"Yes, Ben, what is it?"

"Maureen, I wonder are you possibly free this evening, I have something to discuss with you that I cannot talk about in the office?"

"Yes I can meet you this evening, what time and where?" She asks with interest.

"Shall we say about 7.30, will you come to the house?"

"Certainly, Ben, I will see you at 7.30," Maureen replies.

Ben has decided that he needs a confidante in the office and no one is more suited than Maureen Potter who has been with him for some time. An attractive woman in her 40s, Maureen has never married, devoting her life to her career. She is very well connected, having relatives in the civil service including a brother in The Central Office of Information in London. Ben had asked Maureen to move with him, when he relocated to Carswell, and she agreed. She has run his business affairs at the office in a meticulous manner, and was as loyal as anyone could be. He often wonders what he would do without her calm efficiency about him, especially of late.

And so it is after supper that the doorbell rings and Ben ushers Maureen through to the parlour.

"Maureen, how nice to see you again, it has been some time hasn't it?"

"It has indeed, Margaret, I won't ask how you are after what you and the family have been through recently. I am just relieved that you all appear to have come through the ordeal unharmed, especially you, Polly, you have grown since I saw you and so have you all Maisy, Daisy and George."

"Thank you, Miss Potter, it is lovely to see you again," Polly replies.

"Maureen, can I introduce you to a close friend of mine, Peter Forsyth. Peter has been staying with us during these difficult times. I do not know what we would have done without his help."

"Hello, Peter, I have heard a lot about you from Ben," Maureen replies and shakes his hand.

"Margaret, I wonder would you bring some tea into the study, I do not want to keep Maureen for too long if possible?"

And with that Ben goes off to the study closely followed by Maureen.

"It was good of you to come at such short notice, Maureen, but I do need to discuss recent and forthcoming events with you."

"I understand, Ben, I am happy to oblige, how can I help?"

"I am sure that you will have been somewhat perplexed by the events that have occurred to my family over the last few weeks? I did not want to get you involved, although I have always trusted you implicitly, because of the sensitivity of my work and the dangers involved. However, as my business draws toward a conclusion, I do need a confidante at the office that I can turn to in emergencies and who can make contact with my colleagues in this operation. As you will have guessed, the operation is top secret and up to now no one at the office has any details. It has to stay that way in order for it to be successful."

"Of course, I understand completely, Ben," Maureen comments.

"For reference purposes the code name is Operation Seeker, and any business relating to my activities will come under that banner. Before I go on, I will outline briefly what has transpired over the last couple of weeks."

Ben tells of the visit to the cottage in Rye and the discovery of the storage tunnels on the coast outside of New Haven. He mentions the part that Major Baxter will play along with Beatrice Carrington, but does not name Beatrice, who must remain anonymous. He ends by telling her of the pending arrest of Galbraith over the uninvited entry to his house and the assault on Polly.

"You have certainly been busy, Ben, and I sincerely hope the operation will draw to a successful conclusion for you. God knows how hard you have worked on this and what you have sacrificed. These are ruthless criminals that you have faced up to, against some pretty overwhelming odds and you have some successes already. I will do everything I can to help with the Operation Seeker."

"Thank you, Maureen, and I do apologise for having to withhold one person's name from you, their position is so sensitive you really are better off not knowing who they are," says Ben.

"Of course, now I presume that you do not want me to keep any notes on the operation at the office. I can always type them up at home and put them in my safe?" Maureen replies.

"That would be ideal, and perhaps I can give your home number to the Major and Peter should they want to make contact?"

"Yes, that will be okay," Maureen replies.

"Whilst Operation Seeker will be drawing to a close within the next two weeks or so, there is a lot of loose ends, official and unofficial to tie up, and I can think of no one better than you to chronicle relevant information and sort out any accounting that is required. And there is one particular job that I would like you to carry out, on a personal basis. I want you to keep an eye on Phil for me. I may be totally wrong, but I have to be sure that he is completely straight, do you understand what I am trying to say, Maureen?"

"I understand perfectly, Ben, I will do whatever I can," Maureen replies.

"Now this may sound strange, Maureen, but do you own a weapon of any sort?"

"No I don't, are you saying I should have one?" she replies, with surprise in her voice.

"Because you are now close to this operation, I would feel a lot better for knowing that you are able to protect yourself."

"Very well, Ben, can you get me one, I'm afraid my contacts don't include gunsmiths!"

"I will ask Peter Forsyth to get one for you and show you how to use it. Now I must let you get home, Peter will drive you, and he will let you know when he can get you that weapon."

"Thank you, Ben, will we see you at the office tomorrow?"

"I should be in around 10 o'clock,"

Ben calls through for Peter, and asks if he would mind taking Maureen home, and mentions securing a weapon for Maureen as soon as possible.

"I will sort that in the next two days, Maureen, and arrange a time to show you how to use it, there is no point in carrying a weapon if you are not confident enough how to use it," Peter says.

"Thank you, Peter," Maureen replies.

Ben returns to the study and reflects on his conversation with Maureen. It's good to have her on board and she will be a valuable addition to the team he has around him. He returns the teacups to the kitchen and goes into the parlour where the family are gathered.

"Come along, children, bedtime I think, for you young ones," he says.

"Yes, I will come up with you to say goodnight," Margaret replies.

"Daddy, will Peter be coming back later?"

"Don't you worry my dear Polly, Peter will be along shortly," Ben replies with a smile.

After seeing the children off to bed, Margaret returns to the parlour.

"Did your meeting with Maureen go well Ben, it has certainly been awhile since I saw her, and yet she does not seem to have changed at all?"

"Yes, I am pleased that she is now involved with Operation Seeker from the inside, she will prove a valuable member of the team I am sure," Ben remarks.

The next two days are spent clearing the house of the fire damage and having a new garage constructed from prefabricated building parts. There is a lot of cleaning and some decorating required, but by Thursday, it is getting back to normal and the new garage is almost complete.

Ben, meanwhile, receives a report from Birmingham Constabulary detailing what had been seized on the raid at the canal at the weekend. He estimates that thousands of pounds of goods were on board and, together with the other barge that was seized, the total haul was significant. He believes that the operations in The Midlands will be suffering as a direct result of these two seizures. However, there has been a setback, Bill Holder was attacked and badly beaten. His injuries are not life threatening, but he will not be available for some time. Ben is concerned how he might have been discovered, and passes his concerns on to Chief Inspector Jamieson, who assures him he will follow up on the investigation and let him know of any relevant details. He then calls Maureen into his office.

"Maureen, I am going to ask Chief Inspector Jamieson to make contact with you regarding any further details of the two raids on barges in Birmingham, and on my contact Bill Holder who has been rather badly beaten."

"Very well, Ben, I will keep you up to date as and when necessary," Maureen replies.

"Thank you, now as I mentioned when we spoke earlier that Operation Seeker should be moving forward next week. Can you get me some train times to London for Monday and Tuesday please? By the way, has Peter been able to get you a weapon yet?"

"He is meeting me this evening, so I hope to be fully trained before he leaves."

"He is a good man, Maureen, my family is indebted to him, especially Polly."

"Yes, I did notice how close Polly was with him when I was in your parlour."

"She has become very dependent on him however, Margaret and I believe he has helped her to cope with the trauma that she has experienced so we are happy to let her stay close to him."

On Wednesday evening, Ben contacts Major Baxter to confirm the date of the raid as Tuesday 25th August. He also confirms that 2.00 a.m. will be the time that the raid will coordinate with arrests of key personnel in London, and the cottage in Rye.

"I will travel to London on Monday, Major, can you accommodate me from mid-morning?"

"Absolutely, Mr Spencer, I look forward to meeting with you."

"Very good, so until Monday then, good bye for now, Major."

CHAPTER 24

(Operation Seeker: Setbacks)

On Thursday morning, Peter drives Polly to school, as Betty Poulton is not available and Polly is obviously delighted. However, her delight is short lived as on the way to school the car is hijacked at gunpoint. Polly had just finished telling Peter that she hoped to be able to play for the hockey team again.

"Those dreadful men taking me from Stoke Park school meant I lost my chance in the team, but I am hoping to be considered for the next game."

"I am sure you will be fine Polly, what happened—"

Suddenly, the road is blocked by a large saloon car, one man gets out pointing a gun at Peter, two other men go to the passenger side and drag Polly from her seat.

"Keep your hands where I can see them," the man tells Peter as he leans over and removes the ignition keys. Polly is dragged screaming by two men into the back of the saloon, as the other man fires his weapon to distract Peter, then throws his keys into the ditch beside the road, before getting into the saloon which speeds away. Polly is being held down in the back of the saloon by two men who are particularly rough with her.

"Keep her still until we get there," the driver shouts.

One man leans over Polly, holding her by her hair and pushing her down between the seats, while the second man has removed her shoes so that she cannot kick him.

"Keep still and we will not hurt you," the man holding Polly by the hair tells her.

"Let go of me, Peter will kill you for this," she screams.

As if to make his point, the man holding her hair slaps her hard on the face, then squeezes her cheeks tightly. He then grabs her by her shirt and shouts:

"I warned you, girl, now shut up before I really hurt you." Polly continues to struggle as the saloon speeds toward Leicester on the main road, before the driver turns off down a narrow lane leading to the village of Telford Parva, and stops the car.

"We have to keep her quiet or we will attract attention, get the rope from the boot."

The man holding Polly by the hair removes her school blazer, and secures her arms behind her. He then removes her skirt to tie her legs tightly, then stuffs a gag in her mouth. They then shove her down to the floor, place a blanket over her and put their feet on the blanket to stop her moving about. Once she is secured, they move off towards the village. Once again Polly finds herself in a desperate situation with four men who seem more ruthless than any of the other she had encountered. They had no hesitation in hitting her and binding her with rope. She sobs uncontrollably convinced these men will kill her if they do not get what they want from her father.

Peter, meanwhile, takes the spare key, which Ben had told him was beneath the front wheel arch, and drives after the saloon. The abductors are about a mile ahead of Peter he reckons, but he cannot see their car. He drives as fast as he can, staying on the main road, convinced that Polly's abductors must be taking her to a house somewhere.

He reckons that they will not want to travel too far in case they attract attention, their car being a large saloon which would be easily recognised. As he passes the large houses he looks to see if he can see the car in any of the driveways, but without success. He stops to ask anyone in the front of their houses for information, but again no one is able to help. When he asks an elderly gentleman if he has seen the car, he is certain that no car has past his house in the last hour. How can he be so sure, Peter told that he is waiting to be collected by his son who is late!

Peter then turns back towards Cresswell and notices the turn signposted Telford Parva, the only turning between him and Carswell.

The saloon car carrying Polly turns into the driveway of a large house on the other side of Telford Parva. The men carry Polly through the front door and down the cellar steps, dropping her onto the cold damp floor.

"Now listen, Polly, you could be here for a long time, so behave yourself and you will come to no harm," the man says.

Polly cowers away from him as she is manhandled onto an old wooden chair. She continues to struggle and one of the men pulls back her hair slaps her again and warns her.

"Do you really want me to hurt you, because I know how to really hurt you?" He says angrily.

Polly freezes with fear and stops struggling.

"Jim, go and fetch her blazer and skirt from the car, we don't want any evidence left."

Peter meanwhile, turns into the lane signposted Telford Parva driving slowly past each house looking for the large black saloon which he spots in the driveway of a large house on the far side of the village. He parks his car in the entrance to the churchyard and walks back towards the house. The house next door has the curtains partially drawn suggesting it may be unoccupied, so Peter walks up the drive, using the hedge for cover. He then moves toward the back of the building and climbs over a small fence into the next door property where, he is sure, Polly is being held. He tries the door at the back but it is locked, but manages to force open a window in the conservatory. As he moves toward the door he hears voices. The four men are all together in the hallway discussing when they should leave.

"Stay where you are and no one move!" says Peter as he bursts open the door.

One man tries to get to his gun and Peter shoots him in the chest, another attempts to run and Peter shoots him in the leg. The other two stands motionless with their hands above their heads.

"That's better; now where is the girl?"

"She is in the cellar," says one of the men who is uninjured.

"Okay, lead the way, please. You two stay here, if you move before I return, I will shoot you dead, do you understand?"

Both men nod although realistically neither man is in a fit state to move anyway! Ben follows the two men into the cellar and spots Polly tied to a chair.

"You two go over and face the wall with your hands in the air, if you move I will shoot you," says Peter as he moves toward Polly. He removes the gag from her mouth and Polly burst out tearfully.

"Peter I knew you would come."

Peter unties her from the chair and notices that she has been badly bruised about the face and legs. "Polly, quickly put on your blazer and skirt you two, stay still while I tie you."

Her ties the two men together to a pillar in the cellar and locks them in before returning to the hallway with Polly.

"Polly, can you go and find a phone and call the police and an ambulance, the village is called Telford Parva, and the house has a for sale sign in the driveway," says Peter.

Maureen knocks on the door of Ben's office and enters with a shocked look on her face.

"Ben, it's Margaret, Polly has not arrived at school and Peter has gone missing," she says as she hands him the phone.

"Ben, Mrs Williams phoned about five minutes ago to say that Polly had not arrived at school. No one has seen Polly, Peter or the car, it's happening again isn't it?" Margaret says, almost hysterical.

"I will come home straight away, Margaret, try to keep calm."

"Maureen, can you call the police, tell them what has happened, you have the details of my car, and ask them to call me at home when there is any news."

Very well, Ben, I do hope Polly and Peter are safe, you will let me know, won't you?"

"Yes of course, Maureen, and thank you, now I must go," says Ben as he leaves the office after asking Phil if he may use his car.

He arrives home to find Margaret waiting for him in the parlour. She is distraught and fears the worst with both Peter and Polly missing.

"I will contact the police to see if there is any news, dear," says Ben as he walks toward the study followed closely by Margaret.

It is now 10.30 a.m. and they have been missing since they left for school.

Ben is very concerned that Peter is also missing. He would give his life protecting Polly so something has gone drastically wrong with their security arrangements. This latest setback could affect the planned timing of Operation Seeker. He is sure that the culprits will literally stop at nothing in their efforts to stop him, although he is confident that they will have no idea of the proposed raid at New Haven. He can only hope that they find Polly and Peter soon. Ben dials the police number and asks for Detective Inspector Wishart.

"The inspector is out on a call, who am I talking to please?"

"This is Ben Spencer, I reported an abduction of my daughter and colleague about half an hour ago. Can you tell me if there has been any news?"

"Hello, Mr Spencer, it's W.P.C Becky Garrett, I believe t the Inspector is responding to your call," W.P.C Garrett replies.

"No that can't be correct, how does he know where to go?" asks Ben puzzled.

"One moment, Mr Spencer while I ask when the call was received and who called it in."

After a few moments W.P.C Garrett speaks to Ben:

"Mr Spencer, D.I Wishart was responding to a call from your daughter. It appears that Peter Forsyth had asked her to make the call. They are in a house in Telford Parva, Peter Forsyth has shot two of the men and is holding another two in the house cellar. Thankfully, both your daughter and Peter are both unharmed, apparently the same cannot be said for two of the abductors."

"Where are they now, Becky?"

"It would appear that they are on their way back, with a police escort, Mr Spencer."

"Thank you very much for your assistance, Becky, I expect we may see you again to take statements?"

"Margaret, they are both safe," Ben says as he hugs his wife tearfully.

Peter and Polly arrive back at the house, accompanied by the police, to be greeted by a tearful Margaret and a much relieved Benjamin.

"Daddy, Daddy, Peter shot two of the men who took me and left the other two for the police," says Polly hugging Ben and Margaret before hugging Peter.

"Peter, we are forever in your debt saving Polly again, are you okay by the way?"

"Yes I'm fine thanks, Ben, a cup of tea would go down well, please Margaret if you have one."

"Of course, Peter, and perhaps the Inspector would like one?"

"Thank you, Mrs Spencer, I have to ask Mr Forsyth some questions because there has been a shooting, but I can leave the rest of the questioning until tomorrow."

"Please, use the study Inspector," Ben replies.

He then makes a brief call to the office to let Maureen know that Peter and Polly are safe and well, before going into the parlour to join Margaret and Polly.

"My dear Polly, how are you? In the wars again because of me, I really am so sorry," he says with tears in his eyes, his lovely daughter having again been subjected to a terrible ordeal.

"I'm okay, Daddy, I had Peter there to save me, he actually shot two of those men you know?"

"Come along, Polly, let's get you out of those clothes and I'm sure you would like to have a wash, then I will get us all some lunch."

And with that, Margaret takes Polly off up the stairs to the bathroom, leaving Ben sitting at the table with his cup of tea. Meanwhile, in the study, Inspector Wishart is going through the details of Polly's abduction with Peter Forsyth. Whilst understanding Peter's reaction to pursue the men, he expresses concern that he could have made matters worse.

"I can assure you Inspector that my actions in no way put Polly in any danger. Her safety was always my main concern," Peter responds.

"Quite so, Mr Forsyth, and thankfully your actions meant that all four men have been detained, which will be of great help in the investigation. Young Polly has again been subjected to a dreadful attack, and these men will have to pay for their actions."

"Did you recognise any of them by the way, I know that this is not the first time that Mr Spencer has had problems with violent criminals?"

"Ben's position has made him a prime target for the criminal underworld Inspector, and it is for this reason that I am at the house at all times ready to offer my assistance whenever I can. To answer your question, I did not recognise any of the men, but Polly may be able to help you better with that since she was with them for a while before I arrived."

"Thank you Mr Forsyth, we'll leave it there for now, I'll come back later to talk with Polly, so if there are any more questions I need to ask, I will talk to you then. I'll see myself out goodbye."

Peter returns to the parlour to be greeted by Polly.

"Peter, would you like some more tea, I have just been telling Daddy how we held on to those men until the police arrived. The two that you shot were screaming weren't they, and the other two looked really scared in case you shot them as well! It was amazing that you found me."

"Alright now, Polly, let go of Peter, I'm sure he would like to freshen up before lunch also. Peter, can we get together after lunch, I need you input on what happened and your comments will be appreciated on this latest assault on you and Polly."

"Yes, I think that would be a good idea, Ben," Peter replies as he leaves the parlour for the bathroom. Ben meanwhile, calls Major Baxter for an update and put him in the picture regarding the latest attack on his family.

"This has become a war, Mr Spencer, thank God so far all the casualties have been on their side, this man Forsyth must be a hell of a soldier to have on your side, I would like to meet with him when this business is over," the Major comments.

"He is my most loyal colleague who I have known for some time Major, and I look forward to being able to introduce you to him at some time in the future."

"So, are we still on for the 25th?" the Major asks.

"I certainly hope so, have you selected your team yet."

"Yes I have and I will be briefing them tomorrow, I have also requisitioned two trucks for transportation. My team will be ready, Mr Spencer, let us hope that there are no more setbacks at your end."

"I sincerely hope not, Major, I sincerely hope not, I will call you again Friday afternoon for details of where we meet, good bye for now."

After lunch, Ben and Peter go into the study to talk over the events of that morning.

"Peter, what can I say, once again we are in your debt, we cannot thank you enough for saving our daughter, yet again!"

"It was fortunate that I was able to go after them so quickly, they took the keys and threw them in the ditch, but I remember you saying that your spare was under the wheel arch."

"No indication of who they were I suppose?" Ben asks.

"I didn't say as much to the Inspector, but I believe two of them were watching the house from the lane last week."

"They must be Galbraith's men, well that's four more that we don't have to worry about then," Ben replies.

"I don't see them going after Polly again after what has happened Ben, but you and the family will have to be extra careful from now on."

"Do you think they have got any idea what we are planning?"

"I don't see how they can have any idea really, since all your success has been in the Midlands, you are not known in the South of England as far as the racketeers are concerned. I would say that they are trying to frighten you off from carrying out any more raids, in Birmingham and Coventry especially. The two barges that were confiscated must have been a big blow to their operation in the area."

"Yes, I think you are right, Peter, they cannot possibly have any idea about Operation Seeker, their actions are as a result of what has happened in the Midlands I'm sure, so I think we should proceed with the raids on the 25th."

"And I will have a look at the house security Ben, now that the new building is completed."

The rest of the day passes peacefully, but the children have to be told about Polly, when they return from school, since her bruises are noticeable.

"Did Peter shoot them for being nasty to you, Polly, why do they keep picking on you anyway?" George asks with a frown, obviously puzzled by what is happening.

"Daddy, Peter will always be here to look after us when you are away won't he?" Daisy pleads.

"Yes, children, Peter will be here for as long as we need him and I hope that eventually we can carry on as a normal family. However, do not worry about what might happen, you are all safe with Peter, Mummy and I to take care of you, do you understand?" says Ben, hoping his words will console the children.

"Yes we understand, Daddy, we know we are safe with Peter here, will he be taking me to school every day now?"

"Let us do one thing at a time, Polly, why don't you go outside with the others while I have a word with Mummy."

"I have just spoken with Peter about what happened and we are both agreed that it is unlikely that anyone will attempt to take Polly again considering that two of the men were shot. I would like to get Polly back into her routine as soon as possible, Margaret, although I think we should keep her off school until Monday now."

"Yes, she cannot go back tomorrow with her bruising so obvious, and she needs time with us at home to get over this last terrible ordeal."

Margaret looks out of the window at the children playing together, they seem happy and contented, but she worries that the events of the past week or so may have a lasting effect on all of them, and how many more incidents will there be before Ben finally shuts down the criminal activities of these men? She is well aware that the next week is vital to the success of Ben activities and is apprehensive about its outcome. She has always supported Ben in everything he has done at The Central Office of Information, and has seen his position become more important since the end of the war. She now looks forward to the day when he can finally close the file on this business once and for all. Ben decides to go into his office on Friday since he is unsure how many days he will be away next week. Phil asks after Polly and again expresses his concern over recent events.

"The sooner we can shut these people down, the better for all of us, Ben."

"I couldn't agree with you more on that, Phil, meantime I have a few things to do before Monday," Ben replies as he calls Maureen into his office.

Maureen asks about Polly and Peter with concern in her voice. In the short time that she has known Peter, she has formed an attachment that she hopes may develop and she has known Polly since she was a baby.

"I am happy to report that they are both well Maureen, my daughter seems to be able to cope with the terrible ordeals that she has been subjected to providing Peter is able to ride to her rescue! Now, Maureen, I shall be away for most of next week I believe so you will have to hold the fort for me."

"I will be here, Ben, any special instructions while you are away?"

"I just wanted to go over the contacts that you may make regarding Operation Seeker. I have told Chief Inspector Jamieson of Birmingham Police and Inspector Wishart of the local police that you have full authority to take any messages on my behalf. I have impressed upon both of them that you are the only person authorised to take messages for me. I have also asked Peter to keep you updated with Operation Seeker, either by telephone or you may meet at my home if necessary. The main point is maintaining the utmost secrecy at all times."

"I understand, Ben, I will be as discreet as possible."

"By the way, did Peter see you about having a weapon available."

"Yes he did and I am okay with how to use it, although I hope that I never have to."

"Indeed, Maureen, and I am sorry to put you in a position where it has been necessary to offer you personal protection, but I do feel it is necessary in the present circumstances."

"I understand, Ben, and appreciate your concerns for me," she replies. Like many private secretaries, she was very close to Ben, fiercely loyal and totally dependable.

"There is just one more thing, Maureen, I have also given your name and home number to the person on this paper. They have instructions to make contact with you only in the most extreme emergency, and you likewise," says Ben as he hands Maureen the name and number for Beatrice Carrington. He is reluctant to release Beatrice's details but feels it necessary to have a contact should the operation blow up in his face.

"I understand, Ben, I sincerely hope I do not have to make use of this information," Maureen replies as she moves out of the office.

Ben then speaks with Phil outlining what has to be done over the next few days while he is away, and again emphasises the importance of keeping the operation secret.

Then, after a final goodbye to Maureen, he leaves his office just after lunch.

On his journey home he goes over what he needs to do before his departure on Monday.

He has to contact Beatrice Carrington, this evening, to confirm that she has arranged the necessary paperwork for the arrests of relevant personnel. Then, after he has spoken with the Major, Daniel and Conrad have to be informed where they are to meet for a briefing prior to leaving for the coast. And he must spend some time with Peter checking that all necessary measures have been taken to protect his family. However, what he especially wants to do is enjoy some time with his family before the business of the coming week. He arrives home to find Margaret is busy in the kitchen, whilst Polly is helping Peter with the new building, the garage replacement. All the items salvaged from the fire have been put inside, Peter having erected some shelving and a new door to the utility room has been fitted. It is a solid wooden door designed to slow down a fire, and is secured by a Chub lock, probably the most secure lock available. The electrical fittings have all been replaced and a powerful floodlight has been attached above the outside door which is sensitive to movement.

"Would you like some tea, Ben?" Margaret asks as he enters the kitchen.

"Yes please, I see Polly is busy with Peter, I do hope she isn't making a nuisance of herself. Perhaps I ought to speak with her again about monopolising Peter's time."

"I'm sure Peter doesn't mind her company Ben and given what she has been through lately, we should let her be. He seems to have such a calming influence and that can only be good for her."

"I have to agree with you there Margaret, Peter's influence has been so important to her recovering from what has happened over the last couple of weeks. Anyway, I have to make a couple of calls, so I will be in the study," he says leaving the kitchen to call Beatrice Carrington.

"Hello, Beatrice Carrington speaking."

"Beatrice, it's Ben Spencer, are you well?"

"One moment, while I switch your call. okay, hello, Ben, yes I am fine. There has been some delay with the warrants because of Monday being a holiday, they will now be issued for 9 o'clock Tuesday morning. Providing your raids are successful, making the arrests at 9 o'clock will be sufficient. You will just need to be sure that no one is able to make any contact with the key personnel here, you know the names, so that they do not have the opportunity to warn them."

"Yes I understand, Beatrice, I hope to be able to meet up with you next week after Operation Seeker has concluded."

"I would like that, Ben, and there will be a great deal to talk over!" says Beatrice.

"There will indeed, now is there anything else I should be aware of Beatrice before I let you go for the weekend?"

"Everything has been put in place, Ben, all that remains is for me to wish you good luck, and please be careful."

"Thank you, Beatrice, 'bye for now."

He is relieved to hear that the warrants will be ready for Tuesday, bureaucracy can be a problem but thankfully Beatrice has overcome any hitches that may have occurred, so he decides to call the Major now that the warrants have been confirmed.

"Major Baxter speaking."

"Major, good afternoon it's Ben Spencer."

"Ah, Spencer, no more problems I trust?"

"I'm relieved to say there have been no more problems, and that the warrants will be issued for 9 o'clock on Tuesday, for the key personnel in government departments," Ben replies.

"That is excellent, we are now good to go. I suggest that we meet at my club, The East India in St James's at 13-00 hours."

"I will arrange for your two colleagues and yourself to be signed in as my lunch guests. We'll have some lunch, then rendezvous again when we depart, around 21-00 hours I would suggest, but that can be confirmed Monday. I think that about covers it, unless you have anything else?"

"Nothing else for now, Major, look forward to meeting with you for lunch on Monday."

And after saying goodbye, Ben replaces the receiver. *The bricks are falling into place,* he says to himself. One more call to Daniel and Conrad and he will be ready. He makes the call to Daniel and outlines the latest attempt to abduct Polly.

"They seem very determined, Ben, or is it panic over their losses. They obviously did not realise who they were up against in Peter, he is the one man above all else that you always want on your side. How is your daughter recovering?"

"She is recovering well, Daniel, but I do worry that she may be becoming too reliant on his presence, but for now Margaret and I are just glad that he is with us."

"Your family is in the very best hands, Ben, Peter will not let you down."

"I am sure of that Daniel, now regarding Monday, can you and Conrad meet me outside The East India Club in St James's at 1 o'clock? Major Baxter has invited us to lunch there to go over the final preparations for Operation Seeker?"

"We will be there, Ben."

"Okay, Daniel, 'bye for now."

CHAPTER 25

(Operation Seeker: The Raid)

Ben enjoys a quiet weekend with the family before embarking to London on the Monday morning. Margaret had been apprehensive and he tries hard to reassure her that he is on the last stage of his journey, and soon everything should be back to normal, or at least, so he hoped! The children Polly especially, had asked many questions that he answered as best he could. He hoped he would be able to talk to them on Tuesday evening. Peter had spent time with him offering advice on dealing with the kind of villains he would be encountering. Listen to what the Major says, and follow his instructions to the letter was his advice. Be safe and arrive back in one piece was Peter's final comment. The journey to Euston seemed long but Ben was glad of the time to gather his thoughts. He eventually arrived around 11.30 a.m., and contacted Daniel to meet with him outside St James's Park station. Daniel and Conrad greet Ben enthusiastically as they go into the station cafe for a drink.

"Good to see you both again, are we ready for the final push?"

"We're ready Ben, and look forward to being able to finish the job which we started with you a week ago. How are your family by the way, after the latest setback?" Conrad asks.

"They are all well thanks, once again we are all indebted to Peter for his actions.

After chatting generally about the job in hand, the three of them begin their walk to the East India Club to meet with Major Baxter.

The Major is waiting for them at the entrance to the club and ushers them into a private room.

"Good afternoon, gentlemen, and welcome to The East India Club."

"Thank you, Major, can I introduce you to Daniel Bottomley and Conrad Wilberforce, they will take responsibility for the cottage in Rye and all its' contents."

"Good to meet you both, Ben has told me a little about you, now let's get down to business. Your maps and sketches outlining the tunnels will be invaluable to us in this operation. Moving in from both the east and west entrances makes sense, preventing any escapes while giving us the element of surprise," the Major continues.

They then take a closer look at the sketches supplied by Daniel and Conrad which show the two entrances leading to the straight passages running parallel to each other.

"The group entering from the west will travel up the right hand passage, and the group entering from the east will travel up the left hand passage. Anyone trying to move through from one to the other will have their escape route blocked by the group travelling in the other direction. It is imperative that we round up everyone, so that no one can warn London. Any significant changes since you gave Ben your report, Daniel?" the Major asks.

"None that we know of, sir, but there is movement in and out on a regular basis," Daniel replies.

"Good, well I now have forty men for the operation. We will divide into two groups, one for each entrance, and divide as we move into the tunnels to prevent anyone escaping."

"Ben, may I suggest that you oversee the police operation from the west entrance, I will allocate one of my men to the east entrance. I understand there will be about thirty officers made available under the command of Chief Superintendent Walter Gainsworth. I estimate that the operation to take over the tunnels should take about an hour and I understand that a further operation is planned to seal the tunnels so that they cannot be used again. Daniel and Conrad, I have secured a car for you to travel to Rye, I understand that the local police are expecting you but do not know why you are going or what is involved. I will have relevant documents for you to hand over to them when you arrive. Since it is a holiday weekend, it is likely that Williamson will be at the cottage, so be aware. Your contact is Chief Inspector Bill Weaver of Sussex Police. We will have radio communications, Ben, so that you will be aware of our exact move on the tunnels, and to make sure that you are in place at the entrance. Daniel and Conrad, you will raid the cottage at precisely 2.00 a.m. The vehicle I have allocated to you should be adequate to ship the boxes of files back to London. Should Williamson be at the cottage, he

191

will be arrested and arrangements made to have him transported back to London also. I am unsure what will happen to his mistress, but she will be held by the local police until a decision can be made about her involvement," the Major continues. "Now gentlemen do you have any questions, I will go over the main points of the operation again before we leave this evening, but is there anything else you want to know?" the Major asks.

"Where will we depart from, Major?" Ben enquires.

"Ah yes, we will leave from Hyde Park Barracks, I suggest you arrive there around 20.30 hours, present them with these passes, and you will be directed to our assembly point."

"So if there is nothing else, I will leave you for now, you may remain in this room for as long as you wish, and I will meet up with you again this evening."

And with that, the Major leaves the room. The three men sit there for a moment, digesting what has been said, whilst appreciating the significance of what they are about to undertake. For Ben, this will represent the culmination of years of work, but not without some danger to his family. And Daniel and Conrad have proved invaluable to the operations' success so far by giving details of the tunnels, without which they would not have been able to plan the raid. They now need to secure the documents from the cottage, the documents that are needed in order to determine the precise logistics of the criminal enterprise. The names, dates and details of sites where goods are dropped will be the basis for the charges brought against the key players in the black market operation.

"Well, Daniel, Conrad it would seem that we are all set, any thoughts at all?" asks Ben.

"My only misgiving is whether anyone can actually avoid capture in the tunnels. The disused pillboxes may be a way out for anyone who knows of their existence, so I suggest that four men, two for each pillbox, be used from the west entrance group to check that no one is hiding in the pillboxes, and waiting for an opportunity to escape," Daniel comments.

"We will put that to the Major before the west entrance group enter the tunnels."

"We will be meeting up again tomorrow, I presume, Ben?" Conrad asks.

"Yes, Conrad, I have arranged for you to take the files to The Central Office of Information in Hercules House, Lambeth. You will have access to an office, so if you could wait for me there, we can decide how to proceed. I have some reliable contacts there that I can recruit to assist us. None of them are currently aware of what is happening, I did not want to compromise anyone outside of those who knew already of the operation. Once the arrests warrants have been issued and carried out, there will be a great deal of activity at the offices, so we should be able to carry out our business unobserved. I want to remain low key; what I do not want is anyone to know is who instigated the information leading to the arrests. Apart from personal safety, there may be other arrests that have to be considered at a later date, and one of my contacts may be in danger should they be discovered."

"Understood, Ben, fortunately no one will know who Daniel and I are so that is one problem that you do not have," says Conrad.

"And once we have done with the operation we will effectively disappear, so making us available again should you need any further help," Daniel continues.

"I thank you both for your help so far, it has proved invaluable, and thanks for offering your services again should the need arise, now we have some time to kill, so do either of you need to make any calls, I will remain here and have some dinner later?"

"I have a couple of calls to make, and I am sure Conrad will be able to occupy his time with one of his lady friends, am I correct, Conrad?"

"Now that you mention it, there is someone I can call that I have not been in contact with for a while, thanks for reminding me, Daniel," Conrad replies with a wry smile on his face.

"Okay, so we meet at Hyde Park Barracks at 8.30 p.m.?" says Ben as Daniel and Conrad leave the room.

CHAPTER 26

(Operation Seeker is on!)

Ben finally leaves The East India Club and walks the short distance to Hyde Park Barracks.

Then, after introductions to the Major's men, followed by a detailed briefing of the operation to raid the tunnels, the two trucks leave the barracks about 9.30 p.m. for the journey to New Haven. The roads out of London are in poor condition, many have not been repaired since the war blitz, but the army trucks are built for rough roads, so are able to cope. The route south is pretty direct on main A roads and the trucks arrive on the north side of the tunnel entrances, at South Heighton around midnight. The major's men will walk the short distance to the tunnels under cover of darkness and so achieve the maximum element of surprise.

There are sand dunes around the entrances which offer some shelter for the men, who settle in to wait for the Major's signal.

At 2.00 a.m. precisely, the two groups enter the tunnels and begin rounding up the occupants. There is immediate resistance, and the Major soon realises that the tunnel occupants are heavily armed. However, they are no match for trained soldiers, and suffer a number of casualties. Ben hears the gunfire from the east entrance where he is waiting with Chief Superintendent Gainsworth. Inside the tunnels, the occupants try to escape through the cross channels only to come up against more soldiers moving from the opposite direction. Those occupants close to the tunnel entrances run outside only to be met by the waiting police officers and put into waiting police vans. Meanwhile, there are some fierce firefights continuing inside around the east entrance where some of the occupants have tried to escape via a disused shaft. Although they are trapped they cannot be approached without being exposed to their gunfire. Fortunately, the Major had brought along some smoke bombs, which prove very effective in drawing out the occupants who are holding out in some parts of the tunnels difficult to approach. After just over an hour, the tunnels are declared secure by both teams. The occupants have fifteen men with injuries, none of which are too serious, whilst the Major has no casualties among his men. By 3.30 a.m., all of the tunnel occupants are with the police and the Major's men are guarding both east and west entrances.

Ben enters with the Major and is confronted by an astonishing amount of goods being stored.

Boxes of tinned corned beef, jam, biscuits, cooking fats, tins of fats, tins of beans and other vegetables, cartons of margarine and cooking oils and – there is also a large quantity of alcohol. A number of drums of oil for industry, and about 50 vehicles with boxes of spares, are also found. There were also rolls of cloth which would be sold to make clothing which was also still rationed. But the most worrying find was a consignment of guns and ammunition and a huge quantity of coupons used for rationing. There was also a large amount of cash inside a safe. Ben is totally overwhelmed by the size of the find and realises that they had indeed broken up a massive black market operation.

"Major, I think we can be truly proud of our efforts this morning, the criminals have suffered dearly as a result of this very successful operation. There are many thousands of pounds' worth of goods here. You and your men are to be congratulated on a job well done."

"Thank you, Ben, it has been a damn fine effort all round, should keep you busy for a while?"

"Yes and you, too, Chief Superintendent, your efforts have been very much appreciated in all this," Ben replies to the police officer.

"Happy to help, Mr Spencer, look forward to hearing the final count on the confiscated goods," the chief superintendent answers.

"Now, Chief Superintendent, I will leave a contingent of my men with you to guard the tunnels until all the goods are moved into Crown warehouses. I would say that it will take the rest of the week at least. Can you provide a field canteen for them for a few days?" the Major asks.

"Certainly, Major we will look after them never fear, and I will also detail the arrest warrants for you, Mr Spencer," replies the chief superintendent.

The three men, meanwhile, have found a seat in one of the rooms and enjoy a mug of tea. Ben looks at his watch, it is 4.30 a.m., and after the events of the last hour or so he relaxes just enough to suddenly feel very tired. Operation Seeker has gone well at this end; he hopes the issuing of the warrants in London goes as smoothly later this morning.

"I would like to return to London as soon as everything is in place here, Major, will you be staying on to manage?"

"Yes, I will have to brief the men who will be staying here, then I will travel back with the remainder in the truck," the Major replies.

"In that case, can you arrange a car for me, Chief Superintendent?" Ben asks.

"Certainly, Mr Spencer, where are you staying?"

"Perhaps I could freshen up at your club, Major, before going into the Central Office?"

"Certainly, Ben, tell Jack Daley that you are my guest and he will look after you," replies the Major.

They move back to the tunnel entrance as the field canteen arrives and the men enjoy a welcome drink and a sandwich. Ben thanks everyone for their assistance and follows the Chief Superintendent back to his car.

"Wilson, I want you to drive Mr Spencer back to London, it is essential he returns for the second part of this operation in the capital," the chief superintendent tells his driver.

"Certainly, sir, whenever you're ready, Mr Spencer," the constable replies.

Ben says a final goodbye to the Major and the chief superintendent, thanking them again for all their help, before climbing into the back of the large black saloon.

Daniel and Conrad, meanwhile, have made contact with Chief Inspector Bill Weaver, and knock on the cottage door in Rye at precisely 2.00 a.m. They are accompanied by four constables and a W.P.C. After a brief wait, the door is opened by Giles Williamson.

"Mr Williamson, we have a warrant to search these premises," the chief inspector says.

"What on earth is going on, you are making a grave mistake Officer and your superiors will be notified of this," Williamson replies angrily.

"Is Miss Meadows here, Mr Williamson?" Conrad asks.

"Who the devil are you?' Williamson asks.

"These two men are officers of the Crown, sir, with full authority to search these premises and seize any goods, they believe to be relevant to this investigation."

Just then Katherine Meadows appears in the doorway, and instantly recognises Conrad.

"You, I didn't really believe your story when you knocked on my door, what is going on, Giles?"

"There has been some misunderstanding, dear, nothing for you to be concerned about," Williamson answers abruptly.

"We have reason to believe you have information relating to black market activities, and will be removing all relevant files for examination," Daniel answers.

"Constables, will you remove all the files you find, please?" the chief inspector instructs pointing to the cellar door. The two constables begin removing the boxes of files as the Chief Inspector turns to Williamson and Katherine Meadows.

"You two will be held pending our enquiries, I expect that Scotland Yard will want to question you, sir, in due course."

Katherine Meadows is allowed to dress, in the presence of the W.P.C, Williamson is taken in his pyjamas with just his coat covering them.

"We will hold these two until we hear from London, gentlemen, on what to do next; I expect they will make contact during office hours?" the chief inspector replies.

"Yes, I would expect you will be contacted soon after 9 o'clock when the London arrests have been carried out. In the meantime, if you can keep them away from any phones, we do not want them making contact with anyone," Daniel replies.

"As you wish, tell me do you know who will be in charge of the operation at Scotland Yard?" the chief inspector asks.

"The operation will be overseen by Commander 'Jack' Spratt, and the operation is code named Operation Seeker Chief Inspector."

And with that, Williamson and Katherine Meadows are driven away accompanied by the chief inspector, the W.P.C and the constables.

In all there are twenty boxes to be taken back to London, which are put into the black saloon that Daniel and Conrad are using. All the boxes are labelled which will help determine the areas they refer to and the names of contacts in these areas. This information will be vital in detaining those that have been handling and receiving black market goods. They also remove several letters from the bureau, a couple of cases of spirits and several hundred pounds in cash. A brief glance at the letters shows Williamson clearly implicated in the transportation of items from the tunnels. The operation has been very well organised, as you would expect from those with a civil service background, making identification of those involved so much easier. Then, after one final check to make sure that all the evidence has been removed, Daniel and Conrad bid farewell to the Constable and set off for London. It is 3.30 a.m., so with the journey to London taking about two hours, they decide to go back to Daniel's flat in Kensington to rest before arriving at the Central Office of Information for 9 o'clock.

Ben must have dozed off and is woken by his driver telling him they are a few minutes away from St James's Square. He thanks the driver, handing him sufficient money to purchase a good breakfast, before going into The East India Club. He looks at his watch; it is 7 o'clock. Jack Daley shows him where to wash and brings him some breakfast which he takes in the room he had previously used with Major Baxter. After enjoying a good breakfast, he sits and ponders over the night's events. The raid went smoothly and Ben is sure no one from the tunnels was able to escape. He was astonished by the vast quantities of goods that were being stored in the tunnels, and furious that so many citizens were suffering shortages with all these goods being stored for profit and he was determined that the people responsible would pay dearly for their actions.

He very much hoped that today would be the start of events that would see those responsible eventually punished for their greed. Operation Seeker would be remembered by these people for the rest of their lives. Jack Daley enters the room to give Ben a message.

"There is a call for you, Mr Spencer, will you take it in here?"

"Yes thank you, Jack."

"Hello, this is Ben Spencer."

"Good morning, Ben, it's Daniel, how did last night go down?"

"Hello, Daniel, it went very well, no casualties on our side, some of the tunnel occupants were hurt but none badly. We believe that every member in the tunnels was arrested, so there should be no leaks. What was truly amazing was the amount of goods stored there," says Ben, and briefly relates the quantities of goods they found.

"Tell me, Daniel, where are you now?"

"Conrad and I are at my place in Kensington waiting to go to the Central Offices for 9 o'clock. Our night was also successful, and we bagged Williamson as well as his lady friend."

"Brilliant, Daniel, we'll talk more at the office, bye for now."

Ben leaves the East India Club for the short journey to The Central Office of Information in Lambeth, arriving at 8.45 a.m. He has secured an office on the ground floor, at the back of the building. The room has not been used for a while, but is spacious with two large tables. These will be ideal for looking through the boxes of files and putting the contents in some sort of order. The files represent the bulk of the evidence of the operation from the tunnels. This information, together with the confiscated goods, will form the basis for the criminal case against the people involved. Those people were being arrested, at this very moment, in various parts of London. In fact, Ben is aware of some activity outside and notices police and plainclothes officers entering the building.

"What's going on?" Ben asks a member of the office staff.

"There seems to be some sort of raid and some of the staff are being taken away by the police," she answers.

"Do you know what it is about?"

"No I don't I'm afraid, but the staff being removed seem to be from departments dealing with food acquisition and distribution," she answers.

The Central Office of Information worked with various Whitehall Departments and local authorities generally, making it an ideal base for anyone involved in illegal activities. In fact, it was the department's ease of access to many other agencies that had assisted Ben Spencer in his quest to break up black market operations. And, it is for this reason that there would be arrests from this building. Those members of staff being removed by police officers look visibly shocked and some of them were in tears. Ben notices that there are police officers at the entrance to the building preventing anyone from leaving, and there are a number of police vans outside the entrance.

At that moment Conrad and Daniel arrive, and Ben shows them into the office he has taken.

"I will get someone to give you a hand with the files Daniel, then I can have a closer look at their contents. I suggest that we wait for the police activity to be completed before we start bringing in the files. This may take some time since I do not know how many people have been served with warrants. Then once the files have been unloaded, I suggest you quietly leave so as not to be seen to be involved. You and I can meet later for an update, but what I do not want is to have your positions compromised in any way, just in case we have any further work to carry out."

"We understand, Ben, and agree that our best option is to leave as soon as the files have been unloaded," Daniel replies.

The removal of staff from the building takes some time, but eventually, the police disperse, leaving an officer at the entrance. Ben secures two young office workers to help with the boxes of files and when they are all safely in his office, Daniel and Conrad leave the building. Ben realises that he will need some help sifting through the boxes of files, but is reluctant to recruit anyone from the office in case they may be implicated in some way. He does not know anyone there well enough to be trusted with the sensitive information that the files contain. He decides his best option is the contact Beatrice Carrington on this to see if she can help.

"Hello, Beatrice Carrington speaking."

"Good morning, Beatrice, it's Ben Spencer."

"One moment, Ben while I secure the line. Hello, how are you? Did your Operation Seeker raid go well?"

"Better than I could have hoped for thank you Beatrice, I am now in the C.O.I. offices and there has been a lot of movement through here this morning."

"Yes, all the warrants have been executed, and the only main player missing this end is Williamson," Beatrice comments.

"Giles Williamson was arrested in Rye at his friend's cottage."

"In that case, the main players are all in custody, Ben, you now have to prepare the case against them."

"That is the reason for this call, I wonder do you have a couple of trusted colleagues who could help me with sifting through the boxes of files collected from the cottage and the tunnels. I am reluctant to ask anyone at this end?"

"Yes I can recommend two young colleagues of mine, who would be ideal for such an operation. Both very reliable, they have been with me for two years or so since they left college. Their names are Jamie Donaldson and Sarah Mumford; both are just twenty. Jamie joined me about two years ago, on a recommendation from another colleague who knew his father during the war. A sensible young man who wants to make a career in the Civil Service. Sarah Mumford is a very sharp girl who I believe will go a long way. She has been a leading light in one of the departments I control dealing with events in communist countries. She is a fluent linguist in Russian and I predict a successful career in the diplomatic corps for her," says Beatrice.

"They sound ideal, Beatrice, how soon can I expect them?"

"I will call them into my office when we have concluded our conversation, so shall we say after lunch?"

"I look forward to meeting them, Beatrice, we'll talk again later in the week."

Sarah and Jamie arrive at the C.O.I. just after lunch and knock on Ben's door on the ground floor.

"Mr Spencer, my name is Sarah Mumford and this is Jamie Donaldson, Beatrice Carrington asked us to come along and report to you."

"Yes, I'm delighted to meet you both, Beatrice has told me a little about you, so I suppose it's only fair that I introduce myself. First, what I would emphasise is the need for absolute secrecy in what you will undertake on my behalf. Other than Beatrice, no one knows of your involvement in this operation, and it is imperative that it remain that way. Anyone asking, you simply tell them that you are filing away documents from my offices in Carswell in The Midlands, do you understand?"

Both Sarah and Jamie nod in agreement.

"Good, now let me tell you a little about myself and what we are to be doing over the next few days. I have been with the C.O.I. since its inception. Previously, through the war years, I was with the Ministry of Information. My responsibility has been to track down black market operations and the people running those operations. I have enjoyed a certain amount of success but in doing so, I have also made a lot of enemies, and that is one of the reasons why you should not divulge to anyone who and what you are involved with, since there is an element of danger to yourselves in this, do you understand? I cannot emphasise enough how the work involves access to sensitive information that some people would like to get hold of and would stop at nothing to secure that information. "

"We understand, Mr Spencer, and will be careful."

"Good, now what you see here in these boxes is the culmination of successful raids carried out overnight in the South of England. I won't bore you with the details since they are irrelevant. We were also successful in seizing a huge quantity of contraband goods, foodstuffs, arms ammunition, alcohol, ration books and cash and so on. These boxes contain details of names addresses and consignment details for London and possibly beyond. They have to be recorded ready to be used as evidence against the people who have been arrested this morning."

"Have there been arrests here, Mr Spencer?" Sarah asks.

"Yes there have been a number of arrests here, Sarah, and I expect that there have been further arrests in Whitehall also. No doubt there are a number of curious staff members out there, so you need to blend in and be sure to pass off your involvement here as I have instructed. Now let me show you the contents of one of the boxes and suggest how we record what is inside them."

CHAPTER 27

(Operation Seeker: The Execution)

"If we look at the outside of the boxes you will note place names and dates which are self-explanatory. What we now have to do is sieve through the contents to determine who has received what and where it was received. In other words, names, contents and places. You can draw up prospective lists highlighting quantities delivered so that an inventory can be compiled. Another list of names would also be helpful, since there will be many small fish that have to be dealt with to deter others from being tempted into the black market. A list linking names with the places, addresses or warehouses, where the goods were delivered will also need to be compiled. And finally, there will be references to goods smuggled from Europe, so they will need separately recording. You should finish with a composite set of details relating to a very sophisticated black market business. Can I suggest that you begin by identifying the boxes from their geographical notations, and move through London accordingly? Make all of your preparations today, let me know of any stationery items you may require, and commence operations at 9 o'clock tomorrow morning."

"We shall certainly require a couple of adding machines, Mr Spencer, and can I suggest a recording machine so that I may compile the lists when completed?" Sarah asks.

"Yes, that will be arranged for you today, Sarah."

"Is there any possibility that we may know of someone these files, Mr Spencer?" asks Jamie.

"I really don't know the answer to that question, Jamie, but what I suggest is that if either of you recognise a name to let me know please. Now, I have deliberately arranged the large table against the far wall with my desk in front facing the door, so that if anyone enters by accident they will not be able to see any details of file data. Again just a precaution, but I have spent too much time on this operation for it to collapse over a prying eye spotting some details."

"Now I think we have earned some tea, don't you?"

"Let me arrange that for you, Mr Spencer?" Sarah offers.

"Thank you, Sarah. The canteen is ext. 122 and we are in room 15," Ben replies.

Over a well-earned cup of tea, Ben chats generally over the enormity of the task ahead of them, and asks that they make themselves available at 9 o'clock sharp on Wednesday morning.

"I can make a start now if you wish," Sarah offers.

"Thank you for that, Sarah, it may be best to wait until we have the tools which I am hoping to secure before the end of today."

"Very well, Mr Spencer, we'll see you in the morning then," Sarah answers as she and Jamie leave the office.

Ben speaks with the stationery department to order a couple of adding machines, a recording machine and a number of A4 size notepads and pencils to be delivered for the morning.

He also remembers that The Secrets Container is still in his safe at home, and has information pertinent to the operation. He calls Maureen Potter for assistance in getting the container delivered to him.

"Maureen Potter speaking."

"Maureen, it's Ben, I wasn't sure that I would catch you before you left."

"Hello, Ben, how are things going at your end?"

"So far, so good, will talk more on my return, I wonder if you would do something for me? There is a container in my safe at home which I need delivering to the Central Offices in London. Could you collect it and ask Rupert Bolton and James Taylor to bring it along please?"

"Of course, Ben, I will collect it this evening and ask Rupert and James to deliver it tomorrow as soon as possible."

"Thanks, Maureen, I will let Margaret know that you will be arriving, please be careful."

"I will, Ben, don't worry."

"Margaret, it's Ben, how are you and the children coping?"

"Ben, this is a surprise, we are fine, how about you did everything go well?"

"Better than expected, I will tell you more when I return, listen I have asked Maureen to call round this evening and collect the Container and its contents. She will arrange for it to be sent to me."

"Very well, dear, I will have some dinner for her," Margaret adds.

"Thank you, I completely forgot about the Container, the starting point of all this, but now need its contents to be analysed more closely with what I now have in my possession."

"Daddy, Daddy, when are you coming home, we all miss you," says Polly holding the receiver.

"I hope to home for the weekend, Polly, have you been taking care of Peter for me?" Ben asks with a smile.

"Yes I have, Daddy, and the new building is now completely finished."

"That's good, now put Mummy back on please and remember to give a hug to Maisy, Daisy and George for me?"

"I will, Daddy, see you soon bye," says Polly as she hands the receiver to Margaret.

"I will be home for the weekend, Margaret, I have two helpers supplied by Beatrice Carrington, so I hope to be able to put together a lot of evidence relating to the activities of the black market operators, but there is a mountain of documents to look over."

"I understand, Ben, but do let me know one way or the other," Margaret answers.

"Of course, dear, bye for now," Ben replies and replaces the receiver.

Ben realises that he has not made any reservations for this evening, so calls Daniel.

"Daniel, it's Ben, I wonder if you might be able to accommodate me for this evening, I have been so busy since you and Conrad left, I haven't had time to book a room."

"Of course Ben come along when you are ready, and we'll have some dinner."

205

"Thanks very much, Daniel, I will see you in about an hour."

Ben carefully replaces papers open to view, back in a box, and stores the boxes on the floor against the wall adjacent to the door so that they cannot be seen from outside.

He closes the blinds, and locks the door and gives the doorman instructions that room 15 is to remain locked until he returns, then makes his way to Daniel's flat in Kensington.

"Ben, do come in, leave your bag anywhere, would you like a drink before we eat?"

"Thanks, Daniel, a small whisky with water would be fine."

Ben and Daniel enjoy a meal of beans on toast, followed by some cheese and biscuits.

"Sorry about the cuisine, Ben, I tend to make do throughout the week and have a good meal out at the weekend."

"That was fine, Daniel, sufficient for my needs anyway."

"So how did Operation Seeker conclude at the tunnels?"

"Very well, I am happy to say, the amount of goods stored in the tunnels was far greater than I had imagined, leading me to conclude that this black market business is much bigger than I first thought. There were thousands of pounds, possibly hundreds of thousands of pounds' worth of goods in the tunnels, waiting for shipment to various parts of the country. When the tunnel contents have finally been counted, they will represent a damning record against the black market criminals. I have just begun sifting through the contents of the boxes you confiscated from the cottage; fortunately, I have two helpers to assist in what is a massive task. There will be more than enough evidence to make a number of convictions. I am looking specifically for information about the ringleaders in this business. The four names I was given have been mentioned in some of the papers that I have glanced through. I believe that there is no doubt they are the leaders in this operation. What I have to determine is whether there is any one higher in government that is involved, which will be more difficult," says Ben thoughtfully.

"And much more dangerous?"

"I fear you may be right there, Daniel, but that will not stop me from going after them, I have a good team around me, both at work and at home, and I intend to pursue this business to its rightful conclusion, namely the successful convictions of all those involved."

The two men continue their conversations for some time before retiring for the evening.

Maureen Potter arrives home at about 5.30 p.m., and decides to have a bath before going out to the Spencer House. She is delighted to have the opportunity to see Peter Forsyth again so wants to look her best without it appearing too obvious! She enjoys her bath and eventually leaves for the Spencer's at about 6.30 p.m. arriving shortly after.

"Come in, Maureen, it is good to see you again," says Maureen as she opens the front door.

"Hello, Margaret, I hope everyone is well?"

"Yes we are, and please let it stay that way, Maureen, but I just do not know and confess that I am always apprehensive when Ben is away," Margaret replies with some concern in her voice.

They enter the parlour to be greeted by the children, who are sitting round the table.

"Hello, Miss Potter, are you having supper with us?" asks Polly.

"Yes, you will have some supper with us, Maureen, won't you?"

"Well thank you, Margaret."

Peter joins them for supper and Maureen is pleased to see him once again.

"Maureen, how are you? I understand Ben has asked you to arrange to have the container delivered to him? Can we talk about that after supper in the study? "

"Yes of course, Peter, any advice would be appreciated."

And so after supper, Maureen and Peter depart for the study, closing the door behind them.

"I have missed you, Peter, it has been a while."

"I have missed you, too, Maureen, but until this business is over, my time has to be with the Spencer family, I hope you can understand that?"

"I understand completely, Peter, and would not expect you to compromise the Spencer family for me. As you say when this is over, I hope we will be able to see more of each other."

"I hope so to Maureen, now let me get the container from the safe. It may be an idea to place the contents in this old briefcase of mine, it's a bit battered but will serve the purpose, and I have a key to lock it as well."

"I would have preferred that you did not have this at your home overnight Maureen because of its' importance to so many unsavoury characters, so please be careful, at least you have a weapon to defend yourself if necessary."

"Please do not worry, Peter, I will be okay really and I have my weapon and know how to use it."

After placing the documents in Peter's old briefcase, Maureen goes back to the parlour to thank Margaret for supper and say goodbye to the family. Peter sees her to the door, and again tells her to be careful, before kissing her on the cheek as she leaves the Spencer's house. Maureen arrives home safely, pleased at having seen Peter, and had the opportunity to talk with him. She very much hopes that they can become close friends when Peter's business with the Spencer family is over. Maureen did not think that she had been in bed too long when she is woken by a noise downstairs. She looks at her clock which says 2.00 a.m.

She listens intently and realises that someone is moving about downstairs. She gets up from her bed, and moves toward her bedroom door opening it as quietly as she can. She can see beams of light waving about in her front room. Thank goodness that she had hidden the briefcase in a box in her garden shed before going up to bed, a precaution that proves invaluable. The intruders make no attempt to keep their whereabouts secret, making enough noise to waken anyone in the house. Maureen moves down the stairs hoping to be able to reach her phone in the sitting room at the back. She reaches the bottom of the stairs, and turns towards the sitting room as the front room door opens and Maureen is confronted by three men. She makes a dash back up the stairs, but is hampered by her gown, and is grabbed by one of the men, who pulls her back down the stairs and takes her into the front room. One of the other men holds on to her as they push her down onto a chair.

"Keep still, Miss Potter, we don't want to hurt you but we do require some information from you," the man says.

"I have nothing to say to you, please leave my house."

She has barely got her words out when another man slaps her hard across her face and says.

"Shut up and keep quiet or you will be dealt with do you understand?"

Maureen tries to get up from the chair and is immediately set upon by two of the men. One of them grabs her by her hair while another rips off her dressing gown using the drawstring to tie her hands behind her. Maureen suddenly feels very vulnerable, realising that her position is pretty desperate. The third man, who up to now had not spoken, now addresses Maureen.

"Miss Potter, my men have a job to do here, that is secure information regarding the activities of your boss, Mr Spencer. I suggest you give them the information they ask for as quickly as possible. Believe me, they will get what they want one way or the other."

"I am just a secretary; I do not have any information that is of any importance."

And with that comment, Maureen is again slapped hard, by one of the other men and is cut on her lip. Two of the men then grab her and walk her toward the table and retie her hands in front of her. Each man has a riding crop, and while the third man holds Maureen across the table, they pull aside her nightgown and proceed to beat her with the riding crops. Maureen screams as she feels the whips strike her across her bare back and her buttocks. The men strike her a number of times before being told to stop. Maureen is sobbing uncontrollably. Her position, stretched across the table top means that she is helpless in the hands of these three men. They pick her up and sit her back down in the chair.

"Now Miss Potter, we want to know where Spencer got his information to make his raids, he must have a contact in Whitehall, and we also want to know where you have hidden the documents you collected earlier."

"Please, I don't have any documents, I was invited to supper this evening that is all."

Again, the two men grab her and push her down over the table before striking her again with their riding crops. This time they pull her nightgown over her head leaving her almost completely naked. Maureen screams as the crops cuts into her flesh across her back and buttocks and cries out:

"Please stop, I will tell you what you want to know," she says.

The two men grab her and throw her down into the chair, handing her robe to her. She is by now severely bruised across her back and buttocks and bleeding from her beating. She wipes blood away from her cut lip before she is asked again.

"Now, where are the documents, Miss Potter, and please don't fool around with me, I warn you."

Maureen is just about to divulge where the briefcase is when there is a knock on her door.

"Miss Potter, it's Constable Bradley is everything alright in there?" he calls.

And before anyone can respond, Maureen screams out as loud as she can. The three men push her to one side and make off through the back door of the house. Maureen staggers to the front door and collapses into the Constable's arms. He carries her inside and calls for an ambulance.

When she wakes, Maureen is safe in the Carswell hospital, and Peter is by her bedside.

"My dear Maureen, who did this to you?" he asks with concern and anger in his voice.

"They were after the briefcase, Peter, and I would have handed it over but for the Constable knocking on the door."

"You must have annoyed them by not telling them they have given you a terrible beating."

"Peter, I need you to retrieve the briefcase from my shed and give it to Rupert Bolton and James Taylor, ask them to collect it from the house."

"Yes, yes Maureen, I will do as you ask, now please you must rest, I will try and get back to see you this afternoon."

"Doctor, how bad is it, has she been physically assaulted?"

"No, but she has suffered a beating. Her back and buttocks have deep wheals from the beating, and as you probably noticed her face is also badly bruised. She will be in hospital for few days at least."

Peter had driven to the local hospital as soon as the police had informed them of the attack on Maureen. After picking up the briefcase from Maureen's house, he returns to the Spencer household at about 4.30 a.m., very angry at what has happened to Maureen.

"How is she, Peter?"

"She has been very severely beaten, Margaret, the doctor expects her to be in hospital for a few days yet." Peter replies sombrely.

"Oh dear God what will happen next, first Polly now Maureen, does she have any family that need to be told?"

"Both parents have passed away, but I believe she has a brother who lives in France. I will ask her if she wants me to contact him, for now it is best if she just rests."

"I suggest you go back to bed for an hour or so, Margaret, I will stay here for a while."

Peter decides that there is no point in returning to bed, so sits on the sofa and goes over the recent events. The attack on Maureen shows how desperate these men are, hoping to force Ben's hand by targeting a loyal work colleague. He is furious at what has happened, since he feels a degree of responsibility toward Maureen. He is fond of her, but did not expect her to become involved in the events that have occurred in the Spencer household. He decides that he must speak with Ben as soon as he is in his office, since he will now want to move in with Maureen when she returns home and will suggest that Daniel move into the Spencer house in his place, providing he can take a leave of absence from the Ministry.

Peter must have dozed, because he is woken by Margaret asking him if he wants any breakfast.

"What time is it, Margaret, yes please some toast would be fine?"

"It is half past seven, Peter, will you be going to see Maureen today?"

"Yes, I thought I would call in on my way to pick up Polly, perhaps Mrs Poulton can collect Maisy, Daisy and George today?"

"Very well, I will arrange that with Betty, and do give Maureen our best wishes, I will go and fetch some flowers this morning for you to take."

"I am sure she will appreciate that and thank you."

"I know you have become fond of her in the short time that you have known her, so we all understand how you must feel at this moment. You do whatever is needed to care for her and protect her, Peter, Ben and I would expect nothing less," Margaret concludes.

Peter calls Ben at his office at 9.15 a.m. and tells him of the attack on Maureen.

"Oh my God, Peter, I am so sorry, how is she?"

"She is conscious, Ben, but it will take some time for her injuries to heal, as she took a fearful battering," Peter replies.

"You will want to be with her when she goes home, Peter, what can we do to help?"

"I was going to suggest that we ask Daniel to take my place in your house, he is extremely competent and very reliable."

211

"I stayed with him last night, and he has offered to let me stay for the next couple of days, so I will talk this over with him this evening, but I think it is an excellent idea, Peter."

"I am unsure how he will explain his leave of absence, perhaps you can help with that, Ben?"

"I will make some calls; now do you know what has happened to the documents that Maureen was to collect?"

"I have them here, she has asked me to make contact with Rupert and James to arrange collection, so that they can bring them to you," Peter replies.

"I will contact them for you, Peter, and ask them to call as soon as possible today."

"Thank you, Ben, and thanks for the understanding, I will be in touch."

"Peter, Mummy has just told me about Maureen, I am so sorry, will she be alright?" asks Polly who has entered the study looking for Peter.

"I hope so, Polly, but it will take some time, I am going back to see her on my way to pick you up from school this afternoon, so I will know more when I have seen her."

Peter meanwhile, takes Polly to school and returns to wait for Ben's colleagues to collect the briefcase. He browses through the contents and can appreciate the significance of what it contains. There are names and places recorded in some detail, and he is sure that the information will add to the details that Ben has at his office in London. In fact, some of this detail will prove conclusively the part played by the personnel mentioned, since there are copies of memos sent between some of the names. He hears the doorbell and goes to the front door to meet Rupert Bolton and James Taylor. Peter ushers them into the study and hands them the briefcase.

"Ben will have told you about the importance of delivering the briefcase safely?"

"Yes, sir, can I ask how Maureen is, everyone is shocked over what has happened?" Rupert Bolton says.

"She is recovering in hospital, but it will be a while before she is fully recovered, but thank you for asking. Now are you all set to travel to London?"

"We have booked our seats and depart in an hour, so we should be at The C.O.I. offices this afternoon," James answers.

"Good, now I'll ask Mrs Spencer for some tea before you depart."

The two men enjoy their tea before departing for London to hand over Ben's briefcase. They are reminded, by Peter, of the importance of its contents, and to be vigilant during their journey. Fortunately, the journey passes without incident, and Rupert and James arrive at The Central Offices of Information in the afternoon.

"Thank you for being so prompt with the briefcase gentlemen, it was important that I receive it as soon as possible. I do feel responsible for what has happened to Maureen over this, and just hope that she has a speedy recovery."

"A bad business Ben, and the sooner these men are caught and punished the better," replies Rupert.

"Have you had any lunch by the way, if not I suggest you visit the canteen, then call back before you leave."

The two men take Ben's advice, then after saying goodbyes, return to Euston to catch the train back to Carswell. Ben is relieved to have the Container contents in his possession in the C.O.I. offices, after so much has happened because of its existence. He looks forward to reviewing its' contents along with the details taken from the cottage in Rye. Jamie Donaldson and Sarah Mumford begin collating the information from the box files, as Ben instructed. The boxes refer to drops at warehouses, garages, shops and private addresses in Central London, West London, North London, Croydon, Watford and Uxbridge. Outside of London the two cities mentioned are Birmingham and Coventry. There are details of shipments of foodstuffs, jams, biscuits, beans, cooking fats and alcohol. Also delivered are ration coupons and consignments of arms and ammunition. The last items are of particular concern, and Ben decides that any addresses where arms and ammunition have been allocated should be given priority.

Ben and his colleagues continue to go through the box files for the remainder of Wednesday and continue into Thursday. A number of names are mentioned along with McKenzie and Williamson. Galbraith's name is also mentioned along with a senior politician in Birmingham. Much of the detail in the container confirms details from the box files. It was easy to understand why the black marketeers were so anxious to get hold of it. They would not be aware of Operation Seeker, so destroying the contents of the container would have removed all the evidence against anyone involved in the massive black market business operating in the country. Now, many of them will have been arrested and will be apprehensive about their fate. At lunchtime on Thursday, Ben contacts Beatrice Carrington to arrange a meeting with her, to discuss the operation to date.

"Hello, Beatrice, it's Ben."

"Ben, I understand you are very busy, how are things with you?"

"Yes, very busy, Beatrice, I was hoping we might have dinner this evening to discuss what has happened and how we will move forward."

"I have a better idea; why don't I cook something for you?"

"That sounds wonderful, Beatrice, what time?"

"About seven I think. Do you know my address, by the way? I live in Whitechapel."

"Yes, I have been there just once, about three years ago, Beatrice."

"Yes of course I remember now, okay I will see you around seven, Ben."

"Look forward to it, Beatrice, bye for now."

"Mr Spencer, I wonder if I might have a word with you, please?" Sarah Mumford asks after Ben has finished his call.

"Yes, Sarah, what is it?"

"There are some names mentioned here that work in one of the departments in Whitehall that I have been attached to."

"I see well let me have their names Sarah, and I will mention it to Beatrice, who I am seeing this evening, thank you for mentioning it."

"Can I ask, Mr Spencer, will Jamie and I be required next week, perhaps you might ask Miss Carrington? I only ask because we were told that we would be here for at least this week, then our positions would be reviewed."

"Thank you for mentioning that too, Sarah, I will let you know in the morning."

Ben arrives at Beatrice Carrington's home just after 7 o'clock to be greeted by Beatrice.

"Ben, delighted to see you again."

They had been good friends for many years, a relationship built on trust and mutual respect for each other. A woman of striking appearance at 50 years of age, three years older than Ben, Beatrice Carrington worked in Whitehall throughout the war years and up to the present. She had been influential in a number of key decisions with regard to stamping out the black market, and such was her position that she reported directly to the Home Secretary's office. Ben had always kept their relationship secret at Beatrice's request, because of the nature of their business. She recognised that Ben had a special talent for uncovering racketeering, and was pleased to be able to assist him when she could since they were working to a common end, the end of black marketeering forever.

Other than Margaret, no one knew of Beatrice Carrington, and Ben intended that it stay that way, despite the efforts made by criminal elements to force him to divulge her existence. Beatrice was very relieved that she was still able to continue her role in Whitehall, and obviously felt some responsibility for what had happened to Ben's family and lately to Maureen Potter. Since the end of the war, there had been rumours about corruption in government. Indeed, an inquiry into government corruption will take place at some time over allegations made against ministers. Ben's raids and subsequent discoveries will eventually act as a forerunner to any inquiry. Beatrice has been given authority to act as she sees fit in order to discover who are behind the corruption, was it businessmen and civil servants for example? She had made a number of suggestions and placed the details in the container that was hurriedly left in Ben's garden to avoid being discovered. The details were compiled by her, over time, at the direct request of the office of The Home Secretary. Ben was determined to follow up on the information handed to him by Beatrice, along with his own remit to break up the racketeering and black market activities throughout the nation. The events of the past couple of days were bringing his investigations to a significant conclusion.

After dinner, Ben updates Beatrice on the raid in the tunnels and the confiscation of the box files from the cottage in Rye.

"You have done better than I could have hoped for, Ben, though I fear the costs have been too much to bear. The injuries to your daughter and lately the attack on your secretary are unforgivable, and I sincerely hope that the people concerned will be caught and punished accordingly."

"There have been some arrests already, and I hope that the people responsible for the attack on Maureen will also be apprehended very soon."

"I fear that the attacks may escalate with the arrests being carried out today, Ben, so please be extra careful from now on."

"We have arrested the four that I warned you of, namely Miles McKenzie, Giles Williamson, Toby North and John Devonish, together with their men, and I understand that there have also been some arrests in Whitehall, but have not received any details yet. I spoke briefly with Commander Spratt who will send me a full list of those being held, as soon as possible. There are a lot of concerned people in Whitehall at the moment, since many are unsure of what the arrests are for. I will give you the details as soon as they become available."

"I look forward to that, Beatrice, by the way, I am going to lose Peter for a while, he will be taking care of Maureen until she has recovered. He has saved the day on more than one occasion for the family, and Polly rarely ventures from his side. She has coped very well considering what she has been put through."

"So do you have someone to fill in for, Peter?"

"Yes I do, his name is Daniel Bottomley. He was with me when I went down to Rye and New Haven. He has a similar background to Peter who recommended him and also his colleague, for the visit down the south. He is younger than Peter, but I'm confident that he will prove invaluable. I am staying with him at the moment, so will be putting my request for his help to him when I return this evening."

"Have you had any thoughts about police protection?"

"I obviously thought about the police, Beatrice, but decided that it would prove difficult to keep them in the picture, especially in light of the secrecy involved. The police would have to be informed of what is going on, and I must confess that I have found myself withholding information when they have been asking questions. Having them directly involved with my protection could be counterproductive and difficult to reconcile with both the police and the Office."

"Yes I see; it would prove difficult to maintain the secrecy required."

"Just a couple of points to make regarding my assistants, Sarah and Jamie, Beatrice. They asked how long they will be assigned, since initially it was for just the one week."

"They are available for as long as they are required, Ben."

"Yes I thought they would be, the other point that Sarah brought to my attention was these names that she recognised from her department," says Ben, handing the list of names to Beatrice.

"Not quite sure what their involvement can be, but I think it best if they are questioned anyway."

"There is no way they may compromise Sarah and Jamie's positions Beatrice since I have instructed them to tell their colleagues that they are filing data from the Midlands office for the records. I will however reiterate the importance of their work remaining confidential when I talk to them in the morning."

Then, after thanking Beatrice for a wonderful meal and confirming that they must meet again soon, Ben leaves for Daniel's flat.

"Hello, Daniel, I am glad I caught you before bedtime, I wonder if I may have a word? I wondered how you would be fixed for a leave of absence for a week or so. As you know, my secretary was attacked and badly beaten early yesterday and when she is able to leave hospital, Peter, who has formed a bit of an attachment, will be taking care of her for a while. In light of recent events, I am reluctant to leave my family without some form of security for any time, and I was hoping that you might come along and stay at my home for a while. I would say there is very little to do, but recent events contradict that statement. In fact, I strongly advise you to arm yourself adequately in the event of any intruders. Peter has had occasion to open fire on intruders and also on the men that abducted Polly, so it is essential that you are well equipped."

"Ben, I would be delighted to offer my services for as long as I am needed. I have some time off due to me and I will explain your request to my Commander. He is a very reasonable chap and will be only too pleased to help I am sure; how soon would you want me?"

"If you can clear it with your Commander, I would like you to begin immediately. I will be travelling home tomorrow, so hopefully we can travel together?"

"I will talk it over as soon as I get in the office tomorrow Ben and call you."

And with that both men retire for the evening. Next morning after saying their goodbyes, Ben and Daniel go off to their offices. Ben gets into The C.O.I. offices just before 9 o'clock and ponders, for the moment, what transpired last night with Beatrice and latterly with Daniel. He is under no illusions regarding his and his family's safety, after the success of Operation Seeker in the South of England, and is anxious to install Daniel as soon as convenient. And he is also concerned about Sarah recognising names from the box files, and decides he must speak with her about this as soon as possible. It is absolutely vital that secrecy be maintained especially now that names have been recognised.

"Good morning, Mr Spencer," says Sarah as she enters the room followed by Jamie.

"Good morning, both, I have a couple of points to discuss before we start this morning. To answer your question yesterday about length of stay, Beatrice tells me that you can remain here for as long as it takes to complete our task. Hopefully, sometime next week should see the work completed. Secondly, regarding the names that you gave to me Sarah, I take it that thus far you have not recognised anyone Jamie. On no account must you mention your finding to anyone. As I said yesterday, you and Jamie are here, officially, to file away C.O.I. files from the Midlands. Now that arrests have been made there will be questions asked.

"We have to be sure that no one yet arrested gets information that helps them to evade being taken into custody. I apologise for going on about this, but it really is necessary."

"We fully understand, Mr Spencer, and I can assure you of complete confidentiality at all times. I recognise just how important your work has been and how you want to carry it to a conclusion and I want to help you in any way I can and I'm sure Jamie feels the same."

"Thank you very much for that, Sarah, now shall we have some tea before we get down to work.

Ben receives a call from Daniel mid-morning confirming his availability, and agrees to meet up with him at Euston at 2 o'clock to catch the train for Carswell.

"Thanks for being so prompt, Daniel, and thanks for being there for me and my family. Hopefully we shall enjoy a good weekend, bye for now."

For the remainder of Friday morning, Sarah and Jamie continue to chronicle the contents of the box files. They reveal a number of areas that the capital is divided into, ten in total. The markings on the boxes, 'Central London 1946, West London 1947' are self-explanatory and relate directly to the ten sectors. They are Central London, West London, East London, South London, North London, Romford, Croydon, Dartford, Tilbury and Watford. Those named in the files will be rounded up and questioned as soon as possible. Although there are still a number of files to be examined, Ben decides to send what information he already has, on names and addresses, to Commander Spratt.

"Hello Commander Spratt's office."

"Good morning, could you put me through to the Commander, my name is Ben Spencer and it concerns Operation Seeker."

"One moment please."

"Commander Spratt, hello Mr Spencer, I thought I might hear from you before the weekend."

"Hello, Commander, I wanted to give you all the names and addresses that have been uncovered to date as soon as possible. I wonder, could you send a messenger over to C.O.I offices this morning, I know it is short notice, but I have to be away at lunchtime."

"I will get someone round to you by noon, Mr Spencer. He will have a secure case for the information and identification. In fact, I will send my secretary, she is a most reliable member of staff. Her name is Pamela Cunningham. By the way, would you like a copy of the arrest list that I am compiling for Miss Carrington?" the commander asks.

"I would appreciate that, thank you, Commander."

"Okay, Mr Spencer, I will do what I can to let my secretary have a copy available for you when she collects the information later this morning."

Ben asks Sarah to make a separate list to date of names and addresses that he can hand to the commander's secretary.

"Will you make that a priority please, Sarah, and make a copy for me, Commander Spratt's secretary is to collect them around noon?"

Certainly, Mr Spencer, I will have the list ready for her."

"Thank you, Sarah, Jamie, just to let you both know, we shall be finishing at 1 o'clock today, so please clear all documentation out of sight before you leave for the weekend."

"Certainly, Mr Spencer," Jamie replies.

Pamela Cunningham arrives, promptly, at noon and shows Ben her identification.

"Hello, Mr Spencer, I'm Pamela Cunningham from Scotland Yard.," she says with an air of authority. A small, dark -haired woman in her early 40s she continues, "I have some papers for you and I believe you have some papers for me to take back to the Commander?"

"Hello, Pamela, yes, Sarah, is just completing them, can I offer you some tea?"

"Thank you, Mr Spencer," she replies.

Ben asks Jamie to get some tea for Pamela, as Sarah completes the list of names and addresses for the Commander. Ben enjoys a cup of tea with her before seeing her off back to Scotland Yard.

"Can you both stack the boxes this side of the office so that they cannot be seen from the corridor please?" Ben asks Sarah and Jamie.

The boxes are duly stacked as Ben requests, and Sarah and Jamie wait on Ben's comments.

"As I mentioned to you both earlier, we shall be finishing at 1 o'clock and continue business on Monday morning. As I have mentioned already, please be aware of the importance of not talking about your work this week to anyone, Sarah, the names that you mentioned to me this week, is there any possibility that you will meet with any of them over the weekend?"

"None at all, Mr Spencer, I only know them by name, I have never actually spoken with any of them."

"That's very good, and a relief, I might add."

Meanwhile, Sarah and Jamie complete their stacking of the box flies, and Ben wishes them both a good weekend as they leave the office. He has a last look around the office, closes the blinds and locks the door before moving out of the building and hailing a taxi for Euston. He arrives at Euston and makes for the main cafeteria for a sandwich. As arranged, Daniel is waiting for him inside.

"Daniel, hello there, can I get you anything while we are waiting for our train?"

"I've had a sandwich thanks, Ben, but another tea would go down well."

"I do appreciate you helping me out with this, Daniel. I just hope that you have a quiet time during your visit to my home, although I fear we may not have heard the last of the black marketeers attempts to stop me bringing them to justice. In the meantime, the weekend will give you a chance to meet the family and settle into our home."

CHAPTER 28

(Operation Seeker: Ben is targeted)

Ben and Daniel eventually arrive at Ben's home around 6 o'clock to be greeted, as usual by the family en masse.

"Daddy, Daddy you're home at last, are you going to stay, will you play with us after supper?" the children ask in unison.

"Children, we have a guest please be patient, hello, Margaret," Ben says as he embraces his wife among the children!

"I want to introduce you to Daniel, he has been here, briefly, once before now he will be staying with us for a while."

"Please, Daniel, come through to the parlour and have some tea, Peter is waiting."

The family and Daniel make their way to the parlour where Peter greets Ben and Daniel with a handshake.

"Ben, Daniel, it's good to see you both."

"Good to see you again, Peter, how is Maureen progressing?"

"I am hoping to take her home tomorrow, she is recovering well thanks, Ben, but she has been badly beaten and her injuries will take a while to heal. I will go round to her house in the morning to prepare for her return"

"I would very much like to see her as soon as I can, I do feel responsible for what has happened to her, and would like to offer her my sincere apologies."

"I am sure she would welcome you, Ben, if she is released tomorrow, perhaps you could call in the evening?"

"I look forward to that now, Margaret I hope you have excelled yourself with supper, I am famished. In the meantime, Peter, Daniel and myself need to catch up, so we will be in the study."

"I will get Polly to call you when supper is ready."

The three men go into the study to discuss what has happened regarding Operation Seeker, and what needs to be addressed regarding Ben's security. Ben is very aware that the criminals may attempt to harm him and his family in light of the New Haven tunnels raid and the arrests that have followed, and wants to be sure that everything that can be done will be done to keep them all safe.

"Peter, is there anything else that we can do regarding making the house secure? Personally, I think you have done a good job."

"There really isn't anything else, Ben, if these men try to enter we are more than ready."

"Okay, now after supper, we can have a walk round with Daniel so that he can get a feel for the house and grounds. Just then Polly arrives to say that supper is almost ready, and Peter uses her visit to the study to formally introduce her to Daniel.

"Polly, can I introduce you to a very good friend of mine, Daniel Bottomley. As you know, Daniel will be staying in your home in my place while I look after Maureen."

"Hello, Daniel, I hope you enjoy staying with us, Peter has been a very good friend to me, so I know that you and I will get on well."

"I am sure we will, Polly, and rest assured I will take care of you and your family whilst I am here. I will be here at any time you should need me. I know Peter has had to take special care of you, and will be a hard act to follow, but I will do my best."

"Right so let's go and have some supper," says Ben as he leads the way to the parlour.

After supper, Peter and Daniel take a walk round the garden and also round the house so that Daniel can feel his way round. The two men talk at length about what has happened to the Spencer family and decide that vigilance will be practiced at all times to ensure the safety of the family. Peter mentions his role with Polly and how she has become very reliant on him.

"I think that is understandable, Peter, given the number of times you have rescued her. She is a young girl and sees you as the one person who has saved her. Your actions have saved this family on a number of occasions over the last few weeks. The criminals targeting Ben seem to know no bounds in their determination to stop him from breaking up their activities. Ben, for his part, is so determined to win this war that he may not appreciate just how ruthless these people may become, especially now the arrests have begun. For myself, I will be as ready as I can be for what may occur, and would welcome any advice you have."

"When you are in the house just keep your eyes open for any strangers in the lane. Fortunately, very little traffic travels along the lane so any that does is very noticeable. Also, when Ben is at home, it might be an idea to take Polly to school. It will give you a chance to get to know her better, and also give her the kind of protection that she seems to require given the number of times she has been targeted."

"I will show you the room you will have while you are here, and for tonight we will have to share."

"No problem, Peter, I have slept in far worse places as you well know."

The rest of the weekend is spent quietly with Daniel getting to know the children. George forms a particular attachment to him, and Polly asks him lots of questions about Peter and himself.

"Have you known Peter a long time, Daniel?"

"Yes I have, Polly, we have served together and worked with each other since the end of the war."

"I bet you have had lots of fights with bad people, Daniel, and I bet you won, didn't you?" asks George with a frown.

"Lots of fights, George, not always won I'm afraid." Daniel answers with a smile.

On Saturday evening, Ben goes along to see Maureen leaving Daniel to keep watch over the family home. Peter answers the door and shows Ben into the sitting room where Maureen is resting on the sofa. Ben is shocked to see the injuries to Maureen's face.

Hello, Maureen, how are you feeling, my dear?"

"I am improving thank you, Ben, and am feeling so much better with Peter being here."

"I am so sorry that you have become a victim in my affairs, Maureen, I had no idea that they would go to such lengths as this. "

"Peter will stay with you for as long as he is needed, and you must rest and take as long as is necessary with your recovery. What do the doctor's say about your injuries? Are they healing properly?"

"Some of the cuts were very deep and will take a while to heal, they have swathed me in bandages for a few days to keep them clean and stop me trying to scratch. I am more concerned about the marks on my face; I just hope they will heal completely."

"Is there anything I can do for you, Maureen, do you need anything?"

"What will happen with my work at the office?"

"I wasn't expecting you to ask about the office, but don't worry, you might want to suggest who can look after your day to day business, and I will pass on the message. Regarding information that is pertinent to Operation Seeker, I will contact the people concerned and ask them to contact me direct for the time being. We all want you to get well and want you to be safe."

"Thank you, Ben, it would be nice to say hello to Margaret when she has a moment."

"I will pass on your request, I expect she will call round tomorrow, now before I go I would like a word with Peter."

And with that Ben leaves the sitting room and approaches Peter who is sitting on the back porch.

"How is she really, Peter?"

"A very frightened lady, Ben, she cannot understand why anyone would want to be so cruel to another person. It has made her very nervy, for example I am sleeping in a chair in her room at present, because she does not want to be left alone at night. She does not sleep anyway, so it is easier for me to be close by when she wakes from yet another bad dream. I tried to get some idea of what happened, but when she starts to recall the events of that night, she becomes hysterical, so I don't think we will get any real answers from her for quite some time if at all. In the meantime, I will keep her as comfortable as possible, and hope that time heals," Peter replies with concern in his voice.

"Let me know if there is anything you need. I will give you a call tomorrow evening before I go back to London," says Ben as he leaves the house to return home.

"How is Maureen, Ben?" asks Margaret on his return.

"Physically, she is recovering, but the beating she endured has left deep mental scars, which will take some time to heal."

"She asked if you would visit, and I said you would call tomorrow, can I suggest you take Polly along with you, it may be an idea to see how she reacts talking to someone who has had a similar experience?"

"That may be an idea; perhaps you can suggest that to Polly?"

"Where is Polly by the way?"

"I believe she went off upstairs with Daniel and George."

Polly and George had gone upstairs with Daniel to help him with his luggage. George had taken a liking to Daniel as soon as he saw him and followed him around asking questions about where he had been as a soldier and how many bad men he had shot!

Daniel enjoyed his chatter which was so different for him not having any family. So he told him tales of adventures in the desert and what it felt like to ride a camel, stories that George listened to in awe! Polly was cautious with Daniel at first, especially as he had replaced Peter. He was younger but similar in many ways, both being ex-military, their attitudes reflecting their military upbringing. Daniel was perhaps a little more relaxed than Peter and seemed to take in his stride what was required of him. He had no illusions about the dangers he may face being at the Spencers' home but he seemed to accept his responsibility with a calming influence.

"Have you known Peter a long time, Daniel?" Polly asked as she sat on his bed while he unpacked assisted by George.

"We met during the war, Polly, Peter was an officer with special talents and we served in Africa together. He had a reputation for doing things his way which was successful though not always popular with authority. We got into a few scrapes, but we always managed to get back home. We have also worked together since the war, and I expect we will continue again when your father's business is concluded. In the meantime, you and I will get on well I am sure; hopefully we will not get involved in any issues similar to what has happened previously. I understand from Peter, that you have been badly treated by these people seeking revenge against your father?"

"It was horrible, and I will always be grateful to Peter for how he saved me several times from these men," Polly replies tearfully.

"Please, don't upset yourself, Polly, I am sorry that my mentioning it was so unpleasant for you," Daniel replies and puts a consoling arm around Polly.

"Those men were horrid to Polly, Daniel, they also set fire to our house and some of my toys in the garage were burned," George adds, anxious to make his point with Daniel.

"Yes, your Daddy told me all about that, George, perhaps we may be able to replace some of them while I am staying with you."

"Really, Daniel. I must go and tell Maisy and Daisy."

Sunday is a relatively quiet day, Daniel settles into his new home, while Ben makes notes on who he must contact when he returns to London tomorrow. After lunch, Margaret takes Polly to visit Maureen, and like Ben is visibly shocked by what she sees.

"My dear Maureen, we are all so sorry, are you feeling any better at all?"

"Yes I am and thank you both for coming, Polly, I hope seeing me will not bring back too many bad memories?"

"Not really Maureen, I am just so sorry that this has happened to you. I know that Peter will take good care of you, like he did with me, so you are in safe hands."

Polly goes off to the kitchen to put the flowers they have bought in water and uses the opportunity to say hello to Peter. She has missed him not being in her house and tells him so.

"You will be very well cared for by Daniel, Polly, believe me he is a very special young man."

"What do you mean, Peter?" asks Polly puzzled by what Peter has said.

"Daniel was awarded medals for his service during the war years and experienced action in Africa and beyond. He suffered gunshot and shrapnel wounds from his exploits and would have been a high-ranking officer if he had chosen to stay in the military. Typical of Daniel, he felt he could be more useful outside of the military command, and has served with added distinction since the war ended. He has been to Berlin a number of times, officially as an interpreter, where he has been involved in government business not normally mentioned in the news. So, as I said, Polly, Daniel is a very special young man. You and your family really couldn't be in safer hands. Now, I will stay with Maureen for as long as she needs me, but if you want to talk with me you can phone at any time."

"Thanks, Peter, I must get back to Mummy now bye," says Polly as she returns to the sitting room.

"There you are, Polly, I think we will leave Maureen to rest now, perhaps we can call again in the week?" Margaret asks.

"I look forward to that, Margaret."

And with a final goodbye to Peter, Polly and Margaret return home to The Gables. The remainder of Sunday is spent enjoying the summer sun, George asking Daniel what toys might be replaced from the fire, and Polly thinking over what Peter had said about their new houseguest. Ben prepares for an early start tomorrow, and tells Margaret that he should return mid-week, rather than Friday.

"There is still much to be done, but Sarah and Jamie have been very efficient so the analysis of the files from the cottage should take no more than a couple of days, three at the most. I will then only need to return once the proceedings against these people begin in court and that will take some time."

He leaves the house very early on Monday, having said his goodbyes to the children the night before and arrives at the Central Office of Information at 9.30 a.m. where Sarah and Jamie are waiting. During the day, he contacts Chief Inspector Jamieson, Birmingham Constabulary, telling him of Maureen's attack and asking that he contacts Ben direct should the need arise. He also contacts Coventry Constabulary with the same message. He then realises that he needs to find somewhere to stay for a few nights, and finds a small hotel close to The Oval Cricket Ground.

Sarah and Jamie work hard collecting the data from the files which continue to reveal just how vast the operation is. With this point in mind, Ben calls Commander Spratt.

"Hello, Commander Spratt's office."

"Good morning, Pamela, it's Ben Spencer from the C.O.I. is the Commander free at all?"

"Mr Spencer, hello, I will just see if he is free for you."

"Commander Spratt, morning, Mr Spencer, how are you?"

"Good morning, Commander, I'm okay thank you, still ploughing through the files, I wonder if you can help me regarding Operation Seeker and the eventual sealing of the tunnels in New Haven. Since Scotland Yard has overall authority for the operation, can you advise on procedures relating to closing and sealing the tunnels so that they cannot be used again?"

"I understand what you are saying, Mr Spencer, obviously the local authority would have to be instructed on this, and it is my opinion that the instruction would have to come direct from The Home Office," the commander replies.

"I understand, is that something that you would request via your office, or would you prefer that I make some enquiries from my end?"

"That would suit me, I avoid getting involved with Whitehall if I can, Mr Spencer, too much time spent doing too little."

"I think I understand, Commander, I will contact the Home Office from the C.O.I. and get the paperwork authorised. I will keep you informed of progress."

"Thank you, I appreciate that, Mr Spencer, bye for now," the commander replies.

Ben decides the best option is to make contact with Beatrice Carrington on this and knowing that she has a secure line, dials her office number.

"Good morning, Beatrice, it's Ben Spencer."

"Hello, Ben, good to hear from you again."

Ben then asks Beatrice about procedures required to close down the tunnels at New Haven. He impresses on her the urgency of this, adding that it will send a clear message to those involved that their black market operation is dead and buried literally.

"I will treat your request as a matter of urgency, Ben, and get on to the relevant department later today. As soon as I have any information I will let you know. I appreciate your comments Ben and will pass on the need for urgency here. Those people that have been involved in racketeering and black market activities need to be sent a clear message that their operations are finished for ever and will never be restarted again."

"Thanks, Beatrice, I look forward to hearing from you, bye for now." Ben replaces the receiver.

For the remainder of the day, Sarah and Jamie continue to collate the details, names, addresses and shipments from the files. Ben continues to be surprised by the sheer volumes of goods being distributed around the southern area. It is reasonable to assume that some of it is redistributed northwards, but the operation is undoubtedly controlled through London and reaches inside government departments. Whilst there have been a number of arrests already, there will be many more before Operation Seeker is concluded.

Tuesday morning in the Spencer home sees the children getting ready for school, Polly to be taken by Betty Poulton and Molly, Maisy and George by Margaret, who decides to use Ben's car since it is not in use. She needs to go into town after school so the car will be useful. Once the children have all departed, Daniel begins preparing his daily logs, something he has always done from his army days. A man who enjoys routine, and will ensure that all aspects of security at the Spencer's house are regularly checked. Date, time and work carried out together with relevant comments will all be meticulously logged and for Ben to view if required. This is how operates.

He is in the study when the doorbell rings. He moves out into the hallway and sees a figure standing at the front door. He opens the door to be confronted by the postman.

"Good morning, sir, I have a parcel for Mr Spencer."

"He is out at the moment, I will take it," says Daniel taking the parcel into the study.

He pays no attention to the parcel at first then becomes suspicious by the London postmark. Why would Ben have items delivered to his home from London, when he is in London? He examines the parcel more closely, and hears notices a strange noise coming from it. The noise is something he had not come across for many years. He grabs the parcel, and runs to the bottom of the garden before carefully placing it behind the big hawthorn bush, then racing back inside and closing all blinds and curtains at the back of the house. A similar parcel is also delivered to the Central Office of Information at Carswell. Again, addressed to Ben Spencer. Phil Landers takes the parcel, and in the absence of Maureen leaves it on the desk in her office. Maureen's absence from the office on that day would surely save her life. Daniel, meanwhile, ponders his next move. He is certain that the package is an explosive device of some sort, but he has no idea what the time lapse may be before it goes off.

Phil Landers pays no attention to the package that has been delivered and although his office is the other end of the corridor from Maureen Potter's, it is completely wrecked when the package explodes and brings down the ceiling. The damage to the building is extensive, part of the outside wall collapses and several staff are injured, thankfully no one seriously. Carswell did not suffer from any bombing during the war, since it is midway between Coventry and Leicester, so the locals are concerned at what has happened in the town. Margaret Spencer heard the blast clearly, thankfully, she was nowhere near the explosion. When she discovers that the blast is at Ben's offices, she immediately thinks of her home. The Police and Fire Brigade arrive swiftly to the offices of the blast, so Margaret decides, somewhat apprehensively, to return home. Is it really still happening, have the family been targeted yet again by these ruthless gangsters?

Margaret will very soon be confronted with the answer.

Daniel, meanwhile, was about to call Ben at his London office when the device goes off. His quick thinking, placing the device behind the hawthorn bush probably saved the house from more serious damage. A dull roar, followed by glass shattering and the rear of the house being bombarded with lumps of earth can be heard by Daniel from in the study. He waits for a few minutes, to be sure that there is not a second device and to make sure that the ceiling does not collapse on him, before venturing out of the back door to view a scene of utter devastation. The hawthorn bush, that was situated about halfway down the garden close to the wall has disappeared. Where the bush stood is a large hole. The garden wall adjacent to the lane has collapsed with many bricks strewn across the lane. At the back of the house, all the windows on the ground floor have been shattered, and the conservatory is almost completely destroyed, but thanks to Daniel's quick thinking, closing the blinds and curtains, there is very little damage from glass inside the house. There are clumps of earth spread over the area and the vegetable patch is completely destroyed. Daniel decides that there is nothing that can be done immediately, and waits on Margaret's return. Margaret has to leave the car at the top of the lane and makes her way through the debris at the back of the house.

"Oh my God, Daniel, what have they done to my beautiful home?" she says tearfully.

Daniel consoles her and walks her through the debris to a chair in the parlour. He sits down with her and goes off to make her some tea.

"Now, Margaret, please try not to be too upset as we have a lot to do and not a lot of time. I have to secure your home by this evening if possible. Is there anyone you can call to give you some help inside while I tackle the mess outside?"

"Yes I can call Betty Poulton, is the phone line still intact?"

"Thankfully yes, that and just one of the floodlights at the corner of the house. I need you to find me a number for a carpenter and glazier so that we can secure the rear windows before dark, the wall will have to be completely rebuilt so Ben will have to decide what he wants to do about that."

"There has also been an explosion at Ben's offices in Carswell, thank God he was not there today, I saw the damage myself before returning home. These people are going to kill someone before they are finished Daniel," Margaret says with a touch of despair in her voice.

"Now, Margaret, please listen to me. You and I have a lot of work to do starting now; we must not get side-tracked worrying about what might happen. Ben has declared war on underworld racketeers and has been spectacularly successful in that war. Unfortunately, wars have casualties of one sort or another. You and your family have endured more than most people, but you have survived, and you will continue to survive. I will be with you here at all times to give support and together we will beat these people."

"Yes, Daniel, thank you for that, I will contact Betty and get you those contact details, and thank you for being so supportive, I needed that," Margaret replies as she leaves the parlour to phone Betty Poulton. She returns and mentions that Betty will be calling shortly, and Daniel goes to make the calls to the local tradesmen. He is able to get both a carpenter and a glazier to come and look at the damage within the hour. As soon as Betty Poulton arrives, he leaves the two of them women and makes his way to the study to contact Ben.

"Good morning, Ben, It's Daniel, we've had a bit of a setback I'm afraid."

Daniel then proceeds to give Ben the details of the damage at his home from the explosive device, and mentions the second explosion at his offices. He goes to great lengths to assure him that no one has been hurt since the children were at school and Margaret was in town.

"Thank you for your quick thinking in moving the device into the garden, Daniel, but for your actions it could have been a lot worse. You will let Peter know when you have a moment. I will catch the earliest train home today."

"There really is no need for you to leave your work, Ben, especially as you are so close to finishing it. I have already called on the services of a carpenter and glazier to secure the rear of the building, and I will spend the rest of the day securing the rest of the house."

"Yes, you may be right, Daniel, how is Margaret she must be devastated by all this?"

"She has got over her initial shock, I have spoken with her about the need to move on and how important your work is, let me go and get her so that you can have a word," Daniel replies as he goes to fetch Margaret.

"My dear Margaret, how are you?"

"I am coping, Ben, Daniel has been very supportive and convinced me that we must continue fighting this war in order to win it, have you managed to contact your office in Carswell?"

"No I haven't, the lines must be down, do you know if anyone has been hurt?"

"There were some injuries but no one was seriously hurt it appears."

"Well that is good news at least. Now Daniel has suggested that I should stay in London and finish the work here, what do you think Margaret do you want me to come home straight away?"

"I always miss you when you are not here Ben, but Daniel is right, you need to finish the job you have in London, we will clear the mess and make the repairs good. At least I know you are safe where you are."

"I understand that, Margaret, I will try to make contact with the office and will stay where I am unless I am needed there urgently. Either way, I expect to be home tomorrow afternoon. Bye for now, my dear, now can you put Daniel back on the phone please?"

"Margaret and I both agree that it is best I finish here, unless I am urgently required at the office. Do what has to be done to secure the house Daniel; and take care of my family until I return, probably tomorrow afternoon."

"I will, Ben, rest assured everything that needs to be done will be done to secure your property and safeguard your family."

"I will call you around 5 o'clock before I leave the office for an update, bye for now."

This latest attack on his home and family really shakes Ben. The use of explosives is a new method of intimidation. Whilst explosives, usually gelignite, has been used in bank robberies since the war, using it on a house is very rare and proves that these villains have limitless resources at their disposal. On the positive side his work is coming to an end, but he asks himself will his life and his family's life ever be the same again? Daniel meanwhile, is instructing the tradesmen on what has to be done urgently to make the house secure. The police arrive around midday and take a statement from him.

"What made you take the package outside then, sir, although it was a good thing that you did?" D.I. Wishart asks.

"I recognised the sound from the package Inspector, I have heard it before during the war years and since in Germany, it is one of those sounds that you never forget."

"Well I think we will leave you to get on with your clearing up, will you say goodbye to Mrs Spencer for me. Where is Mr Spencer by the way?"

"He is in London on government business; I have spoken with him this morning."

"I wish him well, whatever he is doing must be very important and is obviously upsetting some very nasty people," the inspector replies as he leaves the house.

The carpenters return to make good what frames are damaged and the glaziers leave after measuring up the windows that will have to be boarded as a temporary measure to secure the porch area. The only concern is that the door will have to be replaced and that will have to be specially made, so it will have to be secured with a wedge of some sort.

In fact, the carpenter expresses concern about the safety of the conservatory as a whole, and suggests that Mr Spencer may need to consider having it dismantled and replaced. Nothing can be done about the wall other than to tidy up the bricks blocking the lane and clearing them from the garden path. Any glass that did get into the house via the conservatory and kitchen windows, is soon cleared, and the parlour remains intact, although some of the window panes are cracked. Unfortunately, Ben's new garage will also have to be replaced. Margaret and Betty Poulton leave to collect the children from school, leaving Daniel to oversee the boarding of the windows and examine the crater left from the blast. *If nothing else, it will be a talking point for young George,* he thinks to himself with a smile. While the tradesmen are still at the house, he contacts Peter to tell him of the recent explosions at the house and Ben's office. Peter, congratulates him for his prompt action in moving the device behind the hawthorn thicket, and expresses some surprise at the level of violence that the criminals have escalated to reminding Daniel of just how desperate they are becoming in their efforts to stop Ben from destroying their operations. After asking Peter how Maureen is progressing, Daniel tells him he will keep him informed and puts down the phone. When the children arrive from school, there are many questions that they want answering. George in particular is very vocal toward his new friend.

"How did you know it was a bomb, Daniel, weren't you scared carrying into the garden, what if it had exploded while you were carrying it?" George goes on.

"I am very glad that it did not go off when I was taking into the garden George, and I was pretty sure it was an explosive by the noise it was making."

"What sort of noise did it make?" George asks.

"Well it was a bit like the noise you hear when you wind up one of your toys, that's how I knew, George, and I had heard that sort of sound when I was a soldier in Africa."

"What happened—"

"George enough questions for now, Daniel will be exhausted, let's have some tea," says Margaret.

'It might be best if we stay out of the conservatory until we are sure it is safe, if you want to go outside go through the kitchen but be careful where you walk," Daniel suggests.

Margaret begins preparing some supper and looks out of the kitchen window to a scene resembling a bomb site. She has a tear in her eye seeing what has happened to her beautiful garden. She must not let her children see her upset, although at the moment they are busy exploring, and probably do not understand the seriousness of what has happened. Polly walks towards Daniel who is busy moving bricks into a pile at the corner of the house by the edge of the conservatory.

"Thank you for saving our house, Daniel, Peter would be very proud of your actions."

"Thank you, Polly, we still have a lot of work to do, can I suggest that you make sure no one is wandering off with the wall down?"

"Okay, have you spoken to Daddy by the way, what did he say?"

"He agreed that there was no real point in dashing straight home, since Mrs Spencer and I can handle the repairs being carried out. It is very important that he finishes his work in London as soon as possible. You are well aware of how desperate these men are, Polly, from your own experiences, so the sooner they are all put away, the better for everyone especially your family."

"Can I ask you something, Daniel, what did you get your medals for in the war?"

"Why on earth do you want to know that, Polly, and how did you know about any medals?"

"It was mentioned by Peter when I asked about you, I did not mean to intrude, I was just curious to know who you were since you were going to take his place."

"Yes okay, Polly, I understand you wanting to know a little about me, and when I have a moment I will tell you, but for now we need to concentrate on clearing some of this mess."

And with that they continue to tidy the garden as much as possible before supper. Ben had called for an update and spoken with each member of the family, saying he will be home tomorrow, but meanwhile they must help Daniel and their mother as much as they can. Ben again thanks Daniel for his prompt action which probably saved the house, and signs off adding he will see him tomorrow, probably late afternoon. After supper, Daniel updates his log before making a tour of the house and garden to see how secure it is.

"Can I walk with you, Daniel, please?" asks Polly.

"Me too please?" says George.

"Very well, but, George, please stay close, we don't want you to stumble over all the rubble."

The house is as secure as it can be given the damage, but Daniel has already decided that he will sleep fully clothed on the top of his bed, just in case. He is concerned that the security of the house may prompt another attack, but does not mention his thoughts to anyone. Looking at the conservatory, he believes that it will have to be demolished but for now it will have to remain, and the kitchen windows are not especially secure, but hopefully these problems will be addressed in the next few days. Daniel has done everything possible for now and goes back inside the parlour, followed by Polly and George. The children need a bath after exploring the rubble in the garden, and Polly also decides to have a bath. They all then go to their rooms after saying goodnight, and Margaret goes downstairs to the parlour to join Daniel. Once again Daniel seeks to reassure Margaret regarding the house security.

"Well we should be safe enough for this evening, Margaret, although the conservatory's life is destined to be cut short I fear. Most of the windows are boarded, and I have wedged that door shut," he says pointing to the door that leads to the conservatory.

"Thank you for all your efforts today, Daniel, it has been quite an ordeal for everyone, but your calming influence has helped me and the children."

Margaret decides that an early night will do her good. Daniel decides to stay down for a while; he is not going to go to bed anyway, so wishes her goodnight. After about ten minutes Polly appears in the doorway.

"I just wanted to tell you how grateful I am that you are looking after us, Daniel. Peter was very special to me, but he isn't here now. You have given Mummy confidence that we will be safe with you, and I know Daddy respects you a lot. Thank you for being here goodnight."

"Goodnight, Polly, and thank you," he replies.

The three men easily gain access to the house because of windows not being secure, and make their way, silently, up the stairs to Polly's room. This time, they are able to render her unconscious, and carry her down the stairs through the parlour and into the rubble-filled garden.

Daniel hears footsteps on the rubble and dashes down the stairs. Polly meanwhile wakes, and screams and struggles as the men half carry and half drag her across the rubble towards the lane where their car is parked. Daniel runs outside and strikes one of the men, whilst pulling out his weapon from his belt, then shoots him in the leg. The other two are trying to get Polly into the car, dragging her across a pile of bricks and rubble. The rough ground rips her nightshirt to shreds as she continues to struggle. One of the men holds on to her hair for purchase as they drag her along. She suffers terrible body lacerations, from the rubble, especially her shoulder and legs. Her flimsy nightshirt offers no protection as her attackers drag her along and is all but torn off her. Daniel meanwhile, fires two shots at the tyres to immobilise the car and stop the men from escaping. Fortunately, there is sufficient light, from the one remaining flood that isn't damaged, for Daniel to see clearly. The two men are grabbing at Polly trying to get her to the car. She is struggling desperately not realising that the car has been immobilised. As she manages to break away from the men, Daniel fires again and hits one of them in the neck. Polly is showered with his blood as he screams and falls to the ground. The third man starts to run stumbles on the uneven ground and Daniel grabs him and hits him hard in the face.

"Don't any of you move or I will aim my next shots to kill you!" shouts Daniel.

Polly is screaming hysterically, covered in the blood, her torn nightshirt hanging from her battered body. Daniel holds her closely to him, trying to console her, as he walks her back towards the house.

"It's okay, Polly, it's over you are safe I've got you, here put my jacket over your shoulders."

Daniel is holding Polly, as Margaret appears after hearing the gunshots. Daniel tries to pass Polly to her mother but she clings to him desperately, refusing to let go of him.

"No, please don't let go of me, Daniel, please!" she pleads sobbing uncontrollably.

Daniel turns to the three men on the floor.

"You three men stay exactly where you are if anyone of you tries to escape, I will shoot him dead, do you understand?"

The men nod their heads in agreement.

"Good, now my dear Polly, we need to go inside with you and look at your injuries. Margaret, could you phone the police and call for an ambulance as well. At least one of the men will have to go to hospital, and Polly will as well, some of her cuts are very deep from being dragged over broken bricks and rubble."

"Before you go, do you have any rope in the garage so that I can tie those men while you tend to Polly?"

Margaret quickly fetches rope from the garage and Daniel secures the three men while they wait for the police to arrive. Margaret goes off to the study to make the calls. Daniel, meanwhile kneels down by the side of Polly and inspects the lacerations over almost all of her body. Her legs are shredded with bits of brick and her arms, tummy and chest are also severely lacerated. It would be better if she removed what is left of her nightshirt since it is covered in blood, and ripped to shreds, but Daniel decides to leave it for the moment. She must be suffering from shock as well so Daniel finds an old blanket and a jacket on the settee in the parlour and wraps it round her to keep her warm. Margaret returns and tells him the police will be about ten minutes, the ambulance about the same.

"Margaret, if you have any brandy could you put a teaspoon in some sweet tea and give it to Polly, it will calm you down Polly I promise," Daniel says to her.

"Okay, Daniel, if you think I should then I will," Polly replies.

"Now, will you be okay while I go and have a word with these men?"

"Yes okay, Daniel," Polly replies.

Daniel moves out of the parlour and confronts the three men.

"Who sent you boys to do a man's job, tell me who sent you?" he shouts at the one with the broken nose as he gives it a tweak.

"Ouch! Okay, guv'nor, we dunno who he is, but we reckon he has friends in high places."

"Where have you come from?" Daniel demands.

"We're from Croydon, boss, I can give you a name if you can put a word in for us," the one with the leg wound remarks.

"I will not make any promises other than to say that if I find out that you have not told me something I will find you and hunt you down like a dog. Remember, I am not police so do not have to be concerned with their rules and regulations."

"Devonish is the man you want, John Devonish, it was his men that told us to send the devices and try and get the girl after he had been arrested. We was to take her with us back to Croydon and keep her there. The men's names are George Bacchus and Jack Pearson. Pearson stole the gelignite from an army storage depot, he is ex-army himself and an explosives expert. That's all we know guv, honest it is."

"Good, that will do for now, the police will be here any minute so just stay there," says Daniel as he goes back inside to see how Polly is.

Margaret has given her some sweet tea with brandy and she has a little colour in her cheeks. Unfortunately, as she comes out of shock she feels the pain from her multiple lacerations. Daniel takes hold of her hand.

"Now, Polly, you must go to the hospital to have these wounds treated, they will most likely let you come home again later today, but they have to be bathed, cleaned and disinfected, you do understand don't you?"

"Yes Daniel, you have saved my life tonight and I will never forget you for that," she says as she raises her arm and kisses him on the cheek.

"You are very welcome Polly, and thank you."

Two ambulances arrive, one to take Polly, accompanied by Margaret, the other takes the two men who have been shot, accompanied by a police officer.

Daniel sits down on the floor of the conservatory and drinks his tea reflecting on the information that he has got from the men.

"Hello again, sir, D.I. Wishart, you've had a busy time since we last met?"

"It's been rather hectic, Inspector, I have to agree, I am just relieved that I was able to stop them from taking young Polly."

Your actions were amazing, sir, overpowering three criminals and saving young Polly as well, that was some feat. Did they say anything at all by the way?" the D.I. comments.

"I think they were too busy screaming about their injuries to say much Inspector."

"Yes I understand, anyway I will leave you to it for now, I shall have to come back when Miss Polly is back home, so I will talk to you again at that time if you don't mind?" the D.I. concludes as he moves out of the house via the side where the wall has collapsed.

Daniel looks at his watch, it is 3.00 a.m. He decides to stay down in the parlour so goes and gets a blanket before using the settee to doze off. He wakes around 6.00 a.m. by the sunrise and lies there reflecting on the last 24 hours or so. After about ten minutes he ventures upstairs to the children's rooms and is both amazed and relieved that they are all asleep! Margaret returns around 6.30 a.m., the police giving her a lift from the hospital.

"How is Polly, Margaret?" Daniel asks as she walks through the door.

"She is recovering and a lot calmer thanks to your influence, Daniel. Some of her lacerations are quite deep and she is well and truly in a sorry mess, but most are superficial according to the doctor, but they will take time to heal. She also lost a clump of her hair in the tussle. Fortunately, she did not have any marks to her face this time, she is a remarkable girl really," says Margaret tearfully, as suddenly all that has happened becomes too much.

"Now come and sit down, Margaret, this has been a hell of an ordeal for you," says Daniel as he leads Margaret to a chair.

"I'll make some tea, and I suggest a tot of brandy to go with it."

"Thank you, Daniel, and thank you for what you did earlier, you saved Polly's life today.

"I did what had to be done, Margaret, these people need to be punished for their deeds, and what small part I am able to play I will play the best I can. We need to get in touch with Ben as soon as possible, but must wait until he is in his office at 9 o'clock."

"I will get in touch with Betty and get her to come round and help with the children, my God I had forgotten about them!" Margaret replies with panic in her voice.

"They are fine, Margaret, I looked in on them when you went to the hospital."

"Thank you, Daniel, you really do think of everything," Margaret comments.

The children are told about Polly when they come down for breakfast, but Daniel only briefly relates to the events when questioned by George.

"How many did you shoot, Daniel, did they shoot at you, why did they hurt Polly?" asks George.

"And why has she had to go to hospital, what did they do to her?" ask Maisy and Daisy tearfully.

"Children, please, so many questions, Daniel has other things to do than just answer your questions," Margaret answers.

"It's okay, Margaret, now all of you, Polly has gone to hospital to have some scratches and bruises looked at from falling over on all the bricks and rubble outside. The men who tried to take her were pulling her across the garden which is a bit of a mess at the moment. She should be back home later today so you will be able to talk with her then. Now George, I did have to shoot at the men to make them let go of Polly, and you will see that their car is still in the lane. I shot the tyres to stop them getting away, the policemen took them and they will all be punished for what they did to Polly, and your home."

"But, Daniel, how many of them did you actually shoot?' asks George with a degree of persistence.

"Well that's a story for another time, George, you must go and get yourself ready for school now," Daniel replies as Margaret guides them toward the door and up the stairs.

Mrs Poulton has agreed to take the children to school and Margaret suggests she travel into Carswell to see what she can find out about the damage to the C.O.I. office. She will drive in early so that she can pass the information on to Ben when Daniel makes contact with him at 9 o'clock. Daniel will remain at the house to oversee the work to be carried out by the carpenter and glazier, and suggests to Margaret that they contact a builder to give some idea what will be involved to rebuild the garden wall. So, Mrs Poulton takes the children off to school, after George has had a close look at the car in the lane, and the tyre shredded by a bullet from

Daniel's pistol, and Margaret drives into Carswell to the C.O.I office. The damage is extensive, and a wide area has been closed off in case any more of the building collapses. Margaret talks to the officer, explaining who she is and he allows her through to speak with D.I. Wishart.

"Mrs Spencer, how are you this morning, it's been a hell of a time for you these last couple of days? Your Mr Bottomley is some special person the way he dealt with those intruders, we are most grateful that all three were apprehended."

"Yes indeed, in the short time that he has been with us he has saved my family from danger and possibly worse, we are very much in his debt. I am here Inspector because I was wondering if you might give me an update I can pass on to my husband in London. I expect he will be returning today, and Daniel will be contacting him as soon as he arrives at his office."

"You might want to talk to those two, they both worked at the offices, and may be able to help you with any relevant information," the inspector replies pointing out two young men standing among the rubble that was once the entrance. Margaret introduces herself to Rupert Bolton and Jamie Taylor.

"Hello, Mrs Spencer, a terrible business, but thankfully, no one was seriously hurt. Phil Landers will be along shortly; he will be able to give you more details."

"I was hoping to be able to give Ben a brief update, about when will you have telephones again, or more to the point, where are you going to work from while the building is repaired?"

"We have use of a warehouse the other end of town, and I understand that we should have telephones in by the end of today," Jamie Taylor adds.

"Thank you both, I wonder could you ask Phil Landers to call me at home when he has a moment, I have to get back?"

Daniel calls Ben just after nine and tells him of the attempted abduction of Polly, and the information he got from the gang.

"Daniel, thank you so much for rescuing Polly, I must come home immediately because of this. Let me make a couple of calls, then I will get back to you."

He immediately contacts Commander Spratt and relates the details of the explosions at his house and the attempted abduction of Polly by men from London.

"This business is becoming very sinister, Mr Spencer, you need to return home immediately, I will send my car and driver to you within the next half hour and he will drive you to your home. Perhaps you could call me later today when you have arrived for a more detailed report?"

"Thank you very much for your consideration, Commander, I will wait on your driver and call you around teatime this afternoon." He decides he must contact Beatrice before he leaves. She is devastated by the news that Ben relates to her.

"My dear Ben, what have I led you into, these men seemed determined to resort to any means to stop you, even killing people. Please convey my thoughts to Margaret and your wonderful daughter Polly. How someone so young has been able to endure what she has put up with is a miracle," Beatrice says with alarm and despair in her voice.

"She is truly remarkable, Beatrice, and so is Daniel for reacting so swiftly, and being able to secure details of who these men were acting for when they set the explosives and attempted to take her."

"Now, Ben, you must go home and remain there for the present to get your repairs done and set up your office in Carswell. We will keep in touch regularly for news; I am going to get those tunnels sealed as a priority, and monitor progress regarding the arrests so far."

"Thank you, Beatrice, I will call you at home this evening, bye for now."

Ben speaks with Sarah and Jamie, informing them that he has to return home immediately.

"Sarah, please finalise the list of names addresses and shipments as quickly as possible. I will take them with me and see that Commander Spratt receives them. I need you both to stack the boxes as before when you finish the work, and send me the final list via internal mail."

"Sarah, I need you to take the key to the office home with you and see that Beatrice Carrington receives it. Please deliver the key to Miss Carrington personally, will you do that please?"

"Of course, Mr Spencer."

"Can I thank you both, Sarah and Jamie for the work you have done over the past few days. Believe me when I tell you that it will prove invaluable in seeing that some very bad people will be brought to justice, and the black market business be closed down for ever.

"My family has been targeted by these people on a number of occasions because of my involvement, so please, do not tell anyone, anyone at all of the work you have been doing for me. Remember, it is just filing nothing else," Ben tells them.

"We understand, Mr Spencer," they both reply with a degree of apprehension in their voices.

"And we hope all your family are well when you get home," Sarah adds.

Just then, there is a knock on the door.

"Mr Spencer, Ted Summers, Commander Spratt's' driver."

"Ted can you wait just a moment please, perhaps you put my bag in the car?"

"Very good, sir," says Constable Summers.

Ben phones home and informs Daniel he will be home around noon, then says a final farewell to Sarah, kissing her on the cheek, and Jamie with a firm handshake, and leaves the room with the final list for the commander along with his briefcase.

Daniel replaces the receiver as Margaret arrives home from Carswell.

"Margaret, I have just spoken with Ben, he is returning home immediately, and should be here just after noon."

"Well that is good news, I thought he might decide to come home, given what has happened with Polly and everything else these past few hours. I have some information about the offices in Carswell, or rather what was the offices. They are moving to some warehouse the other side of town. The office controller, Phil Landers will call me when he has a telephone line."

"And I am going to update my logs before Ben arrives so that I do not omit any details. I shall be about half hour, Margaret, and then I will talk with the workmen."

Ben duly arrives at The Gables just before 1 o'clock after a journey which seemed overly long. He offers the driver tea and sandwiches while he surveys the damage accompanied by Margaret and Daniel. He is visibly shocked by the devastation to his home and garden, and struggled not to become emotional. They had all gone through hell over the past few weeks, but this last episode was the testing Ben's resolution to the absolute limit.

"My God, Daniel, I feel like hunting down those directly responsible for this and shooting them dead, I am totally devastated by all this, totally devastated."

Margaret was shocked and upset by Ben's reaction, she had never seen him so angry and sought to console him.

"Please do not upset yourself, Ben, we will bounce back and we will win," she says with conviction.

"Yes, you're right, Margaret, forgive me I just did not realise how bad the devastation would be. We have a lot to do here and, I imagine at the office as well."

Mr Spencer I'll get off back to London, thanks for the tea and sandwiches," Ben's driver calls.

"I'll see you out, Ted, and thank you for the ride, would you be good enough to give this file to the Commander and thank him for his help?" says Ben, as he sees Ted Summers to the door and on his way.

"Very good, Mr Spencer, goodbye."

"Margaret, I wonder if we might have some lunch and sit down and decide on our plan of action?" Margaret makes some tea and sandwiches and they sit in the parlour to go over the events of the last few hours and what needs to be done.

"I have a detailed log of the events which we can look at to Ben, which is yours to refer to at any time. The main priority at the moment is in securing the back of the house from any further intrusion, although I do not believe you will be receiving any unwelcome visitors short term, Ben."

"Yes. I think you may be right, Daniel, glancing at your notes I see you shot two of them, whilst the third had to have treatment for a damaged nose! Any further intrusion would be mad to for anyone to consider. Did you pass on any of these details that the men gave you about who they were working for and where they were to take Polly?"

"It seemed better not to mention any details before running things past you. The Inspector will be coming back again to talk to Polly, so if you wish me to enlighten him then, I can do that."

"I don't think it will be of any benefit to anyone at the moment, Daniel, but I will mention it to the Commander and ask for his advice."

The telephone rings and Ben goes to the study to answer.

"Ben, it's Phil Landers, my God just what the hell is going on here? I understand that we both received a package yesterday, I trust your damage is not too bad?"

"It's pretty bad, Phil, fortunately my colleague who is staying with us, recognised the noise from the package and took it into the garden before it exploded. The back of the house is badly damaged, conservatory will have to be demolished and I will need another garage, the garden itself looks like a bomb crater, and the wall next to the garden has collapsed."

"I believe Margaret spoke with Rupert and Jamie this morning, so you will know that we are being moved to a warehouse in Carswell Road. We should be operational by the end of the week. I will let you know more as I have it, then we can meet and discuss how we move forward. This is a bad business, Ben, I had absolutely no idea that your work was upsetting so many villains or that they would react so violently toward you and the office. How is Maureen by the way, I was meaning to go along and see her before this happened?" Phil says.

"First of all, Phil, Maureen injuries are healing, but the mental scars will take a while. She suffered a terrible beating with riding crops by the men trying to get information from her. Do try and call round, I'm sure she would appreciate your call. She is being cared for by Peter Forsyth, my colleague from London who was staying at my house. They formed an attachment through me and Peter wanted to stay with her until she has recovered. I will give you an update regarding my activities when we can get back together in the new site, I think that will be better than just giving you bits and pieces, and Margaret and I have to go and collect Polly from the hospital this afternoon."

"What has happened to Polly, Ben?" Phil asks with concern.

Ben realised that no one at the office would know of events at Ben's house, and gives Phil a brief description of what occurred last night, and but for Daniel's quick thinking he would surely have lost his daughter.

"My God, Ben, it's never ending isn't it? How is Polly?"

"I believe she has no really serious physical injuries, Phil, but I do fear for her mental state after this last attempt. This time we came very close to losing her forever."

"You must do what you have to, Ben, I will let you know when we are operating from our new offices again, meantime good luck with the repairs."

Ben goes back to the rear of the house to be told by the builder that the conservatory will have to be demolished as soon as possible. Ben asks him to go ahead and clear the debris from the wall so that they can assess what has to be done. Daniel meanwhile suggests some sort of digger may be an idea to flatten the rear area ready for replanting and laying a new lawn. The builder agrees this would be the best way to clear the area once the conservatory has been demolished. And so, leaving Daniel with the tradesmen and after asking Betty to collect the children from school, Margaret and Ben leave to collect Polly from hospital.

The doctor had just finished examining Polly when Ben and Margaret arrive.

"How is she, Doctor? We can take her home I trust?" Margaret asks anxiously.

"You can take her home, Mrs Spencer, but she is still pretty frail. Her injuries are quite extensive and will have to be dressed regularly. I suggest we have a nurse call on you to arrange this. She has become rather subdued while being here; I believe she may have suffered some delayed shock. While I am not sure exactly what may have happened, your daughter will need a lot of care and attention before is able to get back to her normal everyday life. We have tried to talk with her, but she has been reluctant to say anything about what happened to her. She simply mentioned Daniel, and how he saved her life. Anyway, I will let you go now, please call me if I can help in any way at all, bye Polly," says the doctor as he leaves Ben and Margaret with their daughter.

They are both shocked by the sight of Polly. She is very pale with dark rings under her eyes as though she has not slept, and says very little at first. Mrs Spencer has bought her clothes and notices the lacerations as Polly removes her hospital gown. Whilst some are covered, there are others across her chest and tummy which have been left to heal naturally. Her legs too have been mostly left uncovered and are severely lacerated from being dragged over the rubble from the garden wall. She has the top of her right arm covered and the top of her right thigh. These must have been badly torn when she was dragged by her hair over the rubble.

"Come along, my dear Polly, let's get you dressed and take you home," Mrs Spencer says fighting back the tears.

"Mummy is right, Polly, it will be good to get you home, the children have all missed you and—"

"Is Daniel there, Daniel will be there won't he, Daddy?" Polly asks with panic in her voice.

"Yes Daniel will be there, Polly, for quite some time I assure you."

"You promise, Daddy, Daniel will always be there to look after me won't he, you promise, he saved my life you know, I heard those men tell him they were going to take me to London and leave me in a warehouse. He made them tell him and that's what they said.

"He shot two of them that were trying to take me away, I was covered in blood from one of them and they were screaming. Daddy I may never have seen you again if Daniel hadn't been there," she says as she grabs Ben and sobs uncontrollably, releasing her fear and anger from last night's events. It is good for her to cry and release some of the emotions she had been holding onto since the terrible ordeal she had suffered. She finishes dressing and walks slowly out of the hospital, holding on tightly to Ben and Margaret.

"Will you sit in the back with me, Mummy, please?"

"Of course I will, Polly, come along," she replies as they get into the car and head off back home.

Polly holds on tightly to her mother for the journey home and stares straight ahead. Mrs Spencer tells her how they have missed her and will take good care of her until she is better.

"Daniel will be able to take care of me won't he, Mummy?" she suddenly says with a degree of panic again in her voice.

"My dearest Polly, Daniel is now our guest for as long as you wish, he knows that and accepts it. There is a lot of work to be done, and keeping everyone safe is the most important thing for all of us. Daniel is very much part of keeping the family safe, especially you, Polly," Mrs Spencer adds with reassurance and for Polly's benefit.

"Do you think Daniel might take me for a walk when we get home, Daddy, I would love to go for a walk?"

"We can ask Daniel when we get home, Polly, and after Maisy, Daisy and George have said hello, they have been worried about you, too."

The car turns into Crab Tree Lane, and the first thing that Polly notices is the car, still parked waiting to be towed away. She grabs Margaret's arm tightly and shouts, "Daddy, those men have come back again, quickly drive on up the lane before they see you."

"Polly, there is no one here from yesterday, the car has to be taken away by the Police who haven't got round to moving yet. Those men are all in jail, and will stay there for a very long time," Ben replies as he pulls up opposite the front door. Polly steps out of the car and goes into the house between Margaret and Ben, to be greeted by her brother and sisters.

"Polly, Polly we have missed you so much, are you feeling better?" Maisy asks.

"Did those horrible men hurt you, Polly, I hate them and hope that Daniel hurt them as well," George says angrily.

"Where is Daniel?"

Ben looks at her with some concern, then looks toward Margaret as he says, "I expect Daniel is outside with the work men, Polly, he will be in shortly."

"I have to go and see him to thank him for saving me, Daddy, I have to go really I do," Polly replies oblivious to what Ben has said.

Polly walks through to the parlour and outside to find Daniel, who is alongside the wall still moving rubble which is being stacked ready for removal by the builders.

"Daniel, Daniel, I knew you would be here, you saved my life yesterday, how can I ever thank you?" says Polly as she scrambles over the rubble and holds on tightly to him.

"My dear Polly, it's good to see you, how are you feeling now?" he asks, somewhat overwhelmed by Polly's reactions.

"Daniel, please come inside, I have to talk with you and Mummy and Daddy, it is very important," Polly asks, tugging Daniel towards the house.

"Yes, okay, Polly, let's go inside."

Polly takes Daniel into the parlour and asks him and her parents to please sit down as she has something to say to them.

"Mummy, Daddy, I want to tell you what happened to me yesterday and how my life was saved by Daniel, and what he did to those men. I have had time to go over what happened and I have to tell you, because it is very important that you know how much I appreciate what Daniel has done. Had he not fought with those three men to save me, I am sure they would have killed me. It is very difficult to know what to say to someone who did what Daniel did for me. One of the men, told me that I was going away forever as he tugged at my hair, and you know what happened to him, Daniel shot him. They were both saying horrible things to me as they dragged me along and were grabbing at my nightshirt. They said they were going to keep me for themselves Daddy, and they would have taken

248

me away if Daniel had not stopped them. So I need to know that he is going to stay for a while to help me recover, I have felt poorly since it happened, and scared that something else might happen. As long as I know you are here, Daniel, I will be alright," Polly ends by bursting into tears as she sits down on Ben's lap.

"Daniel will be with us for a while yet won't you, Daniel?"

"Most definitely, and you and I will have a long talk about this after supper Polly."

"Polly, can you help me with the supper, but have a word with Maisy, Daisy and George first."

Ben, meanwhile goes into the study to make his phone calls.

"Commander Spratt here."

"Commander, good evening it's Ben Spencer, did you get the file I sent you with your driver?"

"I did indeed, are there many more names do you think?"

"I would say that we have all but completed logging the names and addresses from the files, I hope to be able to arrange closure sometime next week."

"Good, all of the accused will have been formally charged by then and a suitable date for a trial will be next, though this will be a little while yet. The main point, Mr Spencer, is that you have cut the head off the serpent by closing those tunnels. We both know that the black market will still go on while we have rationing of goods, but it will not be organised on a national scale any longer," the commander adds.

"Absolutely, well I will leave you to it now Commander, perhaps I can speak with you again on Friday afternoon with an update?"

"Very good, Mr Spencer, bye for now."

Ben dials Beatrice Carrington's number and waits.

"Hello, Beatrice Carrington speaking."

"Beatrice, it's Ben. Did you get the office key from Sarah?"

"Yes I did, Ben, thank you, how is Polly?" Beatrice asks.

Ben relates to Beatrice how Polly has been since they collected her from hospital. He is concerned just how permanent her scars will be and asks Beatrice's advice.

"All you can do is give her all the care and love she needs, Ben. Your colleague Daniel is key to her recovery and should also be encouraged to give her any support she needs," suggests Beatrice.

"Daniel has become her crutch, without him I fear she would collapse, fortunately he has a wonderful personality and I am confident he will be good for her."

"You will keep me informed, Ben. Now regarding Operation Seeker, the Keepsake, arrests have all been made and the ringleaders have been remanded to stop them fleeing. I believe that there may be at least one more high-ranking civil servant involved and have informed the intelligence division of Scotland Yard of my suspicions. They are monitoring calls and following a number of suspects. Work is in place to seal the tunnels at New Haven, Whitehall will oversee direct to make this happen, we don't want some local council putting up barriers. Meanwhile army personnel are guarding the entrances which have been blocked with sandbags as a temporary measure. So any movement of illegal goods will now have to be local, and the police know of most of the sites that have been used. They will watch them and act accordingly. Everything that can be done is being done, so all that remains is for me to ask you to be extra vigilant Ben, your family has suffered enough, but I fear you may not have seen the last of these attacks."

"I will be, Beatrice, I promise, and I will keep you informed of any new developments, bye for now."

After supper, Daniel has a word with Ben saying he will talk with him later after he has spoken with Polly. He has been overwhelmed by what she has said and wants to reassure her that he will be there to take care of her for as long as necessary.

"Polly, do you want to have that chat, why don't we have a walk down the lane while it is still light?" he suggests.

Polly nods in agreement, and goes out of the front door followed by Daniel. Immediately they are outside, she takes his arm and holds on to him firmly.

"Thank you for those nice things you said about me, Polly, I feel a bit of a fraud, I only did what had to be done to keep you safe."

"I know that you saved me from those men, and I know what would have happened to me if they had got away. Only you and me know what happened, and I have relived it since it happened. I'm frightened Daniel, I don't think I will ever be able to go out again," Polly replies tearfully.

Daniel stops walking faces Polly and holds her to him saying:

"My dear Polly, you will get over this eventually I promise you that. You have had a number of terrible experiences recently and any adult would have suffered from such treatment. You are still young, but you have had to grow up fast in order to cope with what has happened. You have coped very well Polly and you will put all this behind you. And finally, I am here for you whenever you need me."

"I just feel very tired, but I am frightened to go to sleep in case something happens," Polly replies.

"Well nothing is going to happen, Polly, and we can arrange for your Doctor to give you something to help you sleep. Now come along we should be getting you back home."

On returning home, Polly asks Margaret if she would help her wash. It would be difficult to get into a bath, but she does need to wash. Ben asks the children to go upstairs to their playroom for a while, giving Daniel the opportunity to fill in details of the explosion and attempted abduction of Polly. The attempted abduction so soon after the explosion, concerns Ben, confirming that the men in charge of the racketeering were becoming increasingly desperate in their attempts to frighten him into submission. Had anyone been in the house, other than Daniel, they would surely have been killed. The criminals have no concern for loss of life in their efforts to prevent the authorities closing down their operations and Ben is key to the success. He has secured vital evidence and if they can stop him from giving the necessary evidence in court, then all his work will have been for nothing. Polly would surely have been held for ransom in exchange for his silence. Indeed, had they been successful in their last attempt to abduct her, Ben was sure he would not have seen his beloved daughter again. Although he has no military training, he knows how to use a weapon, and will not hesitate to use it should any of his family be put in any danger. The actions of Peter and lately Daniel will send a clear message to the criminals that Ben will protect his family with all means at his disposal, and if this means using force then so be it. He considers the good fortune of having Daniel in the house when the package was delivered, and his timely actions in saving Polly.

"It was indeed fortunate that you recognised that sound from the package Daniel, you saved the house and yourself."

"And your large Hawthorn hedge served as a natural barrier for the blast. We now need to secure the back of the house as soon as possible. Fortunately, the main part from the parlour door and the kitchen door are relatively secure, but do need to be checked, especially as some of the windows are damaged. For the future, can I suggest that any parcels that are addressed to you be placed in isolation by the Post Office?"

"That is a very good suggestion, Daniel, I will get onto that tomorrow. Now I believe you have made relevant notes of what has happened whilst you have been here?"

"Yes I have, force of habit from my work in interrogation making note of everything that occurs," Daniel replies handing over his notes.

"Did you actually get these men to give up names and where they were from?"

"Yes, I think they were a little surprised by my actions in shooting them, but sometimes Ben it really is the only reply to violence. I suppose my military upbringing played a part, but my overall responsibility was always to you and your family. You gave me a job to do and I carried it out as best I could. I was concerned that they would take Polly, and was sure that if they succeeded they would kill her, so I decided on drastic action, namely stopping them at all costs. In the short time I have been here you and Margaret have made me very welcome and I have enjoyed the company of your children. Polly and George particularly have become quite special and lately your daughter has made me realise just what a special young lady she is.

The events that she has endured over the last few weeks have taken their toll, and I will do what I can to help her get back some normality in her life."

"As I have already said, Daniel, we shall all be forever in your debt. Polly will lean on you for a while over what happened, of that I am sure. All I can ask is that you help her as much as you are able for me please."

"Whatever is needed to get her back to being a happy school girl again."

Margaret and Polly enter the parlour, Margaret asking if anyone would like some tea. Polly sits down next to Daniel as Margaret goes off to the kitchen.

"I hope you feel better for your wash, Polly?"

"Yes, Daddy, and I would like to go up to bed shortly, but would like to ask a favour of Daniel."

"Of course, what is it Polly?"

"May Daniel stay with me until I am asleep, I am sure that if he is there it will help me?"

"Would you mind, Daniel?"

"It will be my pleasure, Polly, anything to help."

Margaret returns with the tea and a milky drink for Polly, then goes upstairs to get the other children ready for bedtime. They all descend downstairs to say goodnight with George still asking Daniel for details of what happened.

"When I have a moment, George, we will sit down and I will explain, is that okay for you, only we are all busy trying to get your house back together at the moment."

"Okay, Daniel, but you will tell me about how you shot those nasty men that hurt Polly won't you?" George persists.

"You will find out soon, George, I promise," Daniel replies with a smile.

Polly finishes her drink and asks Daniel if he will go with her to her room. He escorts her to her room and settles down in the chair next to the window.

"Thank you for staying with me, Daniel, I know I will fall asleep easily with you by my side. What do you think would have happened to me if those men had got away, do you think you would have been able to find me?" she asks tearfully.

He moves closer to Polly and sits beside her holding her hand.

"Polly, listen to me, those men didn't take you away, that was never going to happen while I was there, so there really is no reason for you to think about what might have happened. You need to concentrate on getting better, spending time with your family, perhaps having some friends round later. The sooner you are able to get back to enjoying your life, Polly, the better you will feel, do you understand?" Daniel asks, concerned that Polly seems to be reliving the events over and over again.

Having to relate to a young a teenage girl is a new experience for him, so he is having to learn as he goes along. Polly has become very special to him and they have become close because of circumstances. However, he does not want her to become too dependent on him as that might prevent him from carrying out his duties effectively.

"Yes I understand, Daniel, but will you stay with me just for now please?"

"Of course, Polly," Daniel replies sitting back in his chair.

After about twenty minutes or so Polly goes off to sleep, but Daniel remains for another half hour or so, before leaving her room closing the door carefully behind him.

"How was she, Daniel?"

"Sound asleep, Margaret, but I am sure you understand it will be a while before she is back to herself again."

The night passes without any incidents and Polly sleeps through, obviously exhausted from her ordeal. The family are relieved and Daniel too is especially relieved that Polly has been able to have a good night's rest. His talk with her seems to have been effective for now. Ben travels into Carswell to get an update on the move to the new site. It will be operational by the end of the day, Thursday, so Ben decides to leave Phil to arrange the movement of the files that can be salvaged, and arrange an inventory to see what has been lost. He returns home and makes contact with Commander Spratt at Scotland Yard to give him precise details of the last attempt to abduct Polly, and the explosive devices used at his home and offices.

"I am going to arrange for some experts to come and look at both sites, Mr Spencer. They have had experience investigating explosives used in robberies in London and in following up on suspected I.R.A. activity. Perhaps you could ask you colleague to have a close look at your crater and see if he can see anything meanwhile. As an army man he will have had some experience with explosives, I'm sure. The team should be along later today; I was hoping to get them there sooner but they were working elsewhere. Their names are Captain Billy Radford and Sergeant Jack Davies, both are war veterans with knowledge of bomb making and disposal. If you could arrange for them to look at both sites please?"

"Certainly, Commander, I will get them to liaise with the local police, they will be along this morning to talk to my daughter."

"My apologies for not asking after her, how is she?" the commander asks.

"Getting better, but very slowly at the moment, her physical injuries should heal completely, but we are concerned about mental scars from this and the other ordeals she has been involved in."

"Yes indeed, we will do what we have to and see that those concerned are punished, Mr Spencer."

"Thank you, Commander, and I will look forward to receiving your colleagues later today."

The doorbell rings and Ben finds D.I. Wishart, Constable Parsons and W.P.C. Becky Garrett waiting.

"Good morning, Mr Spencer, I wonder if we might take those statements?"

"Of course, Inspector, please come inside, go into the study, I will go and get Daniel and Polly," Ben replies. He is somewhat apprehensive how Polly will react to questioning, but realises that the police will have to take her statement of events at some time.

"But, Daddy, I don't want to have to tell them what happened to me, it was horrible," Polly pleads.

"I know it will be difficult for you, Polly, but the police have a job to do so that these people can be caught and punished for what they did."

"Can Daniel stay with me?" Polly asks.

"I am sure that will be acceptable in these very special circumstances, now come along let's not keep the Inspector waiting," says Ben as he guides Polly, accompanied by Daniel to the study.

"Inspector, I wonder if you would mind if Daniel stayed instead of myself for the interview with Polly, she will feel more confident with him here?"

"Yes of course, Mr Spencer, hello, Polly, Mr Bottomley, shall we begin? We will not keep you any longer than necessary and Polly, Becky will ask you some questions if you would prefer."

The W.P.C. begins the questioning so that the Inspector might talk with Daniel alone.

"Hello again, Polly, I know this must be very painful for you, but we do want to catch these villains so any help you can give us will be good," the W.P.C. begins.

Daniel had already suggested to Polly not to mention the men's names or where they were from. The information would be used by Scotland Yard as part of their ongoing investigation.

Polly describes how she was dragged over the rubble, and how she was badly injured especially as she only had on a nightshirt which was quickly torn to shreds. She says the man who grabbed her hair was mumbling something, but she couldn't understand what he was saying.

"I was terrified what they would do to me, Becky. I had been taken away before, but these men were far worse, they really wanted to hurt me.

The bruising and cuts I have will take forever to heal. If Daniel hadn't shot two of them they would have taken me away. I am certain that Daniel saved me from being killed and I will never forget what he did for me," she ends, with a tear in her eye, struggling to remain calm.

"Okay, Polly, that will be fine, I suggest you go and join your Daddy now while I have a word with Daniel, we won't be too long now," the inspector says.

"How is the clearing up progressing, Mr Bottomley, it must be a big job all round?"

"Yes indeed, Inspector, it will take a while, the conservatory will have to be demolished and the adjacent wall completely rebuilt. As for the garden, what is left of it will have to be replanted etc., but they are a resilient family so I'm sure they will cope."

"Yes I'm sure, now tell me you were able to shoot two of the men to stop them abducting Polly and I understand that the third man has had to have his nose reset after you hit him?"

"Yes I was able to stop one by shooting him in the leg, the one who was dragging her into the car I shot in the neck with the intention of firing a fatal blow. These were desperate men, Inspector, and the situation called for desperate measures, I'm sure you understand."

"Indeed, Mr Bottomley, but how could you see what you were firing at in the darkness?"

"Fortunately, the floodlight at that end of the house was still working, so the whole area was lit."

"And you also shot out the tyres to prevent them driving away anyway?"

"Yes, I was making sure that whatever happened, they would not be able to take Polly."

"And were you able to determine who these men were at all?"

"I can only guess that they were associates of those seeking to disrupt Ben's operations against the black market racketeers. As he has become more successful in closing down their operations, so they are becoming more desperate. Ben may be able to offer you more on that, although I know that he is working with officials from Whitehall and with Scotland Yard.

"In fact, two explosives experts are arriving this afternoon to survey the damage at both sites, and he will be asking you if you would mind escorting them to the office in Carswell."

"Well thank you, Mr Bottomley, you have been most helpful, and can I just say that if I am ever in a tight spot, I may just call on your services," The Inspector says with a smile.

"Anytime, Inspector, now let me fetch Ben so that he can talk to you about the arrival of the explosive experts, bye for now," Daniel replies as he leaves the study for the parlour.

Ben tells the Inspector of the pending arrival of the bomb disposal experts, and suggests they meet at Carswell station.

"I will be in my office for the rest of the day, Mr Spencer, so perhaps you will call me when they have completed their investigations here?"

"Yes, Inspector, now let me see you out."

Polly is waiting for Daniel, and asks him what happened with his interview.

"I did as you asked, Daniel, will I have to tell anyone else about what happened to me?"

She obviously did not enjoy having to relive the events of the night before, and holds on to Daniel for reassurance.

"No you will not have to talk about your ordeal with anyone else, Polly, I promise."

Captain Radford and Sergeant Davies arrive about 2 o'clock and go outside to look around.

"It's good that you have left the crater untouched, Daniel, have you managed to salvage anything at all from the site?" Captain Radford asks.

"I carried out a quick inspection immediately afterwards, and kept some bits for you to look at."

"That is first class, Daniel, first class let's have a look, yes gelignite with a timer, fairly crude but effective in a confined area. Similar devices have been used by gangs in robberies around London," Captain Radford comments.

"Sergeant, could you have a closer look around to see if there are any more parts that can be found?" the captain asks.

"Yes, sir," replies Sergeant Davies.

"Do you think you will be able to identify those responsible, Captain, it would be a bonus if we could tie in these men with some of those already held in custody?" Ben asks.

"It may be possible sir, since there are so few people who have the expertise and contacts to get hold of the explosive," the captain replies.

Does the name Jack Pearson mean anything to you, Captain?" Ben asks.

"Jack Pearson, yes it does, he is a former commando and an expert with explosives, why do you ask."

"His name was offered by one of the men who attempted to take Polly," Daniel answers.

"You have just made my job a bit easier, Daniel, and taken a bomb maker off the streets. We have known of Pearson for some time, but have never been able to pin him down. There has never been anyone who would be prepared to give evidence against him. This may be because no one really knew it was Jack Pearson. We are talking mainly about bank robberies, so there were never any witnesses to his safe cracking exploits, other than his accomplices. Hopefully, the men you have in custody may be able to shed some light on his whereabouts," Captain Radford concludes.

"Well the men you need to talk with are in police custody, and I am sure that D.I. Wishart will be happy to oblige, Captain," says Ben.

CHAPTER 29

(Operation Seeker:
Charges detail & family setbacks.)

Overwhelming evidence has now been gathered which links a number of civil servants with the operation run from the tunnels in New Haven. The tunnels will be bricked up securely within the next few weeks, so cutting off the distribution centre point for that black market operation.

Miles McKenzie and Giles Williamson, who both work in Whitehall have been accused of illegal black market activities, using their positions to seek information about goods shipments and arranging for those goods to be rerouted on to the black market. Both men worked in The Food Ministry during the war years, and have been ruthless in their pursuit of profit, and though suspected had never been charged. Toby North and John Devonish were involved in the manufacture of arms and equipment for the war effort. They had established a network of illegal operations involving misuse of equipment for government use, namely raw materials. They were also known to be importing electrical goods and clothing items for illegal distribution, and were also known to be distributing stolen ration books. Both men employed violence toward anyone who interfered with their activities. These four men were at the forefront of the operation from the New Haven tunnels, and had divided the movement of goods via the areas of London identified in the files from the cottage in Rye.

When the goods in the tunnels had finally been detailed the quantities were staggering.

There were some 100 cases of sugar, 100 boxes of jams, 100 boxes of treacle, 500 cases of tea, 300 boxes of biscuits, 150 boxes of assorted sweets, 100 cases of canned fruit, 500 cases of cooking oils, 500 cases of lard, and 400 cases of Alcohol. Also stored in the tunnels was about 2000 gallons of petrol, some 100 boxes of arms such as pistols and automatic rifles with 1000s of rounds of ammunition and spare parts for trucks and motor vehicles. There was also a large quantity of cigarettes, although cigarettes were not rationed, but were in short supply.

There were a number of men working in the tunnels administering the movement of the illegal goods. They were all apprehended and pointed the finger at McKenzie and Williamson as the men running the operation. There was also obvious collusion inside Whitehall to consider, which Ben hoped would be uncovered by Beatrice Carrington. These arrests might take some time to carry out because securing evidence against them would be more difficult.

However, once concrete evidence was secured, and this could happen with those already in custody looking to get some sort of deals in exchange for information, those concerned could be arrested and charged. In the meantime, there were a number of arrests made in Coventry and Birmingham as a result of the attacks on the Spencer family. Conspiracy to carry out explosions was the most serious offence carried out at the Spencer's home and the C.O.I. offices, and this charge was laid at the foot of McKenzie and Williamson by the three men who were instructed to send the explosive devices. These same men were also accused of breaking into the Spencer's home and attempting to abduct Polly Spencer. George Bacchus and Jack Pearson were arrested for stealing the gelignite and compiling the explosive devices.

Montagu Galbraith was charged with a catalogue of offences as a result of what had happened at the Spencer's home, and with collusion in a number of attempts to abduct Polly, including: attempted murder, concerning the shots fired at Peter Forsyth during an attempted robbery and abduction at the Spencer's home, and arson concerning the fire at the Spencer's home. Three charges of kidnapping of Polly with intent to endanger her life and inflict physical harm. Two charges of attempted kidnapping of Polly with intent to endanger her life and inflict physical harm. One charge of grievous bodily harm with intent to endanger life, for the attack on Maureen Potter in her home and finally, attempted robbery at the Spencer's house.

Whilst he may not have been involved directly in all of these activities, by listing them against him it was hoped that Galbraith would be forthcoming with information about the main culprits. Any information obtained this way would strengthen the prosecution's case against the main perpetrators, and secure long prison sentences for all those involved. Galbraith will be aware of this and his counsel will recommend that he cooperates with the Crown. He is only part of the operation; it is the men at the top that the Crown want to put away and if Galbraith is cooperative it can only be beneficial to his case. Galbraith's men will also be keen to implicate him, if only to save their own necks! He has been responsible for some serious crimes against the Spencer family, not least Polly and faces a long prison sentence, so he will be wanting to cooperate fully with the court.

Whilst the prosecution's case will be complex, the wealth of evidence secured by Ben and his colleagues is overwhelming. There will be documentation of the smuggling and black market operation secured from the cottage of Giles Williamson, and the evidence from those that have been working the operation both from the tunnels and from the clearly defined areas of London. These charges would form the prosecution's case against the defendants when the case is presented at The Central Criminal Court. All that remains to be done is secure the date for the court case and hope that the Spencer family can remain safe in the meantime. While the court case is being prepared, Ben takes stock of his own situation. He has to have a large part of his house and grounds rebuilt after the explosion, he has to consider his position at The C.O.I. once proceedings have been completed, and he needs to also consider Daniel's position. The idea of him leaving the household in the short term is unthinkable, both because of his expertise in handling dangerous situations and because of his relationship with Polly.

Ben realises that Polly will need his reassuring presence for some time yet. This is why Ben decides to speak with Margaret as soon as possible about what should be done.

"What is it, Ben?" Margaret asks as Ben beckons her into the study.

"I think we need to sit down and assess what has gone on over the last few weeks, Margaret, and what we need to do to ensure that we are safe and secure up to and after the trials of these men. They have tried many times to harm us, and I hesitate to say that they may do so again before they have finished."

"Do you really think so, Ben?"

"Yes I do and that is why I have some suggestions that I would like you to consider with me. Firstly, I think it only reasonable that we give Daniel some time off, if only to see if his flat is okay and call in to his office to settle any business that he may have outstanding. His superiors have assured me that they would only wish to review his duties once the Crown had successfully prosecuted those responsible and the case was concluded. So I am going to put the following suggestions to Daniel for his consideration. I suggest that he spends a few days back in London to address any issues that may have arisen whilst he has been with us.

"But, Ben, how is that going to affect Polly, she will be devastated and I am not sure if that will be good for her at all," Margaret replies in earnest.

"I agree with you, Margaret, and that is why I am going to suggest that Polly go with him."

"Well if Daniel is in agreement, I think that is a wonderful idea, Ben, but what about our security while he is away?"

"I have thought about that, too, and I am going to suggest that Conrad Wilberforce spend a few days with us in the meantime."

"Well let's ask Daniel what he thinks about it before we mention it to Polly."

Ben calls in Daniel and puts his suggestions to him and asks his advice regarding Conrad.

"I must admit I was hoping to be able to go home for a few days, but with so much happening, it had completely slipped my mind. It could be just what Polly needs, Ben, a few days away from the house where so many things have happened to her and all of you. For me, I would be delighted to give her some time in London, I take it you have not asked her yet?"

"Not yet, Daniel, we wanted to see what you thought about the idea first."

"Well I would be very happy to give her a break, and to contact Conrad on your behalf to arrange when he can come along in my place."

Margaret calls Polly into the study where she finds Ben and Daniel. She leaves them to attend to the workmen, telling Ben that they can talk later.

"Polly, Mummy and I have been discussing the possibility of Daniel returning to London for a while, he has–"

"But, Daniel, who is going to take care of me, I can't bear to think of you not being here to take care of me," says Polly tearfully.

"My dear Polly, Daniel is happy for you to accompany him so he will still be able to take care of you."

"Really, Daniel, can I come and stay with you?" Polly asks excited about the possibility of being with Daniel in London.

262

"It will be my pleasure, Polly, I am sure you will enjoy the trip."

"Okay, well perhaps you can contact Conrad for me Daniel, and see when he might be available?"

"I will do that as soon as we have organised the workmen Ben, we really need to get the back of the house more secure as soon as possible."

And with that, Daniel and Ben go to the rear of the house to talk over a programme of work to ensure that the repairs and any rebuilding is done as quickly as possible. Both men are concerned with the poor security at the rear of the house, caused by the explosion and the fire. But before any work is carried out, Ben decides to call on a building surveyor to check the stability of the house and its' foundations. He is expected to call today so that any delays to the building work will be minimal. He talks with the workmen before he calls in to the new temporary offices, while Daniel goes off to make a phone call to Conrad. He is delighted to be able to help, and welcomes the opportunity of some work in the field.

"Thank you and Ben for asking me, Daniel, I will be delighted to cover for you," says Conrad.

"How soon can you come along, Conrad?"

"I do have some free time due to me, I can book that today, and be with you around lunchtime tomorrow, how would that fit in with your arrangements?"

Absolutely fine, Conrad, I will make the arrangements with the Spencers, and talk with you when you arrive, see you tomorrow."

Daniel tells Ben and Margaret of Conrad's arrival tomorrow, and goes off to tell Polly and the children about the new arrangements.

"But, Daniel, I won't have anyone to play with me if you go away, so why can't I come along with you and Polly?" George asks.

"Polly and I will only be gone a few days, George, your sister needs to have some time away to help her recover from what has happened. You must be brave for her, George, and Maisy and Daisy as well, will you do that for her?"

"Well okay, Daniel, we understand and we want to help Poll as much as we can to help her feel better," Maisy replies.

Conrad arrives at the Spencer's house around lunchtime on Saturday and is given a warm welcome by everyone, and is questioned about who he is and what he has done by George!

The family enjoy a lunch together, then the three men go into the study.

"Thank you again for helping the family Conrad, especially as I understand, from Daniel, that you are using your own time for this."

"It's a pleasure, Ben, I look forward to the change of scenery, and I have a feeling young George is going to keep me busy!"

"Yes, he looks forward to another male in the house, especially if I am away."

"I will be in London for about five days I guess, this should give me ample time to settle any business at work, and allow Polly to rest and relax," Daniel comments.

"Take what time you need, Daniel, I am only too pleased to be of assistance to you and Ben."

"We very much appreciate your help at short notice, Conrad. There has been a catalogue of incidents over the last few weeks, directed at my family, designed to scare me off from my work. Polly has been specifically targeted on a number of occasions, and but for the heroic actions of Peter Forsyth and latterly Daniel, I believe we would have lost her. The house has been subjected to an arson attack and on Tuesday was severely damaged by an explosion. So please be aware of the environment that you are stepping into. You are most welcome, I just wanted you to be aware of what you may become involved in while you are with us."

It is agreed that Daniel and Polly will travel to London on Sunday, so Conrad will bunk down with Daniel for the one night. Conrad enjoys the rest of the day getting to know the children, and makes some notes regarding what has to be done to make the house secure whilst the building work is carried out. He realises just how vulnerable the house will be with workmen leaving the site unattended and doors being left open, plus the garden being exposed having no wall. He mentions his concerns with Ben, and it is decided that the erection of a new wall will be a priority. In the meantime, some sort of temporary barrier will be erected to close off the garden from the lane.

This is seen as an absolute priority by Ben, Daniel and Conrad. The building surveyor's immediate thoughts are that the main structure of the house is sound, there are no cracks in the brickwork or any of the inside walls. This is a relief for Ben and Margaret, who can now arrange for the conservatory to be removed and replaced as soon as possible, likewise the garage.

Daniel and Polly leave early Sunday morning to get their train for London. This is quite an adventure for Polly, since she has never been to the capital before. It has been agreed that she will stay with Daniel for three days or so returning home on Thursday. This should give her time to recuperate from her recent ordeals. After an uneventful journey, they arrive at London's Euston station at around 1 o'clock and catch a tube for Kensington, eventually reaching Daniel's flat around 2 o'clock. Daniel shows Polly to her room and leaves her to unpack.

The house does seem rather empty without Polly, and it is obvious that the children are missing her organising their day. But, for Sunday at least, they have a new man in the house who needs to be investigated! Conrad has never known a large family atmosphere, he being an only child, so he is enjoying the experience of having children around him. He is a very organised person and finds them jobs to do which keep them occupied and there is certainly plenty of jobs to be done with the house in so much turmoil because of recent events. The children obviously enjoy Conrad's organisation of their day and carry out the tasks he gives them enthusiastically. After supper, George asks him to look at some of his toys damaged and broken from the damage to the garage, hoping he will be able to fix them.

"I will do my best for you, George, let me talk to the tradesmen tomorrow to see if they can help with some bits of timber."

"Will you be able to mend them for me Conrad? I hope you will," George enquires.

"We will do our best, George, now I think your Mummy will want you to start getting ready for bedtime, I believe you have school tomorrow?"

Margaret takes the children to school by car Monday morning, so that she can travel into Carswell afterwards to go shopping. It has been sometime since she has been able to browse around the shops, so parks her car in Spire Walk off the main road. She has told Ben and Conrad that she will be a while, and she drops Ben off at his office on the edge of town. She enjoys being able to have a leisurely look around, although with so many shortages, there is not a great deal to look at. However, she purchases some buns from the bakery and some sausages from the butcher's shop. She also gets some flowers to cheer up the chaos currently surrounding her home. She strolls back to the car, not paying any attention to the large saloon parked close by. She is just about to get into her car when the man approaches her.

"I wonder can you tell me where the Council offices are? It's a bit confusing with all the rubble in the High Street," the man asks.

Margaret is about to direct him and doesn't notice the other man getting from the car. As she turns her back to show him the directions, she is suddenly grabbed by the two men who push her towards the large black saloon. They are joined by a third man, and Margaret is easily overpowered and bundled into the car. She has dropped her shopping in the struggle as well as her car keys. It all happens so quickly that she has not let out any screams and suddenly she is on the floor and the car is moving off out of town. She struggles violently until one of the men covers her mouth with a cloth containing chloroform or something similar, and she passes out.

When she finally wakes from being drugged, she is strapped to a bench, her arms and legs wide apart, tied to the ends of the bench. Apart from feeling very vulnerable in this position, her legs and arms soon begin to ache from being extended. She is seated in the middle of an old warehouse, dark and damp and at least one level from the ground floor. There is nothing in the large room, save for a door in the corner leading to a smaller room. After what seems a long time, four men enter the room.

"Now then, Mrs Spencer, your husband is going to pay dearly for his meddling, he is costing my business a lot of money. If he doesn't pay, you will suffer lady," she is told.

"My husband will not pay you anything."

One of the men produces a cane and hits Margaret several times across her legs and chest.

She screams with pain as the man goes on.

"Don't interrupt, lady, your husband will pay, if he does not, he will never see you again do you understand?"

"But first we need to encourage you to persuade your husband how serious we are," he says.

With that two of the men grab Margaret, and take her into the room in the corner and close the door behind them. Margaret returns after about half an hour. She has bruising on her shoulders, red marks on both her wrists and additional bruising on her thighs. She has been violently sexually assaulted.

"Now, Mrs Spencer, we are going to call up your husband shortly, and you will tell him what has happened to you, tell him to pay the ransom and not to give any evidence at the trial, do you understand?" the man says.

Conrad has been busy with the workmen and doesn't notice the time. It is only when one of the workman mentions lunch that he checks his watch and realises that Margaret has been gone over three hours. He immediately phones Ben with his concerns.

"I will contact the police to see if they can locate my car, Conrad, please stay by the phone if you wouldn't mind and I will call when I hear anything."

"I will wait on your call, Ben, if Margaret should turn up meanwhile, I will call you, bye."

Ben calls back after about fifteen minutes and tells Conrad that his car has been found, unlocked in a side street with groceries scattered around the roadway.

"Margaret has obviously been taken, Conrad, I am coming home so that I am available should the police find out anything. I will be with you shortly."

Ben arrives home and asks for any news, but nothing has happened since he last spoke with Conrad. There is really nothing they can do until they hear some news either from the police or from the men who have taken Margaret. He must contact Daniel, but decides to leave it for a little while in case he receives any news. He does, however contact Peter Forsyth.

"I am so sorry, Ben, what can I do to help?"

"Can I call you when I have some details, Peter, at the moment all I can do is wait by the phone?"

And with that Ben replaces the receiver and waits for news of his beloved Margaret. After about half hour, the police contact Ben to tell him that they have a witness who saw Margaret talking to two men in Spire Walk, and then being forced into a large black saloon. They have also been told by another passer-by that a similar car was seen travelling west. It could be travelling to Coventry or Birmingham, but they have no notion of exactly where. Ben thanks them for the news and replaces the receiver. A moment later, the phone rings again.

"Mr Spencer, we have your wife," a voice says at the other end of the line.

"If you harm her, I swear I will kill you," Ben responds angrily.

"Shut your mouth, Spencer and listen, I want 25,000 pounds from you if you want to see her again, and your word that you will not give evidence at any trials," the man says.

"I will not give you any assurances, now let me speak with my wife," Ben demands.

"Ben, it's Margaret, do not give in to them," she pleads tearfully.

"Margaret are you alright, have they harmed you?"

"That will be all for now, Spencer, think over our demands, we will call you again so stay close to the phone."

"I told you he would not give in to your demands," Margaret says to the man who contacted Ben.

"That is too bad for you, lady, you'll wish he had."

And with that he and one of his accomplices drag her into the room in the corner, closing the door behind them.

At 5 o'clock after no more news has been received, Ben calls Daniel and tells him that Margaret has been taken. Daniel is devastated and Polly becomes hysterical.

"Daddy, Daddy, you must find her you must, I will get Daniel to bring me home straight away."

"It might be better if you stay where you are overnight and come home with Daniel in the morning, let me speak with Daniel again, Polly."

Ben suggests that he brings Polly home tomorrow, they can arrange whatever time off he may need when he is back.

"I will be with you until Margaret is returned, Ben, and have no fear we will find her."

The men return with Margaret and tie her down to the bench. She is covered in even more bruising and dirt from being held down on the floor. Her hair is matted with grease and grime, and her dress is torn and she is also severely dehydrated from screaming.

"We will be back later after we have spoken again with Mr Spencer. Let's hope he sees some sense next time for your sake," she is told.

At 9 o'clock that evening, Ben is contacted again by the men asking him if he has changed his mind about their demands.

"What exactly is it that you want from me?" Ben asks looking to buy some time.

"I have told you what we want, Spencer, have you given our demands serious thought?" the man replies angrily.

"You must appreciate that it will take some time to raise the money even if I agree to your demands?"

"Mr Spencer, if you want to see your wife again you will get the money first thing in the morning. I will call you again at 10.00 a.m., goodnight," the man concludes.

The man who spoke with Ben approaches Margaret.

"It seems that we have to be a bit more convincing, Mrs Spencer, to help your husband make up his mind. When we are done you will speak to him and convince him to give in to our demands. If he refuses we will keep on until he does, do you understand? Okay, you know what to do with her?" he says as the three men grab Margaret, kicking and screaming, and carry her into the room in the corner, closing the door to shut out her screams.

After about an hour, they emerge from the room and drag Margaret to the bench and tie her as before. She is extremely distressed having been continuously violently assaulted by the men. She is dressed only in her underwear, her dress in shreds, her body dirty and covered in bruises, especially her back and buttocks. She begs for some water but her pleas are ignored.

"We will return in the morning, I hope your husband has made up his mind about you by then," the man in charge says as they leave her in the darkening damp warehouse.

She is cold from sweating, trying to fight off the men who were assaulting her. Her injuries are becoming severe from contact with a concrete floor and from being tied up repeatedly. As the time passes she begins to hear noises squeaks and can make out rats as they run across the floor. She screams, hoping to frighten them off, but as the night progresses they become bolder, attracted by the scent from her open wounds. Despite her efforts, she is bitten several times and becomes hysterical as she feels the rats running over her body. Eventually dawn arrives and the rats disperse leaving Margaret to examine her wounds.

She has been bitten a dozen times at least and the bites have become swollen and painful. Her main concern is being dehydrated, although her injuries are now becoming a real problem. Around 9 o'clock the men return.

"Well, you look a bit of a mess, but here you are, I've bought you some water," the man says, and pours water over Margaret from a jug. The water is freezing cold on her body, but at least she manages to swallow some.

The next morning, Ben decides he must call Margaret's family, her sister Pauline and her brother John. They need to know what is happening. They are both distraught when Ben tells them what has been happening and they ask him to call as soon as he has any news at all. Meanwhile he waits for the call from Margaret's abductors knowing that they will expect some favourable news regarding their demands.

At precisely 10 o'clock the phone rings.

"Good morning, Mr Spencer, what do you have for me this morning?" The voice asks.

"I need to speak with my wife to be sure she is okay."

"You are not in any position to make demands," the man replies.

"Now listen to me, without me you have nothing, sir, now I will not agree to anything unless I can be sure that my wife is okay, so I ask again put my wife on the phone," Ben demands.

There is a long silence followed by a husky reply from a voice that Ben barely recognises.

"Ben, please help me, please help me," Margaret pleads.

"Margaret, is that you, what have they done to you?" shouts Ben.

"She is a bit croaky from the cold, Mr Spencer, now what have you done about our demands?"

"I say again, if you have harmed my wife at all, I will hunt you down and shoot you like a dog."

"You are obviously upset, Mr Spencer, I will call you again a little later and discuss how you can best get her back, but just remember your delays are not helping Mrs Spencer."

"For God's sake, I don't care anymore, there is nothing left that you can do to me, so do your worst and be damned," Margaret screams and bursts into tears.

"Take her away," the man says as the they drag her into the room in the corner again, closing the door behind them.

It is just 1 o'clock when Daniel and Polly arrive home, and Polly rushes into Ben's arms.

"Daddy, what has happened, have you heard any news about Mummy?"

"I'm afraid not, Polly, they have made certain demands which I cannot meet at present."

"Is there anything I can do, Ben?"

"I wonder would you collect the children from school Daniel, I need to be here in case the men who have Margaret call again?"

"You sit tight, Ben, it will be no trouble to collect the children, perhaps Polly can get some tea for you?"

"Of course, I will make some tea and see what we have for Maisy, Daisy and George."

Just then, the doorbell rings and Ben answers the door to Pauline, Margaret's sister.

"My dear, Ben, has there been any news about Margaret?" She asks holding on to him.

"Nothing yet, Pauline, just a repeat of their demands for a ransom and guarantee that I will not give evidence at the pending trial. Come into the study, Pauline, and let me introduce you to Daniel"

Meanwhile, Margaret's condition is causing some concern with one of the men. She now has severe lacerations over her back and buttocks from her treatment, has bruising to her shoulders, arms and legs and is bleeding from the rat bites. She has become delirious because of the brutal physical assaults and is mumbling incoherently.

"You need to ease up on her, Tommy, we can't afford to lose her yet," the man says.

"I expect Spencer to agree to our terms when I next make contact with him, I will leave it until about 8 o'clock to make him sweat. Get her some water meantime and cover her with something."

Daniel collects the children from school and tries hard to console them about Margaret's abduction. Polly, too, is very supportive and with her Aunty Pauline talks to the children to convince them that Mummy will be home soon. Supper is a very quiet affair, and Ben is beginning to fret on

271

why the men have not made contact. Then, just after 8 o'clock the phone rings.

"Mr Spencer, you have almost run out of time, what can you tell me? Will you meet my demands?"

"What have you done to my wife, is she hurt?"

"She is sleeping at the moment so I will not disturb her but will tell her that you asked after her, now about my demands," the man persists.

"Do you really believe that you can force me to refuse to give any evidence and that it will make any difference?"

"Okay, Mr Spencer, now listen carefully, I will call you again at 10.00 a.m. tomorrow. If you do not give me the guarantees that I have asked for I will kill your wife, do you understand?" the man replies and puts down the receiver.

Ben sits motionless and realises that he will have to give in to their demands or risk never seeing his beloved Margaret again. He calls in Daniel and Conrad and tells them of the demands and ultimate threat to Margaret's life.

"I really do believe I have no choice you know; I cannot risk Margaret's life."

"What do the police say, Ben, don't they have any leads at all?" Daniel asks.

"At this moment they cannot say whether Margaret is in Coventry, Birmingham or whether she has been taken to London."

Pauline insists on staying overnight, so a camp bed of sorts is erected in Polly's room for her. Conrad will sleep on the sofa in the parlour for the time being, although it is unlikely that anyone will sleep tonight any way. Pauline helps with the children at bedtime, and Polly stays until Pauline herself goes up. The three men sit in the parlour going over what they might be able to do to stall the men holding Margaret.

Then, suddenly the phone rings, Ben looks at his watch, it is 1.30 a.m.

"Hello, Ben Spencer speaking," he says rather apprehensively.

"Mr Spencer, it's Bill Holder in Birmingham, I'm sorry to call you so late, but I overheard something in the pub earlier which may be about your Mrs Spencer," Bill Holder replies.

"I don't follow, Bill, what are you trying to say?" Ben asks in anticipation.

"Well there has been a lot of talk about goods being seized and people being arrested in Brum and in London. There are a lot of unhappy blokes around at the moment because they don't have anything to sell. Anyway I heard this bloke talk about how things will get better because his boss was gonna fix things."

"What else did he say, Bill? Any names or places mentioned?"

"One of the blokes mentioned an old warehouse in Fazeley Street. There are a lot of old warehouses down there, ideal places to hide things."

"Do you know where these warehouses are, Bill? Could you take me there?"

"Yeah, I know where they are, and I could show you the way there, Mr Spencer, anything to help."

"Okay thanks, Bill, now listen to me, can you be in the Bull Ring for 8 o'clock tomorrow morning?"

"Yes I will be there, Mr Spencer, I will see you then, but please do not be late in case anyone asks me any questions about being there."

"We will be there in plenty of time, Bill, and thank you so much for this, you will not regret it I promise."

"I am pleased to help you, Mr Spencer, I don't want anything for that."

"As you wish, Bill, we will see you tomorrow at 8 o'clock, and thank you again."

Ben is almost in tears as he relays his conversation with Bill Holder to Daniel and Conrad.

"My God, Ben, that is wonderful news, we will need to start out around 6.30 a.m. or even earlier so as not to keep your colleague waiting, so I suggest that we try and get a few hours' sleep."

"I will certainly try, Daniel, and I'll set my alarm just to be sure."

None of them actually sleep at all, and Ben starts organising their departure around 5.30 a.m. It has been agreed that Conrad will stay at the house while Daniel travels with Ben to Birmingham. Ben goes upstairs to wake Pauline and tells her the news. She is obviously delighted and wishes Ben good luck and prays that they will find Margaret safe and well. Meanwhile, he prepares for the trip to Birmingham, taking his pistol from the study.

"I will leave you to organise the workmen for me, Conrad, and keep my home and family safe please until we return," he tells Conrad.

"I will keep everyone safe, Ben, go and find Margaret and bring her home safely," Conrad replies.

And with that Ben and Daniel set off for Birmingham in silence, knowing they have a chance of finding Margaret, albeit a slim one. They arrive at The Bull Ring about 7.45 a.m., and stay in the car until 8 o'clock when Ben walks towards The Woolpack pub, where he finds Bill Holder waiting.

"Morning, Bill, come with me the car is just round the corner," says Ben as he directs Bill to the car.

They quickly move off east and arrive in Fazeley Street after about half hour. There are warehouses mixed with some houses and corner shops. As they drive slowly down the street, they notice one car parked outside a warehouse which is obviously not in use.

Many of the ground floor windows are broken and there is no one about, which there would certainly be at this time of day if the warehouses were being used. Ben parks his car in a side road and leaving Bill in the car, the two men walk slowly back to the warehouse where the saloon is parked. After looking round to be sure they have not been seen, they look for a way in and see that the main gate is unlocked. They move inside, listening for any noise that might indicate that the building is being occupied, but hear nothing. They find the stairs and move up to the first floor which is also unoccupied. The four men have been at the warehouse since 8 o'clock, trying to get some sense out of Margaret, who by now is barely conscious and completely unaware of who she is or where she is. She has been attacked by rats again, and her lips are crusted from dehydration.

"Shouldn't we try and clean her up a bit, Tom, she looks a bloody mess?" one of the men asks.

"Listen, Bill, our job is to get the money and the deal from Spencer, I don't care what she looks like, she is not our problem, or won't be for much longer if Spencer does not see sense."

"Mrs Spencer, can you hear me, it won't be long now, your husband will either pay the ransom or you will pay with your life do you understand?"

There is no response from Margaret Spencer, just a garbled noise from her lips. She is in some state of semi consciousness and covered in filth from the warehouse floor.

"What time are you gonna phone Spencer, Tommy?" one of the men asks.

"I told him I would call him at 10 o'clock, so we'll give him the time that I promised. We ain't in any hurry, once he gives us the okay, I will tell him where to leave the money. The main thing is to get a written message from him about not giving any evidence. When we have that we can go and get paid for the job."

Just then there is a clatter behind them as Daniel and Ben burst into the room.

"Stay where you are all of you," shouts Ben.

The men turn around startled and three of them run toward the door, Daniel fires and hits one of them in the leg. The leader goes for his weapon, whilst turning to face Daniel and Ben, and trying to use Margaret as a shield. Daniel is too quick for him and fires his weapon twice hitting him in the arm and shoulder. The two uninjured men freeze and put their hands in the air, the leader screams with pain from his two wounds. Daniel rounds up the four men and puts them in the room in the corner after checking them for weapons. He reaches for the phone and contacts the police and ambulance service, telling them they will require two ambulances. He then restrains the two men with some rope from the office and places the injured men outside the door, telling them to remain on the floor until the police arrive. Ben meanwhile, dashes across the room and becomes distraught when he sees the state that Margaret is in.

"My good God what have they done to you, my dearest Margaret?" he cries.

Margaret opens her eyes and shows a flicker of recognition.

"Ben?" she replies, then collapses unconscious as Ben frantically tries to revive her as he unfastens her bonds.

He gently lays her back on the bench, and covers her with his jacket and the old blanket.

Thankfully, the ambulance arrives very quickly, and Margaret's wounds are tended to before moving her.

"Daniel, I am going to hospital with Margaret, I will get her transferred as soon as possible to Carswell, can I get you to finish up here, take Bill back and return home after you have talked with the police?"

"Of course, Ben, you go with Margaret, I will take care of things here."

The ambulance personnel spend some time with Margaret before they move her. They have to set up a drip because she is so badly dehydrated, and cover her with a hospital gown after treating the rat bites. Looking at the bruising to her legs, they realise that she will have to be thoroughly examined, having been subjected to a serious physical assault. Daniel, talks with the police at length, mentioning Chief Inspector Jamieson as being familiar with Ben's activities. The D.I. recognises Ben Spencer's name, and tells Daniel that he will inform the Chief Inspector of what has happened. He asks that he, Daniel, and Ben make a formal statement to their local police who will be contacted by Birmingham Constabulary. Daniel thanks him for his cooperation and leaves to collect Ben's car and Bill Holder. The two men with bullet wounds are relayed to the Accident and Emergency hospital.

Ben, meanwhile, travels with Margaret to Birmingham General Hospital so that she can be looked at as quickly as possible. Her wounds are so severe that they need to be tended before any decisions can be made regarding her general demeanour. She has been given oxygen so is now conscious. Ben talks to her and strokes her forehead, but receives little response. She just stares ahead and sobs uncontrollably. When they arrive at the hospital she is looked at by a senior registrar, who decides that she be given a sedative to calm her. Hopefully, after she has rested she may be coherent, and be able to assist the doctor's regarding what has happened to her. Daniel, meanwhile goes back to the car and drives Bill back to The Bull Ring.

"I heard the shots, guv'nor, is Ben okay?" he asks.

"Yes Ben is okay, a couple of the men who took Margaret are a bit worse for wear I'm afraid, and Margaret herself has been badly treated. Tell me, Bill, did you manage to get any names when your colleague mentioned this to you?" Daniel asks.

"Yes I did, they are Tom Cotter, Bill Willis, Ted Chaplin and Cedric Tubbs, they are all well known in the Birmingham area, I wrote them down for Mr Spencer. Cotter is a vicious sadistic character who has hurt a lot of people. Mr Spencer's successes have cost people in Birmingham, and have made him a lot of enemies. Cotter moved in when Galbraith was arrested, so everyone knew who he was especially round the canals and the Bull Ring pubs. It was his men that gave me a good hiding, so I'm really glad to have been able to help Mr Spencer with this one."

Daniel pulls up in Moor Street and Bill turns to get out of the car.

"Tell Mr Spencer I do hope that Mrs Spencer gets well soon, now I think I need a drink, good bye, sir," says Bill, as he walks towards the Woolpack Inn.

The sedative given to Margaret wears off after about an hour. She opens her eyes to see Ben at her side.

"Margaret, it's Ben, how do you feel, my dear?"

"Ben, where am I what happened to those men, are there any rats here, they came every night and kept biting me, Ben, please don't let them bite me anymore Ben!" Margaret replies with panic in her voice.

"You are in hospital, Margaret, you are safe now, nothing and no one can hurt you," says Ben fighting back his tears.

"Mr Spencer, I'm Dr Pattinson the hospital Senior Registrar, I would like to conduct a thorough examination of your wife to determine her injuries and how we might proceed. She has obviously been very badly treated, and we need to know exactly what has happened to her, but before I can do that I need a nurse to wash her."

"Very well, Doctor, I will leave you to it, and talk to you in a while I trust?"

"The nurse will let you know when we have finished," the doctor replies as he draws the curtain around Mrs Spencer's bed.

Ben meanwhile goes off to find a phone and call home. He is delighted to have rescued Margaret, but fears that her injuries both physical and mental, may be permanent. He prays that she will get better soon whilst realising the monumental task the family will have caring for her.

"Hello, Pauline, we've found her, she is in hospital and the doctor is looking at her now."

"Thank God for that, Ben, did you manage to get the men who took her?"

"Yes we did, Daniel shot two of them and held the other two until the police arrived. I am waiting on the Doctor's decision about Margaret, so will call you again as soon as I know something, can you put Polly on please?"

"Daddy, you found Mummy, I knew you and Daniel would find her."

"Yes, Daniel shot two of the villains so they will not be going anywhere except prison after they are discharged from hospital. Now I need you to take care of the children with your Aunty for me, and see that Conrad gets everything he needs can you do that for me, Polly, please?"

"Of course Daddy, but hurry home with Mummy please!" Polly answers.

"I will; 'bye for now, Polly."

"Mr Spencer, Dr Pattinson would like to speak with you please," the nurse tells Ben.

Ben knocks on the door and enters the office of Dr Pattinson Senior Hospital Registrar.

"Mr Spencer, please sit down, your wife has indeed suffered terrible injuries by these men, and has a number of rat bites as well. Most of the lacerations will heal over time, but there may be some internal injuries from the sexual assaults on her. She cannot or does not want to remember how many time these assaults took place, but from the external bruising to her legs and thighs, there were a number. Because of this she has been severely traumatised and will have to be carefully monitored over the coming weeks."

"Will she recover from all of her injuries, Doctor?" Ben asks.

"I hope so, Mr Spencer, 'though I have to say, I have no experience in treating any women that have been victims to such a brutal physical attack. You and your family will be her best therapy in this, you will need to be strong for her," the doctor replies.

"How soon can you move her to the local hospital, Doctor?"

"As soon as I have completed my report and secured an ambulance for you, Mr Spencer, you can be on your way. I expect your local hospital will keep her in at least overnight," Dr Pattinson replies.

"Thank you, Doctor, very much."

"Thank you, Mr Spencer, I hope it all goes well for you, good bye."

Ben finds a phone and calls home to tell Pauline that he hopes to be taking Margaret to the local hospital shortly. Daniel answers the phone and tells him that they have the names of the perpetrators and the police will pass the details on to Chief Inspector Jamieson.

"That is good work, Daniel, can I ask you to hold the fort until I return, not sure how long I will be, I have to wait for the doctor to complete his report before he will release Margaret."

"Take as long as you have to, Ben, we'll see you soon."

Ben puts down the phone and goes back to be with Margaret and wait for their transport back to Cresswell hospital.

The Spencer household is gripped by turmoil mixed with relief over the rescue of Margaret from her captors. Daniel and Conrad discuss how best they may protect the family while waiting for a date for the trial, at the same time not wishing to shackle them into severe restrictions on their movements. The children have to go to school, and Ben still has work to do, although they both agree that if the people concerned had wished to harm Ben, they would have done so before now. Threats to his family would usually be more effective in putting pressure on him. They discuss a plan of action which they will go over with Ben on his return. Meanwhile, Margaret is moved to Carswell hospital in the afternoon, arriving around 5 o'clock. She has improved a little and is talking with Ben and asking when she can go home.

"The doctors have agreed that it would be best if you were to stay in overnight, and we can take you home tomorrow providing you are well enough to be moved."

"I feel so tired and wretched from head to toe, Ben, but I do so want to go home as soon as the doctor will allow me to."

"We all want you back home, my dear Margaret as soon as possible, now let me check what time it would be best for me to collect you."

"No don't go for a moment, Ben, please. Now that I have rested, I have begun to realise what happened to me, you do know what those men did to me?"

"Yes, dear, the doctor told me what has happened to you, and I know it will be hard for you to accept and try to forget, but we will all help you and take care of you Margaret do you understand?" Ben confirms.

"I will never be able to forget or understand what happened to me Ben, those men took away what was most precious to me and I will hate them for that until the day I die, but I know that life must go on, and I will try, Ben, I will try," Margaret replies tearfully.

"I know you will, my dear, now perhaps you should rest now, let me go and check when I may collect you tomorrow."

Ben goes to talk with the doctor who suggests Ben call him around 11 o'clock tomorrow, Thursday. Ben goes back to Margaret with the news and after a tearful goodbye, he leaves the hospital for home, arriving around 6.30 p.m. He is met by Pauline and the family who all ask earnestly about Margaret.

"Mummy is recovering well children, can I suggest we all go into the parlour, Pauline I wonder if I might have a cup of tea, I have not had one since this morning. Polly, perhaps you and Pauline can organise something to eat, anything really, unless you have already eaten?"

"We have been waiting for you, Daddy, but everything has been prepared, it will be about half an hour before it is ready."

"Thank you, Polly, now I am going to freshen up, I feel rather grubby from today's events in dirty warehouses, we need to have a talk about Mummy as soon as we are all ready," says Ben as he goes upstairs to the bathroom.

Ben returns from the bathroom, feeling refreshed from his wash, and enjoys his tea. The family are all waiting on him, together with Pauline, Daniel and Conrad.

"When is Mummy coming home, Daddy, we miss her so much?" says Maisy.

"Mummy will be coming home tomorrow children so you will not have to wait much longer before you see her. But you will have to be especially good for her because she will need a lot of rest and help to get better."

"Has she had to have lots of operations, Daddy, and will she be able to help me with my shoe laces?" asks George.

"Mummy has had to have lots of care from the doctors because of her injuries George, but I am sure we can find someone to help with your shoelaces," says Ben with a smile.

"And I will stay as long as I am needed, Ben, Margaret must be given all the help that she will obviously need. I just need to go home and collect a few items for my stay."

"Thank you for that, Pauline, I know Margaret will really appreciate your being here. Conrad, perhaps you would take Pauline home after dinner?"

"Certainly, Ben," Conrad replies.

After sitting down to their meal, Conrad takes Pauline home to collect what she may need for her stay, whilst Polly amuses the other children before bedtime. Pauline only lives a few miles away and Conrad returns with her after about an hour. The younger children are now ready for bedtime which is organised by Pauline and Polly. Once the children are bedded down, Pauline and Polly return to the parlour.

"Now that Pauline is to be with us for a while, I would like to make a few suggestions regarding what needs to be done before Margaret comes home.

We need to look at the sleeping arrangements for Pauline and Conrad. I will get a single bed delivered for you Pauline, and Conrad can use the camp bed and share with Daniel for the time being, is that okay with you, Daniel?"

"So long as he does not keep me awake snoring!" Daniel replies with a smile.

"And you, my dear Polly, will be able to help Pauline with Mummy and the children, when you come home from school. Daniel will take you each morning, and collect you in the afternoon.

"I will arrange for Mrs Poulton to take and collect Maisy, Daisy and George each day, so that you can be here for Margaret, Pauline. Conrad and Daniel, can we have a chat in the morning about security, and where we are with the repairs. I would like to get some idea of when we can get the wall at least rebuilt, so that the perimeter of the property is more secure?"

"Mummy will be alright, won't she, Daddy? She will get better soon?" asks Polly who is obviously concerned at what has happened.

"My dear Polly, your Mummy was physically abused by these men repeatedly, more than that it is difficult for me to explain to you exactly what happened to her. It would be very distressing for all of us, and you may not really understand," says Ben struggling for an explanation that Polly would understand or would want to understand.

"Let's be grateful to Daniel and your Daddy for rescuing your Mummy, Polly, it will only upset you more if Daddy talks about what happened," says Pauline realising that Ben is finding it difficult to explain to his young daughter the brutal physical assault suffered by Margaret.

The next morning, after Daniel has returned from taking Polly to school, the three men meet in the study. Ben had phoned the hospital, and will be collecting Margaret around lunchtime after she has been examined again and her wounds dressed.

"Pauline will bring us some tea shortly; I want to hear your ideas about keeping the house and occupants safe. This last attack on Margaret has made me realise that we have to review all aspects of security. I cannot allow these people to continue harming my family, the attacks on Polly and now Margaret must be the last attacks on anybody, and once the house has been repaired, I want it to stay that way. So, how can we make our security more secure?" Ben asks.

"Taking Polly away for a few days would have been good, Ben, but it was only going to be a temporary measure. Firstly, let's make certain that no one leaves the house alone. I will accompany Polly to and from school, and Conrad will accompany anyone else, for example, if Pauline needs to go anywhere, then Conrad will go with her and likewise with Margaret, when she has recovered. I suggest that you be extra vigilant too Ben, and be sure to carry your pistol with you at all times," Daniel comments.

"You may want to make the garden more secure Ben, even with the wall rebuilt, it is still rather exposed, so I suggest a more secure fence at the bottom with a stronger gate, and more floodlighting would be good," Conrad comments.

"Okay, gentlemen, well we shall get that organised, I will speak to my colleague in Whitehall this afternoon for an update on court dates. The sooner we can put the culprits behind bars the better. We all know that the black market will continue until all rationing has ended. But I intend to break up the organised criminal element so that the public is not held to ransom. Conrad, can you move the bed from Polly's room please, I am hoping for a delivery of a bed for Pauline this afternoon and then the sleeping arrangements should be sorted?"

"Leave it with us, Ben, you check on Margaret so that you can collect her as soon as possible."

Ben contacts the hospital and is told that he can collect her around noon, and would he bring her clothes. Ben asks Pauline if she would select suitable items for him to take to the hospital.

"Can you sort out a pair of trousers instead of a dress for Margaret, Pauline, she has a lot of bruising on her legs as well as the rat bites that she suffered and will want to keep them covered?"

"Oh my God, Ben, she was bitten by rats?" says Pauline.

"Yes she was left overnight in a warehouse with rats running wild, she was tied to a bench and virtually naked, making her an easy target for them."

Pauline holds back her tears and hands Ben the clothes before disappearing into the bathroom.

Ben understands how she must feel, having heard about Margaret's plight, and decides to leave her for now, and goes off to collect Margaret. Ben brings Margaret home to be greeted by a tearful Pauline.

"Margaret, I do hope you are feeling better, let's go into the parlour, I will make you some tea, and then we will have some lunch, was my choice of clothes okay only—"

"It was fine, Pauly, really and thank you," replies Margaret as she is helped into the parlour by Ben.

She sits down on the settee and Ben lifts up her legs so that she is as comfortable as possible. Ben is glad that there is so much going on as the distractions will benefit her. They will give her other things to dwell on and help to push aside the terrible ordeal that she has endured. She knows there will be questions, not least from the children, especially Polly, but for now she can sit in her parlour looking out at the devastation and actually appreciating all that is happening around her! Daniel and Conrad are busy helping the builder with the wall, which has become a priority. It has been decided that the height be increased to 12 feet, and a more secure gate be fitted. All of the old wall has been cleared, and the builder has cleared the ground to prepare for the foundations, which will have to be deeper and wider to accommodate the extra weight.

"Is there anything special you would like for lunch, Margaret, how about some eggs?"

"Thank you, Ben, eggs will be fine, I am rather hungry, so perhaps some toast please?"

Margaret enjoys her lunch, and says hello again to Daniel and Conrad.

"I'm sorry that your break was cut short, Daniel, hopefully we can arrange another one soon for you with Polly?"

"That is not important for now Margaret, taking good care of you and the family is, we can talk about anything else when the time is more favourable."

"What was the verdict on the conservatory, Ben, I presume you can get another one soon?"

283

"It is something you and I can talk about, Margaret, it will have to be specially made so perhaps you may want to think about an alternative design of some sort?"

"Yes, that will give me something to do, Ben, and what about the workshop alongside the house?" Margaret asks.

"It is secure for now; I have to decide what is the best way forward with this when I have some time. Now, I have one or two things to attend to in the study, can I leave you with Pauline for a while, I will be just across the hallway?"

The men move from the parlour, leaving Margaret with her sister looking out over the garden.

"I will talk about what happened with you eventually, but I do need some time, I am having difficulty understanding what happened myself Pauly," says Margaret breaking the silence when the three men leave the parlour.

"I can only imagine –"

"No, Pauly, please do not try and imagine what happened, you really have no idea and will only upset yourself, I need you to be with me and help look after my family, just for a while please, will you do that for me?"

"Of course, Margaret, one thing at a time, I just want to take good care of you for as long as you like that is all," Pauline replies.

Meanwhile Ben is asking Daniel and Conrad for an update on proceedings in the garden.

"I was hoping you could clear a space at the bottom end close by the stream so that Margaret might sit outside and get some air from time to time."

"I can do that, Ben, it won't take long now that the crater has been filled in."

"Okay, thank you, Conrad, now I have to make some calls so I'll leave you two to get on if I may, Daniel, you will be collecting Polly later won't you?"

Daniel confirms as he and Conrad leave the study. Ben lifts the phone and dials Beatrice Carrington's number.

"Hello, Beatrice Carrington."

"Beatrice, it's Ben, Ben Spencer."

"Hello, Ben, a moment while I transfer to a secure line, so how are you, I was going to call you about the trial?"

"Yes, I was hoping for an update, since I have had a nasty set back here concerning Margaret She was abducted and rather brutally assaulted by a group of men."

"My God, Ben, I am so sorry, how is she?"

"She is home now, but it will take time, Beatrice, a long time for her to recover. My reason for calling you was to invite you to my home so that we can discuss in detail the trial and what needs to be done etc., would you be able to get a few days off?"

"I would be delighted, Ben, and meeting outside London may be a good idea. I have a driver who could drive me up to the Midlands."

"That's marvellous, Beatrice, I don't really need to keep you any longer except to ask how soon we can expect you?"

"I will travel up tomorrow and be with you around lunchtime, remind me of the address again please."

Ben recites his address to Beatrice and replaces the receiver. He must call Maureen to ask how she is and ask her a big favour.

"Hello, Peter, it's Ben, how is Maureen, I am sorry I have not been in touch recently, Margaret was taken on Monday, and I have just got her back from hospital."

"Hello, Ben, how are you coping with this, you must be praying that it will soon be over. Your family has been through hell with these people?"

"Indeed, Peter, but we carry on, we have to see this battle through to the end, now I wonder if I might have a word with Maureen?"

"Yes of course she will be glad to hear from you, I'll go and get her."

"Hello, Ben, it's Maureen, so sorry to hear about Margaret."

"Thank you, Maureen, but how are you now, are you feeling any better?"

"I am feeling much better thanks to, Peter, who has been my rock, looking after me, what can I do for you?"

Ben tells Maureen about Beatrice Carrington's proposed visit tomorrow and could she possibly help him with accommodating her for a couple of nights.

"I wouldn't normally ask, but we are full to bursting at the moment with two of Peter's colleagues and Margaret's sister staying with us."

"Of course, Ben, I look forward to meeting her, I know you are very fond of her and I am pleased to be able to help."

"Thank you so much, now will you and Peter come over for dinner tomorrow evening, it should be a pleasant change for all of us?"

"Thank you, Ben, that will be a very pleasant change, about 7 o'clock?"

"7 o'clock will be fine, I look forward to seeing you both, now could you put Peter back on the line, bye for now?"

"Looking forward to seeing you all, Ben, what can I do for you?" Peter asks.

"Yes, it will be good for all of us, I have just asked Maureen if Beatrice Carrington can stay with you as I simply have no more room here. And I need to know that she is safe while she is here."

"I will organise a room for her, and I assure you I will take good care of her."

"Thank you so much, Peter, now I had better start arranging the dinner requirements, see you tomorrow evening, bye for now."

Ben talks with Pauline and Margaret about the arrangements for tomorrow and is pleased with Margaret's response. She welcomes the opportunity to see Maureen, and Beatrice again and appreciates that the evening will be therapeutic for her. Polly will also be pleased to see Peter.

"How would you feel about going shopping tomorrow, Margaret, I am sure it would be good for you providing you feel well enough of course?"

"I want to get back to some kind of normal life as soon as possible, Ben, and a visit to the shops will be an idea way to start, now Pauline and I will have to make a list."

Daniel meanwhile goes to collect Polly from school, and Pauline goes along to collect Maisy, Daisy and George. There will be a lot of hugs and kisses when they return and see Margaret.

And there will be lots of questions, too, but Margaret so wants to see them again that she will not mind the questions at all. Ben is relieved at her response to having friends to dinner, and it will give everyone the chance to enjoy their time together. Meanwhile, the children arrive home from school and surround Margaret with hugs and kisses, telling her how much they missed her.

"We are all so happy to see you again, Mummy, we knew that Daddy and Daniel would find you and bring you home."

"We missed you so much, Mummy, Didn't we Maisy? Didn't we Daisy?" says George tearfully.

"Thank you children, it is so nice to be back with you again, now shall we have some tea?" Margaret sits down to tea with her children chattering to her, enjoying their being with her and, for the moment, forgetting the events of earlier in the week. It will be these everyday meetings with her children that will help her to get better as soon as possible, better than any medicine in fact.

George soon goes off to find Daniel, and Maisy and Daisy help Pauline in the kitchen, leaving Polly sitting with Margaret.

"I hope you do feel better today, Mummy, I know that you must have been very badly treated by those men, what did they do to you and why did they keep you for so long?"

"The men believed that keeping me prisoner would force Daddy to change his mind about getting them put on trial. They treated me very badly, Polly, but for now, I really do not want to talk about what happened. I want to get better, and you, Maisy, Daisy and George can help me by being here for me."

"Okay, Mummy, we will do whatever you think is best for you."

"Thank you, Polly, now I need to talk with your Aunty Pauline, so let's go into the kitchen," says Margaret.

She has decided that she needs a bath to ease some of the ache from her bruising, but will need some help dressing her wounds. So, leaving Polly in charge, Pauline goes with Margaret to help her bathe. As Margaret removes her clothing, her sister gasps at the extent of her injuries. The severe bruising on Margaret's thighs leaves her in no doubt what has happened to her sister. And the marks on her wrists and ankles show how long she had been kept tied to the bench. Then there were the rat bites which looked particularly nasty.

"My dear Margaret, I am so sorry, you must have gone through hell with those men."

"I just tried to black out what they were doing, Pauly, as though it were a bad dream that I kept having over and over and over again.

Unfortunately, the pain from it happening continuously never went away, neither did knowing just when it was going to happen again. Each time they returned I knew what to expect, I knew they would take me into the small room, two of them each time. They would abuse me as though what they were doing was part of a plan of action. They never spoke once during all the time they were with me and when they were finished, they moved to one side to make way for the next one.

"I am sure that they were ready to kill me if Ben and Daniel had not found me, but how long they would have kept me before that happened I just shudder to think about," says Margaret with fear in her voice and tears in her eyes.

"They will suffer for what they have done to you, Margaret, thank God they were all taken, and thanks to Daniel for shooting two of them, at least they would have suffered some pain."

Pauline helps Margaret to dress the most severe wounds with the ointment that the doctor had given her, and Margaret puts on fresh clothes keeping on her trousers to hide the rat bites and the marks on her ankles. She felt better for her bath and also for being able to talk with her sister.

The following morning, Friday, Ben calls Commander Spratt to see if there are any pressing matters regarding arrests. He also updates him on the recent attack on Margaret and confirms that the men will be tried separately, in Birmingham, for the attack.

"Yes that is absolutely correct, Mr Spencer, we at the Yard are concerned solely with the conspiracy charges surrounding the racketeering of rationed goods."

"The assaults on your family will be dealt with locally, but of course your prosecution barristers will bring it up at the trial as evidence of the type of men we are dealing with. The defence will try and prevent it from being used, but I imagine the Crown will question you in detail about what has happened, so you need to be prepared for this. We are dealing with violent, desperate men, Mr Spencer, who need to be put away, the sooner the better for everyone. Incidentally, the two men that were named regarding the explosions at your home and your office, have both been arrested and charged with conspiracy to commit explosions," the commander says.

"So are there any more arrests to be carried out at all?"

"Not to my knowledge, I understand that the Crown's case is being prepared, your colleague in Whitehall will be able to give you more precise information," the commander replies.

"Thank you for that, Commander, I will keep you in touch regarding anything else relevant at my end, bye for now," says Ben as he replaces the receiver.

He also makes contact with Chief Inspector Jamieson of Birmingham Constabulary, who confirms that relevant charges have been made against the four men who abducted Margaret, and they have all been remanded. He expects the case to be heard in about four to six weeks. Margaret will have to give evidence, but he knows that a number of painful events will have to be recalled over the coming weeks to ensure that those responsible will pay for their actions. Polly especially, will have a particularly difficult time, having been abducted more than once, along with Maureen who was subjected to a particularly nasty assault. While Ben waits for Beatrice to arrive, he decides to call the office for an update.

"Hello, Phil, it's Ben, how are things in your new 'home'?"

"We are back in business now, Ben, but what about you; how is Margaret after her ordeal?"

"She is on the mend, but it will take some time. Now, is there anything urgent that I should know about?"

"Nothing urgent, Ben, you need to spend time with Margaret and getting your home back together, we will cope here, never fear."

"Thanks, Phil, and by the way we have determined who the culprits were that planted the explosives. Captain Radford recognised their method, and they have been arrested."

"Good news then, Ben; keep in touch and let me know if there is anything you need, bye for now and remember me to Margaret."

Ben had received some details of the damage to the offices in Carswell, and it is apparent that the building will have to be demolished. So the new home is likely to become permanent for some time until suitable office space can be found. Fortunately, many of the records kept at the building related to local business, details of items seized, names of local racketeers, and records of arrests and convictions were not damaged. The office had been in existence through the war years, so the records were extensive. However, none of the records lost relate in any way to Operation Seeker, which are all in London.

Margaret and Pauline take Maisy, Daisy and George to school by car so that they can go into Carswell to shop for this evening's meal. Margaret is a little slow walking, but the trip to town can only do her good after her ordeal. They are able to get two rations of minced beef, using both

Margaret's and Pauline's allocation, to be able to make a cottage pie. Everything else required, potatoes, peas, carrots, etc., are relatively plentiful in the countryside. They also purchase some apples for a bread and apple pie for pudding.

"I would like some tea before we go back, Pauline, I'm feeling rather tired."

After enjoying a cup of tea, they return to the car and take the short drive back home.

"How was the trip, Margaret, were you able to get something for dinner?"

"The trip to town was just what I needed, Ben, but I do need to sit for a moment, I'm feeling rather tired." She sits quietly in the parlour while Pauline attends to some sandwiches for lunch.

In the meantime, the builder has obtained some fencing which can be erected as a temporary measure to ensure that the garden is secured from the lane. It has been decided that a number of the bricks may be reused to save time waiting for supplies of new materials. Like everything in post war Britain, building materials are in short supply, so Ben decided that reusing some of the bricks will save time. New doors, from the parlour to the conservatory area and from the kitchen to the garden, have been ordered, and will be available next week. Daniel meanwhile, has fitted extra lighting which floods most of the garden with lighting. However, the front of the house may need to have a light of some sort, since the lane is rather dark and secluded.

"I believe we are doing all that can be done for the moment, Daniel," says Ben over lunch.

"Okay, Ben, Conrad and I will see what we can do outside in the meantime."

Just as Daniel is leaving the room, the front door bell rings, and Ben opens the door to Beatrice Carrington.

"My dear Beatrice, it is so good to see you again, please come inside."

"Hello, Ben, can we first look after Tommy, my driver before he returns?"

"Of course, come inside, Tommy, and I will get you some lunch," Ben answers.

Tea and sandwiches are given to Beatrice's driver, who then leaves to return to London. After family introductions and some lunch, Beatrice follows Ben into the study to discuss the trial and matters arising. She has some disturbing news to give to Ben, news which could influence how they proceed with their pursuit of black market criminals.

"I have made some startling discoveries recently, Ben, regarding black market activity. It would seem that corruption and racketeering has got to the very heart of our government, so you will have to be so very careful until the trial has concluded. I am confident that my position is safe, but everyone knows who you are and what you are doing. I am sure you are doing everything possible to protect your family, but you must consider the strong possibility that you will be targeted personally, since you will be giving evidence, and have documentation that is so damaging to these people."

"Your family has endured the most terrible abuses since you began to gather the relevant evidence that will put these people away. They have tried to stop you by harming your family, not you personally, but I believe that will be their next move. Corruption in high places means that government agents may be used to target you, Ben, and believe me they will be ruthless in their efforts to bring you down. These men are usually ex-military, mercenaries for hire to the highest bidder."

"What do you suggest, Beatrice, how long do you think it will be before we can begin giving evidence? That is key to all this isn't it, how long are we going to have to wait before these people are exposed?"

"It will be a while yet, two or three weeks at the earliest. Regarding your safety, can I suggest that Daniel or Conrad escort you everywhere from now onwards, as an added precaution? They have both shown themselves to be very capable?"

"God, Beatrice, I had no idea that this would escalate to such a level. We are going to be able to bring these people to justice aren't we, is there any way that they may have to stop us going ahead with the trial?" Ben asks with concern.

"I cannot see how the trial can be halted in any legal way, Ben, it could be delayed, you could be indisposed, indeed anyone called to give evidence could be indisposed. You must also be aware of any loopholes in your presentations Ben. Daniel and Conrad must be kept out of any proceedings to avoid questions of how they entered Williamson's cottage and the New Haven tunnels. The information that was acted upon from simply from a 'reliable source' no names need be divulged."

"I understand, Beatrice, then we must protect key witnesses, especially those that have agreed to give evidence so as to get their sentences reduced. I can give you a list of the people concerned, can you arrange for some sort of watch to be placed on them, ideally without their knowledge. If they think they are in danger, then there is a good chance they will recant?"

"I will speak with Commander Spratt on this. I do not want to involve local police directly, but my own position can remain secure if the Commander will go through channels on our behalf. Meanwhile, I will get the necessary clearance from the Home Office and see how they might help us with the trial preparation."

"That sounds promising, meantime Beatrice can I ask you not to mention the threats to me to anyone, I do not want to worry the family any more, especially Margaret who has been subjected to a terrible assault by these criminals?"

"Yes of course, Ben, the last thing Margaret needs at this time is to start worrying about you."

Ben is interrupted by a knock on the door and Daniel entering.

"Just off to collect Polly, Ben."

"Thank you, Daniel, perhaps you can take Beatrice to Maureen's when you return please?" replies Ben. As Daniel leaves the room, Beatrice gives Ben some more news.

"Just as disturbing at the moment, Ben, are the government's concerns over goods being smuggled into Britain from U.N. relief agencies. Cloth and leather goods even food items including meat are being diverted to the black market. Those behind these operations are outside of our authority however, it is rumoured that the Soviets have set up a network of black market smuggling into the country using their communist members here in Britain so we hope to get some leads from our contacts within the party. What I would say, Ben, is that any information you may come across relating to the German smuggling operation, you pass on to me. I do not think that it would be wise to pursue the German connection. You need to concentrate on securing the convictions from the operation out of New Haven. You have been very successful so far, let us get over the trial before you look at any other fields."

"Indeed, Beatrice, and I have no knowledge of any German operations, so for me it is best left alone until the trial has concluded, perhaps then I can make some enquiries through the C.O.I. They will have some knowledge of this, I am sure."

Daniel returns from collecting Polly and collects Beatrice's bag.

"We will see you later Beatrice, thanks for the update, perhaps we can talk some more tomorrow. Daniel, I wonder if I might have a word with you and Conrad when you get back?" Daniel nods and goes off with Beatrice to Maureen Potter's house, giving Ben a few moments to digest what Beatrice has told him.

He had never considered his own safety was in jeopardy, and was shaken by what had been said. He instinctively opened the desk drawer, and checked his weapon. He decides to ask Peter's advice on whether he should have a second weapon as a precaution. His way of life is about to change drastically until all of the criminals he has brought to trial have been put behind bars.

"Hello, Daddy, Mummy says would you like some tea?"

"Thank you, Polly, that would be nice," says Ben smiling at his daughter and thinking just how well she was coping with her own ordeals and now with Margaret's. The last thing he wants to happen is another upsetting incident involving himself!

"Here you are, Daddy, will you be much longer, I think Mummy was asking after you?"

"Not much longer, Polly, I just need a word with Daniel and Conrad, then I will be finished for today."

"Okay, I'll tell Mummy you will be through soon."

"Come in Conrad, you too, Daniel, I just need to have a word with you before I can settle for the day. I have just received some rather disturbing news from Beatrice regarding my own position.

"It seems that the black market operations in the country extend as far as government. Our successes are making people in high places nervous of being discovered, and they are taking drastic actions. They have been making enquiries about using mercenaries for hire, ex-military types who will do anything for money."

"They know no boundaries and are answerable to no one. If these men are coming after me then I will need one of you by my side at all times gentlemen."

"I have heard about these mercenaries for hire, Ben, let me make some enquiries, I may be able to find out who they might be and what they may be planning."

"Any information would be a help for all of us. If this change of emphasis means that my family are out of real danger, then I regard their

293

move as a plus for us. With one of you with me at all times, I believe we can handle whatever they throw at us."

"Providing we can organise the day so that one of us will still be here to watch over the home and any occupants, then we will cope, but we will have to be watchful, if we are to combat ex-military."

"What about additional weapons Daniel, should we consider having a second weapon to hand?"

"It would do no harm, Ben, and ensure that there is a weapon to hand at all times, Smith and Wesson revolvers would be a good choice, I will make the arrangements."

"I will ask Beatrice if we can secure a government issue for these under the present circumstances," Ben comments.

"You will need to keep your car inside the garage from now on Ben and make the garden side of the garage secure as well so that your car cannot be tampered with. And when you go into Carswell, we need to be sure that the car is parked in a secure spot or in the main street where there are people passing by at all times," suggests Conrad.

"Okay, gentlemen, I think we have covered most points, thank you for your suggestions, now I think we can relax for a while before we all get together for dinner this evening."

So the three men depart from the study and Ben goes off to be with Margaret. She had enjoyed her visit to town with Pauline, but was rather tired so had gone upstairs for a nap. Ben made some tea and took a cup upstairs for her. She had obviously enjoyed her rest and Ben was pleased to see that she was getting better every day.

"I would like to have a bath before dinner, Ben, I wonder could you help me, I am still rather sore?"

Ben helps her get ready for her bath, visibly shocked when he sees the bruising on her body. He had no idea just how badly she was injured, noting how she winced as the water covered her bruises and lacerations. The good signs were regarding the rat bites, they seemed to be healing at least. The children are getting excited at having a house full for dinner and are questioning Ben about who will be there. George, especially, is keen to know who will be arriving.

"You know everyone who will be coming, George, Peter, Maureen and Beatrice you have seen before don't you remember?"

"Yes I remember, Daddy, will Peter be able to play with me, he always did and it has been a long time since I saw him?"

"Well let's wait and see, George, now we'll have some tea, then I expect Mummy will want to get you all ready for our guests."

"And I am really looking forward to seeing Peter again, Daddy, he is a very good friend."

"Just make sure that you don't take up too much of his time, Polly please."

Peter arrives, with Maureen and Beatrice, just before 7 o'clock, to be greeted by Ben and Margaret. Maureen is slowly getting over her ordeal and offers Margaret her sympathy for what has happened to her.

"Thanks, Maureen, now let's all go inside and enjoy the evening."

George is delighted to see Peter and grabs him to one side.

"Peter, Peter come and look at my toys please!" says George.

"George, Peter will see you before he leaves, now go along and sit down. Hello, Peter, it's so nice to see you again."

"It's good to see you too, Polly you are looking well, I understand that Daniel has been taking good care of you?"

"Yes he has, and I am going to stay with him when Mummy is feeling better?" she says.

"That will do you good, Polly, and Daniel will entertain you I am sure," Peter replies.

Everyone is in the dining room, and Margaret is directing where each should sit. She has sat Polly between Daniel and Peter, with Maureen the other side. The other children are sat between Pauline and Conrad who is next to George. Everyone enjoys Margaret's meal of Cottage Pie followed by a Bread and Apple pudding. Considering the restrictions Margaret has done remarkably well to set a meal for seven adults and four children.

Afterwards, George grabs Peter, Maureen chats with Margaret, and Polly stays close to Daniel.

"I was wondering if we might have another chat tomorrow Beatrice, if you wouldn't mind, there are still some things to discuss."

"Of course, Ben, I'll call around 11 o'clock is if that's okay?"

Pauline and Conrad watch over Maisy and Daisy, and Pauline asks if Conrad might give her a lift home tomorrow to sort out her washing.

"Whenever you are ready, Pauline," Conrad replies.

The rest of the evening passes by very quickly before Maureen, Beatrice and Peter depart.

"Until tomorrow, Ben, goodnight," says Beatrice.

On Saturday morning, Conrad takes Pauline back home to organise her laundry and say hello to her husband. She expects to be with Margaret for about another week, so takes a few more clothes back with her. Ben and Daniel assess the building work to be done and tidy up where they can. At least they have a secure fence in place albeit only temporary.

Beatrice duly arrives around 11 o'clock to be met by Ben who ushers into the study. Margaret brings them tea, and leaves them to their discussions. It is important that they spend time discussing strategy for the pending trial.

"The container is still in the C.O.I. offices in London, Ben, is that correct, because it might be best if I retain it ready for the trial?"

"Yes, it is, Beatrice, perhaps you can arrange for Sarah Mumford to collect it if I give you the office key?"

"Okay, now as you know, some of the names mentioned in the documents have now moved into positions of authority. There are council leaders, civil servants even police officers who are implicated. When their names were first added, they were in lowly positions in councils and in government, but they used their positions to gain access to information which they used to divert and sell on vast quantities of goods and ration stamps. Civil servants in the supply and food ministries were in ideal positions get information about shipment and storage of goods, and those working in council offices would have been able to monitor movement in their areas. So the information recorded in the documents stored in the container is going to put several people away who occupy high ranking positions in public office."

"I understand why they have been so desperate to get hold of the container, Beatrice, and until the trial is over and they have been punished, I know we are at risk."

"The other point, Ben, is whether any of your methods of securing the information in the container can be questioned at all?"

"I certainly did not engage in any illegal activities, but I did meet with a few unsavoury characters who offered me information in exchange for leniency if they had been operating in the black market. We are only talking about small time operators who tipped me off when they were receiving goods. I would then use the same tactic on the middlemen to try and get details of the main operators. That was the basis of my operations against the racketeers, it was simple and it worked."

"If that is so then we have a very strong case, Ben, one which will hold up to any scrutiny, and which exonerates you and your methods. You have spent years pursuing these people and now have all the evidence to convict them. Once I have the container, I will discuss its contents with the Home Secretary's office so that they are aware of its importance and what will be divulged when the trial begins."

"Now will you stay for lunch, Beatrice, before you leave, Daniel will take you to the station as soon as you are ready?"

"Thank you, Ben, my train leaves at 2 o'clock so lunch would be very nice."

The next two weeks pass by without incident, giving the Spencer family time to settle down into some normality with their lives. Polly goes back to school on Monday and slowly seems to put aside the ordeals that she has gone through, although she is never far from Daniel's side. It is hoped that she may still be able to spend a few days away with Daniel in London as soon as the house has been secured.

Margaret is still quite frail from her terrible ordeal, and Ben knows that it will take some time for her to be able to accept what has happened to her. Whilst her body may heal eventually, the mental scars will be with her for many months. Her sister has been a great help with the children and making sure that Margaret gets plenty of rest time as the doctor suggested. Ben takes her for short walks most evenings just to be with her and talk about nothing specific just chat about everyday things. Trying to be normal and hoping that it helps Margaret's convalescence.

The work on the house continues apace. The wall is eventually completed and a secure gate fitted. The new wall is ten feet high and made up of a mixture of new bricks and those that could be salvaged when the old wall was demolished. The conservatory, after some delay has arrived and is being erected. This should not take too long, and Ben is hoping that once it is in place, the garden flood lights can be fitted, so that the whole of the garden will be lit. Ben is able to go into work and get up to date with what has happened. The new site is proving more practical than the old, having more space, and a large area at the rear for parking and deliveries. He spends most of his time preparing for the pending trials. He will have to give evidence relating to events at his home, and will also be called to the conspiracy trial relating to the sale of goods on the black market. This will almost certainly take place at The Central Criminal Court of The Old Bailey. Ben is assisted by Maureen, who has now returned to work part time. Ben was reluctant to allow her to return, but both Maureen and Peter assured him that a few hours a day would be good for her.

Ben is in contact with Beatrice a number of times to ensure that his evidence will be as detailed as possible, and the defence team will have no reasons to ask for any delays. She has received the container of documents from the C.O.I. and has locked it away in her safe. Only Beatrice herself knows the combination of the safe. And the children are beginning to settle down to the way of life they had always been used to before the events of the last few weeks. They have stopped asking Margaret questions and really never quite understood what had happened to her. Margaret wants to keep it that way, she does not want them to dwell on the incident, she just wants them to have a happy life. Sadly, the events of the next few days will shake her resolve, the family are about to be subjected to their most serious setbacks in Ben's fight against criminal racketeers.

CHAPTER 30

(Operation Seeker: Disaster for the Spencers)

Daniel drove Polly to school on Monday as usual, before returning to the house. It was then Conrad's turn to take the car and drive Ben into Carswell. Polly was excited since it was the School Sports Day, and she was to run in the relay, and also take part in the high jump. Being a tall girl for her age, she had always been a good athlete, and was confident that she may win a prize. It was a pleasant September day and a great number of parents were present to cheer the children on. There were a number of parents with cars and vans, so no one paid any attention to the large van parked near the school pavilion entrance. The changing rooms were accessed by a door at the side of the pavilion and was unsighted from the playing field. After the relay race Polly went and changed her shirt. She had tripped during the relay and her shirt was covered in dirt. As she left the changing room, she was approached by a woman.

"Bad luck, dear, are you alright you took quite a tumble out there?" commented the woman smiling.

"I'm okay thanks, just a–"

But before Polly can finish her sentence, two men appear and grab her. One puts his hand over her mouth, the other grabs her round her legs as they half carry and half drag her into the back of the van. The woman follows and gets into the passenger seat as the van drives out of the gates. No one has seen anything, since everyone was watching the events on the sports field. The two men, meanwhile, tie Polly's legs together and put a gag in her mouth. She struggles desperately, until one of the men slaps her hard across her face, splitting her lip.

"Keep quiet it will do you no good to struggle, no one can hear you," the man says.

They drive for about an hour before stopping in a disused factory yard. The men take her inside to a room with an old settee, and a large glass window. They remove her socks and shoes, tie her hands behind her, and throw her down on the settee.

Ben and Conrad travel into Carswell on Monday to Ben's new office. They have decided that it may be the best option to take the car back home and return when Ben is ready. The car can then be put safely into the garage during the daytime, reducing the risk of it being tampered with. The journey from Ben's house to Carswell is only a short one and there is very little traffic about.

The truck comes from the side road and hits Ben's car, which is turned round facing the car behind them. Two men leap from the car and grab Ben, hitting him on the head. He falls to the ground unconscious. Conrad meanwhile, has been injured by flying glass and the force of the impact with the truck has damaged his shoulder. Before he is able to draw his weapon he too is hit across his head and slumps into his seat. Ben is dragged from the car into the back of the waiting vehicle and driven off together with the driver of the truck, which is left by the side of the road. The whole thing is over in about two minutes and no one saw anything. Again, the car travels for about an hour before arriving at the disused factory yard. Ben is placed in the room next to Polly and tied to a chair.

After about an hour, four men return to the disused factory, and enter the room where Ben is tied to the chair. He has a terrible headache but is otherwise unharmed.

"Take a look in the other room, Spencer," the man asks.

Ben looks through the glass and is devastated at seeing Polly, clad only in her underwear, in the other room.

"Don't you think my daughter has suffered enough from your actions, you've got me, why don't you let her go home," he pleads.

"That is not going to happen, Spencer, we want you to be able to see everything that is happening to her and you won't be able to stop us."

"My God what sort of people are you, she is only a child?"

"She is your daughter, Spencer, and we will do with her what we have to until told otherwise."

"What do you want from me just tell me so that I can take my daughter home," says Ben pleading.

"You and your daughter ain't going anywhere for a while, so make yourself comfortable."

"Can I speak with my daughter please, at least let me speak with her?"

"No you cannot speak to her, but you get to watch what happens to her. She doesn't know you are here and we won't be telling her." he replies as he leaves the room. Ben peers anxiously through the window and sees the four men enter the room where Polly is being held.

The phone rings and Margaret answers in Ben's absence.

"Hello this is Margaret Spencer."

"Mrs Spencer, it's Mrs Williams from school, I'm afraid there's been an incident at the school playing fields. Polly is missing, I'm afraid she may have been taken. "

Margaret is speechless and begins to shake, then answers, "Oh God, do you have any more details Mrs Williams?"

"I'm afraid we don't, the police have been informed of course, but nothing else at the moment."

"Thank you, Mrs Williams, I will let you know when I hear anything."

She immediately contacts Ben's office, but to her dismay, he has not arrived.

"We were expecting him a while back, Margaret, but he has not arrived yet, can I get him to call you when he arrives?" Phil Landers asks.

"I think Polly has been taken again, Phil, so please get him to come home as soon as he arrives," replies Margaret tearfully.

"Oh my God, Margaret, I am so sorry, can I help at all?"

"If you can just ask him to come home please."

She leaves the study as the doorbell rings and Conrad enters the hallway with a bad cut on his head and obviously in pain from his shoulder.

"Ben has been taken, Margaret, they rammed my side of the car with a truck, and made off with Ben in a car, before I could get out to help him. Then they hit me over the head. I managed to get a van driver to bring me back. I must contact the police before –"

301

Conrad suddenly stumbles and collapses onto the hall floor. Margaret calls Daniel from the garden and they carry Conrad through to the parlour, laying him down on the settee.

"Take care of him, Margaret, I will call the police and can we contact your doctor to have a look at him please?"

"Of course, the number is on Ben's desk."

The four men sit down facing Polly, and stare at her menacingly.

"What do you want, why are you looking at me like that?" Polly asks, trembling, and wondering what is going to happen to her.

"We are wondering what we should do with a pretty girl like you," the older man says.

"Yeah, and you can amuse us, miss, what's your name by the way?"

"My name is Polly, and I don't want to talk to you, leave me alone, My Daddy will kill you if you touch me," Polly screams at him.

The men begin to laugh, knowing that Ben Spencer is in the other room and cannot help his daughter.

"Come here, Polly, let's have a look at you, I said come here!" he shouts.

"Now you listen to me, young Polly, you behave yourself and nothing will happen to you, we don't want to hurt you."

"You be nice with us and we will be nice with you," he says as he pulls her close to him and kisses her on the cheek.

"Get away from me, you horrid man!" says Polly and kicks him on his legs.

"You really should behave yourself, Polly, I'm afraid you will have to be taught a lesson in good manners," he says as two of the men grab hold of her and push her down onto the settee.

Meanwhile Doctor Wilson arrives at the Spencer's house and examines Conrad.

"Nothing broken, Conrad, but you will have a heck of a headache for a while. Your shoulder is bruised from the bump, but nothing is broken. Just don't do any heavy lifting for a day or so, and you will be okay. I will leave you something to ease your headache."

"Thank you, Doctor, I am obliged," Conrad replies as the doctor leaves the room.

"I will call your local garage and ask them to tow the car in, Margaret, perhaps they can let us have one to rent for a few days?"

"Thank you, Daniel, the owner is Jonathan Crump, he is very helpful, I am sure he will find us something," she says.

D.I. Wishart arrives after he had visited Polly's school, and expresses his sympathy at what has happened.

"I am sorry to hear about this latest setback with your daughter, Mrs Spencer, I hope we are able to find her and Mr Spencer very soon."

"Thank you for your concerns Inspector, please find them quickly for me."

Conrad details what happened to D.I. Wishart, although he has to admit that details are rather sketchy.

The two men barely spoke, carried out the attack swiftly and effectively and it was all over within minutes. All Conrad was able to remember was the make of the car, a black Humber saloon.

"Well thank you, Conrad, please let me know if you think of anything, or the abductors make contact," he says as he gets up and departs.

Daniel sits down with Conrad and goes over what happened, hoping to get an idea of who the men were that took Ben.

"From what you have said, Conrad, I reckon they are ex-military, they moved swiftly and without saying much. Ramming the car was the best way to stop it and make you and Ben easier to overcome. The attack was ruthless; they could easily have caused you serious injury in the passenger seat. They were interested only in taking Ben at all costs," Daniel comments.

"Do we have any idea where they may have taken Ben and Polly, Daniel, any idea at all?"

"They would not have wanted to travel too far in case anyone saw the car. I think they may have taken them somewhere in Birmingham, as they did with you Margaret, but exactly where, I really have no idea," Daniel replies.

"Can you speak with the police officer that Ben has dealt with in Birmingham, Chief Inspector Jamieson, he may be able to help?" Margaret suggests.

"I will contact him straight away, I know that Ben tipped him off about two consignments of goods, so he will want to help I'm sure," says Ben as he goes off to the study to make the call.

"Chief Inspector Jamieson's office."

"Would you tell the Chief Inspector that a colleague of Ben Spencer wishes to speak with him urgently please?"

Meanwhile, the men holding Polly are angry at her response toward them.

"You need to be taught some manners, young lady," the older man says. Two of the men hold her down while he hits her hard with a cane. He hits her several times before the men holding her sit her down on the settee and give her back her skirt.

"Let that be a lesson, Polly, now are you going to behave or do we have to punish you again?"

"Leave me alone, you beastly horrible man, I hate you," says Polly as she bursts into tears.

"Well we shall have to punish you again for being rude now, Polly. Lie her across the table."

Polly is terrified and screams as loud as she can as the man hits her again with the cane several times, then a second man joins in. They continue for several minutes and Polly becomes delirious with pain and fear. They finally stop, tie her to the table and leave the room.

"Now, Mr Spencer, you now know what we are capable of," the older man says as he joins Ben in the adjoining room.

"God what sort of men are you that would treat a child in that way?" Ben answers in despair.

"Mr Spencer, we have been hired to do a job, we do this all the time, we kill people if we are commissioned to kill, it's our job to get results at any cost. Do you understand? We believe that we can get what we need from you by using your daughter. When we are convinced you are ready to meet with our associates, we will release Polly. We shall have one more session with her, then we'll arrange some food for you before leaving you until morning," he concludes.

The older man then re-enters the room where Polly is being held.

"Now, young Polly, my colleagues will now deal with you for your rudeness and bad behaviour toward me. Tie her to that beam and take off her shirt and skirt but you can leave her vest."

Polly is suspended from the ceiling She has several marks across her bottom already. The men proceed to cane her across her back and legs, gagging her so that her screams are muffled. When they eventually stop, Polly is barely conscious. The men sterilise her wounds, before leaving her on the settee.

"We will bring you something to eat and drink shortly Polly, for now I suggest you rest up," the older man says. Two of the men return later and stay with Polly while she drinks the water, but she leaves the bread and cheese, and lies back sobbing.

"Here is your food, Mr Spencer, we have finished for today, so I suggest you rest. Your daughter is unaware that you are here and these rooms are soundproof so you will not be able to contact her. You will however, still be able to see her through the one-way glass."

Daniel, meanwhile, speaks at length with Chief Inspector Jamieson, hoping he they may have some suggestions as to where Ben and Polly may have been taken.

"I will ask my men to talk with their informers, but from what you say these men are not local, and certainly act as though they are ex-military. They are obviously well organised, making them difficult to trace, Daniel. We have to hope that someone may have seen something suspicious or noticed the car." the chief inspector comments.

"Can you ask your men if any of them know a Bill Holder. He was able to find out where Mrs Spencer was being held, he may have some ideas. I would very much appreciate it if you could ask him to contact me please?"

"Leave that with me, Daniel, I will get back to you, bye for now," says the chief inspector.

Daniel, meanwhile, contacts Jonathan Crump at the local garage and asks him if he can help with a vehicle to rent for a while. Mr Crump is very helpful and arranges to bring a vehicle to the house in the morning with the relevant papers. It is a vehicle he has for sale so is in good condition and ready to use. Meanwhile Margaret asks Mrs Poulton if she would collect the children from school. She has to somehow prepare herself to tell them that Polly and Daddy have both been taken. She sits down with her sister and bursts into tears. She has by no means got over her ordeal, and now she has this latest terrible business to endure.

Daniel takes the opportunity to speak with Conrad, who is dozing on the settee.

"How are you feeling, my friend, head still buzzing?"

"I'm okay, Daniel, shoulder is a bit sore, but no matter, any ideas about finding Ben and Polly?"

"I am hoping that they are being held in Birmingham and Chief Inspector Jamieson's men can come up with an address through their informers. One of them may know of Bill Holder, he is our best chance of finding them at the moment."

"It is still a hell of a long shot, Daniel, do you think we should speak to Beatrice Carrington, she may have some ideas?"

"Yes, good idea, Conrad, first I must tell Peter what has happened, then I will contact Beatrice," says Daniel as he goes off to the study.

Peter is very upset by what has happened and tells Daniel to keep him informed. If he can help with any rescue attempt he will be only too pleased to participate he says.

"I'm afraid we have no clues to their whereabouts at the moment Peter, but I am exploring a number of options, I will keep in touch and let you know if you can help further," says Daniel as he replaces the receiver, then dials the number for Beatrice Carrington.

"Hello, this is Beatrice Carrington speaking."

"Beatrice, it's Daniel Bottomley calling from Ben's home, I am sorry to bother you are you free to talk at the moment?"

"One moment, Daniel, while I secure the line. Okay, what is it, has something happened?" she asks with concern.

"Ben and Polly have both been taken in separate incidents, Ben from his car and Polly from school and for the moment we have no idea where may be, I was hoping you may have heard something?" Daniel asks.

"I know that ex-military men have been hired to take Ben, and that they are operating under instruction from the highest level. They have been given full licence to do what is necessary to secure the information that Ben holds in the container. The people whose details are chronicled in the documents are panicking as the trial draws near, they know that only

Ben has the information, and I believe they will kill him to get it if necessary. I am sorry to sound so dramatic, Daniel, but that is how serious this latest setback is. Polly is probably being used to force Ben to give up the information; God knows what they will do to her."

"Do you think you can find out who these men are, Beatrice, and would you also be able to find out who they are reporting to?"

"I will do what I can Daniel and get back to you later this evening when I have anything, please give my best to Margaret," says Beatrice as she puts down the phone.

"Good morning, Mr Spencer, I trust you slept well, I have brought you some tea and toast. Now, what will happen today is that we will continue to punish your daughter to persuade you to stop your meddling. My men will be firm, but not too harsh remembering she is only young, but you will appreciate that this is all your fault," he says.

"My God, I will give you what you want, anything, just let her go for God's sake, as you said you would please," Ben pleads.

"It doesn't work that way, Mr Spencer, I have to wait until I am contacted before I can release Polly, and you can then provide my superiors with the information they are seeking. I am sorry but that is how it works. Meanwhile we continue with our work," he says as he leaves the room.

Polly is slumped on the settee, half conscious when all four men enter the room. They untie her and give her something to drink and some toast. Polly by now is hungry and welcomes the toast they have given her.

"Thank you," she says gratefully.

'My pleasure, Polly, we don't want you to get hungry while you are with us. We are sorry about this but now we must continue, I hope you understand, I have asked my men not to be too harsh with you. But your Daddy is being stubborn and interfering in the business of my boss. He must be punished for his actions and the best way to punish him is to hurt you. So what is happening to you is not our fault, it is your Daddy who is to blame. Carry on men," he says as he leaves the room and his men begin giving Polly yet another beating, tying her to the beam, and beating her with canes across her back, bottom and legs. She is now bleeding from a number of marks across her back and bottom, and her arms are aching from her being suspended from the beam. After what seems an age the men stop and release from the overhead beam.

"Now then, Polly, perhaps we should have a break for a while," he says as they both leave the room. Polly slips on her skirt over her torn pants and collapses on the settee. She really does not know what is happening to her anymore and just lays there and weeps, convinced that they will kill her when they have finished. There really isn't anything more they can do that they haven't already done. She is cold and dirty from the old settee and finally she slips into a fitful sleep.

"Okay, Mr Spencer, that's it for today, I will fetch you and Polly something to eat before we leave, is there anything else I can get for you?" he asks with a grin.

"I have only one thing to say to you, sir, when I am free I promise I will not rest until I find you and shoot you dead. Believe me I promise you that."

"Good bye for now, Mr Spencer."

By the Wednesday morning, Daniel, Conrad and the whole Spencer family are desperate for news about Ben and Polly. The children are asking questions and are so upset that Margaret phones their school to tell the Headmistress that they will not be attending for the next day or so.

"We have had a serious family upset which concerns Mr Spencer and Polly. I cannot give you any more details I'm afraid, I hope you will understand?"

"Of course, Mrs Spencer, I heard about the incident involving Polly, I do hope you find her soon, please let me know when the children will be returning," the headmistress replies.

"Yes, I will and thank you," she then follows Daniel and Conrad go into the study to discuss what can be done. She is desperate for some news about Polly and Ben.

"I am going to call Chief Inspector Jamieson shortly, hoping he will have some news. If nothing is forthcoming soon, I am tempted to go to Birmingham and see if I can locate Ben's contact Bill Holder. I know it will be like looking for the needle in a haystack, but unless we hear something soon, we have no alternative but to start looking ourselves. I don't suppose Ben has a number for Bill Holder does he, Margaret?"

"I think that Bill always contacted Ben, and they always met in Bull Ring pubs."

"Then that is where I will start if we have no news by this afternoon, now let me call the chief inspector."

As their abduction enters the third day, Ben is becoming more apprehensive about what will happen to them. Why are they keeping them so long, especially as he has said he will give them whatever they want? Is it just their way of prolonging his agony at seeing what they are doing to his daughter, increasing the tension before finally getting rid of her? Ben decides he must go on the offensive and demand that he is allowed to speak with the man in charge. He notices that the men are late, it is after 11 o'clock when they finally arrive. He has been looking at Polly through the window and is devastated by her appearance. She has been badly beaten by these men over two days and he can see some of her wounds are serious. Her vest is torn from the beatings and he can see cuts on her legs. She is slumped on the settee, half asleep, apparently mumbling to herself. She is in desperate need of medical attention, and when the men eventually arrive he screams at them about his daughter's condition.

"Are you idiots aware of the state my daughter is in? Your treatment of her has left her with serious physical injuries and she is mumbling to herself. It will do your cause no good if she dies on you, and rest assured you will get absolutely nothing from me if that happens," he says firmly.

"Nothing is going to happen to Polly, Mr Spencer, we will wash her and clean any wounds before we carry on today, now have some tea and toast, sorry we are a bit late this morning," the older man, the man in charge, answers.

"Will you at least let me attend to her wounds, I am sure that will help your efforts if I spend some time with her?" Ben replies desperate to see Polly and address her situation.

"No, no, Mr Spencer, we can't do that, we are supposed to be punishing you not agreeing to your wishes and demands. We will continue dealing with your daughter as I see fit, you have my word that we will be sure not to overstep the mark, but the punishment has to be severe to show you how serious we are; do you understand, Mr Spencer?" he says with firmness, leaving Ben in no doubt of his intentions as he leaves the room. All four men enter Polly's room and wake her from her stupor, shaking her roughly.

"Come along, Polly, it's time again, tie her to the beam please. Now, you look a bit of a mess so we are going to give you a wash before we continue," he says, and with that one of the men returns with a bucket of water and throws it over her. The shock of the cold and the wet causes Polly to scream and gasp for breath. One of the men wipes her face, while the older man examines the cuts on her legs and bottom.

"You have a few cuts, Polly, but nothing that won't heal eventually, now we need to get on with things we are late this morning," he says as two of the men begin to strike Polly again with the canes.

The water dripping from her now makes the pain from the canes even worse and she is gagged again. After only a few minutes the men stop, and remove the gag from her mouth. She is given some water then left suspended from the beam while the men leave the room. Ben is sitting slumped in his chair having decided that he can no longer watch what is happening to his daughter. However, the men enter the room and force him to look through the window at Polly, hanging from the beam, her underwear in pieces, soaking wet and bleeding.

Jonathan Crump delivers the car to the Spencer's home around noon, a large saloon in very good condition. Mrs Spencer signs the necessary paperwork, agreeing to rent the car for two weeks. The garage will be able to assess what damage has been done to Ben's car in the meantime. Daniel meanwhile, makes the call to Chief Inspector Jamieson, and receives some encouraging news.

"Daniel, good morning, we may have some news. It seems that there has been talk about an abduction of a senior government figure who is being held for ransom. The villains are not local, no one has any idea who they are, so that would substantiate your thoughts that they have been sent from London," says the Chief Inspector.

"Any ideas where they might be held, and have your men been able to find Bill Holder?"

"I'm afraid not, but I thought we might talk with some of those that we have in custody from previous attempts on the Spencers' home. They might know this chap Bill Holder," the chief inspector replies.

"That sounds like a very good idea."

"I will arrange that as soon as possible, Daniel and call you back with any news, bye for now." Daniel passes on the information to the rest of the family with a degree of optimism.

"What do you think, Daniel, is there a chance that one of these men may know Bill Holder, and even if that is so, what chance that he will know where Ben and Polly are?" says Margaret with despair in her voice.

"Margaret you must remember that it was from information received from Bill that we were able to find you, so let's try and be optimistic about the Chief Inspector's suggestion."

"Yes of course you're right Daniel, this is the best news so far," says Margaret tearfully.

The children look on quietly before George decides it is time to say something.

"When are you going to find the men who took Daddy and Poll? Daniel, you are going to find them, aren't you?" he asks tearfully.

"We certainly are, George, and very soon I hope, now why don't you go with Conrad and see what toys he may be able to help you with?"

Maisy and Daisy cling close to Margaret who decides that she will go into the garden with them and see how work on the new wall is progressing.

"Do you really think that you will find Ben and Polly, Daniel?" Margaret asks when she is alone with Daniel in the parlour.

"We have to believe that they are alive, and if so we will find them. Ben is no use to them if he is dead, and he will give them nothing if they get rid of Polly. They are using her as a means of forcing Ben to give them the details from the contents of the container. He will make absolutely sure that Polly is released before he agrees to anything. My real concern is what they might do to Polly to force Ben to give them what they want. This is the third day, and I am becoming very concerned for her."

The men return to Ben around 5 o'clock, and Ben is curious where they might have been.

"For God's sake let my daughter down from that beam, her shoulders will dislocate if they haven't done already."

The men leave Ben with some tea and sandwiches and go into Polly's room cutting her down from the beam and putting her on the settee. She is unconscious.

"She is in a bad way, sir, perhaps you had better take a look at her?" one of the men suggests.

The older man holds Polly in his arms and gives her some smelling salts to bring her round. She opens her eyes, but gives no signs of recognising him, staring ahead with a blank look on her face. They lie her on the table face down, and clean up her wounds which are numerous and becoming infected.

"Now then, Polly, we need to clean you up before we continue," the man says.

Polly is shivering continuously from the soaking she was given and the fact that she is wearing only her badly torn underwear. She is given some tea which helps and slowly she comes round to realising where she is. She is actually being held by the older man while one of the others offers her some tea. She is also given a meat paste sandwich which she eats ravenously.

"Where am I, what are you doing to me, who are you, why am I here?" Polly becomes increasingly agitated as she slowly begins to realise what is happening, but is too weak to resist in any way.

"Now you just lie there and rest for a while, Polly," the older man says smiling.

Then after about ten minutes or so after she has had a warm drink and a sandwich the older man turns to her.

"Now, are you ready then, Polly, we have to finish what we started with you, you do understand what is going to happen to you don't you?" he says smiling.

"Are you going to kill me? You are, aren't you? You are going to kill me." she says becoming agitated.

"No, Polly, we are not going to kill you, not yet anyway, we have lots of other things we can do first. Then when your Daddy has given us what we want, then we will kill you, my dear," the older man says.

"We will have to tie you to the beam again I'm afraid, let me help you up," he says.

"No please don't beat me any more please!" Polly pleads.

"My dear Polly, we have to, but it won't be for long so try and understand it has to be done, okay, gentlemen, carry on if you will, I will watch from next door, give her about ten minutes then cut her down and put her on the settee," he says as he leaves the room and joins Ben in the adjoining room.

"Your daughter is coping very well, you should be proud of what she is doing for you," he says.

"I have nothing more to say to you, sir, other than the fact you disgust me," says Ben.

As the afternoon goes by, Daniel becomes more and more concerned at no news. At 5 o'clock he calls the Chief Inspector again, but despite extensive efforts from informers and despite contacting those in custody, no information has been forthcoming.

"If these men are from London, Daniel, chances are that they will not be known to any locals at all. They are shadows. Your best bet is to try and make contact with your Bill Holder. We have tried his address but he has not been seen there for some time," the chief inspector says.

"That is probably because he was attacked recently, someone found out about his passing information which led to your seizure of the barges full of black market goods."

"I see; no wonder we cannot find him if he is in hiding."

"Well thank you, Chief Inspector, please let me know if you hear anything, good bye for now," says Daniel as he replaces the receiver. He speaks with Conrad and Margaret and suggests that he asks Peter to accompany him to Birmingham to see if they can locate Ben and Polly. Conrad is disappointed not to be going along but with his damaged shoulder he would only be a hindrance.

"Talk to Peter, Daniel, ask him to bring Maureen here while you are gone."

Daniel calls Peter who agrees to go with him as soon as possible.

"Maureen and I will be with you very soon, Daniel, we can then head for Birmingham immediately."

Daniel is relieved to at last be doing something. He appreciates it may come to nothing but it will be a start. He cannot just sit and wait for something to happen. Then as he is preparing for the visit to Birmingham, the phone rings.

"Hello, this is Daniel Bottomley speaking."

"Daniel, it's Bill Holder, I understand you have been asking about me? I may have some information about what has happened to Mr Spencer and his daughter."

"My God, Bill, it's good to hear your voice, I am sorry if you have been bothered by half the police in Birmingham trying to find you, but we are desperate can you help?"

"A mate of mine who drinks in the Nechells district, told me about four blokes using a disused factory this week. He was suspicious because they had cockney accents. Why would four blokes from London suddenly start using an unused factory in Birmingham, we reckon they must be hiding something. When I heard the law were looking for me I thought about Mr Spencer."

"That is wonderful news, Bill, can we meet in about an hour or so, say 6.30 p.m.? Would you be able to find out exactly where this warehouse is and show us, it will be myself and my colleague Peter?"

"Okay, Daniel, can we meet outside The Woolpack Inn like before? I will see you there. We can drive to my mate's place and he can tell us where the factory is, see you soon," says Bill. Daniel dashes out of the study to find Margaret.

"Margaret, I have good news, we think we know where Ben and Polly are being held."

"Oh, Daniel, please let it be true, where are they?" Margaret asks with tears in her eyes.

Daniel tells Margaret and Conrad about his telephone conversation with Bill Holder, and says he will be travelling to Birmingham with Peter as soon as he arrives. Peter and Maureen arrive about fifteen minutes after the telephone conversation, and after checking they have everything they need, including weapons and ammunition, Daniel and Peter leave for Birmingham.

They arrive at the Bull Ring just after 6.30 p.m. and spot Bill outside The Woolpack. He gets into the car and directs them to his friend's house in the Nechells Area. Bill's colleague is suspicious of Daniel and Peter, thinking they are police, but is reassured when Bill convinces him that they are close friends of Ben Spencer, a very good friend of his. Bill's colleague tells Daniel that the men have been using the old factory for about a week now, and he knows that it has not been used for anything since the war, like a number of factories in the area.

"I was suspicious about them from the start, Bill, who would want to use any of those old factories, the best thing that can happen to them is to demolish them, and the sooner the better if you ask me. Anyway, the factory is in Nechells Park Road Bill, their car should be out front if they are still there," Bill Holder's colleague says.

"Thanks, mate," says Bill.

Polly is once again subjected to a beating by two of the men. She screams in agony before collapsing. The men carry on until they are told to stop by the older man. They cut Polly down and dump her on the settee. She is almost naked, her underwear cut to pieces by the canes, so the men put her shirt and skirt back on her. Then, the older man glances at her and decides to leave her there until the morning. They are waiting instructions, so do not need to do anything else with her today.

"Well, Mr Spencer, Polly is sleeping now, so we will not disturb her further today and we have put her clothes back on for her. But you need to start giving us some details. My colleague will be contacting me tomorrow and I need to be prepared."

Daniel and Peter spot the car in the factory yard, park further up the road and tell Bill to wait until they return. They move swiftly toward the entrance, and go to the back of the building to find an easy way inside. They find a broken window so are able to lift the catch, open the window and climb inside. They hear voices from the other end of a long corridor and make their way towards them, just as a door opens and two men emerge, see Daniel and Peter and fire at them. Peter returns fire and hits one of the men in the shoulder. Daniel and Peter run toward the end of the corridor as the second man fires randomly in their direction before disappearing behind the door. Both Daniel and Peter run toward the door and fire shots through before opening it.

"Stay exactly where you are nobody move, Ben move over to the side," Daniel shouts.

Another man reaches for his gun and is shot in the leg by Daniel.

"Stay still both of you, Ben where is Polly?"

"She is in the room next door," says Ben as he dashes from the room.

Peter checks the phone and surprisingly, it is working. He calls the police asking for the chief inspector, then asks for an ambulance as quickly as possible.

"See if there is anything to tie these two with Daniel," says Peter.

Ben meanwhile comes back into the room, his face red with anger.

"Peter, let me have you weapon please."

Peter hands Ben his weapon, Ben walks over to the leader of the men who have been holding him and Polly, and orders him to get down on his knees. He then aims and shoots him in the head, hands back the weapon to Peter, and returns to Polly.

"Daddy is that you, I am so tired, Daddy, please help me, Daddy." Polly whimpers.

Daniel has covered her with his jacket as Ben holds her to him while they wait for the ambulance. They both realise that she is close to death from the beatings and the cold that she has endured. The ambulance arrives after about five minutes and takes Polly, accompanied by Ben, to The Children's Hospital in Steelhouse Lane about five minutes away.

Peter, meanwhile has secured the one man uninjured with the rope used on Polly, while they wait for the police.

"You gentlemen would do well to remember that it was me who shot this man when he went for his weapon do you understand?" Peter says.

"Whatever you say, guv'nor," the man replies.

The police arrive and find one man dead and two men injured from gunshot wounds.

"You must be Daniel, Chief Inspector Jamieson, very pleased to meet you."

"Chief Inspector, this is my colleague, Peter Forsyth, Ben has gone in the ambulance with his daughter, she is badly hurt from a beating at the hands of these men."

"We would very much like to go and see Poll, Chief Inspector may we call on you afterwards to give our statements?" Daniel asks.

"You can use the Steelhouse Lane Station, across the road from the hospital."

The police take away the men involved, and Daniel calls Margaret with the news. Margaret bursts into tears of joy, and asks Daniel if he would ask Ben to call her from the hospital as soon as possible. They return to the car to be greeted by Bill Holder anxiously awaiting news.

"We got them, Bill, thanks to you and your friend, Ben has gone to the hospital with his daughter, she is in a bad way I'm afraid. We cannot thank you enough and I know that Ben will be contacting you very soon."

"I'm glad that I could be of help, Daniel, tell Ben I will contact him in a couple of days when he has had chance to recover."

"I will do that, Bill, now let's get you back to The Bull Ring, my guess is that you are ready for a drink," Daniel replies.

Daniel and Peter drop Bill Holder back in the Bull Ring, and proceed to the hospital to see Polly.

They park the car and go into the hospital to be shown where Polly is being cared for in a side ward. Both men are shocked by what they see and what Ben relates to them. Polly has been subjected to the most brutal attack by the men trying to secure information from him. Ben has not been harmed physically, but has been forced to watch the attacks on Polly, which have left him devastated. Polly has been sedated, giving Ben the opportunity to talk with Daniel and Peter.

"Peter, Daniel, how on earth did you manage to find us, I am indebted to you yet again."

"It was your colleague Bill Holder again, we tried to find him through the Police, using their informers, and he was tipped off by a friend that they were looking for him. When he heard about strangers from London using a disused factory for no obvious reason, he guessed it may have something to do with you. He phoned the house and we came to Birmingham as soon as we heard.

"His contacting you, and your rescuing Polly and I, has saved our lives Daniel. Those men would have killed us as soon as they had the information from me. Beatrice was right, they are mercenaries for hire. We must find out who hired them and see that they too are punished."

"I think they will be more than happy to cooperate with the police, Peter and I will be giving our statements before we return to Cresswell. I will try and see what I can find out about them, it will be useful for Beatrice Carrington to know who hired them."

"Perhaps you might both go along since Polly will be asleep for a little while yet."

"Yes okay, Ben, we will come back when we have finished," says Peter.

Peter and Daniel go across to the Steelhouse Lane Police station, and introduce themselves to the desk sergeant.

"We've been expecting you gentlemen; I will tell the Chief Inspector you are here."

The sergeant returns and shows them into the office where the chief inspector is waiting along with a W.P.C. who will take down their statements.

"Gentlemen, thank you for being prompt, how is Polly, do you have any news yet?"

317

"She has been sedated for the time being, I hope we shall get some news when we return, thank you for your concern," Peter replies.

For the next half hour or so, the two men outline the circumstances behind finding Ben and Polly, and then the detail of the struggle to eventually free them. Peter confirms that it was he who shot the ringleader dead, since he was threatening to shoot Ben. The chief inspector accepts their version of events without any reservations, since there is no reason for him to think otherwise. He is familiar with Ben's activities in the National Interest, and was appreciative of the tip offs that Ben passed on regarding criminals operating on the canals. He is also aware that these interviews are merely routine prior to the men in custody being returned to London.

"Well that seems in order, gentlemen, again thank you for coming, is there anything I can do for you meanwhile?" the chief inspector asks.

"Yes as a matter of fact, Chief Inspector, would it be possible to speak to the men, off the record of course, only for a short period?" Daniel asks.

"Off the record, I suppose that will do no harm, and anything we can do to help Mr Spencer's cause, we are more than willing to do. I think the two injured ones have been patched up, so I'll get them fetched up from the cells. The W.P.C. will direct you to interview room no.1, good luck."

The three men sit opposite Daniel and Peter, looking a little apprehensive.

"Gentlemen, this interview is unofficial, is not being recorded so anything you say will remain confidential, do you understand? Firstly, what are your names, please?" asks Daniel.

"Arthur Bellamy, Frank Phelan and Freddie Carter, our dead colleague, our Commander was George Chisholm," they answer.

"Thank you, now were you made aware of who Mr Spencer was by your superiors?" Daniel continues.

"Yes we knew who he was, and what his job was, we were told to get some information about secret documents, and torture his daughter to persuade him. Once we had the information, we were to dispose of both of them," Arthur Bellamy replied.

"And who were you to give the information to?" Peter asks.

"Before we give you any names we want to know what we can expect from the law in return," Bellamy comments.

"Let me just say this to you, if you cooperate with names it can only be good for you, your actions against Polly Spencer will get you ten years' hard labour, so you need to look at your options.

"Write down any relevant names on this piece of paper, and we will see to it that the prosecution is made aware of your cooperation. You should give out the information again if required when you are interviewed by Scotland Yard. You don't need to tell them of our conversation, do you understand?" asks Daniel.

"Yes, sir, we don't tell nobody about giving out names, understood," Bellamy replies.

"That's it for now, gentlemen, just remember what we said concerning the execution of your commander, he was threatening Mr Spencer's life, and we had no alternative but to kill him, understand?" The three men nod in unison as Daniel and Peter get up and leave the room. They tell the desk sergeant they have finished, and leave for the Hospital. Ben is sitting outside Polly's room waiting for the doctor to finish his examination of Polly. He eventually emerges from Polly's room looking very sombre.

"Mr Spencer, your daughter has received a terrible beating sustained over several days, I believe, and is in deep shock from the experience. She is barely lucid at present, although she may recognise you. The wounds to her shoulders back buttocks and legs are severe and will take some time to heal. They will need to be dressed regularly, but they will heal over time. I noticed other wounds on various parts of her body in various stages of healing, what on earth has happened to you, Mr Spencer?" the doctor asks with concern.

"Over the past few weeks my daughter has been abducted twice and dragged from the house in a failed attempt at abduction. This last abduction is the third time that she has been taken. I will not go into any details as to why this has happened, other than to say that there are desperate people who will do anything to stop me doing my work for our government."

"I understand, Mr Spencer, you can appreciate why I had to ask given the dreadful state of her injuries?"

"Of course, Doctor, may we see her now please?"

"Just you, Mr Spencer, let's see how she reacts, then perhaps your colleagues may follow if she responds to you."

Ben goes into the room and sees Polly who is staring at the ceiling blankly.

"Polly, my dear it's Daddy, how are you feeling?" he asks fighting back his tears.

There is no response from Polly, who continues to stare, her face as pale as snow, her eyes red with black rims beneath.

"Daniel and Peter are here, too, we all want to say hello to you, can you understand what I am saying, my dearest Polly?" Ben asks with concern.

There is still no response from Polly, and Ben turns to leave the room, thinking he might get Daniel to talk to her. Daniel goes into the room and sits beside Polly holding her hand.

"Polly it's Daniel, Peter and I found you and came for you and Daddy, you are safe now, but you need to get well, then you and I can spend some time in London again."

However, there is no response from Polly, just a blank stare. Then, as Daniel turns to leave the room, Polly responds.

"Please don't go, Daniel, please stay with me, is Daddy okay? And Mummy? Is Mummy okay? Daniel, I don't want you to ever leave me again, will you promise me?" Polly asks with fear in her voice.

"Nobody is going to leave you, Polly and I will stay with you for as long as you want. You must rest now, would you like something to drink?"

"Just stay with me, Daniel, I am so tired but cannot sleep unless I know you are here close by."

Polly eventually goes off to sleep, and Daniel slips quietly out of the room.

"She is in deep shock, Ben, I think she believes that if she is left alone she will be taken again, God we should have killed those men when we had the chance," says Daniel visibly upset by Polly's state of mind.

"We need those men to bring down the culprits in high places, Daniel, though I completely understand your reaction. Can I make some suggestions here, Ben? It might be an idea to contact Margaret, and return home with me. The children need to see you and know that you are okay. Then you can return tomorrow with Margaret. Daniel can stay here with Polly, and call you if there are any changes that you should know about," says Peter.

Ben agrees with the suggestions put forward by Peter, and goes off to talk with the doctor and call Margaret. The doctor says that Polly will have to stay in hospital for a few days yet, but agrees that she can be moved to Carswell tomorrow afternoon. Ben and Peter leave for home around 9 o'clock after looking in on Polly who is sleeping soundly. Ben will return, with Margaret, around 10.00 a.m. tomorrow, after the doctor's rounds, and hopefully will be able to travel with Polly back to Carswell Hospital. Daniel meanwhile, settles in to spend the night at the hospital with Polly. The staff find him a blanket and they offer him a drink and some sandwiches. The hospital is very quiet, having settled down for the night and he is relieved to see Polly sleeping, without any assistance, and falls asleep himself. He is woken, suddenly, by Polly calling his name. She has obviously woken from a deep sleep and is disorientated.

"Daniel, where are you?" she shouts.

"I'm here, Polly, right beside you, you must have woken from a deep sleep."

"Is Daddy here, Daniel, and can I talk with Mummy please?"

"Daddy has gone home to fetch Mummy, they will be here soon, then once the doctor has given the all clear, you can be transferred to Carswell hospital so that you are nearer to home and your friends and family. Now, shall I ask the nurse to get you a drink?"

It is nearly 7.30 a.m. so there should be someone around who can get a drink for Polly.

"Yes please, I also need the nurse for the toilet."

The nurse enters and takes Polly to the toilet in a chair and Daniel asks her what is the routine for Polly regarding her treatment.

"The doctor will come and look at her in about half an hour, her wounds will be looked at and dressed. She can then have some breakfast, but I will fetch you both some tea while you wait for the doctor."

"Thank you very much for your help, nurse," Daniel replies as she wheels Polly out of the room.

The doctor arrives to look at Polly as she is drinking her tea along with Daniel. She is beginning to show signs of recovery, greeting the doctor with some enthusiasm.

Hello, Doctor, thank you for taking care of me, Daniel has told me I may be able to move to a hospital nearer home later?"

"I hope so, Polly, I'm pleased to see you are much improved this morning."

"Daniel stayed with me so I knew I would be safe. He always looks after me."

"Now let me take a look at you, Polly, Daniel if you wouldn't mind please?" the doctor says pointing to the door. Daniel gets up to leave when Polly interrupts.

"No please, Doctor, please I want Daniel to stay with me if you don't mind?" she pleads.

"Very well if you insist, Polly, so long as it makes you feel comfortable Daniel can remain."

The nurse removes Polly's hospital gown to reveal her body covered in deep cuts and lacerations. They are particularly severe on her buttocks, and her wrists are badly injured from being tied up for so long. Daniel is deeply shocked by what he sees. He has witnessed severe injuries during the war, but never such injuries on someone so young. She has undoubtedly been subjected to severe beatings over the three days she was kept a prisoner, and will carry the physical scars for a very long time. The mental scars she may well carry for much longer. The nurse tends to the most severe using soothing creams to ease the pain for Polly. Daniel marvels at the courage of this young girl. He knows that he along with her family will be needed to help Polly in the weeks to come. When the nurse has finished, she puts Polly's gown back on and goes off to get her some breakfast.

"Well now, Polly, how do you feel after a good night's rest?"

"I feel better thank you, Doctor, but I knew I would with Daniel by my side. He will look after me won't you Daniel?"

"Absolutely, Polly, absolutely," Daniel replies with a smile.

"I wonder if I might borrow Daniel for a moment, Polly, do you mind?"

"Okay, Doctor, but please don't keep him for too long," Polly smiles.

Daniel follows the doctor out of the room and listens to his comments about Polly.

"Your presence seems to have a remarkably calming effect on Polly, Daniel, she seems almost serene when you are close by; you will have a major part to play in her recovery."

"I was fortunate enough to be able to foil a previous abduction attempt from her home, and since that night she has become very reliant on my being close by, it's as if she believes that nothing can happen to her providing I am with her. Unfortunately, this last abduction was from her school, so I was not there for her. Her family has endured terrible ordeals by criminals trying to stop Mr Spencer from doing his job. Polly has been abducted twice before and her home has been subjected to an arson attack and an explosive device. My job is to give them protection until Mr Spencer's work is done, and circumstances have meant that I have become attached to Polly in all this. My colleague Peter, who you met, has also been assisting with security at the Spencer's house."

"God, this family has been through hell, Daniel; Mr Spencer did mention these points to me yesterday. Regarding your relationship with Polly, my judgement is that your presence will greatly help her get through this ordeal. Her injuries will eventually heal, but the mental scars are more of a concern. This is where your calming influence will be so valuable. As you know, we are going to transfer her to a local hospital this afternoon. She will be kept there for a few more days before she is allowed to go home, so please stay close to her, your being there will make all the difference. Now you had better get back to her before she wonders where you are."

"I will do my very best for her, Doctor, and thank you for your comments," says Daniel as he returns to Polly's room.

Ben and Margaret arrive just after 10.00 a.m., and rush to see Polly.

"Hello, Mummy, I am so pleased to see you," she says tearfully.

"My dearest darling Polly, what have they done to you this time?" Margaret says with tears in her eyes.

"Everything will be okay now, Mummy, Daniel is taking care of me."

Ben, meanwhile has found the doctor and asked him for an update on Polly's condition.

"She has made great strides, Mr Spencer, Daniel's presence seems to have completely rejuvenated her, I see no reason why she cannot be transferred to your local hospital later today."

"That is wonderful news, Doctor thank you very much, I wonder if we might have some tea?"

"Certainly, I will get nurse to bring you some into Polly's room."

After some lunch and the formalities relating to transfer to Carswell, Polly is placed in an ambulance and despatched to Carswell. Ben and Margaret travel with her and Daniel takes the car. He has to promise Polly that he will drive straight to the hospital to be with her when she arrives.

On the drive back to Carswell, Daniel reflects on the rescue of Ben and Polly. He knows that he will have to spend some time with Polly as part of her healing process, whilst carrying out his duties, together with Conrad, to make sure that the members of the Spencer family are kept safe. This last abduction indicates the desperation of these criminals. No one is safe whilst the ringleaders are free to make further attempts on Ben and the family.

Daniel, a battle hardened soldier, had never seen anyone resort to such brutality against a young girl, a child, in order to service their own ends. Ben's actions in shooting George Chisholm were understandable, and should send a message to anyone who is planning any further attacks. With these thoughts going over in his mind, he parks the car and goes into Carswell Hospital to wait for Polly to arrive. As soon as Polly is settled, Daniel speaks with Ben.

"Ben, I am going to the house shortly to clean up after today's events. I will bring Maisy, Daisy and George back with me as soon as they are home from school."

"Thank you Daniel, but you had better tell Polly where you are going!" he replies with a smile.

So Daniel goes off to the house leaving Ben and Margaret with Polly. Maisy, Daisy and George have arrived back home from school, and full of questions about what has happened.

"Daniel, is Poll okay? Did those nasty men hurt her? How many did you shoot?" asks George full of questions as usual.

"When can we go and see Polly, Daniel, we miss her so much?" asks Maisy.

"Okay, children, as soon as I have had a wash and changed my shirt, we can all go and see her. Now off you go and get ready while I have a word with Conrad and Auntie Pauline."

"How is she really Daniel?" asks Pauline with concern in her voice.

"She is remarkably resilient considering the savage beating that she has had Pauline, your niece is an amazing girl, most adults would have not coped with what Polly has been subjected to these last few days, and on several previous occasions."

"She will need a lot of attention from you Daniel, she does so rely on your presence to give her confidence after what she has gone through recently," says Pauline.

"Is there anything I can do at all Daniel?" asks Conrad.

"Just keep Pauline and the home safe while we are at the hospital Conrad," says Daniel as he goes to the bathroom to wash and change.

His shirt has blood spots from the encounter at the old factory, and his jacket is dirty from the factory floor, when he tied up the men. He washes, puts on a change of clothes, and collects the children. After saying goodbye to Pauline and Conrad, he leaves, with the children for Carwell Hospital. The children dash into Polly's room and rush to her side, all talking at once. Polly's face lights up when she sees them, they, too, will play a large part in her recovery process.

"Polly, Polly, we have missed you so much. When can you come home?" Daisy asks.

"Can Polly come home today, Mummy, please?" George pleads.

"Only when the doctor tells us George, and not before," replies Margaret.

"I knew Daniel would find you Polly, he always does doesn't he Daddy?" says George holding on to Daniel's hand.

"Yes, George, Daniel and Peter saved us and we are all very grateful to them, now you stay with Polly while I go and speak with Daniel a moment."

"The doctor has told Margaret and myself that we can probably take Polly home tomorrow afternoon. They want to be sure that she is healing properly, so will keep her in overnight."

"However, the doctor has said that she must stay in bed for a week at least to allow her body to recover and give her the rest that she needs after her terrible ordeal. I mention this to you now Daniel knowing how much Polly has come to rely on you. You will give her the time that she needs from you I'm sure, I just wanted to put you in the picture."

"I will give Polly all the time she needs, Ben, I want her to get well as soon as possible, and I did promise her that I would take her back to London."

"Thank you, Daniel, now I suggest that you stay a little longer when I leave with the children, I will come back and collect you," Ben suggests.

"Can I ask you how you are coping with all this, Ben, it is obvious where Polly gets her strength from, you have been through hell these last few weeks yet seem to have coped unscathed."

"Believe me, Daniel, I have not had time to think about what has happened too much, but this last episode with Polly, was the last straw for me. My actions against their ringleader surprised and shocked me I have to say, but I had promised myself that I would finish him if I ever had the chance."

"You did what any parent would have done in the circumstances, Ben, you have absolutely nothing to be ashamed for."

"Thank you, Daniel, now you had better get back to Polly, she will be sending out to find you!"

Ben and Margaret leave with the children after about an hour, leaving Daniel to remain with Polly for a little while longer.

"How long can you stay with me, Daniel?" asks Polly sounding concerned.

"I will stay with you for a while yet, Polly, don't you worry, you are in very safe hands here."

"I am coming home tomorrow, Daniel, then I know I will be safe because you will be there, I just wish you could stay with me tonight," Polly replies, sounding disappointed.

"Best if I go home tonight, Polly, we have to get your room ready for when you come home. I am going to try and arrange some sort of communication for you. That way if you want anything you will be able to contact Mummy downstairs. And I believe we are going to rearrange the bedrooms so that Pauline has the room next to the bathroom and Conrad and I have the room next to yours. That way, I will always be close by."

"But you will stay with me at night, Daniel, please, promise me, I really need to know that you are there when I wake," says Polly, with panic in her voice.

"Polly, I will always be here for you no matter what. Whatever I can do to help you get over this terrible ordeal, I will do. I care for you very much and nothing will ever happen to you while I am here, and I will be here for as long as is necessary."

"Can we go back to London when I am better, Daniel?"

"Yes we will be going to London, to finish our trip, as soon as you are well enough, so that is something to look forward to for both of us. Now I think you had better rest a while."

Polly lies back, closes her eyes and drifts into a deep sleep. Daniel sits looking at her and again reflects on his responsibility toward her. She will rely on his support even more after this latest incident and will be very demanding of his time and need him to be there whenever she needs his support.

They have grown very close so he will not be burdened in any way by her demands. In fact, he may well relish the challenge that young Polly is offering him. She has become the sister he never had, and he is enjoying their special relationship. Polly sleeps for about two hours, and wakes just as Ben returns to collect Daniel.

"It's nearly 9 o'clock, Polly, so we will leave you to rest for the evening and see you in the morning my dear," says Ben.

"Will you come in the morning too, Daniel, please?"

"Yes, I will come in the morning, Polly, for an hour or so, then after lunch Mummy and Daddy will collect you and bring you home. Sleep well," he says and kisses her on the cheek.

"Good night, my dear Polly," says Ben as he holds her to him, before both men leave the room and return to the house. Margaret has prepared Daniel some supper which he is grateful for, not having eaten since lunchtime. After chatting with Ben, Margaret, Conrad and Pauline for about an hour, Margaret addresses him directly.

"Daniel, before you retire for the evening, can I just say something? Although we have only known you for a short time, I feel that you are very much part of our family, and I hope will continue to be so for some time yet. You saved my life, and yesterday, with Peter, you rescued Ben and Polly. Without you, I do believe our daughter would not have survived her terrible ordeals. Our home is your home, Daniel, for as long as you like, we can never repay you, all I can say is thank you, thank you so much," says Margaret with a tear in her eye, as she moves toward Daniel and hugs him tightly.

"Thank you, Margaret, you are very kind, and all I would say is that it has been a pleasure to have helped you and the family and I hope, in some small way, I have been able to contribute to Ben's bringing the racketeers to justice."

The household retires for the evening, enjoying a comfortable night's rest after the worries and anxieties of the last few days. Next morning, Daniel, Conrad and Ben get together in the study for an update on what needs to be done over the next week or so before the local trial and the trial at the Criminal Court in London.

"Over the next day or so, I need to update my evidence notes regarding the abduction of Polly and myself to pass on to Beatrice Carrington. She in turn will be able to pass them on to the Crown Prosecutors for them to use in evidence. I want to see these men punished to the maximum, along with those that gave them their orders. This has become more than a black market trial, the charges of kidnapping and grievous bodily harm to a minor will now be added. This last attempt to extract information from me will show the court how contemptible these people are and I hope they will get the punishments they deserve," says Ben.

"I am sure that will happen, Ben, apart from the racketeering, physical assaults against children are looked on very severely. It is unfortunate that Polly will need to give evidence, but I will help her understand just how important it is," Daniel replies.

"And she is sensible enough to know how important it will be for her to tell her story."

"Perhaps it may be an idea for me to take over the school run, Ben, Daniel will be on hand here, and I believe that it is important to keep all the children safe."

"That is a very sound idea, Conrad, we have to accept that these people are capable of anything. And should Margaret or Pauline need to go into town, perhaps you would be good enough to accompany them?"

"Absolutely, Ben."

"I need to set up some sort of buzzer for Polly, Ben, there is probably something I can use in the garage. There was a bell on the old back door I believe, maybe I can salvage that if I can find some cable," says Daniel.

"There should be some cable left by the electricians who fitted the flood lights."

"Good, well I think that covers most points, Daniel you are off to the hospital later this morning, and then Margaret and I will collect Polly after lunch and bring her home."

And with that, Daniel and Conrad leave Ben in his study to continue preparing his evidence for the pending trials. Daniel finds what he needs to set up some sort of buzzer, which he will do later, then leaves for the hospital just before 11 o'clock. Polly is sitting up in her bed, a huge smile on her face when Daniel enters the room.

"Hello, Daniel, I am so pleased to see you, how is everyone at home?"

"They are all fine, Polly, and looking forward to seeing you later, how are you did you sleep well?"

"Not really, I had nasty dreams, and I kept seeing the faces of the men who hit me, they were saying horrible things about me, telling me to behave, I kept waking up then falling asleep, but then having nasty dreams again, I don't want to go to sleep again, Daniel, I know they are waiting for me to go to sleep so that they can say horrible things to me," Polly says with tears in her eyes as she grabs hold of Daniel.

"Now, Polly, you must not let those dreams upset you so, they were only dreams, nothing else will ever happen to you I promise," Daniel replies, concerned by her anxiety.

"I know and when you are here, I feel safe and well, but last night I was so lonely and afraid."

"You will feel so much better when you are back home, Polly, and I will be nearby at all times. We are going to get you better as quickly as possible and when you are well enough, we will have a few days away in London, so that is something for you to look forward to."

"How soon can we go away, Daniel?"

"Well you have to heal first, Polly, the doctor's will need to look at you a few times to make sure that all your cuts and bruises heal properly, then we can decide."

"Why can't we go to London now, Daniel? I will still be able to heal in London, you will be there to keep me safe, and no one will know who I am. Please, Daniel, take me to London now?" begs Polly, becoming agitated.

"Polly, Polly, listen to me now. I know you trust me to keep you safe and be with you whenever you want, don't you?"

"Yes, Daniel."

"Okay, well we must get you well before we can go anywhere, Polly, the doctor has insisted that you remain in bed for a few days, that was a condition he gave on allowing you home. We all love you very much and want you to get well, but it will take some time and I'm sure some of your friends would like to see you, Polly, and don't forget how much Maisy, Daisy and George have missed you. Your Mummy and Daddy have also suffered over the last few weeks and need your support," Daniel replies hoping that Polly will understand.

"I will try, Daniel, I will help Mummy and Daddy and I know that Maisy and Daisy and George have missed me lots, so I will spend some time with them as well, but I still want to go to London with you as soon as I am better, so that will be okay won't it?"

"That will be something that we can both look forward to, Polly."

Daniel manages to arrange some lunch, and asks the Doctor if he might have a word. He is concerned about the anxiety that Polly is showing.

"I wasn't sure whether Polly had mentioned her bad dreams, Doctor, she seems frightened to go to sleep in case she sees the men who abducted her in her dreams. I would hope these bad dreams might subside when she moves back home?"

"I am sure they will, Daniel, and of course you will be close by. She has come to rely heavily on your presence, and will continue to do so for some time. It is obvious that you have a very special relationship which has developed through the events of the last few weeks, and you rescuing Polly on more than one occasion. She sees you as a father figure and a shining knight always there to rescue her, whatever the circumstances. You will have to accept the fact that she is totally reliant on you for the present. Her needs will diminish over time, she is very young, but for the moment she is vulnerable and needs you to be there for her."

"Yes of course, Doctor, I understand and thank you."

Ben and Margaret arrive shortly after lunch, with Polly's clothes, and having thanked the doctor take Polly home. They agree to keep Polly in bed for most of next week, and arrange for the family G.P. to call in the meantime. Polly arrives home to hugs and kisses from Maisy, Daisy and George. Conrad and Pauline greet her with affection as well. After all the greetings are over, Margaret takes her up to her room and gets her settled in bed. Daniel has moved her bed against the wall so that there is space for an easy chair and a small table. As soon as Polly is settled he goes in to see her.

"Now that you are settled, Polly, I will fix a buzzer for you. That way you can be heard downstairs should you need anything."

"Thank you, Daniel, that will be very useful, but you will be here any way most of the time won't you?"

"I will certainly be here some of the time, Polly, especially in the evening, but you will have other visitors, Maisy, Daisy and George, your Auntie Pauline and of course some of your school friends."

"As long as I know you are close, Daniel, I will be okay," she says as Daniel goes off to fix a buzzer for her to use.

Daniel fixes the buzzer for Polly which sounds in the parlour when pressed. This will allow her to attract attention without having to shout, although unless all the doors were open, it is unlikely that she would be heard anyway. Margaret gets into the habit of leaving the parlour door open when she is in the kitchen so that she will be able to hear should the buzzer. For most of the afternoon, Polly's time is occupied by the children. They have missed their big sister so much and want to make up for lost time. They play some games, then ask Polly to read them a story. They love Enid Blyton Stories, and can relate to the characters and the dog. In fact, they have played out games in the garden using the names of some of the characters. Polly greatly benefits from this time spent with the children and enjoys being with them again.

And so for the next week, Polly remains in bed, as the Doctor instructed, and spends time with all members of the family, a visit from her school friends and of course lots of time with Daniel.

Margaret and Ben also spend time with her just sitting with her reading and talking. Ben has to spend some time at his office as the trials get closer, but Margaret finds herself seeking solace with Polly, after her terrible ordeal which has been somewhat overlooked recently. Remarkably, Polly gives Margaret just the support she has needed, and mother and daughter forge a close bond based on their experiences.

"No one will ever be able to understand what happened to us, Polly, only you and I really know, that is why we can help each other."

The children, too, are excellent therapy, providing Polly with the routine around the house that she needs to help her get back to normal. Every day, after Conrad has collected them from school, they descend on Polly, wanting to play games and listen to stories. All this family activity is good for her and can only help with her convalescence.

It is the night periods that prove to be most difficult, and Daniel finds himself having to stay with Polly throughout most nights. She goes off to sleep, then wakes in a panic, which can only be consoled by Daniel holding her in his arms until she goes off to sleep. This means uncomfortable nights, armchair with Polly sleeping on his lap. However, at least she sleeps and when in his arms, she sleeps soundly through the night and Daniel finds himself enjoying a nap during the afternoons, when the children are with Polly, to make up for his loss of sleep. On Wednesday Polly is surprised by her three best friends, Valerie, Veronica and Clare. The girls press her about what has happened, but Polly sidetracks their questions by asking about school and what she may have missed.

"I can't talk about what happened yet because the horrid men responsible have to stand trial, so I have to wait until then before I tell what happened, you do understand?"

"Okay, Polly, we just want you to get better and come back to school," Valerie replies.

"I believe Mummy is going to call the school and ask for some work for me, could you bring it round, Val, please?"

"Of course, Polly," she replies as they hug before departing. After they have left, Polly bursts into tears. Seeing her friends has just proved too much for her.

That evening, Polly has a bath, Margaret is hoping that it may help her with her sleep. By 9.00 p.m. she is sleeping soundly, and everyone hopes that she will have a good night's sleep after an enjoyable time during the day. Daniel must have dozed off forgetting to put on the night light.

Polly awakes screaming and Daniel goes to console her. She is thrashing about with her arms and legs, half-asleep and half awake, calling Daniel's name. He manages to calm her down and puts her back into bed, holding her tightly as she curls up beside him and goes into a deep sleep. Daniel wakes around 6.30 a.m., and tries to move off her bed, but she wakes and asks him to stay. Eventually, Polly drifts into a deep sleep, allowing Daniel to cover her with a blanket and sit back in the armchair to get some well-deserved sleep for himself. He sleeps for about an hour or so before being woke waked by the sounds of the children moving about. He opens the door so that the sound drifts into Polly's room.

"Good morning, Polly, I'm off to have a wash and brush my teeth, would you like me to get you some breakfast?"

"Yes please, Daniel, whatever Mummy is preparing will be okay for me."

After visiting the bathroom, Daniel goes downstairs to get some breakfast and Margaret asks him about Polly.

"She had some bad dreams, Margaret, I am a bit concerned about how she is reacting at the moment, I know she will need time, but she seems to becoming even more reliant on my being with her."

"Well the doctor will be calling this morning, perhaps you should speak with him about your concerns?"

Daniel agrees, takes Polly her breakfast, and tells her that Mummy will be up to attend to her as soon as she got the children ready for school. Pauline and Conrad say hello, and ask her if she requires anything, since they will be going into town after taking Maisy, Daisy and George to school.

"If you can find me a magazine, Aunt Pauline, please."

Daniel joins Ben in the study to mention his concerns about Polly and Ben agrees that Daniel should mention this to the doctor when he arrives.

"I have to go into my office this morning, Daniel, I want to see what has happened over the last week. Can I leave you to take care of everything here please?"

"I will be here, Ben, I have the buzzer to fix for Polly, and we need an update on the conservatory. I will check the house and grounds generally to see if there is any area where we can improve security. We have to be very conscious of what could still happen, with the main trial at The Criminal Court still a week or two away."

"Do you think that we are still at risk, Daniel, God I wonder what they could possibly do next?" he says.

"I believe that it is your property that will be most at risk, they have tried a number of times to abduct one or other family members, and know that we will always respond with force. This will make them look for a softer target, and the house is just that.

"However, if we make it as secure as we can and be alert to any strangers, we will be okay. Whilst the house is in a quiet area, any strangers, on foot or in a vehicle of any kind, will be quickly noticed. With both Conrad and myself around, we can endeavour to ensure that at least one of us is always watching the garden and the lane beyond."

"I will leave the details to you and Conrad, Daniel, I know you will do everything possible to keep the home a safe place for all of us."

The Doctor arrives just after 9 o'clock and goes up to Polly's room with Margaret. He asks Polly about her bad dreams and suggests a sedative to help her sleep.

"I am okay when Daniel is with me, Doctor, but if you think the sleeping draft will help then I will take it if I need to."

"Well I believe it will be a help, Polly, and Daniel will not always be here you know."

"But, Doctor, Daniel has told me he will be with me for as long as he is needed, and I feel safe when he is here," Polly replies almost protesting at the doctor's comments.

"Now, Polly, we know that Daniel is here for you, just concentrate on getting better, now let Doctor Wilson check on your cuts and bruises," says Margaret, not wanting Polly to become upset over the doctor's comments.

After examining Polly, and telling her he will call in again in a few days' time, the doctor accompanies Margaret into the study. He writes out the prescription for the sedative and hands it to Margaret.

"How bad are her wounds, Doctor? Will they all clear up over time?"

"I'm sure they will, Margaret, but it is obvious that she has had a fearful beating, mentally she is very fragile however and her dependency on Daniel is rather worrying."

"I believe that Daniel wanted to have a word with you about that, I will go and get him," says Margaret as she leaves the study to find Daniel.

"Hello, Daniel, I am pleased to have this opportunity to speak with you about Polly, I understand that you wanted a word?"

"Yes, Doctor, whilst I enjoy being part of her convalescence and do care for her very much, she has become almost obsessive toward my being with her since the last abduction. We both know that she has suffered terribly, not just this last time, but a number of times previously and I am concerned that she has become very frail mentally. It seems that only by being in physical contact with me can she feel safe. I will always be there to protect her for as long as necessary, but we both know that I will not be with her forever."

"Yes indeed, Daniel, do you think that Polly sees you as more than a friend who is caring for her, is she forming a physical attraction to you do you think?"

"I am a former army officer doctor, most of my adult life has been in the army, organised and structured, I am not married, nor do I have any sisters, so I am not really qualified to know what sort of feelings Polly may have towards me. I have to say that your comments are a little confusing. I love Polly very much and would protect her with my life, but that is part of my remit being here with the Spencer family in these extraordinary circumstances.

"As for Polly, what has happened to her will leave scars for a very long time. I am doing what I can to help her overcome the terrible ordeals she has been through. Now, I cannot tell you how these ordeals may have affected her emotions other than to presume that they must have. For me I see her as a frail young girl who seems to draw strength from my presence, can you understand that, Doctor?"

"I understand perfectly, Daniel, and thank you for saying that. I would just say that you may need to be aware of any changes in Polly's feelings toward you, especially while she is in her present state."

"Thank you, Doctor, I will be aware of Polly's attitude toward me and respond accordingly, let me see you to the door."

Daniel sees the doctor out and returns to the studio to think over what the doctor has said to him.

Ben returns to his office to be greeted by Phil Landers and Maureen, both relieved and delighted to see him back safe and well. Maureen especially, knowing from experience, is particularly relieved that both he and Polly are okay.

"How is Polly progressing, Ben? That poor girl has been through hell the last few weeks, and you too must have suffered dreadfully for her."

"She is coping Maureen, it will take time, and Daniel is there with her for most of the time which helps. We are a little concerned at her dependence on him, but for the moment we just want her to get well, whatever it takes."

Ben has been allocated an office at the end of the building and Maureen has an adjacent one with an adjoining door. She has also arranged for Ben to have a secure line installed for his conversations. He decides to take advantage of this and calls Beatrice Carrington. He apologises for not contacting sooner, giving her details of his and Polly's abduction.

"My dear, Ben, how are you and how is Polly, these people know no boundaries to their wickedness?"

"We are recovering, Beatrice, I am unharmed anyway, it was Polly that was subjected to a terrible ordeal at the hands of the four men. I am sure that they will provide evidence against the main culprits in exchange for a lighter sentence. One of them escaped justice, however, I shot him dead. Daniel was able to have a word with them, courtesy of Birmingham Police, and they assured him that they knew the names of the men who had organised the abductions and instructed them to harm Polly."

335

"Well it's good to receive some positive news in all this Ben, now the trial will commence in two weeks, initially there will be the reading of the formal charges against all of those involved. The Crown will push for an early start to proceedings, and all of the main perpetrators will be remanded. So I estimate that you will be called to give evidence in about three weeks. Now the Crown may decide that they want to talk to Daniel and to Peter, regarding the raids on your home.

"Whether the Crown or the defence call on Polly, Margaret or Maureen is doubtful, especially since they have more than enough evidence to secure convictions and any evidence they gave if questioned by defence barristers would be detrimental to their cases. However, Polly should be prepared for your local trial which should be quite soon."

"The sooner this is brought to a conclusion the better Beatrice; it is becoming very wearing to everyone in my family. One point I would just mention. I would like to recommend some sort of reward and commendation for my contact in Birmingham. His name is Bill Holder, and it was information supplied by him that resulted in Margaret being found as well as Polly and myself."

"Then he most definitely deserves some recognition, Ben, if you can let me have an address, I will see to it that he is suitably recognised."

"One other point, Beatrice, will the local trial impact at all on the Criminal Court Case?"

"The Crown will be advised, and may mention it as additional 'ammunition' if you like, but it will not affect proceedings in any way."

"Thank you, Beatrice, I will keep you informed and get you that address, bye for now," says Ben as he replaces the receiver. He will look up Bill Holder's contact address as soon as he returns home and get Maureen to send the details to Beatrice as soon as possible. Meanwhile, he asks Maureen if she can get details of the trial dates, in Birmingham. He mentions that she may be called, although the men concerned were never apprehended.

"Whatever needs to be done, Ben, I feel strong enough to go to court and tell my story, I want to see these people punished for their actions."

Phil Landers knocks on Ben's door and asks for a moment of his time.

"Come in, Phil, thank you Maureen, what can I do for you?"

"I wanted to update you on events of the last week or so, Ben, if I may? There have been a number of illegal goods seized in the local and Leicester areas, nothing spectacular, but significant in that we are taking more and more villains out of the black market business. I spoke with D.I. Wishart after one successful arrest, and one of the men made reference to the attack on Maureen. I expect the D.I. will be in touch with Maureen on this very soon."

"That is really good news, Phil, Maureen and I were just discussing the upcoming trial and the fact that her attackers had not yet been apprehended. She will be delighted to hear the news."

"I will give you a copy of the details of the recent raids with a breakdown of those responsible and the values of goods seized."

Ben thanks Phil, and takes time to reflect on what Beatrice had told him about the possible trial start date. Was it all really coming to an end? All the hard work, the destruction of his home, the terrible attacks on Margaret and Polly, and Maureen, were those concerned soon to be severely punished for their actions both toward them and for their black market activities over many years? He certainly hoped so for his family had suffered enough for his pursuit of those who sought to gain from the Nations shortages. Their greed had created much hardship and they were soon to pay with their liberty for their despicable actions.

Ben was feeling rather satisfied at the moment, and set off home confident that he and his family would soon be able to start having a normal life again.

Daniel, meanwhile, sits and ponders over his conversation with the doctor regarding Polly's demeanour. He will look after her as much as is required. Her recovery takes precedent over everything else at present. If she becomes obsessive toward him, he will handle it. Whatever is needed to get Polly back to her normal happy self will be done. He continues to think about this as he goes about his day, first setting up the buzzer for Polly, then walking the garden perimeter to assess the security of the garden and house. He is confident that with the floodlights operational, and the newly erected fencing at the bottom of the garden, coupled with the newly erected wall, that every precaution has been taken to make the house safe. The conservatory windows will be installed within the next few days, completing all the work that needed to be done. And Ben has instructed the Post Office not to deliver any packages addressed to the house. Conrad returns after what seems a rather long shopping trip with Pauline, and goes off to collect the children from school. Daniel completes fixing the buzzer and goes upstairs to look in on Polly.

"Daniel, where have you been, will you stay with me for a while?"

"Of course I will, Polly, I have been rather busy, tell me what did the doctor say, are your wounds healing as they should be?"

"Doctor Wilson said they were, would you like to see?" says Polly as she removes her nightshirt to show Daniel the bruising and wheals across her back and legs. Daniel is shocked to see just how badly the wounds look, and wonders how long it will take for the injuries to completely heal.

"Let's hope they soon heal, Polly."

"Stay with me please, Daniel, for a while anyway. How soon will we be able to go to London and stay at your flat? I'm sure that Conrad could cope if we were to go away for a few days."

"We will go as soon as the doctor feels you have recovered enough; I am here, Polly, so you concentrate on getting better before we go anywhere."

"Okay, Daniel, but you will stay with me for a while won't you?"

Daniel sits with Polly talking about what they might do when they go to London. Daniel feels that talking to Polly about the trip to London might help her look forward to it for when the time arrives.

Polly's friend Valerie arrives around 4 o'clock, bringing her some schoolwork, so Daniel happily leaves the two girls to chat while he catches up with Ben and Conrad. He confirms with Ben that the security of the house is all but complete, and reiterates the idea that Conrad and himself spend time during the day walking around the perimeter and looking for any strangers in Crab Tree Lane. Ben updates him on news, from Beatrice, regarding the trial at The Criminal Court, and informs him that the Birmingham trial is set to start in just over a week's time. This means that Polly may be called to give evidence at that time and Ben asks Daniel for his advice on how soon she should be told.

"I suggest that we talk with her on Monday, Ben, hopefully, the Doctor will let her get up for a few hours a day by then. We should ask him for his thoughts on whether she will be ready for the ordeal of a trial so soon after her latest abduction."

"Very well, Daniel, the doctor will be along, probably Monday so we can discuss it with him then."

Both men then move off toward the garden to look at the work completed, collecting Conrad, who was with Pauline in the parlour, on the way. Margaret is already in the garden, spending time with the children on the new swing which has arrived. The garden is slowly coming together and Margaret reflects on what plants she will be able to get when planting begins again. Valerie leaves after about an hour, and Pauline and Margaret begin to get supper ready. The children spend some time with Polly, and Daniel remains in the garden enjoying the peaceful early evening sunshine. Ben receives a call from D.I. Wishart around 5.30 p.m. asking if he might get statements from Ben and Polly for Birmingham Police and Ben asks if he would call around 9 o'clock Friday morning. The family, together with Pauline, Conrad and Daniel, enjoy their supper after which Margaret goes to spend time with Polly. She suggests that she have a bath which should help her relax, and take the sleeping draft that the Doctor has suggested. After she has bathed and taken the draft, Daniel goes in to sit with her. After about half hour, Polly falls asleep, so Daniel goes back downstairs, hoping that she might sleep through the night. The family sit and chat after supper trying not to dwell on what has happened. Margaret seems to have recovered some from her ordeal. Ben and Polly's abduction must have helped her in some way. Having to fret over their wellbeing took her mind off her own terrible ordeal. And Ben has so much going on that he has not had time to think about his own ordeal, or the fact that he killed a man. Then, around 10 o'clock, Polly's buzzer sounds. Daniel goes upstairs to find Polly in some distress.

"Daniel, I woke and you weren't here, why weren't you here, Daniel?" she sobs as she clings tightly to him.

"Polly, come along, I was only downstairs with Mummy and Daddy, anyway I am here now," he says giving her reassurance.

"Will you sleep here tonight, Daniel, I want you to sleep with me, then I will be safe."

"I will be here with you for as long as you wish, Polly, now shall I get you a warm drink?"

"Yes please."

Daniel goes off to get Polly a drink and collects one for himself before saying goodnight to everyone and going back to Polly's room. He has managed to get an additional blanket in case the night turns chilly.

"Here you are, Polly, this should help, and I am with you now."

"I am fine now, Daniel, I must have slept rather deeply from what the doctor gave me. When I woke I wasn't sure where I was and felt frightened."

"Well you are safe now, Polly, so relax and just remember I am just here, goodnight, my dear. "

"Goodnight, Daniel."

Daniel had no idea how tired he was, and soon drifts off to sleep himself. However, his sleep is short lived. He is woken by Polly groaning, then sobbing, then calling out, "No, no, no, please."

Daniel goes to her and calmly talks to her while she is still apparently dreaming.

"Polly, it's Daniel, you are quite safe, my dear, quite safe," he murmurs to her.

Polly wakes up and clings to Daniel pleading with him not to leave her alone.

"Please, Daniel, please don't leave me," she sobs.

Daniel climbs onto her bed and takes Polly in his arms before wrapping them both in a blanket. He realises that this may be the only way he can console her. And though Daniel is extremely uncomfortable, he manages to calm her down and slowly her sobs ease off as she falls asleep. He has no sleep all, since Polly becomes more and more agitated as the night progresses. She moves around pushing off the blanket and finally ends up lying across him with her head nestled into his shoulder and her arms around his neck.

"Good morning, Polly. How do you feel? I hope you slept well," says Daniel smiling.

"I didn't sleep very well, Daniel, sorry if I kept you awake," she replies obviously a little dismayed finding herself sprawled across him.

"Thank you for being with me all night, Daniel, I had some weird dreams and I can remember talking with you about something before I was interrupted, but you saved me and held me tight, then I woke up."

"So long as you got some rest, Polly, that is all that matters." He realises that she is rather embarrassed by the position she found herself in and seeks to reassure her. He does not want her to become upset over nothing, her rest and recuperation are most important, no matter how they are achieved.

"Will you sit with me for a while after the children have gone to school, I really need to talk to you please?"

"Of course, Polly, but don't forget you have to give the police a statement later," Daniel replies.

D.I. Wishart and W.P.C. Becky Garrett arrive around 10.00 a.m. and Margaret answers the door and shows them into the study.

"If you would wait just a moment, Detective Inspector, my daughter has been confined to bed after her ordeal so you will have to conduct your interview in her room. I am sure you appreciate that she is rather frail at the moment, so if you could be brief I would appreciate that very much. One more thing, would you mind if Daniel stays with her during the interview?" Margaret asks.

"Not at all, Mrs Spencer, I understand that she has become rather dependent on him through her ordeals, and I welcome his being there if it will help her during my interview," the D.I. replies.

"Thank you, now please follow me."

Margaret leads the way upstairs to Polly's room followed by the D.I. and W.P.C. Polly is sitting up in her bed, with Daniel beside her. As the police officers enter the room, she immediately grabs hold of his hand.

"Hello again, Polly, I hope you don't mind if Becky and I ask you a few questions about what happened to you and your Daddy?" the D.I. asks.

"I will try and answer your questions, but please don't ask me what those men did to me, please," says Polly tearfully.

"Now, Polly, we only want a few details and we will stop if you want us to at any time," the W.P.C. replies hoping to put Polly at ease.

"But don't you understand, Becky, those men beat me every day for three days. They used canes on my back, bottom and legs and took it in turns. They enjoyed hurting me, really they did, they just kept hitting me with the canes over and over and–" Polly bursts into tears and turns to Daniel, holding on to him tightly.

"Please, Daniel, I don't want to talk anymore, please," Polly sobs.

"Okay, Polly, we will leave it there for now, I am so sorry for upsetting you," the D.I. says with concern.

"Daniel, will you stay with her please, shall we go back to the study?" Margaret says tearfully to the police officers.

"It may be best if you spoke with my husband, Detective Inspector; he was there and was forced to witness what happened to Polly. It will be a big enough ordeal for her if she has to give evidence in court without going over it again here," Margaret answers tearfully.

"Of course, Mrs Spencer, I am sorry if we upset her, she has obviously been badly affected by what happened to her and I hope she gets well soon. We can talk with Mr Spencer at his office."

"Thank you for your understanding, Chief Inspector, let me see you out."

Margaret sees the police officers to the door, then returns upstairs to find Polly still firmly holding on to Daniel. She is sitting across Daniel with both her arms around him and her eyes closed.

"Polly, Mummy is here to see you."

Polly stirs, but hardly moves from her position on Daniel's lap.

"I'm okay now, Mummy, really I am, Daniel is taking care of me. "

"Very well, my dear Polly, but you must let Daniel get on with some of his work, he cannot be with you all of the time," Margaret replies, concerned over the way her daughter clings to him. She must speak with Daniel about the total independence that Polly has on his being by her side. The way that she holds him almost childlike is very disconcerting for Margaret and she must speak with Daniel about this as soon as possible to try and devise a way that Polly's complete reliance on him can somehow be reduced.

Daniel stays with Polly for about an hour. She does not move from her position on his lap. Her outburst to the Police officers had triggered the nightmare of her time with the men who abused her so badly. Slowly, Daniel moves her back into her bed and leaves her sleeping. He joins Margaret in the parlour having tea with Pauline. Conrad is situated at the bottom of the garden, checking the lane for any strangers.

"How is she, Daniel?"

"She is sleeping at the moment, Margaret, the questioning obviously proved too much for her triggering the memories of her captors and her treatment."

"How do you think she is getting on is she improving, only it seems as though she has become totally dependent on your being by her side at all times. And this would include virtually sleeping with her throughout the night as well," says Margaret with some concern in her voice.

"I must confess to being a little concerned myself about how much her dependency on me has become, Margaret, but for the moment I am happy to be able to give her some sort of peace. I am no expert, so I have no idea how long it may take, but if I can make the difference then I will do my best for her."

"You cannot begin to know how much we appreciate what you have done for her, Daniel. Had you not been here we would surely have lost our beautiful daughter forever. She obviously loves you very much, and makes that very clear from how she wants you to be with her all the time. If you are happy with the way she is progressing, and do not mind her taking up so much of your time, then we are happy for you to continue being with her. Hopefully, as she recovers her mental strength, she will become less dependent on you being with her."

"I am sure that in time she will recover and be the normal happy school girl that you and Ben know her to be."

Daniel goes out to join Conrad, taking in what Margaret has said and wondering whether perhaps he has allowed Polly to become too close to him. He just hopes that her dependency will slowly diminish over time as the recent events become a distant memory. Polly sleeps for a while then gets on with some of her schoolwork apparently none the worse for the earlier upset. Daniel calls in on her in the afternoon, and is pleased to see that she is getting on with other things. He does not actually go back into her room until about 10.00 p.m., and thankfully Polly has her first really good night's sleep since she came from the hospital. The whole family enjoy the weekend. Doctor Wilson calls Saturday morning and tells Polly that she can get up for half days from Monday. This is just what she wanted to hear and is delighted with the news.

"We shall be able to go for walks, Daniel won't we? You did say you would take me for walks."

"Yes, Polly, we can go for short walks they will be good for you."

Polly has two good nights' sleep on Saturday and Sunday, much to Daniel's relief as he was beginning to feel the effects of sleepless nights himself. Whilst he had still remained in Polly's room, she had not disturbed him, and on Monday morning was showing clear signs that she was feeling much better. She chatted with the children before they went off to school, telling them that she would be up when they came home so they could all go into the garden. The children were delighted that their Polly was going to play with them again. They had missed her so very much this last week. Ben goes off to his office where he has arranged to meet D.I. Wishart at 10 o'clock.

"Good morning, Detective Inspector, can we get you some tea?"

"Thank you very much, sir. I hope we didn't upset your daughter too much, last Friday?"

"Polly is very fragile at the moment, Inspector, it doesn't take much at all to upset her, so mentioning the events of last week would have been too much for her.

"I was forced to witness the cruelty of the men towards my daughter. They beat her constantly over three days and seemed to treat the event as though it was a normal daily occurrence for them. I begged them to stop and agreed to give them all the information they were seeking, but they seem to be working to a schedule, and would not change what they were doing. Polly has sustained severe wounds to her back and legs which will take some time to heal. She was suspended from a beam for periods of time while two men hit her with canes. My God, Inspector, you cannot imagine what she went through on my behalf," Ben concludes with tears in his eyes.

"You have my sympathy, Mr Spencer, I understand how difficult this must be for you, just a couple of questions relating to the shootings then I will be off. Can you give me a brief idea of what happened regarding the men who were shot?"

"Two of the men were shot and sustained injuries the third man, who was the obvious leader, was shot dead. Peter felt he had no alternative since he was threatening me with a pistol. The injuries to the other men were a result of Daniel and Peter rushing into the room. They were fortunate not to have been hit themselves."

"Well thank you for your help, Mr Spencer, I wish you every success in the upcoming trial, those men will surely go away for a long time. Goodbye and good luck to you," the inspector replies as he leaves Ben's office.

He felt a degree of guilt regarding his part in the shooting, but decided to go along with Peter's comment that he be responsible so that there could be no complications at either trial. It was absolutely essential that no complications occur regarding the mass of evidence gathered against the criminals. The trial, in Birmingham, was due to start one week from today, so it was important that no adjournments were secured, since the trial at London Crown Court was not too far away.

After lunch, Polly gets dressed, with some help from Mrs Spencer, and goes downstairs and into the garden, where she finds Daniel. She has selected one her best dresses to put on, and Mrs Spencer spends some time brushing her hair. Polly sits next to Daniel on the bench and asks him when they can go for a walk.

"We can go after supper, Polly, you will want to spend some time with Maisy, Daisy and George first won't you?"

"Okay, Daniel," she replies.

Having spent some time with Maisy, Daisy and George, and enjoying a walk with Daniel, Polly goes off to bed quite early. Mention of the upcoming trial, had upset her and Daniel took some time to console her before returning home. Daniel deliberately avoids any talk of Polly, not wanting to get involved in her condition and his relationship with her. He eventually goes upstairs around 11 o'clock, to find Polly sound asleep. Perhaps she is finally being able to enjoy proper rest. Daniel goes off to sleep himself, but is suddenly woken by Polly. She has got from her bed and is pleading with him to get in with her.

"Daniel, hold me, please hold me," she sobs, with sweat pouring from her.

Daniel lies with her and holds her in his arms, covering her with a blanket. He does his best to console her, not sure what could have brought on this latest panic attack.

Polly holds Daniel so tight that her nails dig into his neck. The one advantage of Polly going off to sleep with Daniel, is that he also manages to get some sleep, although he does get rather warm with Polly lying on him for six hours or more. When Polly wakes, she is sweating through her bad dreams and also because she has been lying on top of Daniel for so long. She moves from him and turns on her side before drifting off to sleep again, giving Daniel the opportunity to go to the bathroom and wash. He goes downstairs and makes himself some tea before returning to her room. He looks at his watch, it is 5.30 a.m. He sits in his chair and tries to understand what is happening with Polly. Instead of becoming less dependent on him, she is in fact becoming more dependent. He is not getting enough rest himself, which he needs to be alert at all times round the family, having to attend to her throughout most nights. And Polly is becoming totally reliant on his sleeping with her rather than him just being in her room. He decides that he must talk with her about this; she must understand that he cannot be expected to stay with her every night.

Polly eventually wakes about 7 o'clock and seems very refreshed from her night's rest. She does not mention being with Daniel, so he does not mention anything about it.

"Good morning, Daniel, I slept very well, what about you?" she says with a smile.

"Yes I slept well too, Polly."

"Gosh I am hot and sweaty, I think I will have a bath later," she says.

"I will see what is for breakfast and I need to change my clothes," Daniel replies noticing how creased his trousers and his shirt are. Conrad takes the children to school, and returns to find Daniel with Margaret in the study.

"I thought I might look at our weapons while the children are away at school, Daniel. They have all been used recently so could benefit from being stripped and cleaned," he suggests.

"Good idea, Conrad, see if there is any lubricant in the garage."

"How was Polly last night, Daniel, I heard some moving about, did she get up at all?" Margaret asks.

"Yes she did, she got rather upset so I had to lie with her again, she only seems to be able to relax if I am in with her. She holds on to me so tightly, that she actually scratched me on the neck," Daniel replies showing Margaret the deep scratches.

"Well I am sure you will speak to her about her dependence on your presence, Daniel, and I hope things will improve when she returns to school. She will have her friends around her and schoolwork to concentrate on," Margaret adds as she leaves the study.

Margaret's comments convince Daniel that he must talk with Polly as soon as possible. In fact, since he has nothing specific to do before lunch, he decides that there is no time like the present. He goes upstairs and knocks on Polly's door before entering. Polly is busy with some of the schoolwork that she has been given, and is obviously delighted to see Daniel.

"Daniel, come and sit with me, I did not expect you until later," she says with a smile.

"I have just been chatting with Mummy, Polly and we are both a little concerned about me having to sleep by your side each night," says Daniel with some firmness in his voice.

"But, Daniel, I have to have you close to me, it makes me feel safe."

"I understand, Polly, and I will be with you in your room at all times, but you have to start sleeping on your own, do you understand?"

346

Polly gets from her bed and goes over to Daniel, sitting on his lap.

"But I need you to be close to me, I just feel so frightened if I cannot feel you close by, Daniel," Polly replies as she buries her face in Daniel's neck and begins to sob uncontrollably. Daniel holds her as her sobbing gradually subsides, then carries her back to her bed.

"Okay, Polly, let's leave things as they are for now, I do not want you to upset yourself for no reason. I will leave you to get dressed now, then after lunch we can go off for a walk together."

"Thank you, Daniel, I look forward to that very much."

Daniel goes downstairs to join Conrad who is busy in the garage. He has both of his weapons stripped and has managed to find a light oil for lubrication. Daniel hands him his spare weapon and leaves him to his work. He wanders down to the edge of the garden to check on any activity in the lane but there is no one about. Regarding Polly, he has to concentrate now on preparing her for the possibility that she may be required in court next week, not a task he is going to enjoy given Polly's demeanour. Over the next day or so, Daniel carefully coaxes Polly into accepting that she may have to give evidence in court next week. The fact that she was abducted twice before being taken, with Ben, to Birmingham, and was seriously assaulted twice more in her home could make her a key witness for the Crown in seeking the maximum sentence against her perpetrators. The fact that Polly will be classified as a minor will mean that the sentences will be the most severe. Unfortunately, she will be asked to tell what happened, and Daniel is concerned how she may react. She has tried to shut out what has happened to her, now she will be asked to catalogue the events in some detail.

"But, Daniel, I cannot tell strangers what happened to me, nor can I be expected to be with those men who hurt me so much, I just cannot," she sobs and holds on tightly to him as they walk along the lane outside the Spencer's home.

"It may be the only way we can punish these men, Polly, and you do want to punish these men don't you?"

"I suppose so, it just seems so unfair that they will be allowed to look at me again and try and say it did not happen, now can we go home please?"

They return in silence and Polly goes up to her room, Daniel decides to leave her alone for a while. She will have to accept that in order to punish these men, she may be asked to tell her story, however painful. He will continue to coax her over the weekend, and hope that she will be strong when the time comes. Over the next few weeks, Ben Spencer's hard work, over a number of years, will come to a satisfactory conclusion. Daniel has to make sure that everything goes smoothly at home. Polly's welfare and how she copes over the next few weeks will be his responsibility, only he has the influence to be able to prepare her and support her through what will be quite an ordeal for her. He looks in on her around 10 o'clock to find her asleep, so goes back downstairs to talk about the upcoming trials. Everyone is becoming a little edgy, not least Margaret, whose dreadful ordeal has been somewhat overlooked by other events.

Ben has spoken at some length with her, and she is extremely apprehensive about what she may be asked.

"You will have to tell them what happened, Margaret, it will be very painful for you but it is the only way that we can see the culprits punished. I will be with you at all times, my dear," says Ben hoping to reassure her.

"Thank you, Ben, I will do what I have to, but I am dreading the trial and will praise the day when all this is over."

"How is Polly coping with all this, Daniel, I understand, from Margaret, that you have had a difficult time with her recently?"

"Like Margaret, she is apprehensive about facing those that treated her so badly, but I am confident that she will manage, Ben," replies Daniel, trying to sound convincing.

"I hope so, Daniel, I hope so."

Daniel spends some time over the next couple of days, Friday and Saturday, persevering with Polly, and gently convincing her that she will be absolutely safe when she goes to court. He will be with her and so will members of her family. Slowly, it seems, she begins to gain confidence, and even concedes that she must give the evidence needed to put the men away that have treated her and her family so badly.

Meanwhile, Ben receives a call from Bill Holder who sounds very excited.

"Mr Spencer, I just wanted to thank you for my reward. I also got a letter from The Chief Constable of Birmingham, thanking me for helping you and your family. One hundred pounds, Mr Spencer, I'm rich!"

"I'm delighted for you, Bill, you deserve it, without your information we might not have been having this conversation."

"Well thank you anyway, and I keep my eyes open for you," says Bill.

Ben contacts Beatrice Carrington to confirm the trial go-ahead in Birmingham on Monday.

"Let's hope it does not last more than two weeks, Ben, the Old Bailey conspiracy trial is due to start in three weeks," Beatrice comments.

"It should be over well before then, Beatrice, although there are a number of charges to consider, the evidence is overwhelming. I will keep you up to date with anything that may be relevant at your end."

"If you would, Ben, the Crown does not like last minute surprises, good luck Monday," says Beatrice as she replaces the phone.

Ben has one final call before he is finished for the weekend.

"Hello, Peter Forsyth speaking."

"Peter, it's Ben, how are you?"

"Okay, Ben, what can I do for you?"

"Just checking about next week, Peter."

"Daniel and possibly Conrad too may be required to give evidence in the trial in Birmingham, and I am concerned about the house security while we are away. Maureen could come here direct from work or just be with you if she is not in work."

"It will be a pleasure, Ben, we will enjoy the change and it will give me a chance to see the children again and your newly built home!"

"Thanks very much, I will give you a call and let you know when I have more detail."

Ben, Margaret, Polly and Daniel then go over what will happen on Monday.

"It should be a relatively easy case to follow since the evidence is overwhelming and is not in dispute. We just need to make sure that these people get the maximum punishments for their treatment of our family and Maureen, too, of course," Ben continues.

"Will all of the men be there, Daddy, those that hurt me and Mummy and tried to burn down our house?"

"Yes, they have all been arrested, and they will all be made to pay for what they did to us all."

"But will they be able to talk to us, I don't want to talk to them, Daddy," Polly asks tearfully.

"No they cannot talk to you directly, Polly, they will have someone talk for them."

"So they will be able to tell him what to say to me, they will tell him to make me say what happened to me, I know they will, Daniel, please I don't want to talk about what happened to me," Polly continues becoming particularly agitated as Daniel puts his arm around her to comfort her.

"My dearest Polly, the men who will be answering you questions will not be allowed to upset you, but you will be asked a few questions, so please don't worry about it," Ben replies rather unconvincingly.

Margaret looks at Daniel as if needing him to give Polly reassurance.

"You don't have to worry about anything, Polly, I will be there to take care of you. It will be over very quickly and we shall be able to come back home."

"But, Daniel, I am scared, really scared that the men will go over what they did, I really don't want to have to remember being dragged downstairs, dragged outside, and being covered in blood from that man that you shot, then being taken by those men who beat me with canes. They will enjoy seeing me get upset, I know they will, I can't do this anymore," she replies and runs from the room in tears. Daniel looks across at Margaret, unsure whether he should go after her.

"You had better go to her, Daniel, you are the only one who can calm her, try and get her to go to bed, it has been a long day for her."

Daniel goes upstairs to find Polly lying on her bed sobbing into her pillow.

"Now come along, Polly, you have no need to upset yourself. It will all be over before you know it."

"But, Daniel, I cannot bear the thought of those men looking at me again, I really can't."

"Why don't you have an early night, Polly, I will help you get ready for bed, and we can talk again in the morning."

"Okay, Daniel," says Polly taking off her clothes and putting on her nightshirt. Daniel goes back downstairs and resumes the conversation about the court case in Birmingham.

"I have put her to bed, Margaret, let's hope she enjoys a good night's sleep."

"Her behaviour is worrying, Daniel, I fear this case may be almost as bad for her as what has actually happened. I will talk to the Crown Prosecutors about procedures regarding the questions they can ask a child."

"We can only hope that she is not subjected to any unpleasant cross examination."

"I believe she will cope, Margaret, and I will keep coaxing her over the weekend," says Daniel.

The family begin drifting upstairs around 11.30 p.m., and Daniel is pleased to see Polly is sound asleep. So he wraps a blanket around himself, and settles in the armchair. He is woken suddenly by Polly pulling at his hair, and scratching him as she shouts out, "Please stop, please stop hurting me, go away, go away."

Daniel, who is half-asleep, desperately tries to get hold of her, but finishes up holding her down on the floor. She is thrashing about ripping at Daniel's vest still apparently asleep! She is still trying to hit out at him, and makes his nose bleed from her blows, as Daniel desperately struggles to get a hold of her. He grasps her nightshirt and manages to lift her. Just at that moment Polly wakes up. Daniel has her in his arms, her nightshirt, covered in his blood.

"Daniel, Daniel, what has happened, why is my nightshirt covered in blood, and what has happened to your face and nose?" she asks sobbing hysterically.

"Polly, you are safe, you have had a bad dream, now let me put you back to bed."

"Don't leave me please, Daniel, please don't leave me," she pleads as she holds on to his arm.

Daniel sits beside her and Polly, once again, curls herself around him. He pulls a blanket over them, and settles down to yet another uncomfortable night. He lies there, as Polly drifts off to sleep and begins to wonder if he will ever be able to break Polly's dependency on him. Each time he manages to drift off to sleep, Polly disturbs him, pulling at his vest and again scratching him, this time on his arm. He tries to move her off him, but she clings to him too tightly, so he puts his arms around her hoping that she will feel safe now and settle into a restful sleep. When Polly awakes she is puzzled by her bloodied nightshirt. She looks at Daniel and notices the scratches on his arm and chest.

"What's happened, Daniel?"

"You had a particularly bad nightmare, Polly, and I'm afraid you gave me a bit of a beating while you were asleep."

Polly notices Daniel's scratches and bite marks and his bloody nose. Margaret, who had been woken by the noise earlier, opens Polly's door and is shocked and dismayed at what she sees.

"Daniel, what on earth has been happening?"

"I'm afraid Polly attacked me while she was having a bad dream Margaret."

"And what happened to your nightshirt, Polly?"

"I must have torn it during my fight with Daniel, Mummy, I am so sorry for all this trouble I have caused you, Daniel," Polly replies tearfully.

"Well, I had better attend to your scratches and your nose, Daniel, and Polly find yourself another nightshirt."

Daniel goes into the bathroom with Margaret and has his wounds dressed. His nose has stopped bleeding, but the scratches are quite deep, and he winces as Margaret applies antiseptic. When Daniel removes his vest she notices a number of deep scars on his back and a particularly bad scar on his side.

"What are these scars you have over your back and this one on your side?"

"Leftovers from the war, Margaret."

"Okay, well I have treated your scratches as best I can, it would have been better to let the doctor treat them, but explaining how you got them could prove difficult. I really am becoming concerned with Polly's behaviour toward you, Daniel. You must keep trying to get her to become less dependent on you, for both your sakes."

"I understand, Margaret, and I am also concerned with her behaviour and her total dependency on my being by her side all the time. Night-time has become difficult, but my being with her seems to be the only way to calm her. I have spoken with her about it but this; her only comment is that without me there she does not feel safe."

"I will speak with her, Daniel, and see what I can do to make her feel safe," says Margaret, and leaves Daniel to make her way to Polly's room.

"Hello, Mummy, how is Daniel, I am so sorry for hurting him, I didn't mean to honestly," she says sitting up in bed still wearing her nightshirt covered in blood.

"Daniel will soon heal, Polly, but you really must stop insisting that he is in your bed."

"But why not, Mummy, I need Daniel to be with me to feel safe, I cannot bear it when he is not holding me tight and keeping me safe. Please, Mummy, let him stay with me."

"Let's see how you are after the trial, but you must try and let Daniel get some sleep on his own, Polly, do you understand?"

"Yes, Mummy, I will try."

Margaret leaves Polly and goes downstairs to get breakfast. Daniel returns to Polly's room and finds her sitting in bed still in her nightshirt covered in his blood.

"You really should change your nightshirt, Polly."

"Okay, Daniel," replies Polly as she goes over to her drawers and gets herself another nightshirt.

"Stay with me, Daniel, I am so embarrassed by what has happened."

"I know you didn't mean it, Polly, but I am rather worried about your behaviour, you seem to be reliving what has happened to you over and over again. Your Mummy is also worried about you. You must try and relax, nothing is going to happen to you when I am in your room with you."

"But, Daniel, I need you to be with me, I really do."

"Let's leave things for now, Polly, I was going to ask your Mummy if I could take you out to Bradgate Park for the day, what do you think?"

"Yes please, Daniel, just you and me that would be wonderful," Polly replies hugging him.

"Now you get dressed, and I will talk with your Mummy, come down when you are ready."

"I think that is a good idea, Daniel. Getting Polly away from the house for a few hours will give you a chance to talk with her, and prepare her for tomorrow," says Margaret, when Daniel suggests he take Polly to Bradgate for the day. So after breakfast, Margaret prepares a picnic lunch for them and they set off for Bradgate Park around 11 o'clock. Daniel decides that he will tell Polly a little more about himself to get her thoughts off everything that have happened recently. They walk for about half an hour before sitting down for lunch.

"You remember Peter mentioning medals to you a while back, Polly? Well, let me tell you a little bit about myself, I think it's about time. My father was a civil servant, and I never had any relationship with him during my early years. I spent most of my time at home reading, mostly about the British Empire, and at school I enjoyed all sports. I joined the army 1939, when I was eighteen, and spent time in Africa and in Europe. I received commendations for fighting in Africa, but was injured while in Europe. I came home and have worked with the army, tracking down deserters. So there you have it, Polly."

"Thank you for telling me, Daniel. Were you badly injured?"

"Not really Polly, mostly shrapnel, and just one wound from a bullet but nothing serious."

"When will you have to leave our house, Daniel? I know you will have to eventually."

"I have unlimited leave attached to your Daddy's department, so I will stay as long as I need to."

"But when you do eventually go back to London Daniel will I be able to come and live with you?" Daniel was not expecting Polly to ask about living with him and is at a loss how he should respond.

"You can certainly stay with me in your holidays, Polly, but I am not in a position to become your guardian, and anyway, you have your family to take care of you. You are only 13 years old and need your family around you."

"But you would have me if you could, Daniel wouldn't you?"

"You have become very precious to me, Polly, and I love you very much, but you have a family that also loves you very much so let us leave it at that."

"Perhaps when I am older, Daniel, perhaps I can make up my mind when I am older?"

"Yes, Polly, now are you feeling better, and ready for tomorrow?" Daniel asks with some apprehension. He wants to change the subject, and he has to get Polly focussing on the trial.

"As long as you are with me, Daniel, I will be okay, I just don't want those horrid men looking at me again."

"You must not concern yourself with who is there, Polly, all you will have to do is answer any questions truthfully. There won't be too many, but you have to give your evidence about what happened to you."

"Daniel, can we go home now please?" replies Polly rather sharply. Again she has caught Daniel unawares, unsure whether she is upset or just tired.

"Of course, Polly, we can go home right away," says Daniel as they pack the picnic bag and return to the car. Polly is very quiet on the way back, in fact she hardly says a word, and when they go into the house she goes upstairs into her room, and closes the door.

"Did you have a good day, Daniel?" asks Margaret as Daniel enters the kitchen.

"Well I thought we were having a good day, but as soon as I mentioned the trial, she asked to come home. She barely spoke on the way back and has gone straight to her room."

"Could you go to her, Daniel, you are the only one who can do anything at all to help prepare her for this trial. I am sorry to burden you so, but you really are the only one that she will listen to?"

Daniel taps on Polly's door and walks in. Polly is lying on her bed face down sobbing.

"My dear Polly, what on earth is the matter?" he asks. Polly gets up and collapses in his arms, once again wrapping herself around him and pressing her face into his neck.

"Daniel, don't leave me, please don't leave me."

"Okay, Polly, nobody is going to leave you now please calm down. Perhaps you should go to bed, it has been a big day for you and tomorrow is another big day as well," Daniel replies. And with that Daniel leaves Polly to get ready for bed, telling her he will bring her some supper later. He goes back downstairs and tells Margaret that Polly has gone to bed. when Daniel takes her supper, Polly is asleep, so Daniel returns to the kitchen. It is only 7.30 p.m. so if she wakes and wants anything she will ring. Daniel goes into the garden and chats with Conrad about the trial, and how much he is looking forward to it all been over. The last few weeks have been hectic and placed a great deal of responsibility on both men, not least Daniel.

"You certainly have a lot of work to do with Polly she is still pretty frail, Daniel. How is she?"

"Well, when we were at Bradgate Park, she asked if she could come to London and live with me!"

"Good God, what on earth did you say to her," says Conrad startled at Daniel's comments.

"I said she could stay for a holiday but that was all, she has a wonderful family that will take care of her."

"And how did she respond to that?"

"She has said very little since and when we returned she went up to bed."

"What about you, Daniel, would you like to have her with you all the time?"

"She is a beautiful girl, Conrad, but I am not qualified to care for a 13-year-old girl full time."

"You are practically caring for her full time now, Daniel, there would be very little difference if she were with you in London surely."

"But would it be ethical Conrad, having a young girl with me in my home?"

"Why don't you find out when all this is over, Daniel, if you really want her to be with you that is."

"Thanks Conrad, I may take your advice and do just that when all this is over." Daniel goes inside and decides to look in on Polly. She is sleeping soundly so returns downstairs to join the rest of the family. The discussion is centred around the case beginning tomorrow. It is agreed that Peter Forsyth will bring Maureen round early tomorrow morning to travel with Ben, Margaret, Polly and Daniel to Birmingham by train. It is agreed that Conrad will stay at the house with Peter whilst Daniel is with the family at the trial in Birmingham.

"I would think that the trial should last no more than four or five days at the most.

"The evidence is pretty overwhelming and the written evidence that will be offered concerning Polly, Maureen and Margaret's injuries will be compelling. I hope that I am able to talk to the Crown Prosecutors and ask them to limit the questions they put to Polly. I am concerned that she may break down and the case be adjourned. Daniel, I am hoping that you can give her the support that she needs to see this through. I am aware of the burden of responsibility that she places on you and I hope that you will continue to give her the confidence that she obviously draws from your being with her."

"I will do my best, Ben, Polly will be ready I am sure."

"Thank you, Daniel, now I suggest we get an early night we have an early start tomorrow."

Daniel goes quietly into Polly's room and settles down in the chair. He looks across at Polly and reflects on his conversation with Conrad. How would he cope with a 13 year old schoolgirl living with him? Whilst he has no problem himself, he harkens back to the doctor's comments about Polly's changing behaviour toward him as she gets older. She is a sensible girl, but she has been badly affected by what has happened and Daniel needs to beware that his emotional crutch does not become more than that. Meanwhile there is a court case to consider. Thankfully, Polly is sleeping soundly, Daniel eventually goes off himself, and Polly sleeps through until morning. Daniel is relieved as he also had a restful night for the first time in a while.

CHAPTER 31

(Birmingham Trial and matters arising)

Ben had determined that Monday was to be preliminaries where the charges will be read out and the accused asked to plead. However, witnesses may be required, so Ben, Margaret, Maureen, Daniel and Polly arrive at Birmingham Crown Court and wait on their instructions.

"There are a long list of charges to be read, as well as written evidence to be recorded. So it may be some time before you are called if at all," the officer of the Crown tells them. And he is correct, the list of charges being extensive.

Montagu Galbraith is accused of conspiracy to kidnap, entering the Spencer's home illegally, holding the occupants at gunpoint and violently assaulting Polly Spencer. He is also accused of attempted burglary at the Spencer's home and he is further accused of being complicit in all the abductions and attempted abductions of Polly Spencer, namely:

The first abduction from the bus stop in Carswell:

The second abduction, from School playing fields in Coventry:

The third abduction, from the Spencer's house during an attempted burglary and arson attack:

The fourth abduction, at gunpoint from a car taking Polly to school. Polly taken to a house in Telford Parva, a village on the way to Leicester:

A fifth attempted abduction of Polly from the Spencer's house, causing her grievous bodily harm:

Galbraith is further accused of arranging the arson attack on the home of the Spencers.

He is finally accused of arranging for explosive devices to be sent to the Spencers' home and the offices of the C.O.I. in Carswell. Attempted murder is added to this charge.

After the charges have been read, Galbraith is returned to the cells.

Jimmy Spears, Don Wilson, Billy Jones and Eddie Fulbright are accused of conspiracy to kidnap and violent assault on Polly Spencer, namely:

During illegal entry of the Spencer's home:

During her captivity after she was abducted from school playing fields in Coventry:

Rebecca Faversham is accused of being complicit in one of Polly's abductions.

After the charges have been read, the three accused are returned to the cells.

Jack Overbury, William Burgess and George Beacham are accused of conspiracy to kidnap and grievous bodily harm on Polly Spencer, namely:

During the attempted abduction from her home after the explosion.

After the charges have been read the accused are returned to the cells.

Ben Taylor, Jake Houston, Johnny Turner, and Pete Frobisher are jointly charged with serious offences against Maureen Potter namely:

Attempted burglary:

Grievous bodily harm:

After the charges have been read, the accused are returned to the cells.

Four men, Tom Cotter, Bill Willis, Ted Chaplin and Cedric Tubbs are jointly charged with serious offences against Mrs Margaret Spencer namely:

Conspiracy to Kidnap:

Violent physical assault:

Grievous bodily harm:

After the charges have been read, the accused are returned to the cells.

Medical evidence relative to the assaults against Polly Spencer, Mrs Margaret Spencer and Maureen Potter are read out to the court as verified by local hospitals. The injuries inflicted on them were severe and draw gasps from the court. The fact that Polly is only a 13 years old child is

359

particularly significant, since violence against children is considered especially despicable.

Fire investigators outline details of the arson attack on the Spencer home, and explosive experts give details of the devices used at the Spencer's home and the C.O.I. offices in Carswell.

After all of the charge details have been completed, the judge gives his summation of the case against the accused.

"The accused stand charged with a catalogue of offences, nearly all of which have been against the Spencer family. This trial will be unique in as much that I cannot recall any family being submitted to so much violence against the person and property. It is a tribute to their resilience that they are here today ready for this trial to commence."

"And I would add that the young daughter especially deserves a word of recognition for her enduring so much at the hands of these men. The evidence is overwhelming based on the detail provided by doctors and Fire officers and explosive experts. We will listen to relevant questions, but I tell the defence council now that I will not tolerate any questioning that I deem to be upsetting toward anyone, especially Miss Polly Spencer The child has been terribly abused over the last few weeks, and I insist that you appreciate that. Your questioning of Ben Spencer may have to be in closed court, since the work that he has been involved with is pertinent to a case due to be heard in the Central Criminal Court in London, at a later date. I suggest that we now adjourn for today and commence hearing evidence tomorrow at 10.00 a.m.," the judge concludes. And with that, he leaves the courtroom.

"Well, as I expected you were not required today, Mr Spencer, but some of you will almost certainly be called tomorrow. I suggest you return to your home and I will see you all again tomorrow morning at 10.00 am," the Crown representative concludes.

"Thank you for your help, we will be here at 10.00 a.m.," Ben replies.

And with that, the Spencers, Maureen and Daniel return to New Street Station to catch the train back to Carswell. Very little is said on the way back, nothing has yet transpired so there really isn't anything to discuss.

"Well the trial will begin in earnest tomorrow, now that all the preliminaries have been done," says Ben. The family with Daniel and Maureen return home arriving about 5 o'clock. Thankfully, all is well, Pauline is preparing supper and Conrad and Peter have been reviewing the security.

"Hello, Peter, how are things, nothing to report I trust?"

"No, Ben, Conrad and I were just discussing whether we can improve on your security, but it seems all is in place now, I cannot see any one getting near the back of the house unseen or unheard with the floodlights and the alarm."

"That is good to hear, Peter, now will you and Maureen stay for supper?"

"I think Maureen will want to go home, Ben, a bath and a change of clothes and so on, thank you."

"Of course, have some tea before you go anyway."

Daniel goes with Polly to her room and asks her if she is okay after today. She has been very quiet and he hopes she will be focussed for tomorrow.

"I just want it to be over, Daniel," she says as she sits down on his lap.

"It will be over sooner than you think, Polly, why don't you have a bath before supper?"

Polly agrees, and Daniel returns downstairs leaving Polly to have her bath. He does not want to get too close to her for the moment. He knows that she is worried about the trial, so he will stay close by and hope that all will be well. After enjoying a good supper, the family settle down in the garden and in the parlour. Pauline stays close to Conrad, and the children ask Daniel and Polly to play in the garden. Daniel willingly obliges, the children providing a welcome distraction for Polly.

"Polly seems to be coping well, Ben, I do hope she does not get upset tomorrow."

Margaret had not told Ben about how she found Daniel in Polly's bed with her after she had attacked him, he had enough to be concerned with and it was not important at the moment, although, once this trial has finished she may need to talk to him about Polly's talk of going to live with Daniel permanently.

"I am sure that Daniel has fully prepared her for what is ahead, and I am confident that our daughter will cope. When you consider what she has endured, the trial is nothing by comparison. How are Maisy, Daisy and George coping with all this Margaret, I had completely overlooked the fact that they too are involved in what is going on?"

"They seem to be carrying on and not taking too much interest, but I am sure there will be questions eventually."

Polly seems to be enjoying spending time with the children, so Daniel leaves her with them to go off and speak with Margaret as soon as he gets the chance. He wanted to know what Ben said about Margaret finding him and Polly her bed.

"I thought it best not to mention it, Daniel, you and I know that it does not need to be discussed any further for the moment."

Thankfully, Polly has a restful night again, and Daniel believes that she may well be getting back to normal at last. Today will be critical, since she may well be put into the witness box. How she will react is difficult to say, but he will be as close to her as he is allowed when she is giving evidence. So, on Tuesday morning they all return to Birmingham Crown Court.

"Can you please say your name for the court?" the usher asks after Polly has been sworn in.

"Polly Spencer," she replies.

"How old are you, Polly?" the Crown representative asks.

"I am 13, sir."

"Now, Polly, what happened to you the first time you were taken from the bus stop in Carswell?"

"I was taken to a house in Coventry and tied up to a bench and left"

"And did these men hurt you at all?"

"They pushed me down in their car and threatened to hurt me if I did not do as they asked."

"And what about the second time you were abducted, Polly, did they harm you then?"

"They hit me, and threatened nasty things to me while I was in the cellar, they said they would really hurt me if I was not a good girl for them. I was terrified of them, but thankfully Miss Faversham stopped them from hurting me anymore."

"When they came to your house the first time, what happened then?"

"First they kept all of us except Daddy upstairs. Then two of them came and told me to take of my dress socks and shoes and go downstairs with them. Mr Galbraith told them to take me into the dining room and teach me a lesson. They hit me, then grabbed me and forced me down across the table. If Peter had not come in and pointed a gun at them they would have hurt me more I am sure."

362

"Now leaving out the other abduction for a moment, Polly, there was an attempt to take you again after the explosion at your house, is that correct?"

"Yes, those three men took me from my bedroom and wrapped me in a rug to carry me down stairs."

"And what happened when you were downstairs, Polly?"

"The men dragged me across the bricks trying to reach their car, Daniel shot two of them and they dropped me onto the ground."

"And you were badly injured, Polly?" the Crown representative asks, passing details of her injuries to the judge.

'Yes, my nightshirt was ripped into bits and my back and legs were injured by the bricks. They dragged me across the bricks and wouldn't stop. I told them to stop but they wouldn't," Polly replies tearfully.

"Yes thank you, Polly, I am almost finished now, can you just confirm for me that there was another abduction, when you were kept for three days, which will be covered at another trial? "

"Yes I was abducted again from my school playing fields."

"Thank you, Polly, that is all for this witness, my lord."

"Do any of the defence team wish to ask this witness a question?" the judge asks.

"The defence has no question to ask of this witness, my lord."

"In that case we will adjourn for lunch."

Polly leaves the witness box and rushes over to Daniel.

"Polly, you were very brave, I knew you would be, wasn't she wonderful, Margaret?"

"Daddy and I were very proud of how you were in the courtroom, Polly, you were indeed very brave."

After lunch, the Crown representative calls Maureen Potter.

"Can you tell the court your name, please?"

"My name is Maureen Potter."

"And I understand you are Mr Spencer's personal secretary?"

"Yes, for about four years now," Maureen replies.

"Will you relate the circumstances that occurred last month at your home in Milton Parva for the court please?"

"I had been invited to have supper with the Spencers and to collect some important documents from Mr Spencer to be delivered to London."

"And can you tell the court what the documents were, briefly please, Miss Potter?"

"Yes, they contained names, places and dates of transactions carried out by black market racketeers. Criminals that Mr Spencer has been pursuing for a number of years."

"So, sensitive information that would be valuable to the courts if they were to be successful in prosecuting black marketeers?"

"Yes I believe so, although I have not seen the documents personally, I only know of their value from Mr Spencer's comments."

"Very good, Miss Potter, now can we go to the night in question, can you tell us what happened please?"

"I returned home from the Spencer's and went up to bed soon after."

"You were alone in the house?"

"Yes, the house belonged to my mother who died some time ago."

"Please continue, Miss Potter."

"I was disturbed by a noise, it was about 2.00 a.m. as I recall, coming from downstairs, so I put on my robe and went down to see if there was anyone there. I heard people moving about in the front of the house and tried to get to the phone, which is in my sitting room, but the intruders stopped me. There were three men so I knew that it was no use to struggle."

"And what happened next, Miss Potter?"

"The men demanded to know where the documents were, I told them I did not have any documents, and they slapped me across my face. They then sat me down in a chair and tied my hands behind my back. They kept asking me where the documents were, and I told them I did not have any documents and didn't know what they were talking about, so they hit me again several times," Maureen replies, struggling to stop herself from breaking down.

"Are you alright, Miss Potter?" the Crown representative asks.

"Yes I will be okay, thank you."

"Then please continue."

"They then tied my hands in the front and marched me over to my dining table. One of the men held me across the table by my hands, while the other two tore off my robe and began to beat me with riding crops. They hit me several times and–" Maureen became very distressed and began to weep.

"Miss Potter, would you like a break to compose yourself?" the judge asks.

"Thank you, sir, I would appreciate that."

"Fifteen minutes, gentlemen," the judge replies.

Maureen sits down with some water and calms herself, knowing that she must continue and not allow her emotions to hold up proceedings.

"I just wish Peter were here," she says tearfully to Margaret.

"You will cope, Maureen, you always do."

"Are you quite fit to continue now, Miss Potter?" the Crown representative asks.

"Yes thank you, I will be okay."

"Then please continue, you last mentioned how you were held over a table and two men beat you with riding crops, is that correct?"

"Yes, after a while, I am not sure how long, they stopped, and sat me back down on the chair. Again they demanded I tell them where the documents were. When I refused they hit me again then took me back to the table and beat me again. They kept on hitting me with their crops, I screamed out with the terrible pain and told them I would tell them what they wanted to know if they stopped hitting me," says Maureen struggling to compose herself.

"Take your time, Miss Potter."

"Thankfully, my screaming attracted the attention of the local policeman. He must have knocked on the door, and the men ran off. I managed to get to the door and open it before collapsing. The police officer called the ambulance to take me to hospital. "

"And how long were you kept in hospital, Miss Potter?"

"For about two weeks, and I was away from my work for a further two weeks."

"And I believe that as a result of your experience you now have someone staying with you, is that correct?"

"Yes, I do not feel safe being on my own anymore."

"My Lord, there is a copy of the extensive injuries inflicted on Miss Potter for your reference. Thank you for your evidence, Miss Potter, the defence does not have any questions so you may go now."

"The Court will now adjourn until 10.00 a.m. tomorrow," the judge announces.

After a difficult day at court, Ben, Margaret, Polly, Daniel and Maureen return home by train. The conversation is muted, no one wishing to dwell on what was said, or to talk about tomorrow. Margaret holds on tightly to Ben, her mind racing at the prospect of having to relive her experience at the hands of the four men who abducted her. She has to be strong, but knows how painful it will be. Just seeing the men was difficult. Supper was a quiet affair, and afterwards Ben goes with Margaret for a walk down the lane.

"How are you feeling, my dear? You must be worrying I am sure, but we have to be brave and face these wicked people."

"I know, Ben, I will do what I have to do, but God I am dreading having to recall my time with those men. What they did to me, the smells from them, the rats, it was a nightmare, Ben, a nightmare," replies Margaret as she sobs in Ben's arms. They walk back and find that Polly has gone up to her room, and Daniel is still in the parlour chatting with Peter. Margaret is pleased to notice that Daniel has not gone with Polly. The more space he can give her the better it will be for both of them. Pauline goes out into the garden with Margaret, and asks her how she is going to cope with tomorrow.

"I have to cope, Pauline, I have to be strong for Ben, for Polly, for everyone. I need to see these men put away for a long time, and be able to move forward with Ben so that he can finish his work. He has spent so much of his life in bringing these wicked people to account, now we must make sure that nothing stops him from doing that."

"I can only admire your positive attitude, Margaret, I just don't think I could have coped with what you have had to put up with not just yourself but as a mother and a housewife as well. Ben should be very proud of you."

"I don't think I have had the chance to thank you for all your help Pauline, your life has been turned upside down staying here on a virtually permanent basis. I hope it will not be for too much longer, although you can stay for as long as you wish of course."

"I have enjoyed being able to help, Margaret, and Conrad has become a very good friend during my stay here."

"Yes I had noticed that, Pauline," Margaret replies with a smile.

Wednesday arrives after an uneventful evening, much to Daniel's relief. Today was going to be very difficult for everyone and it was important that they are prepared. Maureen is not with them, having completed her evidence, so Ben, Margaret, Polly, and Daniel arrive at Birmingham Court to be met by the Crown representative.

Margaret enters the witness box just after 10 o'clock.

'Can you tell me your name, please?" The usher asks.

"My name is Mrs Margaret Spencer."

"Mrs Spencer, can you tell the court what happened to you approximately five weeks ago?"

"I had gone into Carswell to do some shopping, and was returning to my car when I was approached by two men asking where the Town Hall was. I was about to start explaining to them when I was grabbed from behind. They put a cloth over my face which had some kind of drug on it. I passed out, I had no idea how long, and when I awoke, I was in some sort of warehouse tied to an old bench. After a while, four men came into the room," says Margaret, beginning to feel tense at what she is about to recall.

"Please go on, Mrs Spencer," the Crown representative says.

"One of the men starts talking about my husband meddling in their affairs and how he must pay for their losses. They threatened me saying if he doesn't pay I will suffer. When I tell them he will not give in to them, one of them beats me with a cane across my chest and legs. They then tell me that they will make me suffer even more and two of the men take me to a small room in the corner."

"Then what happened, Mrs Spencer?"

"They pushed me down on the floor, and violently physically assaulted me for about half an hour. When they had finished they took me back and tied me to the bench again. They tell me I must tell my husband what they have done to me, but I do not."

"Did they make contact with your husband?"

"Yes they wanted to tell him that they had me and that he must cease his actions regarding the pursuit of those involved in black marketeering, and I think they also demanded some money but I am not sure. I was feeling pretty groggy so did not catch everything that was said."

"Then what happened, Mrs Spencer?" he asks.

"Three of the men took me into the room and took turns to violently physically assault me. I begged them to stop, but they ignored me and just kept on and on with it until they were finished," Margaret replies and begins to struggle with her words.

"Are you alright, Mrs Spencer? Would you like to stop?"

"Yes I am okay, thank you," Margaret replies.

"Please go on, Mrs Spencer, what happened next?"

"When they had finished with me, after about an hour, they tied me back to the bench and left me until next morning. The room was very dark and cold, but the worst thing about the night was the rats.

"I was bleeding in several places from the beating and from being on a concrete floor on my back. They had removed my dress and my underwear was ripped and torn. I was bleeding from cuts and the rats must have got wind of the blood. I was bitten several times by them, the squeals were terrible, horrible, I thought they would eat me alive," she says becoming very distressed recalling the events.

"My lord, may we have a short break, Mrs Spencer is clearly distressed?"

"Yes of course, we will adjourn for fifteen minutes for Mrs Spencer to recover," the judge orders.

Margaret rushes to Ben and bursts into tears. Polly too is crying and Daniel puts his arm around her to console her.

"My God, Ben, this is killing me, having to go over the events of those days bit by bit, I cannot take much more really."

"You have been remarkable so far, Margaret, please hang on and finish it, then we can go home," Margaret returns to the witness box to continue.

"Are you feeling better, Mrs Spencer?" the judge asks.

"Yes thank you, sir," Margaret replies.

"Can you tell the court what happened next, Mrs Spencer?" the Crown representative asks.

"The men returned the next morning, they did not offer me any water and they again threatened me before they made contact with Ben. I was allowed to speak to him, just enough to let him know that I was alive. Then after the call was made, the assaults continue, two men again taking me into the small room and pushing me down on the concrete floor and taking turns to attack me. I lost consciousness at one stage, and when I came around, one of the other two men was on top of me. By this time, I didn't really care anymore what they did to me. I was numb to just about everything that was going on, my body was battered and bruised, and I was bleeding from the rat bites. They told me that Ben would pay up in the end, and then they would kill me, so I didn't much care what they did to me anymore.

"They continued with the physical assaults for a while, I can't remember for how long, they just kept on taking turns, then they tied me to the bench and left me to the rats. They came as soon as it was dark and began biting me again. No matter how loud I screamed, because I could not move, the rats just bit me as much as they wanted.my legs and thighs everywhere. When the men returned on Wednesday morning, I was delirious and didn't know much about anything. I just waited for them to take me into the room, do it all over again, and get it over with. My hair matted with dirt and grease from the floor, I was covered in dirt and grime and almost naked, my underwear in tatters. Then, thank God I remember Ben and Daniel arrived and they shot two of the men before the others gave up as you might expect. I was barely conscious, but I just remember Ben holding me and talking to me before I passed out. When I eventually woke, I was in hospital."

"Thank you, Mrs Spencer, we appreciate how difficult and painful this has been for you and your family. I have no further questions, my lord," the Crown representative concludes.

"Yes thank you, Mrs Spencer, we will adjourn for lunch, a little later than usual, and I will begin my summations in the morning. I expect to begin delivering sentences on Friday, and I warn many of the accused that they can expect severe sentences," the judge remarks.

At the end of the third day, everyone returns home drained of emotions after Margaret's harrowing evidence. Ben is very tense and sits close to Margaret on the train home. Polly holds Daniel's hand and stares blankly out of the window. When they get back to the house no one says very much, and Polly goes upstairs. Daniel decides that it may be best to give her some time alone. Whilst the last three days have been difficult for everyone, they will have affected Polly more than most because of her tender years. Supper is eaten in relative silence and Ben goes to his study afterward to contact Beatrice Carrington with an update on the trial. Margaret goes and enjoys a long bath, while Daniel talks with Conrad about the events of the last three days.

"These evil men must pay heavily for their treatment of this family Conrad, the evidence I have heard these last three days has been shocking, their behaviour more like beasts than humans."

"Where is Polly, Daniel?"

"She went straight to her room when we got in, so I have left her to spend time on her own."

"Have you given any more thoughts to the suggestion of Polly living with you on a permanent basis?"

"No, not really, it was my intention to talk it over with Margaret and Ben when the trial is over, probably this weekend. I would love to have her with me, Conrad, but I realise the implications. I have to wait and see how she is over the next few weeks, whether I can help her to break this total dependency on me."

"It is complicated, Daniel, and as Polly gets older her feelings toward you may change quite dramatically, you need to think about that."

"Yes I understand that, Conrad, she may begin to think of me quite differently from how I think of her. And that could be a worry for both of us."

"I am sure you will find a way, you obviously care for her and if being with you gives Polly the strength that she needs to recover from what has happened to her, then I believe you should consider having her live with you. You will have to discuss this with Ben and Margaret and of course Polly herself. But she has suffered terribly and being with you may be the only way she is ever going to recover. "

"Yes thank you for your observations, Conrad, I appreciate what you have said and will seriously consider it. Well, I think I will go up now, it has been a difficult day and I hope I can get a good night's sleep."

Daniel goes up to Polly's room about 10.30 p.m. to find her sleeping. After about two hours, Daniel is disturbed by Polly moving around the room in her sleep, mumbling as if afraid of something as she heads toward the door. She is dripping with sweat and her mumbling gets louder as she resists Daniels attempts to get her back into her bed.

Finally, he manages to get her back into bed by holding her round her waist and pulling her toward him. Slowly she stops struggling, but keeps mumbling about something.

"Kill them, kill them, Daniel, help Mummy, please help Mummy," she screams and pulls and tugs so violently that she pulls Daniel out of the bed and onto the floor. She is thrashing about beneath him when she awakes from her nightmare.

"Daniel, Daniel what is happening, those men were hurting Mummy?" she says tearfully.

"It's okay, Polly, you have had a bad dream, let me put you back in your bed," he says as he lifts her gently and puts her back into bed.

"Stay with me, Daniel, please stay with me," she pleads.

"Yes, okay, Polly, I will stay with you until you are asleep," He replies and pulls the blanket over Polly who is now sitting on his lap. They both drift off to sleep, then suddenly Polly begins to shake. Again she is dripping with sweat which Daniel can feel through her nightshirt. He tries to calm her, but without much success.

"Polly, it's me, I am here with you."

"She starts to thrash about on his lap, digging her nails into him and shouting about Margaret being hurt as she wrestles Daniel from the bed onto the floor. She is kicking at him as he tries to hold her and stop her from hurting herself. He holds on tight to her using her nightshirt to grasp her and stop her getting away from him, as Margaret comes into the room, disturbed by the noise, to be confronted by a chaotic scene. Bedclothes are strewn across the floor, with Daniel grasping hold of Polly by her nightshirt. She is on top of him thrashing about and trying to free herself whilst still asleep despite what is happening.

"Oh my God, Daniel, what is happening to my daughter? Polly you must wake up!"

Polly wakes, startled to find herself on top of Daniel on the floor. Margaret helps Daniel get her back into her bed, and picks up the sheets.

"Mummy, I thought those men were going to hurt you again."

"No one is going to hurt me or you, my darling daughter, now please, you must try and get some sleep, it will very soon be morning."

"Okay Mummy, can Daniel stay with me please?"

"Daniel will stay with you, Polly, but not in your bed."

"But, Mummy, I need him close to me, I cannot sleep unless he is with me, I am afraid, Mummy please let Daniel hold me safe, please, Mummy," Polly becomes almost hysterical in her pleas for Daniel to be by her side. She is sobbing and becoming agitated, as Daniel looks toward Margaret for advice on how he should react. He desperately wants to go to her but waits for Margaret, who seems unsure what she should advise.

"Please, Mummy, don't leave me on my own, I need Daniel to keep me safe, Daniel please come and stay with me."

"Yes, very well, Polly, Daniel may stay with you, now please try and get some rest my dear," says Margaret as she gives in to Polly's requests. Daniel moves to Polly's side and comforts her as she lies beside him and drifts off to sleep.

Margaret is unsure what to make of seeing her daughter in Daniel's arms in her bed. For now, there seems little that she can do, since it would seem that this is the only way Polly can be relaxed and calm. She has obviously been affected by Margaret's evidence and has been reliving this in her dreams. Margaret leaves the room and returns to bed wondering what the answer is to all this. Should she call the doctor, or more importantly talk with Ben about his daughter's behaviour? She has kept all this from him knowing that he has to focus on the conspiracy trial in a week or so. *There would be time enough to talk about Polly*, she had thought. Now, she is not so sure. And with these thoughts in mind, she drifts off to sleep.

Daniel, meanwhile, lies with Polly and ponders just what to do about her absolute reliance on his being with her. Once the conspiracy trial has finished, perhaps her staying with him over a period of time might be a consideration. Whatever the outcome, it is clear to Daniel that Polly will be a big part of his life for the foreseeable future. As he looks down on Polly, sleeping soundly in his arms, he appreciates just how much a part of his life she is now. Whatever decisions are made, they will be best for Polly; that has to be the deciding factor he says to himself as he drifts off to sleep. He wakes around 7.30 a.m. and Polly is still sleeping soundly. He manages to move without disturbing her and goes to the bathroom to wash and shave and he will need a change of clothes after the night's activities. After breakfast, the children get ready for school, Pauline will take them and Conrad will drive. Margaret is anxious for the opportunity to talk with Ben about Polly as soon as possible, and whether they should consult the Doctor over her distressing behaviour. She tells Daniel of her concerns, and he agrees that she should most definitely talk to Ben. Polly, meanwhile bounds downstairs apparently none the worse for the events of last night. She doesn't mention last night so Daniel and Margaret decide it is best left for the moment. As soon as the children have gone off to school, Margaret goes into the study to talk with Ben.

"Would you have a moment, Ben, I need to talk with you about Polly?"

"Of course, she had a bad dream again last night I presume, you getting up and going to her room?"

"Yes she did, but she seems okay this morning, but my concern, Ben is her being so reliant on Daniel's presence by her side that is more worrying."

"I am sure that she will grow out of her reliance, Margaret, given time, she is only 13 at the moment so sees Daniel as her special knight in shining armour, her hero if you like, as she gets older she will think differently I am sure."

"Whilst what you say may be true, Ben, but how far does hero worship spread, in Polly's case she has to have Daniel beside her in bed before she can sleep, is this the normal behaviour of a girl toward her knight in shining armour?"

"What on earth do you mean, Margaret?" replies Ben obviously shocked at Margaret's words.

"Daniel is having to sleep with our daughter, Ben. She will not sleep unless she is in his arms and so he has to be with her in her bed. This is happening every night, they are sleeping together, Polly in Daniel's arms and I see no way of that changing at the moment," says Margaret, obviously concerned with the situation.

"I had no idea she had become so dependent on Daniel, Margaret, and I can't pretend that I am happy with this, in fact I am shocked to say the least. But you must have talked with Daniel, what is his position, is he happy to continue the relationship at the moment?"

"Daniel only wants to do what is best for Polly, Ben, he obviously cares for her very much. But are you happy for this to continue for the moment? It must be difficult for Daniel, he only wants to do what is best for us, but there are implications should she mention her sleeping arrangements with anyone else. Whilst she is a very sensible girl, she obviously does not appreciate what people will say about what is happening, however innocent it may be. And there is another point for us to consider. Polly has expressed a wish to go and live with Daniel in London as soon as she is able."

"Perhaps we should be talking about this with Polly and Daniel, I am finding it difficult to take in what you are saying about our daughter," Ben says with bewilderment.

Margaret calls Daniel and asks him to bring Polly to the study, telling him that she has told Ben about his sleeping in Polly's bed and her talk about going to live with him.

"Hello, Daniel, my dear Polly how are you? Mummy tells me you have had another bad dream."

"Yes Daddy, it was horrible, but Daniel was with me so I was okay after all."

"Yes that is what I wanted to have a word with you about, Polly. Mummy tells me that Daniel is actually with you in your bed for most of the night, is that true?"

"Yes, Daddy, I must have Daniel with me or I am so afraid, I need him to hold me so that I know nothing will happen. I am afraid of being alone, Daddy I dream about those horrid men and what they did to me, only if I can feel Daniel by my side do I feel safe and secure, please don't take him away, Daddy please," says Polly becoming tearful and agitated.

"My dear Polly, no one is going to take Daniel from you, we all need him and I want him to look after you for as long as necessary, but his being with you in your bed is rather disturbing."

"But why, Daddy, I don't understand, why can't Daniel be with me and keep me safe forever?" says Polly, obviously puzzled and confused by Ben's comments.

"As you grow older, you will understand, Polly, now Mummy and I do not want to upset you, so we will leave the talk for now you go along and do some school work while Mummy and I speak with Daniel," Ben replies, resigning himself to the fact that, for now despite his concerns he does not wish to upset Polly further.

Polly leaves the study and Ben turns to Daniel looking for inspiration.

"What are we to do, Daniel? My daughter has become totally independent on your being by her side while she sleeps, it really is disturbing, I do not know what to do for the best. Our daughter's welfare is the most important thing in the world, but this seems to be a heavy price to pay?"

"Ben, we all agree that it is Polly's welfare that is the most important thing to consider. You and Margaret need not be concerned about my intentions. I will care for your daughter every way I can for as long as she needs me. I admit that our relationship may be rather difficult to understand, I am a little overwhelmed by it myself, but if we consider only Polly's welfare above anything else, then I will to continue to grant her wish. I honestly believe Polly will recover, but am under no illusion about how long it will take. What I am sure of is that by allowing her to be with me as she wishes can only help in her eventual recuperation. If you impose rules on her, I fear they may make things worse and be detrimental to her recovery."

"Yes I understand that, Daniel, now what's this about her wanting to live with you in London?"

"Polly believes, in her mind, that when I am no longer with her, she will not be safe. This is her thinking ahead; she is fearful of a future without me. I understand how she feels and I have given some thought to this. Nothing can happen until the conspiracy trial is over, but when it is over, I am happy to have Polly with me for a long holiday. I will make arrangements with the lady who looks after my flat, to watch over her during the day, since eventually I will have to return to my position in Whitehall. I only want to do what is the very best for her."

"Margaret and I will need to talk further about this, Daniel, but I see no reason why she should not spend some time with you. She was due to do so before if you remember, before Margaret was taken. You obviously care very much for her Daniel, and Margaret and I know what you have done for her. We will never be able to pay you for that. So if by being with you will make her the happy and contented daughter that we know her to be, then so be it. I will leave it to you to talk about this with Polly, and thank you very much for taking care of her for us."

"My absolute pleasure, Ben," Daniel replies as he leaves the study.

Polly is waiting for him in the parlour and rushes to meet him.

"Daniel, Daniel, what did Mummy and Daddy say, will you stay with me, come and talk with me in the garden?"

"Your Mummy and Daddy love you very much, Polly, and only want what is best for you."

"But will you stay with me, Daniel? I need you to be with me."

"I will be there if you want me, Polly, eventually you will grow out of your dependency on me I'm sure but for the moment we will leave things as they are."

Polly is delighted and hugs Daniel.

"I knew you would stay with me, Daniel, I knew you would," she says smiling.

"And Mummy and Daddy will consider your staying with me for a long holiday when all this is over. So you see, Polly, you have everything to look forward to."

The remainder of the day passes without incident, Polly enjoys time with her siblings when they return from school and Daniel talks with Conrad about his discussion with Margaret and Ben.

"It has to be that way, Daniel, Polly needs you to get her through the terrible ordeal she has been through, and Ben and Margaret appreciate that," says Conrad.

The remainder of Thursday passes quickly, Polly has a good night's sleep, as does Daniel, and they all set off for Birmingham on Friday morning to listen to the verdicts.

The judge begins his summation just after 10 o'clock.

"This has been one of the most harrowing and disturbing cases that I have ever presided over. How one human being could subject such pain and suffering and indignity over another human being, as was the case here, I fail to understand. Miss Polly Spencer, Mrs Spencer and Miss Maureen Potter were treated with such wickedness that it is testament to the human spirit that they survived. That one family could be put through such a catalogue of fear, to further the ends of criminal gangs operating in the black market, is almost beyond comprehension. And yet they have survived and Mr Spencer will I am sure be successful in bringing down the main perpetrators in this business. I will now begin passing sentence, bailiff, please bring up Montagu Galbraith to the box," the judge orders.

"Montague Galbraith, it is apparent from the evidence presented that you ordered the actions against the Spencer family, and Miss Potter, to directly furnish your own ends and those of your masters in London. You showed no mercy and were prepared to go to any lengths, including murder, to stop Mr Spencer from continuing his work against the black market in this country. You forcibly entered the Spencer's home, and you ordered the assault on their daughter in her own home. You also instructed your men to abduct their daughter on a number of occasions and held her against her will. When this failed your accomplices entered the home of Miss Potter, and subjected her to a horrific assault. You ordered the abduction of Mrs Spencer and your men subjected her to three days of wicked physical assaults. You had your men set fire to the Spencer's home and again attempted to abduct their daughter in the confusion. You then arranged for explosive devices to be delivered to Mr Spencer's home and place of work. This action risked the lives of many people, which you completely disregarded," the judge says.

"On the charge of conspiracy to murder by using explosive devices and of arson I sentence you to ten years' hard labour. On your complicity in the kidnap of Mrs Spencer, I sentence you to seven years, on your complicity in the abductions of Miss Polly Spencer, I sentence you to 7 years and on your complicity in the violent assault on Miss Maureen Potter, I sentence you to five years. Finally, I further instruct that these sentences run consecutively, take him back to the cells," the judge directs the bailiff.

"Please bring up Tom Cotter, Bill Willis, Ted Chaplin and Cedric Tubbs," the judge instructs.

Margaret grips Ben's hand tightly as she faces the men who savagely assaulted her.

"Your actions against Mrs Spencer are beyond any words that I could find. Wicked, despicable, inhuman – they all fit. Taking a woman's dignity in the way that you did during Mrs Spencer' captivity and complete disregard for her welfare is beyond contempt. Not once during the time that you held her prisoner, did you show one ounce of compassion, you used her for your own gratuitous pleasures then discarded her like rubbish to a bin. You will each serve seven years' hard labour, take them down to the cells Bailiff," the judge concludes.

"Bring up Ben Taylor, Jake Houghton, Johnny Turner and Pete Frobisher," the judge instructs the bailiff.

"Your actions against Miss Maureen Potter can only be described as heinous. To subject a human being to a beating, using riding crops was wicked. That you carried out this beating repeatedly to a defenceless woman is inexcusable. Pity that we do not still have floggings as punishments; you would have received some of your own medicine. For your actions, I sentence each of you to seven years' hard labour. Take them to their cell Bailiff," the judge concludes.

"Bring up Jimmy Spears, Don Wilson, Billy Jones, Eddie Fulbright and Rebecca Faversham to the box, please Bailiff," the judge instructs.

Polly winces and grips Daniel's hand so tightly she draws blood. He whispers words of encouragement to her telling her it will soon be over.

"You four men I hold in deep contempt for your despicable behaviour to a school girl of just 13 years. Grown men violently treating young children I find disgusting especially when the child is female. God knows what thoughts went through her mind when she was alone with you. In fact, were it not for the actions of your colleague Rebecca Faversham, I believe the charges against you would have been more severe. Your brutal handling of a young girl, with complete disregard for her welfare, shows you to be without any mercy. I find myself wanting to give you the maximum sentence that I am allowed, so sentence each of you to ten years' hard labour. Take them down to the cells bailiff, Rebecca Faversham will remain in the dock. Your actions in preventing these men from abusing Miss Polly further during her abduction does you credit. In fact, she actually mentioned how understanding you had been toward her to the local police.

"I see no real benefit from giving you a custodial sentence and sentence you to two years' probation. My advice to you, Madam, is to choose your acquaintances carefully in future. Bailiff, take her to be registered then she will be free to go," the judge concludes.

"Before I conclude proceedings for the day I would like to offer my sympathies to the Spencer family for the terrible ordeals that we have heard of in this trial. You are indeed a very special family and I wish you Mr Spencer good luck in your continued pursuit of the criminal element running the black market in our country."

The judge ends his statement to the Spencer family and leaves the courtroom. Everyone is relieved it's over, and satisfied that the criminals got what they deserved. They travel back to Carswell, looking forward to an enjoyable weekend with the family. It's as if a heavy burden has just been lifted from the family, and they can now begin to live some sort of normal life. There is still the conspiracy trial for Ben to prepare for, and Polly and Ben will have to go to court for the trial of the men that abducted and held them for nearly three days. But, for now the family will enjoy a good weekend together. Polly will spend time with Maisy, Daisy and George again, and Margaret will enjoy being a housewife. Ben, too, will enjoy being with his family and friends.

Monday morning soon arrives and Ben gives some thought to the trials that are coming up in The Crown Court in London and The Central

Criminal Court, The Old Bailey. The trial against the four men who abducted him and Polly is due to commence one week from tomorrow Tuesday.

The trial at The Old Bailey, probably two weeks after that. Polly will have a particularly harrowing time, having to give evidence against the men that treated her so badly. Daniel will have to be close by her side through all this, and Ben decides he must speak with him.

"Daniel, as you know Polly and I will be giving evidence in the Crown Court next week. Once again I find myself having to rely on your relationship with Polly to get her ready for what will be a very difficult time for her. As a parent, I have to be somewhat concerned about the relationship that has developed between Polly and yourself, but I do appreciate how you have helped her get through the terrible ordeals she has had. If keeping my daughter safe and well means accepting the arrangements that are in place, then so be it. Margaret and I trust you implicitly and know that you would never do anything detrimental to Polly's welfare."

"Thank you for your vote of confidence, Ben. I must confess, I too find my relationship with Polly somewhat confusing, but it seems to be working. This weekend she has been spending time with the family and has slept soundly without me by her side. I will do what I can to get her ready for the trial, but I know it will be difficult," Daniel replies.

"Do you have any ideas how we can relax her and help her through this, Daniel, I would welcome any suggestions really?"

"Well I had considered asking you and Margaret about taking her away for the coming weekend. That would surely take her mind off the trial for a while."

"I hadn't thought of that, let's ask Margaret what she thinks," says Ben as he opens the door to the kitchen and calls Margaret into the study and tells her of Daniel's suggestion.

"We trust you completely, Daniel, and any suggestion that you think may be good for Polly, we are happy to go along with. Polly is going back to school tomorrow, so I would ask you not to mention this for a day or so, to allow her to focus on school."

"Very well, Margaret, I will not mention it until Thursday when I collect her from school."

"Thank you, Daniel, and thank you again for taking care of her," she says as she returns to the kitchen. She thinks over what she has just agreed to as she prepares vegetables for tonight's supper. Polly comes into the kitchen looking for Daniel and Margaret tells her that he is in the study discussing the Old Bailey Trial. So Polly goes off to her room to finish the schoolwork that she has before going back tomorrow. Daniel finds Conrad in the garden and tells him of his suggestion to Ben and Margaret.

"That is an excellent idea, Daniel, taking Polly into a completely different environment will be good for her, and soften the blow about the trial. God knows it will be difficult for her. But be aware that you will be alone with her my friend, she is an impressionable young girl."

"I know what you mean Conrad and know the limits. I believe I know her well enough to be able to read any unusual signs she may show toward me."

Polly has another restful night and gets up early ready for her return to school. For the first time for a while the family sit down to breakfast before Pauline walks with Maisy, Daisy and George to school, and Daniel takes Polly to her school. She never stops talking on her way to school and Daniel is pleased to see her so happy.

"Enjoy your day, Polly, I will see you at 4 o'clock," says Daniel as Polly dashes into the school gates looking for her friends. Daniel drives back to the house, satisfied that Polly is really getting back to some normality. Going back to school will be the tonic she needs to get on with her life.

Daniel spends the day clearing up his clothes, having a bath and spending some time in his room reading. He collects Polly at 4 o'clock and is puzzled by her strange behaviour. She doesn't say a word to him when he asks her how she has enjoyed her day. As soon as they arrive home Polly goes straight to her room and remains there until supper.

"How was your first day back, my dear?"

"It was okay, Mummy."

And that is all she says at dinner until she tells Margaret that she is tired and goes up to her room.

"Has something happened, Daniel, why is she acting so strange?"

"I have no idea, Margaret, she has not said a word to me since I collected her from school."

"Perhaps she is overwhelmed by the day, going back after a long time and being asked lots of questions I am sure. Will you go to her later, Daniel, and see if she is okay for me please?"

"Of course, I will go up later and see if she wants anything."

The family sit talking, specifically about the Old Bailey trial. Ben hopes that he will be able to get some idea of the timetable, because both Conrad and Daniel may be called along with himself to give evidence, so he will have to arrange for Peter and Maureen to stay at the house while they are away in London.

"It will be like planning a military operation, Ben, but we will cope and it will all be worthwhile," says Daniel. Around 10 o'clock, he decides to go up to see if Polly is okay, and wishes everyone a good night. When he enters her room, he is surprised to see Polly asleep on her bed still wearing her school clothes. Daniel carefully removes her blazer and skirt and lies her down in her bed. Polly hardly stirs still fast asleep, so he settles in the chair and soon drops to sleep himself. He is woken by Polly, mumbling something about not hurting her anymore.

"Please don't, please don't hurt me anymore," she sobs.

Daniel goes over to her and quietly consoles her. Polly turns towards him and holds on tight. Now she is awake and very distressed. She curls up on his lap and moans about being hurt as she drifts back to sleep. Daniel pulls the blanket over them, something he has done before, hoping his presence will comfort her. Thankfully, she sleeps through to the morning. She could not recall Daniel putting her to bed or her bad dream, so Daniel does not mention it. Then, on the way to school he discovers the reason for her behaviour yesterday.

"I am so sorry for ignoring everybody yesterday, Daniel, I was very upset by what had happened at school. I tried hard to avoid questions, but one of the girls in my class was very persistent saying her Daddy was a reporter on the Carswell Times and would like to know what has been happening to our family. I didn't know what to do so I just ignored her and I think that made things worse," Polly recalls.

"You did right, Polly, now you go into school and I will speak with Mrs Williams."

"Thanks, Daniel, I knew you would know what to do."

Daniel drives through the school gates this time instead of leaving Polly at the gate. He says goodbye to Polly and enters the front of the school into the reception area. He introduces himself to the school secretary and asks to speak with the headmistress on a matter of some urgency.

He enters the headmistress study and introduces himself.

"Thank you for seeing me, Headmistress, my name is Daniel Bottomley and I am a close friend of the Spencer family."

"How can I help, Mr Bottomley?" she says pointing to a chair.

Daniel relates his position with the Spencer family and how essential it is for Mr Spencer's work to be kept confidential. He touches briefly on what has happened to the family as a direct result of Mr Spencer's work and continues, "Because of the series of events that have occurred to the Spencer family over the last few weeks, my colleague and I are living with them as protection against anyone seeking to harm them. My role is taken up with looking after Polly, who has been particularly targeted by people who would seek to undermine Mr Spencer's important work for the Government. Now I understand that one of her classroom colleagues is the daughter of a reporter on the local paper?" says Daniel

"Yes, Jennifer Carter, her father is the editor of the *Carswell Times*," Mrs Williams replies, "It appears that he may think he has some sort of story to pursue via his daughter, I wonder if you might be able to have a word at all? It would be such a relief for the family after all that they have been through, Mrs Williams."

"Yes of course, Mr Bottomley, I know that Polly has indeed been through a difficult time, having spoken with Mrs Spencer. I will see to it that Jennifer and Mr Carter do not bother Polly or her family about this," she replies with authority.

Daniel thanks her for her understanding and leaves the school to return to the Spencer's house, telling Margaret of his visit to Polly's school, and Margaret thanks him for taking the trouble to deal with the problem on her behalf. Thursday and Friday pass without incident and Ben continues to prepare for the conspiracy trial, and talks with Beatrice Carrington.

"You will be called, Beatrice, will it be difficult for you, since the accused will know that you may have implicated them?"

"I will most probably be giving my evidence in closed court, Ben. My superiors do not feel it would be safe for me, or beneficial for the continued fight against the black market for my name to be released. Although the conspiracy trial will put away some key conspirators, the fight will continue, for you and for me, so my being identified will serve no purpose."

"I understand completely, Beatrice, I wonder if I might stay with you when I am in London for the trial, it will be good to reflect, and you will at least have someone around?"

"Of course, Ben, I would be delighted to have you stay for as long as necessary, call me again when we have definite dates, bye for now."

Polly is obviously excited about the weekend, and quizzes Daniel about where they are going and what will be happening.

"Where are we going and when will we be leaving, Daniel, what hotel will we be staying in?" Polly asks, excited at the prospect of being with him on her own.

"Slow down, Polly, I thought we might go to Stratford on Avon, it is a beautiful town and there are lots of places to visit."

"I have never been to Stratford so I am really looking forward to going."

"We can leave on Friday, after school, I have borrowed a car from your local garage, so we should get there in time for supper."

Meanwhile, Margaret is happy to be able to spend some time with her sister and discusses how long she will be able to stay.

"I will stay as long as you want Margaret, I am in no hurry to leave," Pauline says.

"Thank you, Pauline, your being here has been a great help to me and the family, perhaps we can talk again once the trial has ended. I know Ben is busy preparing for it. When it has finished, I am hoping to spend a few days away with him, and I would appreciate your looking after things."

"A break away with Ben would be marvellous for both of you, Margaret, something to look forward to after all the turmoil of the last few weeks."

Daniel and Polly leave for Stratford around 6 o'clock and arrive at the hotel, just the other side of town, soon after. The hotel has quite a few guests and Polly is rather overwhelmed by the size of the place and the people staying there. To save any embarrassment, Daniel has decided that she will be his niece for the weekend, which Polly finds rather amusing.

"I just do not believe anyone will think you are my Uncle Daniel," says, laughing as they unpack.

"It doesn't really matter, Polly, it just saves anyone being inquisitive, what we don't want is for your real identity to be discovered."

And so, after washing and changing, Polly goes down to dinner with Daniel. The dining room is large, the hotel has over seventy rooms, and is about three quarters full. Most of the guests are in their fifties, and some are rather curious of a young man with a very young girl. After dinner, they enjoy a walk in the hotel grounds. Although the hotel is only about three miles from the town centre, Daniel decides they should leave their first visit to the town until tomorrow.

"Travelled far have you?" Daniel is asked by a military type, who sits down beside Daniel and Polly.

"Not far, about two hours, spending the weekend with my niece Polly before she goes away for the summer."

"And where are you off to, my dear?" the retired busy body asks.

"George, I hope you are not bothering those young people?" a powerful voice calls.

"My wife, Elizabeth, no not at all dear, just passing the time, delighted to have met you," he says as he moves on. Polly giggles as Daniel breathes a sigh of relief.

"Come on, Polly, let's keep walking or we will be questioned by more busy bodies."

"I think it was quite funny, where am I going for the summer?" she replies laughing.

After wandering around the grounds for about an hour, they both go inside and return to their rooms. Daniel has secured adjourning rooms with their own bathrooms. Daniel calls Polly into his room before she prepares for bedtime.

"Polly, I hope you will be able to sleep soundly through the night. I will leave the door ajar, but you really must try and sleep without my being beside you. Promise me you will try?"

"Okay, Daniel, I am sure I will, but you will be there if I want you?"

"Yes, Polly, now off you go," Daniel replies, as Polly goes off to her room. Daniel sits down reading for about half an hour before looking in on Polly who is sound asleep. The following morning, he is relieved that Polly has slept undisturbed and wakes her just after eight.

"Daniel I think I will stay in bed for a while, I feel so tired."

"Now come along, Polly, we have lots to do today; you must not waste any of it in your bed."

"Okay," she replies and goes off to the bathroom while Daniel returns to his room.

After breakfast, and avoiding the attentions of two elderly spinsters, they drive into Stratford. Polly wants to have a look at some of the shops, which have all kinds of bits and pieces, antiques, old books, paintings and all kinds of clothes, old and new. She is in awe of so many different things to look at and wants to find something she can get for Margaret. She settles on a small painting of Stratford showing the river and the Shakespeare Theatre, and a book about Shakespeare and his birthplace. They go along to the Theatre and get tickets for the evening performance of The Merchant of Venice. Polly is keen to see a Shakespeare play, as she has just begun taking Shakespeare as part of her English literature classes. After lunch Daniel hires a boat, and they spend the afternoon on the river. Daniel has always been keen on boats and did some rowing himself. The Avon is a beautiful river and Daniel enjoys the time on a boat while Polly just sits and takes it all in. Eventually however, they return to the mooring, and go back to the car. They have to be at the theatre for 8 o'clock so have an early dinner back at the hotel. Not too many guests take an early dinner, so they have the dining room almost to themselves. The waiter is somewhat inquisitive and also shows an interest in Polly.

"Is everything satisfactory, Miss, can I get you anything?" he asks as he hovers over her.

Polly is amused and smiles politely. "My Uncle and I have everything we need thank you," she replies with a smile, then bursts into giggles as he moves away.

Daniel looks on and is delighted to see her enjoying herself so much. This is the Polly that he hopes will be restored when all the terrible ordeals that she has been put through will eventually become distant memories.

"Come along, Polly, we don't want to be late," he says finishing his tea.

The visit to the famous Shakespeare Theatre is something Polly will remember forever. The walls of the entrance are adorned with photos of famous theatricals, and the auditorium is small making the audience appear almost part of the production. She soaks up the atmosphere and is completely enthralled by it all. She claps loudly at the end, and looks forward to being able to tell her friends about her visit.

They arrive back at the hotel around eleven and retire to their rooms. Daniel says goodnight to Polly and is soon sound asleep, the glass of wine during the interval obviously helping. Later, as he begins to come out of a deep sleep, he realises that Polly is beside him. She is sound asleep, so must have been there some time. He is rather concerned as he leans over her to switch on the bedside lamp.

"Polly, wake up please."

"Daniel, what is the matter?"

"Polly, how long have you been in here?"

"I am not sure why what is wrong, Daniel?" she enquires with a puzzled expression on her face.

"Polly, my dear Polly, you must not get into my bed, it is not healthy for you or for me. I have a duty to care for you and have the trust of your parents to look after you. Looking after you does not include having you in my bed."

"But you come into my bed lots of times, Daniel, I don't understand," Polly replies tearfully.

"Only when you have been upset by a bad dream or something similar, I do not sleep in your bed, Polly, nor would I expect to," Daniel replies, realising that the conversation is becoming difficult, but he must try and get Polly to understand. She holds on to Daniel and begins to sob uncontrollably as he tries to comfort her.

"Polly, please do not upset yourself after such a lovely evening, I am sorry but this must not continue," Daniel says firmly.

"Daniel, please, please don't, I want to stay with you," says Polly, who is becoming hysterical, not understanding how serious it would be for Daniel if they were found together, a point that he appreciates.

"Okay, Polly, you can stay with me this time, now please stop sobbing, you are getting yourself upset and I do not want you to become upset again," he says as he resigns himself to letting Polly stay with him in his bed. He looks at his watch, it is just 2.00 a.m.

"Now Polly, listen to me please, you can stay with me this time, but I need you to promise that you will not do this again do you promise me?" Daniel insists, being as firm as he dares.

"Okay, Daniel, I promise, now can we go to sleep please?" Polly replies.

So Daniel switches off the lamp and Polly goes off to sleep in his arms. He lies there for a while, concerned at what has happened. He cannot tell Margaret and Ben about this and he suddenly finds himself questioning his relationship with Polly. He lies, with her cradled in his arms trying to resolve his dilemma, being very aware of her presence beside him. Finally, he drifts off to sleep after deciding that he must talk with her about what has happened before returning home. He rises early and packs ready for their departure after breakfast. Polly sleeps soundly, and he finally wakes her telling her to pack ready to leave after breakfast.

"I wish we could stay here longer, Daniel, it's so peaceful."

"I thought we would have a long walk by the river this morning, Polly, what do you think?"

"I would like that," says Polly as she goes into her room.

After saying goodbye, Daniel and Polly drive into Stratford. Polly is bubbling over, any upsets and fears she may have are far away at present. Yet somehow, Daniel has to be firm with her regarding her behaviour towards him last night. They walk round the park by the river in the warm sunshine, and find a quiet covered bench where Daniel sits down beside her.

"Polly, I have to have a word with you about last night, you do know that, don't you?"

"Yes, Daniel, I suppose so, if you must. I just don't understand what was wrong, I had a wonderful sleep," Polly says with a sigh.

"It was where you slept that is the problem, Polly. You must give me your word that it will not happen again," he says sternly.

"Please don't be angry with me, I am so sorry if I upset you, Daniel."

"Polly, you did not upset me, and I am pleased that you slept so peacefully for once, but 13-year-old girls must not spend the night in an adult's bed. It is wrong and not allowed."

"But, Daniel, we have spent lots of nights together, I do not understand what was so different about last night," replies Polly looking puzzled.

"You will have to take my word on this, Polly, providing it does not happen again, and you do not mention it to anyone, then we will say no more about it, and enjoy what is left of the day."

"Okay, Daniel, let's carry on with our walk and find somewhere to have something to drink."

So nothing more is said, and Daniel decides to move on and put what happened from his mind, at least for now. They enjoy the rest of the day, exploring the walks by the river before finding somewhere to have some lunch. After lunch, they make the journey back home, Polly chatting about what a wonderful time she has had with Daniel, and he does not want to spoil her enjoyment. She will have some difficult times over the next few days so her being happy and relaxed is real therapy for her. When they arrive home she chats to Margaret about the wonderful time she spent with Daniel, and both Margaret and Ben thank him for his time and efforts with their daughter.

The trial of the four men accused of abducting Ben and Polly Spencer will be especially harrowing for both father and daughter. Polly, yet again, will have to give unpleasant details about what happened to her, and Ben will have to recall those details since he was actually a witness to the events. Daniel will be in court to give support to Polly, but he is apprehensive about how she will react to the event, Margaret, too, will find it difficult to control her emotions.

The four of them, Ben, Margaret, Polly and Daniel had gone to London the day before, Monday, to be ready for the trial start on Tuesday. It was agreed that Polly would stay with Daniel at his flat in Kensington, while Margaret and Ben would stay in a local hotel. Polly being with Daniel would offer her the best support possible before the ordeal of giving her evidence. Daniel decides that Polly should have an early night and sees her safely in bed before returning to his sitting room for a nightcap. He is really unsure of how Polly will react when asked to tell the story of her abduction and the terrible ordeal she went through. He will be close by to give her support, but she will be on her own giving the details. He finishes his drink and looks in on Polly, who is sleeping, before going off to bed himself.

His sleep is interrupted by Polly calling his name. "Daniel, Daniel, where are you, please come," she cries out.

Daniel dashes into her room to find Polly sitting up in her bed, bathed in sweat. Daniel sits beside her and holds her tightly.

"It's okay, Polly, you are safe now, go back to sleep," he says as Polly curls up beside him and drifts into a deep sleep until he wakes her.

"Come along, Polly, I have made some breakfast, go and get ready."

"Okay, Daniel," says Polly going off to the bathroom. After breakfast they make their way to the Crown Court where they meet with Ben and Margaret around 9.30 a.m.

"How is she, Daniel?" asks Ben taking him to one side.

"She is okay, Ben, I am sure she will be okay," replies Daniel with some conviction.

The usher introduces the accused and reads out the charges.

"George Chisholm (Deceased), Arthur Bellamy, Frank Phelan and Freddie Carter, you are jointly charged as follows: Conspiracy to kidnap, grievous bodily harm and physical assault of a minor."

The judge enters the court and begins his introduction to the case. "This evidence presented in this case will be especially harrowing, because the witness is so young. Offences against minors can be distressing to record, and I ask you to listen to the evidence carefully and consider your verdict accordingly. The Crown will now call their first witness," the judge concludes.

Polly is called to the witness box by the Crown representative.

"Can you tell the court your name please?"

"My name is Polly Spencer."

"And how old are you, Polly?"

"I am 13 years old."

"Polly, will you tell the court what happened on the Monday of four weeks ago?"

Polly relates how she was at her school sports day and went to the changing rooms, to change her shirt, when she was approached by a woman. As she stopped to talk with her she was grabbed by two men who forced her into a car. They gagged her and tied her legs together before driving off.

"They took me to an old warehouse and took off my shirt and skirt, then they hit me with a cane across my back and bottom," Polly replies tearfully.

"Please continue, Miss Spencer," the Crown asks.

"The four men took turns to beat me with canes, they tied me to a table, then they tied me up to a beam on the ceiling. They kept beating me, across my back and bottom … Daniel, please," Polly sobs.

"Miss Spencer, would you like break?" the judge asks. Polly nods and dashes to Daniel sobbing.

"Thirty minutes' recess, everyone," the judge instructs. Polly is weeping in Daniel's arms as they move from the court into the waiting room. Margaret fetches her some water, and they all try and console her.

"I'm sorry, Mummy, I just had to stop, I feel so wretched remembering those horrid men and what they did."

"You have nothing to be sorry about, my dear Polly, does she, Daniel?"

"Nothing at all, you have been very brave, Polly, having to recall what happened must be so painful for you," says Daniel holding Polly close to him for reassurance.

"Thank you, Daniel, I am feeling better now."

"Are you ready to continue, Miss Spencer?" the usher asks Polly.

Polly nods and the Crown representative continues:

"Do you remember how long the men kept you a prisoner, Miss Spencer?"

"They took me from the school playing field on Monday and Daddy and I were rescued by Peter and Daniel on Wednesday evening."

"So, these men were beating you with canes for three days is that correct?

"Yes they would beat me then leave me for a while, then come back and beat me again, again, they wouldn't stop, I begged them to stop but they kept on–" Polly bursts into tears as an usher rushes to support her.

"We will adjourn for lunch and determine then whether Miss Spencer is fit to continue," the judge instructs. Polly rushes to her family and into Daniel's arms. They calm her down and walk from the court into the fresh air and find a small restaurant close by for some lunch. Polly goes with Margaret to freshen up while Daniel and Ben order some tea and sandwiches.

"She has coped remarkably well so far, Daniel, and I am so glad that you are here for support."

"I am always ready to support her, Ben, I just hope that she will not have too much longer in the witness box."

After lunch they return to the court and Polly is asked if she is ready to continue.

"Yes thank you, sir."

"Now, Miss Spencer, did these men say anything when they were treating you so badly?"

"The only one who spoke was the one who was shot by Peter. He kept telling me what they were going to do to me to teach Daddy a lesson, and he told me that they would kill me when they were finished. "

"And what happened when you were finally rescued, Miss Spencer?" the Crown continues.

"Daniel and Peter came and shot two of the men, then they called the police and an ambulance took me to hospital."

"And how long were you in hospital, Miss Spencer?"

"I was in hospital in Birmingham, for two days I think, then I was moved to Carswell to be near to home, I think I was there for about two and a half days."

"My lord this is a copy of the medical reports outlining the injuries suffered by Miss Spencer," the Crown representative says as he hands over a file to the judge, and one to the defence.

"Thank you, Miss Spencer, that is all the questions I have for you, will you wait there a moment please?" the Crown representative asks.

"Miss Spencer, I am a defence representative, I have just a few questions I would like to ask. Tell me would it be true to say that just one of the accused gave any instructions about what they should do, and also spoke to you, is that correct?" he asks.

"Yes," replies Polly.

"And that was George Chisholm deceased?"

"Yes, he was the horrid man who enjoyed watching the others beat me," said Polly tearfully.

"Thank you, Miss Spencer, that is all, the defence has no further questions for this witness your honour."

"Very well, thank you, Miss Spencer, you have been an exceptional witness and I offer you my sympathies for what you endured. We will adjourn for today and hear Mr Spencer's evidence tomorrow," the judge concludes.

Ben, Margaret, Polly and Daniel leave the court, and go to a cafe a short walk away for some tea. It has been a long day for all of them, not least Polly, and they are relieved that it is now over.

They enjoy some tea and cakes and talk about the evening.

"Do you have any plans at all, Daniel?" Margaret asks.

"I thought I might take Polly a walk around Kensington Gardens."

"Oh yes please, Daniel," says Polly with a big smile.

"Well it's only just after 4 o'clock, so I suggest we all go and have a look round now, what do you say, Margaret?" says Ben.

"Yes, we have plenty of time before dinner. You will be having dinner with us, Daniel?" Margaret asks.

"Yes of course, so let's enjoy our tea before we go off to Kensington Gardens," says Daniel.

So after tea, they get a taxi to Kensington gardens, and enjoy a leisurely walk around. It is all new to Polly who seems to be overwhelmed by the sheer size of the gardens. Some parts are not open, having sustained damage in the 'blitz' but the gardens are still very impressive. Ben and Margaret obviously enjoy their time together, and Polly is just happy that her ordeal at court is over, and she can enjoy her walk with Daniel. He invites them all back to his flat before Margaret and Ben depart for their hotel. They all arrange to meet again for dinner around 7.30 p.m.

Polly asks Daniel if she can have a bath, she feels quite grubby after giving her evidence today.

"Of course, Polly, you remember where everything is from your last visit I trust?"

Polly goes off to the bathroom and enjoys a bath, while Daniel thinks ahead to the conspiracy trial and beyond. Once the trial has been concluded, his work at the Spencer household will be over. He will have to make arrangements soon, if Polly is to stay with him, since he has never had a long-term occupant in the flat, so it will be a new experience for him, especially as it will be a 13-year-old schoolgirl! He has thought over the responsibility of having her with him and is confident that they will both benefit from being with each other. Polly will be with the one person that she feels safe with, someone who has saved her life more than once, and is an inspiration to her. Daniel will be able to give her back her own confidence and at the same time draw from her presence, a very special friendship.

Daniel has no female relatives, other than his mother, and has enjoyed more and more Polly being with him. Yes, the circumstances have often been harrowing because of what has happened over the last few weeks, but he has still enjoyed her being around. She has become very special to him. Polly enjoys her bath and puts on her shirt and skirt ready to go to dinner. Daniel is reading the paper which he bought on the way back from the gardens. Polly browses through the collection of books that he has before they leave for dinner, arriving at the hotel just on 7.30 p.m.

"Do you think you will finish your evidence tomorrow, Daddy, and can we go home if you do?"

"I would think that we will be finished tomorrow, Polly, so you should be able to go back to school on Thursday."

"Will you come back to hear the verdicts, Ben?"

"Yes I will, Daniel, I want those men to see the look of satisfaction on my face when they get put away," Ben replies with a stubborn note in his voice.

The conversation was very light after the ordeal of the trial, and Ben talks about the future after the next trial.

"Do you know, I am beginning to see an end to all this, Daniel? We have all suffered more wickedness and upsets over the last weeks than most people would have to endure in a lifetime. We have survived and have much to look forward to, let's drink to that," Ben says as he raises his glass.

"How soon can I go and stay with Daniel, Mummy, you did say as soon as the holidays are here?"

"Yes Polly, the holidays will soon be here, and it was agreed that you could then go and stay with Daniel. For how long will depend on a number of factors, but we have suggested four weeks then see what happens after that."

"But I will eventually be able to go and live with him won't I Mummy?"

"One thing at a time, Polly, you enjoy your long holiday with Daniel first."

"It won't be long, Polly, you will have to tell me if there is anything I need to get for you before you leave in the morning, bedding, towels and so on, I have only had to manage for myself so I have no experience of this at all.," smiles Daniel.

The meal was enjoyed by everyone, and Daniel leaves with Polly around 9.30 p.m.

"Thank you for the meal, Ben, we will see you around 9.30 a.m. tomorrow," says Daniel as he leaves the Spencer's and looks for a taxi back to Kensington. Polly holds his arm and asks.

"You will let me stay with you after the four weeks have ended won't you, Daniel?"

"I will always look forward to you staying, Polly, but you must listen to what Mummy says and be guided by her decisions."

"Okay, Daniel," Polly says as the taxi pulls up outside his apartment block.

"Do you want anything before bedtime, Polly, a drink or anything?"

"No thank you, Daniel, I am just tired and ready for bed."

"Well you go and get ready for bed, good night, my dear Polly."

Daniel lies awake out of force of habit, listening to hear if Polly is asleep. He has left both bedroom doors open so that if Polly has a bad dream he will hear. Thankfully, Polly sleeps soundly until morning.

They return to the Court on Wednesday morning and Ben enters the witness box.

"Can you give me your name, please?" the usher asks.

"My name is Ben Spencer."

"Mr Spencer, will you tell the court what happened to you on the dates in question please?" the Crown asks.

"I was travelling into Carswell with my colleague when our car was intercepted, and I was taken forcibly to an old warehouse, which I later determined to be in Birmingham."

"And what happened then, sir?"

"Then, for almost three days, I was forced to witness those men and a fourth, violently assaulting my young daughter. Without question, they enjoyed beating her and inflicting terrible injuries on her," Ben replies, his eyes filled with tears.

"Did they say anything to you?"

"Only the deceased, George Chisholm, spoke and enjoyed telling me how they were going to hurt my daughter and let me see it happening through a window in the room where I was being held. I offered to give them whatever they wanted on the first day, but Chisholm seemed to be working to a timetable.

"I do not know how long they intended to keep us, but any more beatings and my daughter would not have survived, the doctor was sure about that. I cannot understand why they wanted to inflict so much hurt on my daughter rather than me."

"I believe they felt that the pain was worse for you if they beat your daughter than if they assaulted you, Mr Spencer," the Crown replied.

"If that was their intention, I have to say they succeeded. I was completely devastated by what I saw happening, and I will never forgive those men, never for what they did to my beautiful daughter," Ben concludes with tears in his eyes.

"Thank you, Mr Spencer, will you wait there please?" the Crown representative asks.

"Mr Spencer, I am representing the defendants, I won't keep you long, can I ask you about the shooting of George Chisholm? You said in your evidence to the police that he was shot by Peter Forsyth is that correct?"

"Yes that was what I told the police," Ben replies.

"Are you quite sure it was Peter Forsyth, Mr Spencer?" the defence representative asks.

"As sure as I can be, since I was there," Ben replies, somewhat irritated by the question.

"Can I ask where this is going defence counsel?" the judge requests.

"Just trying to establish the facts, my lord."

"Please move on counsel, your question has been answered," the judge replies.

"I have no further questions, my lord, thank you, Mr Spencer," the defence representative concludes. Ben steps down and goes over to Margaret, Polly and Daniel.

"After lunch, I will give my summation," the judge confirms.

The family have a lunch in the same place just around the corner and return to court to hear the judge sum up the evidence of the case.

"I have listened to the evidence presented and thank the members of the Spencer family for their evidence. I have to say, that I found some aspects of the case particularly distasteful. Any offence against a child is completely inexcusable. Serious assault against a child is reprehensible. The accused did not show an ounce of compassion toward Miss Spencer, and to subject her father to the horror of witnessing the assaults on his daughter, is beyond belief. I am not convinced that you acted alone here, and would urge the authorities to continue with any investigations that would bring to justice anyone else involved. I will deliver my verdicts on Friday. This case is adjourned," the judge concludes.

The Spencers and Daniel leave the courts and make their way to the station ready to return home. There is a sense of relief now that it is all over, and for Ben especially, since he can now concentrate all his efforts on the conspiracy trial. Margaret and Polly can begin to enjoy a normal life now that the terrible events have been chronicled and there are only the verdicts to consider. They are expected to be severe. Daniel continues to ponder life beyond the conspiracy trial. When it is concluded, he will sit down with Ben and Margaret and discuss Polly staying with him for an extended holiday. Beyond that nothing can be decided for a while, although he is sure that Polly will ask questions. Meanwhile, they arrive home late afternoon to be greeted enthusiastically by Maisy, Daisy and George.

"Mummy, Daddy, Polly, Daniel, we have missed you come and play with us Polly, you, too, Daniel," they all chorus, and tug at Polly and Daniel towards the garden. Pauline hugs her sister and they walk towards the parlour to be greeted by Conrad.

"How was it, Ben?"

"Very harrowing, Conrad, having to relive the abduction was painful enough for me, what it was like for Polly I can only imagine. As usual, she did not venture far from Daniel's side and he has been very supportive of her."

"He continues to be the rock that supports her, and we are so very grateful to him for taking such good care of our daughter," Margaret adds.

"Any more thoughts on whether she will go and live with him permanently?"

"What we have said is that Polly can stay with him for a long holiday, say four weeks, during her school holiday, and see what develops. Beyond that, nothing has been decided," says Ben.

Pauline and Margaret arrange some supper, and the family settle to a quiet evening.

Polly goes back to school on Thursday and appears relieved that it is all finally over.

"I am really looking forward to the holidays, Daniel, are you?" Polly asks Daniel.

"Yes I am, Polly, to see you looking so much better and enjoying life, as you should at your age, is very satisfying, and I do look forward very much to spending some time with you outside of your home surroundings. But there is some time yet before your holidays start so concentrate on your school work in the meantime," Daniel replies.

"Will you take me out to Bradgate Park again sometime, Daniel, I really enjoyed that day?"

"We shall have to see, Polly, now off you go, I will see you later," Daniel replies.

"Thanks, Daniel," Polly replies leaning over and kissing him on the cheek.

Meanwhile, Ben returns to London Crown Court on Friday to listen to the judge's verdict, confident that the men in the dock will be dealt with severely. He wants to see these men punished to the maximum for their treatment of his daughter.

The judge enters the courtroom to deliver his verdict on the three accused.

"The accused showed absolutely no mercy during their numerous serious assaults on the young child Miss Polly Spencer. Whilst Mr Spencer was not physically assaulted to any degree, the anguish he suffered seeing what was happening to his daughter must have been far worse. Your behaviour toward Miss Spencer could have consequences far beyond this court date. The medical reports suggest that she will carry the physical scars from her beatings for some time to come. As for the mental scars, no one knows how long they will stay with her. The fact that the terrible injuries were inflicted in an attempt to change Mr Spencer's testimony at a forthcoming conspiracy trial, lead me to believe that there are other people involved. I hope the authorities will hunt down those responsible."

"I propose to sentence each one of you men to the same term of imprisonment, for your crimes, namely 7 years for abduction and imprisonment and eight years for the serious assaults on a minor. I instruct that the sentences be carried out consecutively. Take them back to the cells," the judge concludes.

Ben feels a sense of relief and satisfaction at the length of the sentences and that the men will not see freedom for many years. He phones home to give them the news before leaving to return as soon as possible. He can now concentrate fully on the case against the black market racketeers, due to commence the week after next. In the meantime, the family can start living a normal life again. There is still much for him to do of course, regarding the pending trial, and the security surrounding family must remain in place for the time being. How long it remains in place afterward is another matter, although Ben is happy for Polly to be with Daniel for a while, if only to secure her wellbeing. He is happy to go along with the special relationship she has with him, since no one can be sure how long the mental scars of her ordeal will take to heal. Margaret, too, will have to be watched over; her ordeal has been overshadowed by what happened to Polly. She suffered terribly at the hands of the men that abducted her, and she too will need some time to get over the mental anguish that she endured. Margaret and Ben have always been very close, even though Ben has been absorbed so much recently with securing the evidence for the conspiracy trial. He will do his utmost to care for her over the coming months and get the whole family back to living happily. For now, however, he has to concentrate on the trial, and will need to talk with the Crown Prosecutors, who will have all the relevant information in their possession. They will be aware of any tactics that the defence barristers may be considering, to try and undermine Ben's evidence, no matter how overwhelming the evidence is against the accused. Ben will also need to talk with Beatrice Carrington. She is very much the link between the accused and any higher-ranking government officials that may be implicated.

Ben must have dropped off to sleep while pondering all the court details, and is woken by the porter calling out the station name.

"Carswell Station," he calls loudly.

Ben gets off the train, and decides to call in on the office before returning home.

"Hello, Ben, it's good to see you again, how was the case?" Phil Landers asks.

Ben relates the sentencing details to Phil, adding that he is relieved that it is over.

"Good riddance, Ben, they got only what they deserved," Phil comments.

They go over relevant business that is being looked at by the office at present and Phil reassures him that everything is in order. Ben thanks Phil for the update, and asks Maureen if she would come into the office.

"Hello, Ben, how did everything go for you?"

"The trial was an ordeal, Maureen, especially for Polly, I am glad that it is over and that the sentences were adequate, although no punishment could really be enough to fit the crimes those men committed against Polly. Now the reason I asked you in was because I wondered if you had any messages for me?"

"Yes I do, Commander Spratt asked if you might contact him next week before the trial, as did Major Baxter."

"Thanks, Maureen, how are you and Peter getting along by the way?" he asks with a smile.

"Very well thank you, Ben, very well indeed," Maureen replies as she leaves his office. After saying his goodbyes to Phil Landers, Ben leaves the offices and makes for home. Everyone is delighted to see him return safely and are satisfied that the judge's sentences were sufficient.

"It's just a pity that Daniel and Peter didn't finish them all off at the same time, that was surely what they deserved," Conrad comments.

"Anyway it is finished, now what plans have we got for the weekend?"

"Pauline and I are going shopping, but first she needs to go home to sort out her laundry," Margaret replies.

"Valerie is coming round tomorrow, I have to try and catch up with some work," Polly says.

"I thought that we might look at the house now that all the work is completed Ben, and see what can be done about the bottom fence which, I believe, is vulnerable," says Daniel.

"And I intend to relax some, before I begin my week of preparation for the trial," Ben comments.

After supper, Daniel goes up to his room to sort out his clothing and get another blanket. The nights can be chilly, under the clear skies, so he places it on the armchair in Polly's room. He returns downstairs and joins Conrad in the garden.

"How are things, Daniel, how is Polly getting along now the trial is over?"

"She is definitely on the mend thanks, Conrad, although I expect it will be sometime yet before she fully recovers."

"And what about you, do you still intend to have her live with you?"

"Yes I do, Conrad, I have promised Polly, Ben and Margaret that I will look after her for as long as necessary. It will be a challenge, especially if it becomes long-term, given her age.

"I know there could be complications, but Polly is very sensible for her age, and I have gone to great lengths to impress upon her that she, too, has a responsibility in seeing that our relationship must be acceptable. We had a long chat while we were in Stratford on Avon. Thankfully, she is not yet old enough nor wise enough to understand the implications of what she did coming into my bed, and it was a difficult situation for me to explain to her. I suppose the true test will be when she is in London with me."

"Well I wish you good luck, Daniel, she is a beautiful girl, and if being with you will help her to forget what has happened then that can only be good for her."

"And how about you, Conrad, how are you getting along with Pauline?" asks Daniel with a smile.

"Yes, I have to admit I have grown fond of her during my stay here."

"Does she think the same of you?"

"Yes, I think she does, we certainly enjoy each other's company, I think that's obvious."

"It certainly is, Conrad, it certainly is."

Polly is busy tidying her room for when Valerie visits tomorrow, and Ben and Margaret chat briefly about the pending trial.

"I will have to find out if Daniel and Conrad are being called, and ask Peter if he would mind staying. I would not think they would be away for more than two days, but I do not want the house to have no security. I am unsure how long I will be giving evidence, but have arranged to stay with Beatrice Carrington."

"An excellent idea, Ben, you can keep her company through what will be a difficult time for her."

"Yes, her position is critical to the success of the trial, and I am pleased to be able to give her some time. She will most certainly give her evidence in a closed courtroom, but will still feel vulnerable, I am sure."

For some reason, Polly has a restless night and Daniel goes and stays with her until she is asleep. However, as soon as he tries to leave, she grabs him tightly.

"Please stay with me, Daniel, I feel so–" Polly suddenly stops and is violently sick over her nightshirt and Daniel.

"Don't worry, Polly, I will get a towel and clear up the mess," says Daniel as he goes to the bathroom and returns with a flannel and a towel. He removes his vest which is covered in Polly's sick and wipes himself with the towel before returning to Polly. She has replaced her nightshirt and is sitting up in her bed, looking rather pale.

"I am so sorry, Daniel, I don't know why that happened." she says, as she notices the scars over Daniel's back. "What are those terrible scars on your back?"

"Just leftovers from the war, Polly, nothing for you to worry about."

Polly finally goes off to sleep, once again in Daniel's arms. He gets up early to wash properly after the upset with Polly, and goes downstairs to find Margaret, the early riser, making tea. He relates what has happened to her and she is a little concerned.

"I suppose we must accept that she will still have bad dreams, although this is the first time she has been sick isn't it. We have a long way to go, Daniel, and I wonder if you realise just how much Polly depends on you. Some people would see your responsibility too daunting to contemplate. I must say that I was apprehensive myself at how she leaned on you for so much support. But, it seems to work, and I am beginning to accept that we may lose her to you permanently."

"You will not be losing her, Margaret, I will just be taking care of her for you, she is your daughter and loves you and Ben very much. She loves me in an entirely different way. She needs me with her to keep her safe and has grown to love me out of gratitude I guess."

"Thank you for your kindness, Daniel, our daughter is fortunate to have you taking such good care of her," Margaret replies as they sit and drink their tea together.

Polly's friend Valerie calls around 10 o'clock and takes her books up to Polly's room.

"Hello, Poll, you look a bit pale are you okay?"

"I was sick during the night, but Daniel took care of me, and I am okay now thanks."

"Does Daniel stay in your room at night then, Poll?" Valerie asks.

"Yes, Daniel stays with me all the time since all the trouble began, he takes care of me all the time. If I have a bad dream he will stay by my bed to keep me safe," Polly goes on.

"Gosh, Poll, it must be super having Daniel sleep by you when you are frightened."

"I would not feel safe if he were not there, Val, he saved my life you know, and he will always be there to keep me safe. I am going to stay with him in London for the holidays."

"He must care for you very much, Poll, you are very lucky to have a friend like that," Valerie replies. The two girls chat on about Daniel, before concentrating on their school work schoolwork. Polly has missed some important work because of the time she has spent recovering from recent events, and she is anxious to catch up. Valerie has some lunch with the family before returning home. The house settles down to the rest of the weekend which is uneventful. Ben has a busy week planned before the trial and decides he will catch up on his phone calls.

"Hello, Beatrice Carrington."

"Beatrice, it's Ben, how are you?"

"Good morning, Ben, I am fit and raring to go with the trial next week. I have sent all relevant documentation to the Crown representatives. Having spoken at length with the representatives, it has been agreed that I give my evidence in closed court. You and I both know that this trial will not see the end of the trade in black market goods, and we will continue to pursue these people. But is important that I remain anonymous so that I can continue my work without interference."

"Your position has to be kept secret, Beatrice, for the good of the operation, and to ensure your own safety, my personal experience is testimony to that. I am keen now to begin presenting the evidence and get it over with."

"You will be staying with me while the trial is on, Ben?"

"Thank you, Beatrice, I would be delighted, we will talk again to make arrangements, bye for now."

Ben is apprehensive about Beatrice giving evidence, even in closed court. The accused must have a lot of influence, and it is vital that she is protected, that is one of the reasons why he was happy to be staying with her next week. After lunch, Ben contacts Commander Spratt and Major Baxter. Both men are ready to be called when required and have consulted with the Crown regarding their evidence. Major Baxter may have to relate details of the raid at New Haven so his evidence will be important. Commander Spratt is unlikely to be called since his participation was only to oversee the issuing of arrest warrants generally, but will make himself available if required. Ben spends some time in his office on Tuesday, but the family suffer a setback on Wednesday. On Wednesday morning, Margaret collapses while she is making breakfast. An ambulance is called and Ben goes with her to hospital. The doctor is most concerned. She has an infection of some sort, has been violently sick and has a bad headache. The specialist thinks she may have some injuries that are a direct result of her treatment when she was abducted. She will remain in hospital so that further tests can be carried out and she can be monitored closely.

"Mr Spencer, your wife suffered severe injuries as a result of the assaults on her. It appears that while she has continued to run your home and so on, her body has grown very tired and she has caught an infection. I want to keep her in for a few days at least so that we can watch her carefully," the doctor concludes.

"Thank you, Doctor; may I see her?"

"Of course, but try not to tire her, she really has to rest," the doctor replies.

Ben goes in to see Margaret, who is looking pale and frail, as the doctor said she will have to have rest for a while.

"My dear Margaret, you gave us quite a fright," Ben says holding her hand tightly.

"I don't know what happened, Ben, I just felt so tired and faint and I have a terrible headache."

"You need to rest, Margaret, I will bring the children along this evening providing the doctor is okay with that," he says leaning over and kissing her forehead.

Ben returns home, and once again finds himself calling on Pauline to assume the role of housewife for his family. Pauline asks about Margaret, and assures Ben that she will do whatever is required to see that the children are cared for.

"There is a possibility that Margaret will be in hospital while I am away, Pauline I'm afraid, I will arrange for Mrs Poulton to take the children to school, and I will ask Peter Forsyth to hold the fort if Daniel and Conrad are called to give evidence."

"Please do not worry about looking after the family, Ben, I will take care of everything, you need to concentrate all your efforts on the trial. Give Margaret my best when you see her and tell her not to worry, I will take care of everything here."

"Thank you, Pauline, I really do appreciate all of your efforts."

When the children arrive home from school, they are anxious to know about Margaret.

"Daddy, what has happened to Mummy, is she going to get better soon?" chorus Maisy, Daisy and George.

"Mummy will soon be well children, but has to stay in hospital to get some rest."

"But, Daddy, I want to go and see her please."

"Perhaps tomorrow, George, I will call tonight just to take her overnight clothes, then perhaps we can all go and see her tomorrow, now off you go into the garden."

Polly arrives with Daniel and she is very upset by what has happened to her Mummy.

"Daddy, how is Mummy, what is wrong, is it because of what happened to her?"

"Yes I'm afraid it is, Polly, Mummy must have complete rest for a while, how she has managed up to now I do not know, but now she must have that rest and her body given time to heal," Ben replies. Margaret's collapse has put the whole family in turmoil, Polly is very close to her mother and frets over what has happened. Daniel does his best to console her, but in this case, she is so upset that he finds it difficult to know what to do for the best. And Maisy, Daisy and George are very upset, constantly asking questions about when Mummy will be coming home. Ben decides he must talk with the children, and calls them into the parlour with Pauline, Daniel and Conrad.

"Now, children, we are going to have to make some changes next week since I will be away as you know," Ben begins.

"But where are you going, Daddy, and does that mean that you and Mummy won't be here with us?" says George, sounding puzzled and a little upset.

"I have to go back to London next week George to make sure those nasty men who have been hurting go to prison. And, at some time during the week both Daniel and Conrad may have to go to London also to give evidence against these nasty people," Ben continues. Polly grips Daniel's hand tightly, she had not realised that Daniel would be going to London.

"Daniel, how long will you be away, I don't understand?"

"Polly, Daniel may be called to give evidence, along with Conrad, they played a major role in finding where the criminals were storing huge amounts of goods intended for black market distribution. I am going to arrange for Peter and Maureen to stay with you, and Pauline will look after you all, as she has been doing for quite a while now. Polly, you will have to watch over your sisters and George, and help Pauline when she needs you, will you do that for me and Mummy?"

"Okay, Daddy, I will help where I can with everything and help Aunty Pauline. How long will you be away, Daniel, I really will miss you not being here with me?" Polly replies with a tear in her eye.

"Perhaps a couple of days, Polly, but nothing is definite and I will call you in the evening. You have a lot of responsibility with Mummy in hospital, and I know you will be a great help to your Aunty Pauline."

"Okay, now I need to call Peter, to ask him if he will stay should Daniel and Conrad be called, although I am hoping that will not be the case. It will be up to the Crown how they direct me when I give evidence," says Ben as he heads toward the study.

He talks at length with Peter who is pleased to be able to help if required. Maureen, too, will be only too glad to pitch in while Margaret is recovering in hospital. Ben thanks them both, and tells Peter he will be in touch when he has more detail next week.

Hopefully, there will not be a need for Peter to be available, but Ben is just relieved that everything appears to be sorted regarding his absence and Margaret being in hospital. He will be calling on Margaret this evening and wanted to be able to reassure her that everything is arranged for his absence, and for her stay in hospital as long as is necessary. Ben calls into see Margaret in the evening and is pleased that she is sitting up and appears comfortable. He has taken additional nightclothes and toiletries for her, together with a magazine and the local paper.

"How are you feeling, my dear, you gave us a hell of a fright?"

"I am feeling better for the rest, Ben, I still feel tired and I ache all over. Most of my injuries seem to be healing, but I feel so wretched generally."

"It will take time, Margaret, but you will have all the time that you need. I have spoken with Pauline, who will be with us as long as necessary, and Maureen too has offered to help. All the arrangements for next week are in place, so you have nothing to concern yourself with, so just get well," says Ben, who stays with Margaret for about an hour before going to have a word with the doctor on the way out.

"How is she, Doctor?" he asks anxiously.

"Your wife is very poorly, Mr Spencer. She has suffered some internal injuries that have become infected and will need treatment. For the moment, bed rest is what she needs to allow her body to heal."

"Of course; may I bring the children tomorrow? They miss her very much."

"Yes, the children will be good for her, so long as she does not get too tired."

Ben returns home and mentions the doctor's comments to Pauline, then tells the children that they can visit Mummy tomorrow. Polly is very upset about what has happened, and it brings back memories of her own ordeal.

"Mummy will get better won't she, Daddy?"

"Mummy needs to have rest, Polly, her body is very tired from her ordeal. She is relying on you to take care of Maisy, Daisy and George and reassure them, will you do that for me, please?"

"Yes, Daddy, I will look after them, I promise."

"And you must help Aunty Pauline while Mummy is in hospital, she will have a lot to do with both of us away."

"I know, Daddy, and I will do my best for both of you."

Thursday passes uneventfully, and in the evening the children go with Ben to see Margaret. She is delighted to see them all but a bit tearful when they have to leave. Polly, especially is reluctant to go and promises Margaret that she will look after the children and help Aunty Pauline around the house. With the conspiracy trial due to start next week, and so much upheaval in the Spencer household, Daniel takes the opportunity to speak with Polly.

"The next week or so are going to be very busy for the family, Polly, are you ready to take on extra responsibilities for Mummy and Daddy?" he asks.

"Yes, and I will have you to help me, won't I?"

"I will be here, Polly, but you have to do this on your own, take on responsibility while Mummy is in hospital. You must try and understand that I cannot always be by your side, for example, I may be called away to give evidence next week. If that happens, you must be able to carry on with what needs to be done in the home. It will be important that Mummy and Daddy have confidence in you while they are away."

"Yes, Daniel, I know that I will have to take on more responsibility while Mummy is away, why are you telling me about your not being with me, I don't understand why you keep saying that," she replies and leaves the parlour hurrying upstairs to her room.

"She is obviously upset by all that is happening, Daniel, I would leave her for a moment," Conrad suggests.

"You're right Conrad and I need a word with Ben anyway."

It's Saturday afternoon, and Ben has spoken with Beatrice, who has again reiterated her comments about Daniel and Conrad.

"I will speak with the Crown again on Monday Ben, although if the defence is persistent, the judge may have no alternative but to allow them to interview Daniel and Conrad. I suggest you spend tomorrow going over what happened in Rye and New Haven, and make sure that you only say what needs to be said. I don't see any problems with what the defence may ask, but you all need to be prepared," says Beatrice.

"Yes, and what about your evidence, Beatrice, will it be carried out in a closed courtroom?"

"Yes it will, Ben, I will enter and leave by a side entrance and give my evidence given in a closed court. And I will be escorted to and from the courts by car, so my position should not be compromised in any way. My Home Office contact has arranged all of this to ensure that I can continue in my post after the trial."

"That is good news, Beatrice, and I will be with you Monday around 5 o'clock," says Ben.

"Yes, Ben, the porter will let you in if I am a little late, I will tell him to expect you, see you then," Ben reflects on what Beatrice has said, especially regarding Daniel and Conrad, and decides that they must talk as soon as possible.

"Daniel, Conrad, we should have a word about next week should you be called to give evidence."

"What do you think, Ben, will we be called?" asks Conrad.

"I really don't know, but after speaking with Beatrice, we both agree that you have to be prepared and we all three need to make absolutely sure that our statements complement each other. For example, Conrad, I see no point in mentioning your visit when you spoke with Katherine Meadows, and especially, there must be no mention of our illegal entry. As for the issuing of the search warrant at the cottage, we were acting on information received about Giles Williamson. That was how we stumbled across the evidence contained in the boxes. The discovery of the tunnels was acquired by your good old-fashioned detective work. Why were we in Rye? Again we were acting on information received about Giles Williamson. Hopefully, the weight of evidence against Williamson will be enough to dispel any claims that the defence makes about information from undisclosed sources," says Ben.

"Is it not possible that the Crown may want to talk to us about your abduction, along with Polly, to give weight to their case argument? Anyone going to such extreme lengths to prevent you from testifying, must have a lot to hide?"

"I am sure the Crown will want to introduce the abductions as weight to their arguments, Daniel, but I can give them all the detail they need, and they will have the police reports to refer to. Well, I think that covers the details, if you think of anything else, we will talk about it again tomorrow."

Daniel and Conrad leave Ben in the study, and Daniel goes to find Polly. She is busy in the children's room tidying their toys and clothes. Daniel taps on the door and walks in.

"I can see you are busy, Polly, are you okay?"

Polly goes over to Daniel and puts her arms around him.

"I am okay, Daniel, I just keep thinking of you going away to London and me having to stay here. I am sorry, but I love you so much and can't bear the thought of you not being here."

"Now, Polly, you must not upset yourself over this. You need to focus on what has to be done with Mummy in hospital, then think about you and I when all this is over. I care about you very much and your Mummy and Daddy agree that you should spend some time with me in London. You should think about that as something we can both look forward to. Your Mummy and Daddy and I only want to do what is best for you, Polly."

"I know, Daniel, and I do want Mummy to get better, then I will be able to spend time with you."

"Good, now I think we should go down and see what Maisy, Daisy and George are up to don't you?" says Daniel, and so they both go down to the parlour.

The children are monopolising Conrad in the garden, while Pauline is in the kitchen sorting out something for dinner. She had been into the village earlier with Conrad to stock up, where possible, for today and tomorrow. Ben goes to visit Margaret at teatime, and takes Pauline. Margaret is delighted to see her sister, and they both enjoy a long conversation about the household duties. Ben tells Margaret that he will bring the children again tomorrow and leaves for home after about an hour.

"How was Mummy, Daddy? Is she getting better, when can she come home please?" the children chorus.

"Mummy is getting better, but it will be a while yet before the doctor will let her come home. She is still poorly, and needs to rest, something that she would not get if she were at home. Now off you all go and get ready for supper."

The family and everybody enjoy a superb supper dished up by Pauline, who is an exceptional cook. After supper, Ben spends some time with the children, assuring them that they will be in good hands while he is away.

Sunday sees everyone enjoying time in the garden and Ben packs for a week away in London. Daniel and Conrad go over details of what they might say if called on to give evidence. In the afternoon, Ben takes the children to see Margaret, and after spending some time with her, Ben asks Polly to wait outside while he speaks to Margaret.

"I will call you every night, Margaret, promise me you will not worry about anything, I have arranged everything with Pauline, Daniel and Conrad and I will ask Pauline to look in on you. Please get better soon, Margaret, and I will see you hopefully Friday evening," says Ben as he hugs her. The children, too, say goodbye before they depart for home.

Daniel, meanwhile, takes the opportunity to take Polly for a walk along the lane before supper. She seems to be coping very well and is taken to her new role, as assistant to Pauline in running the house, very enthusiastically. She holds on tightly to Daniel as they walk along, and he considers how she has changed since he first met with her. The terrible ordeals that she has endured have matured her somewhat, although she is still only 13-years-old. However, she has had to endure more in the last few weeks than most people would in a lifetime. There are perhaps a few more frowns than there were, but she has grown up as a result of her experiences. This young girl will be an integral part of his life from now onward, and Daniel looks forward to that.

"Have you and Daddy come to any decisions about you having to go to London next week?"

"It will depend entirely on whether I am called, Polly, but I am confident that we shall not be required, but we will have to see what happens. Whatever happens, it will only be one day, so I would be able to get back in the evening."

"And then when Mummy is better, we can see about our holiday."

"We certainly can, Polly, and it will be here sooner than you think."

They return to the house for supper, and then the children spend the last hour with Ben, since he will be gone in the morning before they are up. Lots of hugs and a few tears, some from Ben, but Pauline and Polly eventually see them off to bed. Polly goes up at 10 o'clock, and Daniel arranges to drive Ben to the station in the morning. The rest of the household drift off to bed between eleven and eleven thirty, Daniel is pleased to see that Polly is sleeping soundly, and pulls her blanket over her. He settles in the armchair and soon drifts off to sleep himself. His night is peaceful, and he goes downstairs just after 6.00 a.m. ready to take Ben to the station for the 7 o'clock train to London.

"Thank you, Daniel, I will call this evening from Beatrice's around seven, take good care of my family while I am away please."

"I will, Ben, I hope it goes well, we have all waited a long time for today, have a safe journey," replies Daniel as he watches the train slowly pull out of Carswell Station.

He drives back to the house, and settles down to an early morning cup of tea with Pauline and Conrad.

CHAPTER 32

(Operation Seeker: Old Bailey Trial Part 1)

Ben's train arrives at Euston Station just after 9.30 a.m., and he makes the short journey to The Old Bailey by taxi arriving about fifteen minutes later.

The conspiracy trial will be long and arduous. There is a vast amount of evidence to be considered and many perpetrators to be questioned by The Crown.

The trial will be presided over by Justice Percival Stephenson, noted for his strict discipline regarding the law and how it is administered.

The accused on trial are:

Miles McKenzie, Giles Williamson, Toby North and John Devonish.

The four men are charged with conspiracy to fraudulently divert Crown goods for profit, black market racketeering on a grand scale and suspicion of smuggling.

McKenzie and Williamson, had both been in The Food Ministry during the war years, so had many contacts that they could call upon regarding distribution of goods. These goods were intercepted by gangs and redistributed through a network of agents throughout London. Huge quantities of goods were moved in this way and Ben was able to show the proof of this from the documents seized at the cottage belonging to Giles Williamson in Rye in Sussex. The documentation, was damning in many ways. There were names of agents, dates of transactions and addresses where the goods were transported.

Toby North and John Devonish were very much the enforcers of the operations. Both men were known to police, but had never been charged, as no one was prepared to give evidence against them. They played a leading role in distribution and dealt ruthlessly with anyone who did not arrange and deliver the goods to the selected sites. The Crown would call on evidence from Montague Galbraith, who had agreed to cooperate in return for leniency concerning his role in the black market activities. Whilst his convictions for conspiracy to kidnap, illegal entry, violent assault, attempted burglary and complicity in the abductions and attempted abductions of members of the Spencer family will still stand, any charges relating to black market racketeering against him will be considered against the information he offers in mitigation. His evidence will link both Devonish and North with the transportation of goods from London to Birmingham, where Galbraith was responsible for redistribution.

The storage and movement of goods from the New Haven tunnels was detailed in the boxes of documents that were seized from the tunnels. The Crown spent some time listing the hundreds of tons of foodstuffs, jams, fats, cooking oils, tinned fruit as well as alcohol, petrol and weapons that were confiscated. The list was extensive and drew gasps of astonishment from the gallery.

Defence representatives struggle to dispute any of the evidence presented since the details were conclusive. They were anxious to know how the evidence had been forthcoming, and Ben is cross examined about this.

Meanwhile the Crown continued to list the goods seized from the tunnels which also included some trucks along with drums of diesel fuel. There were also many roles of cloth and a huge quantity of ration books together with a large amount of cash.

"The effort's roundup of men and women complicit in the black market will continue even when this trial has concluded my lord. What this trial will show is the scale of the operation run by the four accused. Their convictions will send out a message that there really is no place to hide for anyone who chooses to cheat and deprive the British people of their everyday needs and requirements," the Crown representative concludes his introduction before calling Ben Spencer to the witness box. Ben is questioned at length about his work during WWII and beyond. He tells of his time at the Ministry of Information, which was continued at the Central Office of Information when M.O.I. was dissolved in 1946. The provision of special information services allowed him to move freely about departments and so determine if any suspicious movement of goods, or sudden shortage of goods was taking place.

"Would it be fair to assume that this has been an ongoing investigation since the war years?" the Crown asks.

"Yes that is correct."

"And when did you break through and secure the mountain of evidence before us, Mr Spencer?"

"That would be when we secured the documentation relating to the movement of goods, names and dates, together with the discovery of the tunnels at Newhaven."

"Yes, tell us about that discovery," the Crown continues.

"Acting on information secured from a source within the Ministry of Food, I was given two names, initially, to investigate, namely Giles Williamson and Miles McKenzie. Myself and two of my colleagues travelled down to Rye posing as land agents, and asked questions about possible land for housing. This gave us the opportunity to move around without suspicion. Moving further down towards the coast we were able to determine that some of the locals had seen trucks moving around by some old disused tunnels near New Haven."

"Can you tell us a little about these tunnels, Mr Spencer please?" the Crown asks.

"The tunnels are situated beneath South Heighton about a mile north of Newhaven. They were a secret intelligence centre for the Royal Navy during WWII. There was no record made of their existence for security reasons. In 1941, the Admiralty used certain South Coast ports for communications with coastal radar stations. HMS Forward Newhaven was one of the locations, and since there was no secure accommodation at Newhaven, the tunnels were excavated to support engineers, signal officers, telephone switchboards and so on, everything needed for a secret observations post. All this was more than 70 feet below a large country house, together with a mile of tunnels, and all the work was done under the eyes of German aircraft. No one really knew that they existed, I can only presume that the accused stumbled on their existence and realised how useful they could be to their operations. They were able to keep their business secret by dressing those that worked in the tunnels in military style uniforms and the trucks were similar to army trucks in appearance. "Ben continues.

"And can you give us an idea of what was discovered hidden in these tunnels please?" the Crown asks.

"There were vast quantities of foodstuffs, corned beef, beans, margarine, cooking oils, jams, and biscuits that I recall. There were hundreds of cartons of these goods, you have an inventory to refer to I believe. Also there was a vast quantity of alcohol, hand guns and ammunition, drums of industrial oils, rolls of cloth, ration books and a quantity of cash."

"And is it true, Mr Spencer, that some of these items had been imported?" the Crown continues.

"Yes that is correct, evidence has been secured, by the authorities that proves goods had been brought in from U.N. aid agencies and from Germany itself."

"Thank you for the moment, Mr Spencer," the Crown concludes.

After lunch Ben Spencer returns to the witness box to be questioned first by a defence representative.

"Mr Spencer, I represent Mr Giles Williamson, can you tell me why you specifically targeted my client?" he asks.

"My office had been watching Mr Williamson and Miles Mackenzie for some time. They both had connections in The Ministry of Food dating back to the war years."

"And your information, where did it come from, who was supplying the information?" the defence asks.

"Some information was supplied by my contacts in the Ministry, some was supplied by informers who were arrested for black market activities, and some was supplied by Montague Galbraith in consideration for leniency in his sentence for black market activities."

"Thank you, Mr Spencer," the defence representative replies, obviously surprised at the detail of Ben's response.

"Mr Spencer, will you remain for a moment please?" the usher asks.

"Mr Spencer, I represent Mr Toby North, and I too would like to know where you got information regarding my client, a respected business man?" he asks.

"Toby North and John Devonish were known to be involved in the theft of government supplies during the war, but again we were never able to prove that they were involved, because no one would give evidence against them. They were implicated in the theft of raw materials initially, then from the evidence in the containers found in Williamson's cottage, the importation of goods stored in the New Haven tunnels."

"Thank you, Mr Spencer," the defence representative concludes, realising there is no benefit in his continuing this line of questioning.

The judge decides that he will adjourn for the day and thanks Ben for his efforts. Ben goes for afternoon tea, before taking a taxi to Beatrice's flat. He sits and looks through the evening paper while waiting for Beatrice and calls home around 5 o'clock to say hello, and update Daniel on the day's proceedings. So far he doesn't think that Daniel or Conrad will be called since the evidence against the accused is so overwhelming. Then, after a meal with Beatrice, he calls Margaret.

"How are you, Margaret, what has the doctor said today?"

"I am feeling better, and the doctor says there is a definite improvement. I am hoping to be home for the weekend. And Pauline came along to see me with Maureen, it was a real pleasant surprise to see them."

"Well that is good news all round, Margaret, I will call you again tomorrow bye for now," replies Ben. After spending a quiet evening with Beatrice discussing the court case, Ben returns to the Old Bailey at 10.00 a.m. to continue presenting evidence for the prosecution.

"Mr Spencer, you mentioned yesterday about evidence you had collected, over time, relating to the black market activities in this country. Where was this information kept?" the Crown asks.

"It was kept in an old metal container, a fairly innocuous looking box. I had left it with a trusted colleague through the war years and immediately afterward. However, a few months back, it turned up in my garden. My colleague had placed it there fearing that it might be discovered and its contents destroyed."

"And since that time, can you tell the court the sequence of events that have occurred at your home and beyond?" the Crown asks.

"My family has been subjected to a catalogue of violent attacks from those seeking the contents of the container. Now of course the contents are of no value, since all the evidence is confirmed in the boxes recovered from Williamson's cottage. But those responsible were not aware of that evidence. They obviously believed that my records were unique, and if they could obtain them, then there would be no evidence to link them with the black market operation. My wife, my young daughter and my secretary were all brutally assaulted by groups of men demanding to know

415

where the container was. My house was subjected to an arson attack and explosive devices were delivered to both my house and my place of work."

"Mr Spencer, are you saying all these events have occurred in the pursuit of the information you possessed in this container?" the judge asks.

"Yes, my lord, indeed their demands were made a number of times towards my wife, my daughter and my secretary, whilst they were being assaulted."

"This information may be worth recording for future considerations," the judge comments.

"Mr Spencer, I represent Mr Toby North and would like to ask you a few questions. For example, will we be given the opportunity to question any of your so called contacts, especially those in high places?"

"I can answer that, sir, you will be given ample opportunity, but any witnesses deemed sensitive, will give their evidence in closed court," the judge replies.

"Thank you, my lord, now tell me, Mr Spencer, has not some of your evidence been obtained by illegal search, on the cottage in Rye for example?"

"I don't think so. I am sure the police had all the relevant documentation, but I cannot be sure of that, you will have to ask them."

"I'm talking about a visit made by persons unknown, prior to the police search," the defence representative comments.

"I'm afraid I cannot help you with that, I only know of the search that as carried out with the local police," Ben replies sounding matter of fact.

"You do not know of a previous visit to the cottage by three men?" he asks.

"No I do not, I have already said, I know only of the search carried out with the local police," Ben replies.

"Can we move on please?" the judge instructs the defence representative.

"I have no further questions, my lord," the defence representative replies.

"Mr Spencer, another word if I may? When did you begin compiling this black market evidence exactly?" the Crown asks.

"During WWII, I worked for the Ministry of Information, which gave me the opportunity to go into other departments freely. I picked up details of many black market operations, mostly being carried out by small time operators. As time went by my investigations led me to believe that these operations were becoming more organised by criminal elements, and that they were obviously getting assistance from people inside government establishments. Some of this information was passed to me by my colleague who has a position in government and is well placed to secure such information. I have always kept the identity of the person secret for fear of reprisals. After what has happened to my family, I believe that was the right decision to take. Even when this trial is over, there will still be racketeers operating in a black market. My job will not stop, and I need my contacts to continue to supply me with evidence"

"Thank you, Mr Spencer," the Crown answers.

"You may stand down now, Mr Spencer, and thank you for your evidence, we will adjourn for the day, court will resume at 10.00 a.m. tomorrow, Wednesday," the judge concludes

The third day is dominated by Beatrice Carrington giving her evidence in closed court. She is collected from her home and enters and leaves the court by a side entrance. Throughout the proceedings she is referred to only as "X".

"Can you tell the court how you became involved in the arrests of the accused please?" the Crown representative asks.

"Throughout the war years, as shortages of so many essential items became so acute, the black market operations grew from small time operators, 'Spivs' as they were known into more organised gangs. There was an upsurge in robberies and violence against some of the small time operators. Working in the Home Office, I was fully aware of this and was asked if I would investigate just how big the black market was, and if it was being run inside any government departments. My investigation could only look for people inside departments; I had no contacts at all. I first met with Ben Spencer through the Ministry of Information. It seemed obvious to me, once I was sure that he was trustworthy, that he could be a worthy ally and a valuable asset in the fight against the racketeers. His dedication and perseverance were commendable. He also had a remit to investigate and bring down black market operators. He had contacts on the street supplying him with information, and it soon became obvious that our paths would eventually cross.

"I wanted to help his fight against these people, knowing that it would help my fight. For some time, Mackenzie and Williamson had been under suspicion. We knew that the losses that were being incurred could only be as a direct result of someone releasing details of time and places of shipments. I gave their names to Ben Spencer in the hope that he would be able to prove what had long been suspected of these two men. I was very pleased when my suspicions were found to be true. I have been able to supply Ben with other information over the last year or so, including warning him of reprisals which his family has suffered," Beatrice concludes.

"And is your enquiry on going?" the Crown asks.

"I believe it will continue until rationing has been eliminated. That will be some time yet I fear, so there is still some work to be done. The Home Secretary is determined to punish anyone who seeks to profit from these shortages whoever they may be," Beatrice replies.

"Thank you will you remain in the witness box please?"

"Can I ask you how you collected your information against the accused?" the defence representative asks.

"By intercepting memos, monitoring calls and setting up surveillance on the suspects. In doing so, we were able to determine precisely what they were up to. What we could not find out was where their main storage depot was for shipments from Europe as well as shipments stolen from Crown bonded warehouses. We were able to link Mackenzie and Williamson with the thefts and the shipments from Europe, and North and Devonish with the distribution of goods around London and The Midlands. Ben Spencer and his colleagues discovered the tunnels, and once they were found the arrests were ordered. Without Ben's efforts, we would have struggled to secure the arrests, since we had very little physical evidence to present," Beatrice concludes.

"We thank you for your evidence; the Crown is indebted to you for your diligence in pursuing the black market criminals."

"We shall now adjourn for the day. Tomorrow, the accused will have their opportunity to give evidence," the judge states.

Beatrice leaves the court by a side entrance to return home. Ben had remained at her flat since he was not allowed into the court along with anyone else. She told him of what had transpired and they both agreed that their evidence was more than enough to secure convictions of the accused.

CHAPTER 33

(Another attack on the Spencers' home)

Meanwhile, everyone at the Spencer house has carried on as normal, the children going to school, and Pauline running the house efficiently. By Wednesday evening, the children are becoming restless, missing Mummy and Daddy. Polly has been very good looking after them and trying to make up for Margaret's absence. Pauline is taking the children to see Margaret after school, hoping that will make them feel better.

"Mummy, Mummy how are you we have missed you and Daddy so much?" they all chorus.

"Hello, children, I am feeling much better and looking forward to coming home very soon. I hope you are being good for Aunty Pauline," Margaret replies hugging them.

"Yes we are, and Aunty Pauline is looking after us, but we still miss you very much," Maisy replies.

"And how are things for you, Pauline, no problems I hope?"

"We are all coping, Margaret, but do want you to come home soon, what is the doctor saying?"

"I am hoping to come home this weekend, but will have to wait on the doctor's decision."

Pauline and the children return home, where Polly has been preparing supper. She has been very helpful to Pauline and with her sister's and brother in Margaret's absence. Daniel notices how she has taken on the additional responsibility very well and believes that she may be changing just a little with regard to her reliance in him. And she is sleeping so much better, too, giving him the opportunity to get some rest. Pauline passes on

419

the message about Margaret hopefully returning home for the weekend. After supper, Ben speaks with Daniel.

"Hello, Daniel, just thought I would give you an update. Today has been Beatrice's day in court. Although I could not be present, since her evidence was given in closed court, I firmly believe that her evidence will be more than enough to convict the accused. They will begin their evidence tomorrow, and I expect the case to go into a second week," says Ben.

"Conrad and I may not be called after all it seems then, Ben?" Daniel replies.

"There is no benefit to be gained by the defence seeking your identities, no more than asking for the police officers on the raid to give evidence. In fact, they do not know who you are so they would not be able to call on you even if they suspect that other parties were involved in the raid on the cottage. So you and Conrad can remain anonymous."

"That's good news, Ben, and I'm sure Polly will be pleased as well!"

"Yes, how is she by the way, I hope she is helping Pauline with everything?"

"She has been very good, Ben, she has got the children ready for school each day, and helped Pauline with meals. She has taken on her responsibilities very well and she is sleeping much better, so I am sleeping much better also!"

"Well that is good news all round, Daniel, bye for now, now; I will give you a call tomorrow and speak with the children."

So the Spencer family settle down for the evening before retiring to bed around 11 o'clock. Once again, Polly has drifted into a deep sleep and Daniel is looking forward to a good night. However, he is woken suddenly, by the sound of breaking glass. Polly's room, being at the front of the house, means that it is above the front door. The glass has been shattered by intruders.

Daniel dashes from Polly's room and wakes Conrad, who has also heard the noise. Daniel goes back to Polly and wakes her.

"Polly, we have visitors, go to the children and stay in their room," he whispers.

Both men approach the top of the stairs and as one of the intruders reaches the top, Daniel fires and hits him in his leg. He goes downstairs in the confusion while Conrad remains at the top to cover him. The injured man has fallen down the stairs and sits motionless at the bottom. Daniel peers through the darkness crouching at the bottom of the stairs beside the rail. A second man moves from the study door and Conrad fires three times, but apparently misses. Daniel whispers to Conrad to stay at the top of the stairs, while he tries to draw out any more intruders into the hallway. He moves to the end of the hall way and carefully opens the kitchen door, moves into the kitchen and approaches the door to the study. He opens the door firing as he does so, hitting one man in the chest but another escapes into the hallway. Then suddenly Daniel realises he has been hit. His left arm has been penetrated just above his elbow, and as his adrenaline level subsides, he gasps and winces in pain. He holds his arm across his chest, and moves toward the door to the hall. Just as he reaches the door, there are a number of shots fired from at least two more weapons. He opens the door and sees Conrad on the ground at the bottom of the stairs. He has been hit twice, in his arm and chest, and there is another intruder with a wound to his head lying on the hallway floor. As Daniel goes into the hallway, he sees a fourth intruder dashing up the stairs.

"Stop or I will shoot you dead where you stand," he shouts and the man freezes.

"Okay, don't shoot guv'nor I surrender," the man replies.

Pauline and Polly appear at the top of the stairs hysterical at what they see when the hall light is put on. There are two men with bullet wounds in the hallway as well as Conrad who is badly hurt. Daniel has also been shot, but is still on his feet, just!

"Polly, go into the study and call for the police and an ambulance, please. You, go and sit next to your two colleagues, and do not make a move," says Daniel to the fourth intruder who is unharmed. As Polly approaches the study, the injured man stumbles into the hallway and is ordered by Daniel to sit next to his colleagues. Pauline has rushed to Conrad's side, shocked by the blood from his two wounds.

"Oh my God, Conrad you've been hit, lie back on the stairs while I get some towels."

Polly returns to Daniel, and she too is horrified when she sees he has been hit.

"Daniel, Daniel you've been hit, let me look," she screams.

"I'm okay, Polly, get me a towel to stop the bleeding, then go to the children, I have to watch over these men until the police arrive," Daniel replies.

421

The police arrive within minutes to a scene of carnage at the Spencer's house. Five men have bullet wounds so another ambulance is called. The most serious injury is to the intruder that Conrad shot in the head, and it is doubtful if he will survive. Conrad's wounds need immediate attention. The wound to his arm is a flesh wound but his chest has the bullet still inside, and he has lost a lot of blood. Pauline is tending to him as best she can, and is covered in his blood from the wounds.

"Please try and lay still, Conrad, you have a chest wound and another wound to your arm," she says with concern etched over her face.

"Pauline, you must go with Conrad to hospital, so you need to get some clothes on quickly."

"Thank you, Daniel," says Pauline as she runs upstairs to change.

Polly is at the top of the stairs with the children, who are obviously terrified at what they see. Daniel asks her to get them back into one of the bedrooms for a moment, to avoid them seeing the scene in the hallway, while Pauline returns to Conrad, ready to accompany him to hospital.

"Bit of a mess, Daniel but I think the score is 3 to 2 in our favour," Conrad says to Daniel with a smile, although he is obviously in some pain.

"We won that one, Conrad, you get off to hospital with Pauline, I'll see you later."

The police meanwhile, have handcuffed the one intruder who is not injured and the ambulance crews are giving first aid to the others. Daniel's arm is a mess but the wound is not too deep. It is cleaned and bandaged and his arm put in a sling. Once the hallway has been cleared of bodies, Daniel calls Polly to bring the children downstairs. He ushers them into the parlour and asks Polly to make them a warm drink. They are obviously very upset over what has happened and what they have seen. Poor George is in tears over Conrad being taken to hospital.

"He will get better won't he, Daniel? He must get better," he insists tearfully.

"Conrad will be alright, George, I hope he will be back home very soon."

Daniel is covered in blood from his wound, when he suddenly realises that he has another gunshot wound to his side just above his hip. No one had noticed this second wound in the confusion, thinking the blood was from his arm.

"Daniel, you have another wound, we must call for another ambulance."

Daniel suddenly feels very tired and decides he must sit down. Again adrenaline has been keeping him going, but now things have calmed down his pain levels have shot up. He asks Polly to get him some brandy from the study. Meanwhile, he removes his vest and uses it to stem the bleeding. A shot of brandy helps, but he does need urgent attention. Thankfully, the ambulance arrives shortly, as does D.I. Wishart, together with W.P.C. Becky Garrett. The ambulance crew want to take Daniel to hospital, but he insists on remaining at the house, so he is stitched up and given pain killers, which seem to help.

"Looks like you've been busy again, Daniel, how are you feeling?" the inspector asks.

"Rather sore and very tired, Inspector, but thanks for asking."

Polly asks the W.P.C. if she will watch over the children while she goes and gets dressed into something suitable, since she will not be returning to bed anytime soon. Not only must she watch over the children, but she has to look after Daniel as well.

"This is a bad business, I take it Mr Spencer is in London at the conspiracy trial, is that correct?" he asks. Daniel nods and the inspector continues.

"And Mrs Spencer?"

"Mrs Spencer is in Carswell hospital, she collapsed last week, her injuries from her abduction have not healed properly. We are all hoping she may be back home for the weekend."

"I'm sorry to her that, I hope she will be well soon, God knows this family have suffered enough," the inspector comments. The ambulance crew leave reminding Daniel that he must have his wounds looked at within the next two days to be sure there are no complications.

"Any ideas who they were at all?" the D.I. asks.

"They were from the south; they had London accents, that is all I can tell you, Inspector."

"I would bet they have links with the conspiracy trial, and were on some sort of revenge mission," the inspector replies.

"You could be right about that, Inspector, I can think of no other reason."

"Anyway, Daniel, I will leave my W.P.C. here to help young Polly. She will stay as long as she is needed. I guess it will be a while before Mrs Spencer's sister returns from hospital. I will call round at lunchtime or thereabouts to see how you are and take your statements if that's okay?"

"Thank you, Inspector, I appreciate your help, Polly will see you out, good bye for now," Daniel replies as the inspector leaves after having a word with his W.P.C.

He looks at his watch. It is 4.00 a.m. He suggests to Polly that she try and get the children back to their beds, although they are still rather shaken. Daniel reflects for a moment on the events of the last hour or so and appreciates how fortunate he has been with his injuries. Another inch or so to the right, and he could have suffered severe kidney damage. As it is, his side is badly lacerated, but not serious, just a mess to look at. However, he has lost a lot of blood from his injuries, so does need to rest for a while.

"I have managed to get Maisy, Daisy and George back to bed, Daniel, I think it may be a good idea if you rested now," says Polly who has become concerned at his condition.

"Yes I would like to rest a while, Polly, will you help me up the stairs we can use my room with Conrad in hospital."

Polly helps Daniel upstairs and helps him onto his bed. She leaves the door ajar so that she will hear if any of the children call, their room being directly opposite. Daniel drifts off to sleep thanks partly to the brandy and the painkillers. He is woken by Polly with a cup of tea.

"Daniel, I have brought you some tea, I have to get the children up now, and I am going to call Mrs Poulton to ask if she will help until Aunty Pauline gets back from hospital," says Polly.

"Thank you, Polly, I do appreciate that, I will be down shortly, but I must wash first," Daniel replies.

"I will take care of you, Daniel, as soon as I have got breakfast for the children," says Polly, who seems to be relishing her responsibilities.

"Very well, Polly, just as you wish," Daniel replies, happy to oblige.

She returns, a few minutes later, and leads Daniel to the bathroom. She carefully bathes his face and body, which is caked in dried blood from his two wounds, taking care not to get any water on his bandages.

"Thanks, Polly, can you fetch me a clean shirt please, preferably a dark coloured one and a pair of trousers?" Daniel asks. Polly helps Daniel with his shirt, and notices that his wound to his side is bleeding.

"Daniel you're bleeding again from the wound in your side," she says with concern in her voice.

"It'll be okay, Polly don't worry, it's probably just seeping past the stitches, I'll keep my eye on it, now off you go while I change, I will be down shortly." Daniel looks closer at the wound in his side which does appear to be bleeding again. He will watch it closely in case he needs to take any action. He goes down the stairs, where the children are sitting very quiet in the parlour. They are obviously in some sort of shock over what they have seen take place.

"Okay, everyone, I think you should skip school for today, you have missed a lot of your sleep and you can help Polly tidy up the house after last night, will you do that?" Daniel asks.

"Yes, Daniel, we will help Polly so you can sit down and have a nap if you want," says George.

"Yes we will take care of you, Daniel, like you have taken care of us," Maisy comments.

"Thank you, I do appreciate that, although I am not ready for a nap just yet," Daniel replies looking at his watch. It is 7.30 a.m. There is a knock at the door and Polly goes to let in Mrs Poulton.

"Oh my gosh, what on earth has happened, Polly?" she gasps as she sees the mess and bloodstains through the hallway and up the stairs.

"I'm afraid we had unwelcome visitors again Mrs Poulton," says Daniel, "and your help to clean up some of the mess would really be appreciated. Pauline is at the hospital with my colleague Conrad, who was hurt rather badly."

"Of course, I'll make a start straight away, Daniel, Polly can you show me where you keep your mops and bucket and cleaning stuff, please?" asks Mrs Poulton. As Polly leaves the room with Mrs Poulton, the doorbell rings and Daniel goes to let in Pauline, who has returned from hospital, looking tired and with her clothes spattered in Conrad's blood.

"How is he, Pauline?" asks Daniel about his friend.

"He is out of surgery, Daniel, they managed to remove the bullet without too much damage," Pauline replies a little tearfully.

"That's good news, Pauline, Conrad is a tough nut to crack, I am sure he will be back with us soon," Daniel replies, hoping to reassure her.

"He lost a lot of blood, Daniel; the doctor says they will keep him in for a couple of days to be sure everything is healing satisfactory. Then he will need some rest for a while."

"And he will be in good hands, Pauline, I am sure of that," Daniel replies with a smile as she goes upstairs to change and wash.

Daniel suggests to Polly that she stays with her sisters and with George while he telephones for the doctor. Then, he will ask Pauline to contact the schools to tell them the children will be absent for the day. However, Daniel's first call is to Ben.

He recites in some detail the events of the early morning, and Ben is devastated by what he is told.

"I will return home at once, Daniel, I will not be needed in court for the rest of this week anyway, and I need to be with you and my family after yet another intrusion into our home."

"Is there anything we can do meantime, Ben?"

"You need to rest, Daniel, perhaps I might have a word with Polly?" Daniel calls Polly and Ben asks her to take care of the children until he returns.

"You have done very well from what Daniel has told me, Polly, once again we are all being targeted by criminals. You will be staying off school with the others today, and I will see you all later. You take care of Daniel until I get home."

"Okay, I will Daddy, I promise," replies Polly as she replaces the receiver. She sees the W.P.C. to the door and thanks her for her help.

"I expect I will see you later today, Polly, for your statement?"

Daniel phones for the doctor who says he will come along before his surgery begins. He sees Maisy, Daisy and George together with Polly and Pauline. They are still very upset, but he believes they will soon recover, as young children usually do and be better for seeing their Daddy when he arrives.

"Doctor, I wonder if you would mind taking a look at Daniel. One of his wounds appears to be still bleeding although it has been stitched?" Polly asks. The doctor calls on Daniel and takes a look at the wound in his side.

"You really will have to rest, Daniel to give this wound time to heal. Please no exertion whatsoever, do you understand?"

"Yes, very well doctor and thank you," Daniel replies as he puts his shirt back on. He has not had any time to thank Polly for all her efforts and calls her into the study after the doctor has left.

"My dear Polly, can I say thank you for all of your efforts over the past few hours?" he says as he hugs her with his good arm!

"Thank you, Daniel, but I had to look after you and Maisy, Daisy and George as there was no one else. And anyway, I wanted to take care of you."

"I am going to suggest that we change the sleeping arrangements while Conrad and I are recovering. Conrad to use your room and you and I to move into the other room."

"Of course, Daniel, I would not expect you to sit in a chair all night while you are recovering from your injuries. I will move some of my clothes into the other bedroom."

Mrs Poulton, meanwhile has managed to remove most of the bloodstains and tidied in the study, as the family settle down for the rest of the day, hoping that it can be reasonably quiet.

Around lunchtime, D.I. Wishart arrives accompanied by W.P.C. Becky Garrett, to take statements. Daniel gives him as accurate account as possible of the events of early morning, from the time that he heard glass breaking.

"Conrad and I went to go down the stairs but were confronted by one man on the landing who fired but missed, I returned fire and hit him, he then stumbled back down the stairs and I followed using him as cover," Daniel recalls.

He then continues telling the inspector how he made his way through the kitchen into the study, where he was hit as he opened the door. He was however, able to hit one of the two men in the study before the other ran into the hallway. He was hit on the head by Conrad.

"He must have dashed out without seeing what was waiting for him, and Conrad hit him as soon as he appeared. Unfortunately, the fourth man got two shots off and hit Conrad before dashing upstairs. I shouted for him to halt, threatening to shoot him if he did not, and he duly surrendered."

"And how is your colleague, Daniel?" the inspector asks.

"He has had surgery to remove the bullet and will take time to recover, but he will be okay I am sure. Conrad is a very resilient person and will be about in no time I am sure," Daniel replies.

"I don't suppose you know who these men were at all?" the inspector asks.

"The only one who spoke had a London accent. I believe they may have been carrying out some sort of revenge attack against Ben for his work against the racketeers and the subsequent trial. They seemed determined to get to family members, what would have happened if they had done so I can only imagine. The men in the dock in London have connections, even in government, Inspector, and their attempts to destroy Ben Spencer know no limits," replies Daniel.

"Yes indeed, now perhaps I could speak with Polly and Mrs Spencer's sister?" the inspector talks with Polly and Pauline with the W.P.C. who is also present. They are both shaken up by what has happened, but are coping well considering what they witnessed.

"We stayed with the children for the most part, Inspector, and only came downstairs when the shooting stopped. The scene in the hallway was carnage, with Conrad and Daniel injured as well as three of the intruders, and there was blood everywhere. Conrad and Daniel put up one hell of a fight considering there were four intruders. I am sure they saved our lives and those of the children," says Pauline.

"They must have fought very hard, Becky, both Conrad and Daniel have been hurt, Conrad especially," Polly adds.

"Well thank you all very much, we will speak with Conrad probably tomorrow, depending on what the doctors say. Goodbye for now," the inspector replies as he and the W.P.C. leave the Spencers' house.

CHAPTER 34

(Operation Seeker: Old Bailey Trial Part 2)

Because of the overwhelming evidence against the men in the dock, gathered from the documentation from the cottage, Ben Spencer's efforts over a number of years and Beatrice Carrington's contribution, the defence will not call on the defendants to speak from the dock. This way, they cannot incriminate themselves through cross-examination. However, before the Crown begins its summary, the judge makes a statement from the bench.

"Before we begin proceedings this morning, I want to mention some information that has just been handed to me. In the early hours of this morning four men broke into the home of Mr Ben Spencer. There was considerable gunfire exchanged between them and two of Mr Spencer's colleagues. When colleagues. When they were finally apprehended, three had been shot and the fourth had surrendered. In protecting Mr Spencer's home and family, his two colleagues were both injured wounded, one seriously. I would like it put on record that if these actions are found to be connected, in any way, with the accused the consequences will be severe. The Crown may now continue with its summation," the judge concludes.

"Thank you, my lord. The facts of this case are very clear and the evidence against the accused is damning. Quite simply, they chose to steal and pilfer goods of every description, many needed by families to feed and clothe their children, and sell them on the black market making huge profits in the process. Miles McKenzie and Giles Williamson used their positions of trust within the Ministry of Food to pass on relevant details of distribution of goods for sale to the public. Toby North and John Devonish were responsible for sales and distribution of these goods which they carried out ruthlessly, inflicting injuries on anyone who interfered with the operation. They organised importation of goods which were then stored in the New Haven tunnels prior to their distribution in London and the Midlands. The accused were very efficient detailing names, places and dates for delivery of their illegal spoils This detail was critical to the Crown's case and we thank Mr Spencer for his efforts in uncovering these details. His tireless efforts put him and his family in grave danger, and you have heard of the catalogue of incidents that have occurred.

"Arson, explosions, abductions and serious assault against family members, all these events were suffered by the Spencer family, and there is no doubt that the accused, though not participants in the actual events, were involved.

"Thousands and thousands of pounds' worth of goods were channelled through the black market racketeering operations run by the four accused. This court must send a message to anyone who thinks that they can benefit from such activities and pass the maximum sentences permitted. In closing I would add that there will be many more arrests and prosecutions, peripheral to the evidence, that will be carried out over the coming months," the Crown concludes.

"The defence representatives will begin their deliberations after lunch," the judge adds as the court is adjourned.

After lunch, the defence begins by emphasising that the accused will not be called in their defence. Whilst this is most unusual, it makes sense in this case, since questioning by the Crown would only be detrimental to their case, with so much evidence stacked against them. What the defence endeavour to show is the bigger picture, that the defendants are pawns in a government cover up of black market distribution for gain. They believe an inquiry is needed into some of the departments, not least the Ministry of Food. It has become obvious, through the trial, that the Ministry was being used to move goods to black marketeers. It must have been common knowledge, yet nothing was done about it by the authorities. The defence claims that nothing was done because of the complicity of key personnel within the Ministry and beyond. They argue that this must be taken into account when handing out any sentences to the accused. The defence representatives ask that it be recorded that they expect the Attorney General's Office to take note of the events of the trial and act accordingly. However, since they do not call any of the accused to give evidence, then no mitigation can be offered in their defence, for their actions. All the defence can offer is to make the court fully aware of the facts relating to the accused being used by persons unknown in high places. In their closing summations, they seek to cast doubt on the integrity of Ben Spencer and Beatrice Carrington, implying that Ben Spencer was complicit with many involved in the black market operations detailed, and that Beatrice Carrington used her position in the Home Office to get information that was not readily available. Whilst they have absolutely no proof of the accusations, they are hoping to cast doubt on their testimonies. They point out that Ben Spencer has been operating in a clandestine world for a number of years, no one knowing what he was doing or how he was getting his information. The defence say that in all that time it is unlikely that he was not involved in some way with black market transactions, if only to secure information. After continuing with this line of doubt and suspicion, the judge intervenes.

"Gentlemen, do you intend producing any evidence at all to substantiate your wild claims against the establishment, Ben Spencer and the witness we will call X?" the judge asks. The defence council chorus no they do not.

"In that case, I ask you to conclude your arguments," the judge replies. After the defence sits down the judge adjourns for the day, saying he will give his summations tomorrow.

CHAPTER 35

(The Secret's Holder, Retributions and Rewards)

The end of the trial is a watershed moment for Ben Spencer and for his family. Having to return home was disappointing for Ben, who would have liked to have been there to hear the closing arguments, but he will be going along to listen to the sentencing pronouncements on Monday.

He arrives back home on Thursday afternoon, to be greeted by his children with hugs and tears.

"Daddy, you're back, it was awful the men shot at Daniel and Conrad and hurt them," says George clinging onto Ben for comfort.

"I was so frightened, Daddy, but Daniel and Conrad saved us didn't they, Daisy?" Maisy says.

"Yes, it must have been very frightening, children, and we are all very fortunate to have such brave men as Daniel and Conrad taking care of us, how are you, Daniel?"

"On the mend, Ben and Conrad is on the mend also, Pauline visited him earlier."

They all move into the parlour, and Pauline and Polly go to make tea. The children stay close to Ben, obviously still recovering from their ordeal.

"Polly has been a great help, Ben, with the children and the house, and looking after me as well!"

"I am sure she enjoyed her responsibilities, Daniel, especially looking after you. You and I will talk later and over the next few days decide how we all move on from here. There will be many changes once the trial has been concluded."

Then, after tea Ben goes to see Margaret, taking Polly with him. Margaret is understandably upset about yet another intrusion into their home, and hearing of Daniel and Conrad being hurt, but is relieved to hear that the trial is now coming to an end.

"How are Daniel and Conrad Polly, will they fully recover from their injuries?"

"Yes Mummy, Conrad will be in hospital for a while, but I will take care of Daniel."

"Yes, I am sure you will, Polly," says Margaret smiling.

"And what about you, my dear, how are you progressing?"

"I am feeling much better, Ben, I will have another check to tomorrow and you should be able to collect me in the afternoon."

"That is wonderful news, Margaret, isn't that wonderful news, Polly?"

"Yes, we miss you so much, Mummy, I am really looking forward to you coming home, and Maisy, Daisy and George will be really happy. They were really frightened by what happened."

Ben returns home with Polly, and tells the children the good news. They are very excited to hear their Mummy is coming home and everyone is pleased that home is beginning to return to some kind of normality at last.

The following morning, the judge begins his summary of events at 10.00 a.m. promptly.

"I find the events surrounding this trial and the evidence presented very disturbing. That a conspiracy to defraud the nation of vital supplies for the wellbeing of its subjects has been in existence for so long does suggest complicity at the very highest level," he begins.

"However, this trial is about the activities of the four accused primarily. It is obvious that they were very well organised, and one can only guess at the profits they secured. It is my intention to see that they will profit no longer from their actions, and any profits they may have acquired be seized by the Crown. The storage facility at New Haven will be sealed very soon so that it cannot be used again for any activities. It is a sad reflection on what we have become to see the site used for such a key role in our fight against the enemy during WWII, to have ended up as a depot used by criminals for their illegal activities. As a nation, we are controlled by rationing of all goods that are required to sustain us because of shortages throughout Europe. This rationing is set to go on for some time. We will survive, because we are British and will continue to get by with what we have and not complain. You men sought to take advantage of our misfortunes exploiting the needs of millions of citizens for your own gain. You have intimidated those around you into silence with threats of violence toward anyone who would try and stop you. And your connection, however tenuous, to the attacks on the Spencer family is all but obvious. This means that you have undoubtedly been complicit in the violent actions upon family members and the house of the Spencer family. Despite the terrible ordeals you inflicted on him and his family, Mr Spencer persisted in his quest to bring you down. For his efforts he is to be commended.

"The black market business in this country has to be stopped, at least the organised trafficking of goods. The man on the street corner, the spiv, will always be there, breaking the law but relatively harmless. What I hope this trial, and the sentences I will subsequently hand out will do, is tell anyone, whoever they are, who seeks to bankrupt our citizens for their own gain will be severely punished. As I have previously mentioned, I intend to authorise the seizure of all assets of the accused including property and ban them from any business involvement in the future. I will confirm this when I pass the verdicts. In conclusion, I will add that you may expect lengthy sentences to be imposed on each of you. I shall now retire and give my sentencing verdicts tomorrow," the judge concludes.

On Friday morning the judge begins his sentencing deliberations to the four accused.

"Miles McKenzie, Giles Williamson, Toby North and John Devonish, you have all been found guilty of the most serious crime of conspiracy. Plotting against the state to fraudulently convert Crown goods for gain in itself would be enough. To do so, when so many citizens are without because of national shortages, is a most serious crime. Racketeering, threats and intimidation were used by you to maintain your activities and secure maximum profits for yourselves. I can only estimate how much your activities may have contributed to the hardships of the citizens of our country. We are rationed with supplies of everyday foodstuffs, cooking oils, tinned foods, fuel and so on. You had thousands of pounds' worth of such goods stored away for distribution and profit on a grand scale.

"Many people will have gone hungry because of your greed, mothers unable to feed their children and the elderly going hungry, just to make you rich. And am sure that the ruthless pursuit of your evil trade, was behind the vicious attacks on the family of Ben Spencer. If this is so proved, when all those involved have been placed before the courts, then it will duly impact upon your time in prison. There is no place in our society for those that would seek to take advantage of the lack of basic foods and everyday items, so that they may profit from our misfortune. They are parasites of the worst order, bloodsuckers that must be crushed. Our country is working hard trying to recover, along with the rest of Europe, from the ravages of war. We will recover eventually, and all the basic food items and other goods, will become readily available to all our citizens once again. Until that time arrives, we will have to continue putting up with fair shares for all by rationing what is available. We cannot allow a few people, in privileged positions, to dictate what we can have and when and how much we will have to pay. You four stand accused of doing just that, and for that you must be punished to the maximum. We have to send a message to would be racketeers that they will not be allowed to hold our country to ransom.

"For the charge of conspiracy against the Crown, you will each go to prison for ten years. For the charge of black market racketeering, you will each serve a further five years, these sentences to run consecutively and all goods and chattels owned by the accused to be seized by the Crown.

"Those are my findings, take them to the cells. This case is now closed."

CHAPTER 36

(The Spencer Family move on)

It is now some three months since the trial at the Old Bailey was concluded, and during that time, the Spencer family has enjoyed some very happy moments. At the end of the trial, the judge thanked Ben Spencer for his untiring efforts in bringing the racketeers to justice, and apologised on behalf of the nation, for the dreadful ordeals his whole family had endured.

Margaret is now fully fit, and the terrible events that occurred are rapidly becoming a distant memory to her. Soon after the trial had finished, she and Ben enjoyed a wonderful holiday in Scotland.

Daniel has recovered completely from his injuries, and he and Polly continue with their special friendship. Polly spent most of her school holidays with Daniel in London, and they have continued to enjoy weekends in each other's company.

She has matured considerably and their special friendship shows no signs of abating. Ben and Margaret, for their part, have been content to see their daughter very happy and completely recovered from her terrible ordeals. They firmly believe that it has been Daniel's presence that has made the difference to their daughter's wellbeing. He has been able to give her the confidence that she needed to move forward with her life, after what has happened. For this reason, they have absolutely no objections to the friendship continuing. What might develop from their friendship remains to be seen. Peter Forsyth and Maureen eventually get married and move down to London so that Peter can continue with his work. She is sorry to leave Ben, but he fully understands her reasons and wishes them both well.

For Ben Spencer, his work is duly recognised by the government, and he is awarded the M.B.E. for outstanding service. His efforts stand out as an example to others how one man can really make a difference. This award is followed, a few weeks later, by an invitation to the whole family to meet the Prime Minister.

"Mr Spencer, this country does indeed thank you for your efforts and appreciates the sacrifices your family made in order for you to bring the criminal racketeers to justice. It has come to my attention that your children had their dog taken from them, by these evil men. Can I offer you and your family this small token of my gratitude?" the Prime Minister says as he hands Ben a Labrador puppy.

"Thank you very much, sir, I know the children will be delighted."

"Thank you, thank you very much," Maisy, Daisy and George all chorus.

"You are most welcome," the Prime Minister replies.

And so the family return home from Downing Street with their new Labrador puppy.

Meanwhile, Ben returns to his work, since the black market is still very active, albeit not especially organised, just petty crooks looking for easy money. His office has been reorganised with Ben as the overall Controller of Operations. He is responsible for delegating all actions taken against black market activities in the Midland Region. He will continue to liaise with London, but it was agreed that he would be more useful leading an operation from the Midlands, which covers a very big area of the country, than sitting behind a desk headquarters.

Daniel and Conrad return to their task of tracking down deserters, especially those involved in illegal activities. There is real concern that some deserters were being influenced by communist propaganda, and this will become a special interest for Daniel in the years to come.